FALLEN

D1826467

HERO

DEDICATION

To Andrea - my wife, best friend and mother of our two children. Ben and Tobias. Always encouraging and supportive.

DISCLAIMER

"Fallen Hero" is a work of fiction. It includes fictionalised portrayals of a variety of organisations and places. It does not depict actual persons, locations, or bodies. It does not represent accurate representation of policies, procedures or working practices, ethics or professional standards used or adopted by such bodies.

PRE-PUBLICATION REVIEW QUOTES

"The book was charming, there was a delightful warmth shown through the characters. The story highlighted the war, in a hopeful uplifting way. The blend of diary and story was in parity and the romance was touching and tasteful. I enjoyed the book very much indeed." C.S. UK

"I finished Fallen Hero yesterday, and I must say I did enjoy reading it! It was an excellent story, that improved as it went along. There was lots going on; comedy and tragedy, romance and excitement. Lovely closing chapters rounded everything off nicely, aah so romantic." D.B. UK

"I enjoyed reading this very much and I think you have the makings of a good novel here......What I really love is that you start straight in on the action. Far too many first timers spend ages building up to the story." J.W. UK

"Thank you for allowing me to read "Fallen Hero" at this stage in the novel's development. I genuinely enjoyed reading the manuscript. The quality of your prose is outstanding and you write with a real sense of place and atmosphere." A.M. UK

"I enjoyed reading the book very much. It flowed well and is definitely a page turner." V.K. UK

"I enjoyed the story of the two families in rural Austria and thought the plot bringing present and past together good. I warmed to the Breitner family and the different episodes described." J.F. UK

At least 50% of all royalties from the sale of "Fallen Hero" will be donated to RETINA UK. This UK based charity has been at the forefront of providing research funding to find an effective treatment and hopefully a cure for inherited progressive sight loss. More information on their work along with an opportunity to make your own donation can be found by calling or visiting

Telephone: +44 (0)1280 815900
Mobile: +44(0)7841 004564
Helpline: +44 (0)845 123 2354
Website: www.RetinaUK.org.uk

Registered Charity No. 1153851

Retina UK, Wharf House, Stratford Road, Buckingham, MK18 1TD

CONTENTS

Sep Breitner lay on his back, his legs pinned under tons of shattered masonry. His body lay limp, on a pile of broken bricks and jagged concrete. Exhaustion saturated every pore of his body. Even trying to lift his head to make sense of his situation defeated him. He abandoned himself to the chaotic thoughts and confused images that swirled around his brain. Each fleeting picture was vague and incomplete, just enough to trigger phantom impressions of something real – a familiar face? A half-remembered building? A group of people: were they friends? Family? Comrades? They spun, crashed and collided in his subconscious. He felt dizzy and nauseous. There was a muffled buzzing in his ear. He tried to grasp on to something – a thought, a sound, an image. But each time it slipped away.

Gradually he sensed a hazy form that lazily fused into something tangible. He wondered whether it was a voice, or a growing awareness of approaching death. *Is this what death is?* he wondered. He recalled someone telling him that a person's life passed in front of their eyes when the end was near. The phrase took hold, endlessly repeating itself in his mind, sounding muffled and distorted until, with a rush, his world abruptly stabilised.

Everything was still and quiet. He wasn't dead – at least, not yet. He squeezed his eyes shut and concentrated. He could hear nothing. No gunfire, no crack of rifle shot or the rattle of machine guns. No terrified screams of men thrust into the horror of battle, or the soul-wrenching wails from the mangled and maimed left trampled and shattered in the mud of no man's land.

No sound! There must be gas. Dread seized him. Should he breathe or cover his mouth? Tired resignation replaced panic. If there was gas, he was already dead. He sniffed the air. It smelled of cordite, stagnant water, putrid flesh, and dust.

He *wasn't* dead. The realisation gave him little comfort. It was only a matter of time. He gingerly passed his fingers across his face and his right eye. He could feel that his skin was swollen, and lumps of congealed blood caked his eye socket.

A sudden shout, followed by answering calls, drifted faintly across from the enemy lines. Sep switched his focus towards the raised ground and shattered coils of barbed wire that marked the English trenches. Small groups of grey soldiers heaved themselves over the parapet. They advanced towards him, their helmets set at careless angles, their rifles slung loosely from their shoulders. None bothered to crouch to avoid the hail of machine-gun bullets their appearance would inevitably attract. Sep felt sorry for them. On open ground they were easy targets.

More soldiers emerged. Looking relaxed, they made their way slowly and methodically across no man's land. Now and again one would stop and stoop before summoning his comrades. The small group gathered and stared morosely at something half-buried in the ground. They waited, talking among themselves, hands on hips or thrust in pockets, smoking as they examined the object more carefully. They picked up small objects and placed them in a bag. Once the task was completed, a coloured marker was planted, and the group moved on. They spread out and picked their way through the barbed wire and across the shell-pocked wasteland, scouring the ground as they went.

Sep couldn't make sense of it. Why were they walking around so casually in full view of the German trenches? Firing lines from dozens of machine-gun positions crisscrossed the entire front. The ground had been designed to be a killing zone. No enemy was supposed to be able to survive, should they stray into it. Yet not one shot rang out.

Curiosity finally got the better of him. He craned his neck to take in more of the scene. The movement caused his body to move – just an inch, but it was enough. A bolt of searing agony shot through his body. He froze, then tried desperately to beat down the pain. His head swam. His vision greyed, and consciousness began to slip away. In the throes of his anguish he heard an animal-like howl, not realising it came from him. The urge to vomit was overwhelming, but there was nothing to bring up except thick, black bile that stuck in his throat. He squeezed his eyes shut.

His shrieks attracted the attention of the English.

"Over here!" a voice cried out.

Sep opened his eyes. Fresh terror seized him as the enemy advanced towards his position with purposeful menace, crouching low, their rifles held at the ready. One fixed a bayonet.

Sep swung his arm around. His fingers scrabbled across the broken masonry in a futile search for his rifle. He knew he stood no chance. The sound of the soldiers' boots scraping across the fractured bricks filled his senses. He squeezed his eyes shut again. An image of his mother swam before him. He prayed hard for a quick end. *Please – a bullet, not a bayonet.*

He waited for the stabbing thrust, or the explosion, that would send him to oblivion. He could smell the familiar stench of sweat, leather and nicotine. The only sound was the heavy breathing of the enemy gathered around him.

Sep risked opening his eyes. Three English soldiers stared back at him. One peered down and examined him more closely. He stood up and looked to move away "He's a Kraut," he said dismissively. "Leave him."

"Don't be an arse, Scottie. He's no threat. Look at the poor bugger. He's in pieces."

"If he's in pieces, Sarge, do him a favour and shoot the sod."

The third soldier sneered. "You going to do it then, Scottie? Shoot an unarmed, injured man?"

"He's a Kraut. We shouldn't waste our time on him. We're here to look after our own."

The sergeant opened his water bottle and waved it in front of Sep's eyes. "Our own are past it. This one's at least got a chance," he muttered. "You want some water, mate?"

Sep tried to stretch his parched, cracked lips towards the bottle.

"I'll get the stretcher-bearers," the third soldier said, and ran back towards the English lines.

Scottie spat and turned away. "I ain't helping no Kraut bastard." He took a few steps, then spotted Sep's rifle half-buried under the rubble. He pulled it out and shook the dust from it before turning, open-mouthed, to his comrade. "Jesus, this bastard's a sniper." He held up Sep's rifle. Its long barrel and telescopic sight provided irrefutable proof.

"So? What difference does that make now?"

Scottie stared, as if he didn't understand what his comrade had said. "He's a bloody murderer. Bloody hell, Sarge, have you got shit for brains? You know the rule."

The sergeant continued to hold the canteen to Sep's lips. "There comes a point, Scottie, when the killing has to stop." He looked at his comrade. "We've already tried to kill this man once. That's enough, isn't it?"

"Not for me it ain't." Scottie's face contorted in fury. He swung the rifle round and slid back the bolt. A bullet clicked into the breech.

"Can I have a cigarette first?" Sep's request came out as a dry, rasping whisper.

The sergeant spun around in surprise. "You speak English?"

Sep nodded feebly, careful not to move too much. The effort of speaking exhausted him. "A little."

"I don't believe it. A traitor and a sniper."

"I am not English," Sep croaked.

Scottie's resolve faltered. He lowered his rifle. Sep could speak their language – that changed things. The man at his feet seemed less foreign. He was suddenly almost one of their own.

The sergeant swung his backpack off and placed it gently under Sep's head. "Where are you injured, mate?"

"Leg – the right one. Right eye – I cannot see. And maybe ribs." Sep's good eye swivelled towards the sergeant. "Please, do not move me. I might have a broken back."

"Crew is on their way." Scottie nodded towards a group of three stretcher-bearers scrambling towards them across no man's land.

"How long have you been lying here?"

The question forced Sep to focus. *How long had it been? Two nights. He was sure it was at least two nights.* "I think you English blew me up two days ago," he said weakly.

The sergeant chuckled. "You've done well to survive."

The bearer team arrived and began the task of freeing Sep from his semi-entombment.

Immediately, Sep's world collapsed in on him. The pain was too much, and he faded out of consciousness.

***

Sep lost track of time. His waking moments were fleeting and full of confusion. He had a dim notion that he was being moved. Lights seemed to be continuously passing over his head, and masked figures with concerned eyes peered at him. The smells of antiseptic, alcohol, salt, shit and vomit permeated the air. He became aware of the moans and screams of injured and dying men, the reassuring feminine voices of nurses, the curt instructions of doctors, and the soft murmurings of a priest. At one point, he was sure he heard his mother pleading with him to stay, and wailed in his panic not to disappoint her.

Finally he woke and opened his eyes. There was a single bright light suspended above his head. Everything surrounding the bulb was pitch black. For several minutes he lay still and stared at the light before realising something was wrong. He couldn't see out of his right eye. Instinctively he tried to raise his arm – but it was trapped. A feeling of panic began to take hold.

A young woman's face swam into his eye line. "You're awake." She smiled at him and gently stilled his flailing arm. She continued to smile. "You're awake," she said again, giving a small nod of encouragement.

Sep stared blankly back at her until it dawned on him, she was speaking English. Why? Where was he? He felt wet and clammy, but his mouth and throat were bone dry. Why was a woman in the trenches? He recalled the three English soldiers, one of whom had been a sergeant. They must have taken him to their first-aid post.

"I cannot see." Sep's voice was on the edge of panic.

"You can see me, can't you?"

Sep blinked in confusion until he focused back on the calm, assured young woman. He noticed the white scarf tied tightly around her head. A nurse! The revelation came as a relief – at least his mind was intact.

"I cannot see out of my right eye."

The woman looked amused. "That's because it's bandaged. It's been bashed about a bit, I'm afraid. Nothing to worry about. Your left arm is strapped down because we're giving you some fluids. Now, can you tell me your name and when you were born?"

The question threw him. Why did she want to know his name? "Sep Breitner," he said, sounding perplexed.

"And your date of birth?"

"Twenty-first of March, 1894."

She beamed at him as if he was a small child who had managed to solve a simple problem. "That's excellent. Now, let me explain. You're in hospital and we're going to look after you for a bit. You've been in a scrap, but you're on the mend." She tucked the sheet up under his chin. "I want you to get some more rest. The doctor will see you shortly." She patted him gently on the shoulder. "Welcome back. You had us worried." Then she disappeared from view. A few seconds later the bulb above him was extinguished, and Sep fell asleep.

He awoke to the sound of voices and something he hadn't heard in a long time – laughter. Not the grim, bitter, cynical laughter he had grown used to in the dark tunnels of the trenches. This laughter was light, full of gaiety and spontaneity. It was a young woman's laugh. He wondered whether it belonged to the nurse. To his surprise, he found himself smiling. He lay still for a long time, drinking in the sounds, before plucking up the courage to assess his condition.

A tube ran from a glass bottle suspended from a metal stand into his left forearm, which was strapped to the bed-frame. He felt incredibly weak. That was to be expected, he reasoned. Gradually, it occurred to him that he couldn't feel anything, apart from a dull throbbing down his right leg. Everything else was numb. He moved his right arm and out of the corner of his eye saw that the sheets moved, but he couldn't feel the material against his skin. He considered trying to move his head, but the thought of the agony that might follow discouraged him. *One thing at a time,* he cautioned himself before closing his eyes and focusing on the sounds and smells of the hospital. Eventually he sensed someone close by. He

9

opened his eye to see the young woman placing a jug and a glass of water on the bedside cabinet.

"Good morning," he said, surprised by how firm his voice sounded.

She jumped back, startled, clutching her chest. "Goodness me, Mr Breitner, you gave me such a start. You mustn't do that. And for your information, it is four o'clock in the afternoon. I take it you're feeling a bit better." She placed a cool hand on his forehead.

Sep risked a cautious nod.

"Here, drink this." She placed a paper straw in the glass and held it to his lips.

It was like drinking nectar. He drained the glass. Never had water felt or tasted so good.

"I'll fetch the doctor. He asked to be informed as soon as you were awake." She looked anxiously at him. "Do you think you're ready to talk to the doctor?"

"Soonest is best."

She gave a curt nod and a thin smile.

Sep listened to her retreating footsteps and pondered her comment. Why wouldn't he be ready to talk to the doctor?

Ten minutes later, a large balding man in a white coat loomed over the bed. A stethoscope dangled from his neck. "Ah! Our mystery man returned from the dead." The doctor didn't wait for a response but plugged the stethoscope into his ears, peeled back the sheets and commenced an examination of Sep's chest. For over a minute he stooped, his face set in concentration. Several times he frowned and pursed his lips. Sep watched with growing anxiety. The doctor's frowns unsettled him. He glanced at the nurse, who had appeared behind the doctor. She returned his look with a warm, encouraging smile. Finally the doctor stood up and nodded enthusiastically, as if he'd just sampled a particularly fine wine. "Heart nice and strong, lungs clear as a bell – excellent, excellent. Now, Mr… er, Mr…"

"Breitner," the nurse said helpfully.

"Indeed, indeed." The doctor took a clipboard of notes and charts the nurse held out for him. "First things first. In case you don't know it, you are currently a guest of the British Army 13th General Field Hospital. You were brought here five days ago, more dead than alive." The doctor reached into the top pocket of his coat and removed a pair of spectacles before donning them and consulting the clipboard. "You had severe crush injuries to your right leg, suspected spinal damage, one broken and three fractured ribs, a broken right eye socket, a badly lacerated left hand and numerous other minor cuts. You had also lost a lot of blood." The doctor peered over his glasses. It was the first time he had looked Sep in the eye. He scowled and glanced at his notes again. "Borderline case, Mr Breitner. Your life was hanging by a thread by the time they got you here. Fortunately for you, I was around to stick you back together." He paused to look at Sep, as if assessing whether or not his patient appreciated his good fortune. "However, as good as I am, even *I* cannot perform miracles. I assume you can anticipate where this conversation is heading, Mr Breitner?"

Sep had no idea what the man was talking about, but felt he ought not to complicate matters by asking.

The doctor continued, speaking quickly. "Unfortunately, I couldn't save your right leg, Mr Breitner."

Sep didn't react. His brain couldn't assimilate what the doctor had just said.

The doctor held his gaze for a few seconds to gauge his patient's reaction. "Fortunately, Mr Breitner, that is possibly the worst news I have for you. You're alive, thanks to your robust constitution, combined with my expertise, the wonder of modern surgical techniques, anaesthetics, and the superb care provided by Nurse Jones."

Sep glanced at the nurse, who lowered her eyes and looked embarrassed.

"You note I said *possibly* the worst news I have, Mr Breitner?"

Sep nodded. He was only half-listening as the realisation of the amputation sank in.

"You have damaged your spine, Mr Breitner. Worst case, you could be partially paralysed. However, the fact you can move your head and arms quite freely suggests to me you may have crushed a few vertebrae." He waved his hand dismissively. "Full feeling and mobility may return in time. We've seen that happen before." He snapped the clipboard onto the end of the bed, swept the remaining sheets away from Sep's prone form and bent his head over the stump of the amputation.

Shock made Sep ignore his previous caution about moving his head, and he craned his neck to see the extent of his injury. Bandages swathed his chest. He looked in mounting terror at the large white dressing that encased his right thigh. His eyes were drawn in horror to the bare expanse of sheet where his lower right leg should be. Nurse Jones had moved to take his hand. He turned his head towards her in appalled bemusement, mute with fright.

The doctor continued to inspect the bandage. "Very sound," he muttered and pressed his nose to the dressing. "No seepage and no indication of infection." He straightened up. He seemed oblivious to the distress his blasé attitude might be having on his patient and continued his blunt summary. "We'll monitor progress, check out that eye of yours, Mr Breitner, and put together a rehabilitation programme for you. In the meantime, we have another pressing issue which we need to sort out." He stared hard at Sep. "We need to process you, Mr Breitner, the earlier, the better. The trouble is, we don't know much about you – what regiment or unit you belong to, or indeed…"

Sep no longer listened. He tried to hold himself together but, despite his efforts, his resolve began to crumble.

Nurse Jones cut in. "Doctor Forsythe, I think it would be better if I took responsibility for these matters, now Mr Breitner is able to communicate."

Doctor Forsythe nodded. "I shall call on you again tomorrow." He picked up his stethoscope and clomped out of the ward.

Sep thought he would choke. His throat had constricted, and he had trouble breathing. He wasn't certain anything was real. He watched as Nurse Jones carefully folded the sheets around him, neatly tucking in the edges and folding back the top over the khaki blanket. When she had finished, she refilled his glass of water and held it to his lips. He drank, his eye unfocused, his mind in chaos. When he had finished, she carefully replaced the glass on the shelf and gently took his hand in both hers.

Sep could not prevent his tears.

She stood next to him, saying nothing, allowing the shock to course out of him.

Eventually he glanced at her, embarrassed. What would she think of him, blubbing like a baby? "I'm sorry," he mumbled.

She squatted so her face was level with his. "Mr Breitner, I'm the one who is sorry. Doctor Forsythe is a good surgeon, but not the most tactful or sensitive of men. He could have handled that better."

He laughed cynically. "There is no good way to give such news."

For a few seconds they looked at each other. He tried to think of something to say that might reassure her that he was back in control of himself.

She broke the silence. "I need some information from you so we can arrange your repatriation."

He looked confused. "Repatriation? What is this?"

She leant back in surprise. "Repatriation. You know – to send you back home."

He looked baffled. "Am I not a prisoner?"

She laughed. "Mr Breitner, the war is over. It's been over nearly a week. An armistice has been agreed. Everyone is going home."

"Mein Gott!" He examined her beaming face, searching for clues that this was some kind of trick. "Mein Gott! Is it really over?"

She squeezed his hand. "Isn't it the best news?"

"Of course. It is difficult to believe." He closed his eyes. He had blanked the possibility of peace from his mind. Most of his comrades had done the same. For four years they had grown tired of the rumours and unfulfilled promises. The war would be over by Christmas, by Easter, by the end of summer. One more push and the enemy would be begging for peace. They would be home before the snows come. Their hopes were always dashed. He had never believed the day would come.

"On all fronts?"

"On all fronts," she said firmly. "Everyone is going home. Including you – once we find out exactly who you are." She stood up and released his hand. "I need to fetch some papers. Won't be a sec."

Sep's mind was in turmoil. Everything was happening too fast. His thoughts drifted back to his comrades. He chuckled as he imagined how they would take the news. His smile grew broader as he pictured their celebrations. Then his smile faded as images of the young men who had not lived to see this day flashed through his mind. He remembered them all – laughing, swearing, drinking and carousing – all of them full of hopes, dreams, talents and life. He felt tears well up.

"Scheisse."

"I beg your pardon?"

Sep was mortified. He hadn't heard the nurse return. "Oh! I am so sorry. I just moved, and it hurt," he said quickly, trying to cover his embarrassment.

She looked concerned. "You shouldn't try to move until you are ready – and until someone is around to help you."

"Yes, of course. I shall be careful."

She studied him for a few seconds before pulling up the bedside chair. She sat and become business-like. "Now, I have your name, Sep Breitner, and your date of birth."

"Joseph Breitner – Sep is short for Joseph," he explained.

"Oh, I see. Well, that's a good start." She scribbled the information down on a form. "What's your rank and regiment?"

"*Leutnant Offizierstellvertreter.*"

"My goodness. You're going to have to spell that. *Leutnant* is Lieutenant?" She gave him a questioning glance.

"Acting. That is what '*Offizierstellvertreter*' means."

"I was going to record that as your regiment."

"No. My regiment is the 4th Tyrolean Kaiserjäger." Sep forced his mind away from his injuries and the black memories.

"And where was your regiment's last position before the armistice?"

"I do not know exactly. I would think in the Dolomite Mountains – on the Italian side of the border – *if* they held on to their lines."

She started to fill in the form, then stopped. She put down her pencil and looked at him sideways. "Mr Breitner, you were captured in Northern France. That's a long way from Italy. Were you not with your regiment?"

"No. I'm with the German army."

"You're not part of the German army, then?"

"Mein Gott, no. I am from Austria, working with the Germans – temporary."

"Well, that explains it. No wonder the Germans keep telling us they have no record of you."

She sighed and got to her feet. "I need to try and find out who we're supposed to liaise with to repatriate you. I have a feeling that will take some time." She clipped the papers together, clasped the clipboard to her chest and stood up. "We need to start building you up. I'll sort out some food. And when it arrives, I expect you to eat every morsel." She looked at him with a serious expression.

He nodded.

She gave a brief smile, then left.

Sep lay back and listened until her footsteps faded away.

He hardly slept. As the night passed, pangs of pain pulsed around his body. He winced again as a stab of agony seized his right leg.

The faint sound of footsteps and the soft murmur of indistinct conversation drifted in through the half-open door. He turned his head to survey his surroundings. He was in a small, sparsely furnished room with three neatly made beds, all empty. A large stone fireplace fronted by an ornate brass guard dominated the room. On the opposite wall was a window, partially obscured by white lace curtains. A cast-iron radiator was set beneath the sill. The walls were decorated with bright blue patterned wallpaper. An ornate clock hung above the fireplace, its soporific ticking counting out the passage of time. The room looked like the lounge of a well-to-do house.

The sounds of activity increased as the hospital swung into its daily routine. He caught a glimpse of someone walking purposefully by, heard the distant crash of steel trolleys being loaded, and someone whistling. As sunlight brightened the room, Sep felt his spirits rise despite the constant spasms of pain.

After what seemed like hours a male orderly entered, pushing a tray containing a washbasin and shaving utensils. Sep managed to respond through gritted teeth to his cheery greeting. The man proceeded to wash and shave Sep with a dexterity that indicated years of experience, all the while chatting non-stop and laughing at his own jokes. He had difficulty keeping track of what the man was saying, partly due to the speed at which he spoke. One word tumbled into the next, and the orderly's thick accent distorted his words. However, Sep grinned and nodded whenever he thought appropriate.

Shortly before midday Doctor Forsythe entered, accompanied by a younger man in a smart military uniform. Sep immediately sensed tension between them. Forsythe casually swept the clipboard off its hook on the bedstead. "This is our German friend, Major." His tone was tight, as if he found the other man's presence offensive. He clearly didn't expect or invite any response from the officer but turned instead to address Sep. "How are you, Mr Breitner?"

"Better, I think, Doctor. But I have much pain." Sep managed to keep his voice level.

"Really?" Forsythe looked interested. "What sort of pain?"

"All over – but my right leg is bad."

The doctor swept the sheets off, donned his spectacles and commenced his examination. Sep felt sharp stabbing and tickling sensations on his extremities as the doctor tested for responses. Once finished, Sep was surprised to see that Forsythe looked pleased. Perhaps the man was human after all.

"Well, Mr Breitner, this may come as a pleasant surprise to you, but your considerable discomfort is an excellent sign that you are unlikely to have sustained any serious spinal injury. We'll administer some morphine to help with the pain."

"You need to discharge this man as quickly as possible, Doctor." The officer jerked his head dismissively in Sep's direction.

Forsythe's smile faded. He bristled. "I'm aware of that, Major. However, this man has serious injuries which will require weeks, not days, of recovery and rehabilitation."

"Of course, Doctor. But I'm under pressure to get our men back to Blighty. I'd rather you medical experts spent your time on our lads." He nodded contemptuously towards Sep. "This man should be sent back to his own people for them to look after. I fail to see why we are treating him at all." He waved his hand around, indicating the room. "He's taking up a complete ward, using limited and precious…."

"Major Peters, exactly when any patient is discharged from this hospital, is my decision, and mine alone. I will decide when this man will be discharged based on my considerable medical experience and knowledge – something I understand you do not possess." Forsythe glared at the major, daring him to contradict him. "The only reason this man is occupying this ward is because military orders require enemy casualties to be treated separately. The fact that an armistice has been signed, and therefore this man is no longer an enemy combatant, yet the military order remains in force, is *your* problem."

The two men stood eyeballing each other. Major Peters gave way first. He placed his cap on his head, turned and stormed out.

Forsythe remained standing, head bowed and breathing hard. Once he'd collected himself, he quickly measured and administered the morphine, took Sep's temperature, and checked each of his dressings. The whole procedure was undertaken in silence. Finally, he pursed his lips, casually dropped the sheets back over Sep's torso, replaced his glasses in his top pocket and addressed his patient. "I'll get the nurses to start getting you upright," he muttered before walking out of the room.

Nurse Jones didn't reappear until late in the afternoon. Another nurse accompanied her: a small, rotund woman with a fetching blush to her cheeks that reminded Sep of the girls on the posters that adorned Brandt railway station, exhorting passengers to sample the delights of the Kärnten lakes.

Nurse Jones was crisp and business-like. "We're going to get you in a sitting position, Mr Breitner. You must let me know at once if you experience any discomfort. Lie back and let us do the work." She glanced across at her colleague, who had positioned herself on the opposite side of the bed. "Ready?" Her colleague nodded.

Sep felt the upper half of his torso begin to rise as the nurses turned the bed-raising mechanism. To Sep, it felt like a resurrection. Even in his semi-numb state, staring for hours at the ceiling wasn't particularly stimulating. He winced as the change in posture placed new pressure on his damaged ribcage.

"Are you all right?" Nurse Jones peered anxiously into his face.

"Yes, yes," he replied quickly, not wanting to give her an excuse to halt the operation.

Between them, the two nurses gripped him under his armpits and gently heaved him upright.

A wayward lock of Nurse Jones's hair brushed his cheek and Sep was suddenly aware of her proximity. He caught a breath of her scent – feminine, faint and transient. It instantly transported him back to his childhood and the warm, comforting embrace of his mother.

Much too quickly the task of repositioning him was completed. Nurse Jones stood back and tucked the loose strands of her hair back inside her headscarf.

Her colleague fussed around him, freeing the tangled creases of his gown from under him and securing the ties. Sep hardly noticed. His attention was on Nurse Jones. Now he could see her properly. She was smaller than he expected, and younger – he guessed mid-twenties. The long nurse's uniform hid her figure, but the curve of her waist and fullness of her bodice suggested she was quite slim. She had a pleasing round face, a pert nose, and delicate laughter lines that hinted at a sunny disposition. Sep wondered about the length of her hair. She was fair, he knew from the strands that had escaped her scarf. He averted his eyes as she looked at him directly.

She gave no indication she was aware of his scrutiny. "How are you feeling, Mr Breitner?"

"So much better, thank you both."

She looked reassured. "We'll fetch you a bell. Ring if you need the commode, or some more painkillers. Apart from that, and something to eat and drink, is there anything else you need?"

"Something to read, if you have anything."

"Only English papers, magazines and a few books, I'm afraid."

"English would be fine – anything. Oh, and some paper so I may write letters to my family, so they know I am safe and well."

"Of course." She smiled at him.

Hazel. Her eyes were hazel. For a second, he held her gaze, delighting in the discovery.

"We'll be back later. You'll need a top-up of morphine to help you through the night."

The Scottish orderly came back an hour later and left him with a small bell, a writing pad, pen and a stack of newspapers and magazines.

He spent the rest of the evening flicking through several back copies of the *Illustrated London News* and *Daily Mirror.* Three well-thumbed papers drew his interest. Two were called *The Wipers Times;* the third, a similar-looking publication, had *The Better Times* emblazoned on its masthead. Sep was fascinated. The stories – gallows humour, spoof adverts, gentle lampooning of officers and disparaging comments about the enemy – struck a chord with him. The articles could easily have been written by his friends and comrades. His attention was so focused that it was only when a jab of agony flashed from his missing limb that he realised the effect of the morphine was fading. By the time Nurse Jones returned, he was drenched in sweat and writhing in agony.

"Mr Breitner, why didn't you ring the bell?" she said crossly.

"I did not want to bother you," he said truthfully. "This is only pain – which I have to get used to."

"For goodness' sake, Mr Breitner, it is my job to look after you." She popped a thermometer in his mouth, which prevented him from replying.

Sep felt a sense of sheepish guilt wash through him.

"Keep that under your tongue. I'll be back in a second." She bustled out.

She reappeared minutes later, clipboard under one arm and a small ceramic bowl in her hands. Sep watched her, his pain temporarily forgotten. She had a confident, organised manner. She expertly prepared the morphine dose and put it to one side, then whipped the thermometer from his mouth and squinted at the reading.

She's short-sighted, Sep guessed, pleased he had discovered something more about her.

"I need to check your dressings."

"Of course." Sep forced the words out through another wave of agony. He was determined not to appear weak in front of her. It was bad enough that she had chastised him for his failure to ring for assistance.

Gently, she peeled back the sheets. "My goodness, you're drenched. You need a fresh gown." She bent over and began a careful, methodical examination of his dressings. "We'll need to change your leg bandages tomorrow and see how well your leg is healing." She stood and moved behind him. "I need you to lean forward a bit. Not too far. I'll support you."

He pushed himself forward and felt her untying his gown.

"Can you raise your arms?"

He did as instructed, and she peeled the nightgown from him, depositing it strategically to preserve his modesty.

"Can you remember what happened to you?"

A black ball of panic appeared from nowhere and a wave of dread washed through Sep. The black ball seethed with nightmarish images of screaming men, bloody body parts, explosions, stabbings, mud, snow, choking smoke … and death. Broken bodies were piled up over a barbed-wire fence and spread-eagled across trench parapets. He felt his heart constrict. A cold sweat covered him. His clenched fists gripped the sheet as he fought to stem his terror.

A fresh fear suddenly cut through his hysteria. He flicked his eyes towards her and was relieved when he saw she had her back turned, unfolding and shaking open a fresh gown. What would she think of him? Her question had been innocent. He ought to be able to answer it. And yet? He squeezed his eyes shut and tried to suppress the horrors. He slowed his breathing and managed to compose himself. He'd survived, for Christ's sake. Hundreds of thousands hadn't.

She turned and looked at him. Her relaxed expression changed to one of concern. "Are you OK?"

"Yes," he replied quickly. "It's just a spasm."

She looked unconvinced.

"I can remember everything up to the explosion. I thought I was under cover. But some English soldiers must have spotted me and asked for artillery to blow me up. They fired twenty shells at me – maybe more. The last one was on target. It landed in front of me. Next thing I knew I was lying on my back, half-buried in concrete and mud."

She moved to help him into the fresh gown. "It must have been terrifying."

"It was. But, after being shot at so many times, you learn how to survive."

She touched the bandage around his eye. "We might be able to take this off tomorrow if the doctors agree."

Slowly, his panic abated. Her face was so close, he could feel her breath on his cheek. He watched her mouth as she talked. Her lips were shapely but not in an exaggerated way. They had a delightful upward curve to them, as if she was hiding an amusing secret.

"If he's not in a bad mood."

She smiled, revealing a row of even pearly teeth. "He's a good man, Doctor Forsythe."

"Troubled, I think."

"What makes you say that?" She looked quizzically at him.

He told her about the morning's confrontation with the major. She listened intently, her face serious. When he had finished, she shook her head sadly. "Clash of cultures. Major Peters wants what's best for the military, Doctor Forsythe wants what's best for his patients – and he's under a lot of stress."

"You think he is sick?"

"No. I believe he is grieving. He lost both his sons. One, over two years ago at Jutland. The other, three months ago, not far from here."

"*Scheisse.* That is terrible."

She nodded sadly. "That's bloody war for you. What's worse is neither body could be recovered. The ship his elder son was on

19

exploded, and his younger son took a direct hit from an artillery round."

The fate of Forsythe's sons triggered some vague thoughts and visions that swirled around the edges of his mind. Once again, he felt the cold sweat break out and the rise of the black ball of terror. Sep knew where it would take him. It wasn't somewhere he wanted to go. With an effort, he suppressed the dark monster that threatened to consume him.

"Are you ready for your morphine?"

Sep forced his attention back to the here and now. He felt the sharp prick of the needle and waited in anticipation for the numbing sensation to kick in.

Nurse Jones dropped the used needle into the bowl and sat down next to the bed. "That's me done for another day."

"It must be hard work for you."

"It used to be a lot harder, believe me." She bent forward and took off her headscarf. A tumble of fair curly locks cascaded over her face. She ran her fingers through them and shook her head vigorously. She was an attractive young woman.

Sep's dark thought evaporated. He was captivated. "How old are you?" he blurted. "If you do not mind me asking?"

"Twenty-one. Why do you ask?"

Sep didn't want to say 'because you look so young'. Instead, he asked, "How long have you been a nurse?"

She frowned. "Three years, eleven months and … twenty-eight days." She grinned. "I volunteered in 1914." She kicked off her shoes, then yawned and stretched her arms above her head. "I'm one of the originals."

"One of the best, I'd say."

She beamed at him. "You know, your English is really good."

He smiled back at her, pleased she seemed at ease in his company. "I can speak it, and read it quite well. But writing?" He shook his head in mock despair. "I'm not so good at writing."

"You should practice." She pulled herself upright and leant towards him. Her expression turned serious. "It might be a good thing to do while you're here. Your recovery is likely to take a while. It will help pass the time."

"What should I write about?"

She spread her hands out. "Anything. But if you decide to write, it should be a happy, positive topic. She held his gaze for a second. "Have you written to your family to let them know you're safe?"

"No – I will do that tomorrow."

"You must, and when you do, imagine their joy when they receive your letter."

He grinned and said nothing. He was beginning to feel drowsy from the morphine.

She bent over, put on her shoes and got to her feet. "I'll arrange for your letter to be sent. With luck, the communication lines will be up and running, and you might be able to send a telegram. I'll wind the bed flat for you now, if you like."

He nodded sleepily.

She continued the conversation as she released the catches holding the winding mechanism under the bed. "Could you write poetry?"

"No, I don't think so. I mean, I was not good at poems at school when writing in German. I will be worse if I try in English."

"Did you have a happy childhood?" She moved round to the winding mechanism. "Can you lean forward a bit?"

He did as she asked and the bed started to descend. "Oh yes. I was lucky."

"Well, there's your subject. Write about your earliest memories – events that made you happy, things that made you laugh."

Sep chuckled. "I could tell you about my first memory."

She raised her eyebrows inviting him to elaborate.

"It's about my grandfather. It's a silly story that has kept our village amused for many years. He had lost some fingers on his left hand. He was a carpenter, you see, and managed to saw through his fingers."

She frowned. "Is this supposed to be a happy memory?"

Sep grinned, already reliving the event in his head. "It is. Anyway, what happened…"

She laughed and put two fingers gently on his lips. "No, you don't. Write it down. Once you have, give it to me to read." She picked up her headscarf. "You get some sleep."

Sep felt peaceful and mildly intoxicated. He wasn't sure whether it was the effect of the drug or the memory of her fingers on his lips.

Pain again woke him. The room was dark. A pale-yellow shaft of light through the half-open door provided some dim illumination. He guessed it was two or three o'clock in the morning. He managed to beat down the spasms of agony for another hour before he cried out. His leg felt as if razor wire was being dragged through his flesh. He began to curse his healing spine and dread the spasms from his recovering nerves, which left him exhausted and dejected. He searched for a distraction from his misery but found he couldn't concentrate on anything. The morphine left him in a distorted half world of reality and fantasy. At times he wasn't sure whether he was alive or dead. On several occasions terror rushed through him, leaving him panic stricken and drained.

In his lucid periods he recognised he was falling into a cycle of self-destruction, a spiral of morphine dependency, self-pity and despondency. He needed to break free. He was alive – and better off than most, he reminded himself. The medical care and attention he'd received was beyond anything he might have expected from an Austrian hospital. He owed it to himself, his family and the medical staff – especially Nurse Jones – to make the best of things. Her image brought him up short. Although he had only been semi-conscious over the past three days, he was sure she hadn't been among the staff who had attended to him. That gave him a strange comfort. At least she hadn't seen him at his most pathetic. He steeled himself. It was time to get a grip, deal with the pain, focus on finishing his letter home – and writing the story for Nurse Jones.

Gradually his world began to stabilise. He became aware of time and the hospital routines. He convinced himself the searing agony was diminishing. He could concentrate long enough to hold a conversation with the staff. He felt he'd reached the bottom of the trough and was now on an upward trajectory.

She returned four days later. She swept in, wearing a long, dark blue, mud-splattered cape, dappled with raindrops. She was breathless.

"I came straight here. Have you written your letter?"

He nodded. "You are wet."

She wiped the rain from her face. "Yes, I know. It's tipping it down. The post truck is about to leave. The driver agreed to wait. You need to be quick." She held her hand out expectantly.

Sep reached over to the bedside cupboard and gave her the letter. "I have no envelope."

"Don't worry; I've got one. Is the address written down?"

"Top left-hand corner. Oh – and I have not got a stamp."

"I'll sort it out." She snatched the letter from him, turned and dashed back out.

Sep stared at the wet boot prints on the ward floor. He found himself smiling. He'd only seen her for ten seconds, yet she had succeeded in brightening his day. He spent the rest of the afternoon watching the door like an expectant puppy. His hopes rose as each person entered the room, only to be dashed when it wasn't her. He was beginning to despair when she eventually returned. He heard her approach, chatting excitedly with her rosy-faced colleague.

"Good evening, Lieutenant. Nurse Handsworth tells me you have been making excellent progress." She smiled broadly at him as she placed the familiar enamel bowl on the bedside table.

"I'm doing well, I think. Thanks to Nurse Mandy."

"Oh! On first name terms, are we?" She turned to her friend. "You'd better watch this one, Nurse Handsworth. He'll be chasing you around the ward once he gets his crutches." She glanced at him under her eyelids.

Sep knew he was blushing.

"The lieutenant is fighting to get better." Nurse Handsworth looked proudly at her patient.

"I would like to get out of bed as soon as possible," He said earnestly.

Nurse Jones put her hands on her hips and regarded him intently. "Look, Mr.... Lieutenant Breitner—"

"Please, call me Sep."

Her head jerked back, and she blinked in surprise.

"It is easier. Besides I am not a real soldier. None of us were."

She looked confused. "What do you mean?"

"I was conscripted – like everyone else in the Imperial Army." He gave her an ironic half-smile. "I am not *Leutnant.* I am a farmer. That is my real job."

"Oh, I see."

"Farmer Breitner is as big a mouthful as Lieutenant Breitner. Sep is much easier … or Joseph, if you prefer." Sep realised he was talking too fast and felt embarrassed. Had he overstepped the mark?

"Well, make up your mind." Her grin disarmed him.

He sighed inwardly in relief. "You choose. Nurse Mandy calls me Sep."

"OK, Sep. The thing is, we have to wait until the stitches on your leg have done their work and the skin has sealed the wound. Do you need anything? How are you with the morphine?"

Sep glanced at the wall clock. "I can last until ten o'clock, I think."

Nurse Jones studied him. "Nurse Handsworth tells me you're very determined."

He laughed. "It annoys me, lying here, being waited on. It makes me feel uncomfortable."

She looked put out. "I hope you're not just lying there doing nothing. You promised you were going to write about your childhood memory."

23

"Oh, I have done that for you." He reached across the bedside table, grabbed the notebook and handed it to her.

She read the first few lines before flipping the pages forward. "My word, you have been busy. Is it finished?"

"Not quite. I have a bit more to write."

She handed the book back to him. "Why don't you finish it, and I'll read when it's done?" She glanced at the clock. "I'll be back at ten. I can take it then if you like."

Sep set to work. A couple of pages would complete the tale, and he was sure he could manage that before the morphine wore off. Once again it was a close-run race. However, his confidence had been boosted. This was a battle he could win. He squeezed his eyes shut and counted down the seconds in his head as he waited for her reappearance. He wanted to appear relaxed and in less pain. It was important to show her he had completed the story, and was overcoming his injuries.

She arrived, took one look at him and moved with calm, practised skill. Sep found a thermometer thrust under his tongue. The morphine was administered with clinical efficiency, the gown stripped from his body and a cool, damp flannel applied to his burning flesh. She worked with a tight-lipped determination that worried Sep. She behaved as if she was angry with him. He watched her out of the corner of his eye, his ability to speak constrained by the thermometer. She was almost rough as she helped pass his arms through a fresh nightgown.

"I should box your ears," she said as his head emerged.

His eyes conveyed his bewilderment.

"Why don't you call, when it's obvious you are in such pain?" She whipped the thermometer out and held it to the light.

"You ought to get glasses," he said gently.

"What?"

"You should not need to squint. Are you short-sighted?" he said quietly.

She failed to hold back a rueful grin. "I have a pair of glasses."

"So why do you not wear them?"

"I need to get in the habit, and I keep knocking them off. It's irritating." She shook her head and waved her hand to dismiss the matter. "Anyway, I'm being serious. Please don't leave it too long next time."

"I will not. But I have to beat this pain. I do not want to live my life needing morphine injections – or any other medication, for that matter."

"You might have to."

He shook his head. "You do not understand. Where I live is a small, isolated village. Medication is difficult to get hold of. The nearest *Apotheke* is twenty-five kilometres down the valley." He gave her a resigned look. "I am thinking ahead – trying to be practical."

"Oh. I see." She considered what he had said for a few seconds as she tossed the sweat-soaked nightshirt onto the end of the bed. "Where do you live?"

"Dopplegau. It's a small village at the end of the Brandterwald in the west of Austria, close to the Swiss border. It's beautiful. Lots of high mountains, rushing waterfalls, lush Alpine pastures. One road in, and a mountain track out that leads over the high pass into the Tyrol." He smiled and closed his eyes as an image of the village swam into his imagination. "One *Gasthaus*, a bakery, a bank, a post office, a small store."

She settled on the bedside chair. "It sounds idyllic."

Sep felt an eddy of pleasure. She seemed to be interested and in no rush to depart. "Do you live in a village – back in England?"

"No, a small market town. More shops than Dopplegau. Certainly not a great place to grow up. Not many jobs for the men, and especially depressing if you're a woman."

"Is that why you became a nurse?"

She nodded. "Partly." She considered the statement before adding, "If I'm honest, I originally volunteered to do my bit – you know, patriotic duty and all that. But once I joined, I found I enjoyed it. It was worthwhile. I learned a lot, met lots of interesting people. I've seen things, that's for sure."

"Have you finished your shift?" he asked.

"Yes. You're my last patient." She showed no signs of leaving, and appeared to be completely at ease in his company.

"You were away four days."

She grinned. "Did you miss my care and attention?"

He laughed, partly to cover his bashfulness. Truthfully, he had missed her. But he decided not to respond to her teasing. "Were you on holiday?"

"I wish. No, we had to arrange a convoy of patients to return to England. We're gradually closing this place and trying to get as many of the lads as possible home in time for Christmas."

"I owe you some thanks, and some money."

She looked offended. "No, you don't owe me anything. It's only an envelope, and I persuaded the post office to classify your letter as military field correspondence, so it cost nothing. With a bit of luck, your family should receive it in the next week." She glanced towards the window. "Your wife will be delighted to hear you are safe."

"No, she will not."

She looked embarrassed. "Oh! I'm sorry."

He laughed. "She will not be delighted, because I am not married. My family, however, I expect will be relieved." He shuffled around to face her. "Are you married?"

"No." She shifted uncomfortably and changed the subject. "So, what about your writing? Are you going to show it to me?"

"Ah yes. It is on the shelf." He pointed.

She got up and retrieved the sheaves of paper. "Can I take it with me? I'd like to read it in my room."

"Where you have left your glasses?" He raised his eyebrows.

She stood for a second scanning the first page. "Joseph Breitner is who?"

"My grandfather."

"And this is a happy story? I don't want to settle down to sleep with anything nasty."

He nodded. "It is an amusing tale. Everyone knows this story in Dopplegau."

"I shall look forward to reading it." She smiled at him. "Goodnight, Sep."

"Goodnight …?" He gave her an enquiring look.

She looked at him uncertainly. "Susan. My name is Susan Jones."

In the soft light of the single bulb, Sep was sure he detected a slight colouring of her cheeks.

The third of April 1897 was the first time the skies had cleared since the winter blizzards had isolated the top of the valley. The snow had retreated to the high mountain peaks and the sun beat down, raising the prospect of a balmy Alpine day. For centuries, the village of Dopplegau had evolved at a glacial pace. But on that day, the weather happened to coincide with a change in the fortunes of the small community, and the Breitner family in particular. It was also the day Father Wagner, the young parish priest, received a disconcerting letter; the day a small family crept like thieves through the village in the middle of the night; and the day Joseph Breitner provided his grandson with his first vivid childhood memory.

Joseph Breitner gazed thoughtfully at the stumps on his left hand. He sucked contentedly on his pipe and considered whether the loss of his third and fourth fingers had handicapped his life. The saw had separated his fingers from his palm with surgical precision. Not content with removing two digits, it had made a determined effort to inflict a similar fate on his middle finger. If he had lost that, his life may well have turned out differently, he conceded.

He squeezed his hand into a fist. Although over thirty-five years had passed since the accident, the phantom presence of the missing fingers was disconcertingly real for Joseph. He smiled to himself. The sensation of experiencing something that didn't exist amused him.

An early start had allowed him to reach his summer farm before dawn and prepare it to receive his small herd of pigs, which he intended to drive to the surrounding middle pastures later in the week. He always enjoyed opening the blinds, clearing the stone chimney, airing the hayloft, exterminating the rats and replenishing the stores. Each completed task meant the banishment of winter and the coming of spring. He'd trimmed the wicks on the lamps and recharged the reservoirs – a task that, despite the steadiness of his normally reliable right hand, had caused him to spill paraffin down his trousers. Although he had much more to do, he was happy to take a break, sup a tankard of beer and while away the next hour or so by playing mind games with his phantom appendages.

He kept his eyes tightly shut and raised his hand to his pipe. In his imagination he could feel the warmth of the burning embers seeping through the polished wooden bowl into his palm. He let the pipe move away from his lips and held it in mid-air, still feeling the imaginary warmth of the bowl.

He turned his head to catch the full rays of the sun and listened with half an ear to the sounds of the valley. He could hear the clear crystal waters of the Ach cascading over the rocks, and the occasional hollow chimes of cowbells high up in the Alpine pastures. Apart from that, the valley was still and peaceful. The birds had long since halted their dawn chorus and had resigned themselves to another day sheltering in the cool of the dense pine forests.

Gradually he became aware of the faint sound of a horse-drawn vehicle. Joseph kept his eyes shut and tried to work out by sound alone what type of vehicle it might be. From the beat of the hooves on the gravel road, he deduced there was more than one horse. That meant a sizeable conveyance, probably at least two kilometres from his vantage point on the bluff that marked the boundary between Dopplegau and the neighbouring village of Gau. He could hear the grind of the coach wheels. Joseph cocked his head. Two vehicles – and perhaps eight horses – were approaching at speed. The urgent cry of a coachman and a fainter response from his companion, followed by the encouraging crack of a whip, convinced Joseph he was correct. At the exact moment Joseph opened his eyes, expecting to have his analysis confirmed, his groin erupted in a sheet of flame.

Left to its own devices, Joseph's numb hand had betrayed its master's trust and allowed the pipe to drop, unnoticed, into his paraffin-soaked lap. For several minutes the glowing embers had smouldered quietly while Joseph's attention was diverted. Then the point of ignition was reached. In an instant, Joseph's manhood risked being barbecued.

Until then, the lead coachman's focus had been on beating his rival in a race to their destination. Abruptly his day took a turn for the better. He stared in amazement at the sight of a middle-aged man on the skyline leaping about and beating his genitals vigorously. The coachman's bewilderment morphed into astonishment as the man frantically undid his belt and dropped his britches.

Joseph's concern was for what his late wife had always referred to as his "winkie". Joseph examined it from every angle, unaware he was under close observation. He sighed in relief. 'Winkie" appeared to have escaped being torched. However, the flames had not spared the tender skin on the inside of his thigh. Already blisters were bubbling up, and searing pain replaced the initial numbness. He needed to cool the skin – and fast. His eye alighted on his half-drunk beer. He grabbed the tankard and emptied the contents over his scorched legs. He closed his eyes in relief. When he opened them, he found himself, "winkie" in one hand, empty tankard in the other, looking directly at the open-mouthed coachman. Joseph decided the best course of action in the circumstances was to act casual. He smiled, raised his glass and waved. The bemused coachman waved back until the realisation that he was in danger of running off the road sent him into a panic. He yanked on the reins and brought the carriage back on track. The small convoy entered the village.

The carriages weren't the familiar battered public stagecoaches. These were elegant, highly sprung vehicles with a coat of arms emblazoned across the varnished doors. The coachmen wore smart foreign uniforms. Large leather trunks were strapped to the roofs of both carriages. The visitors reeked of money and class. Even the horses were well groomed, with sparkling brasswear and highly polished leather harnesses.

Joseph knew immediately who the visitors were. The English had arrived. Although he knew the identity of the guests, most of the rest of the community did not. The arrival of one high-class carriage would be enough to excite interest. Two were guaranteed to cause a minor frenzy. Despite the pain in his groin, Joseph settled down to watch the first of the scouting parties emerge and head for Drössel's *Bäckerei*. Located directly opposite the Adler, the bakery provided an excellent vantage point to monitor the comings and goings from the *Gasthaus*.

Frau Hagspiel, the village gossiper-in-chief, burst from her front door as soon as the coaches had appeared, desperately attempting to tie her scarf around her head while simultaneously trying to draw her coat around her. Joseph couldn't help but admire her determination to be first in position. Other villagers quickly emerged. In less than ten minutes the small bakery was crowded. Joseph chuckled to himself. He could imagine them all weaving and ducking around the small shop window like a flock of wide-eyed owls trying to catch a glimpse of the foreigners. No doubt Frau Hagspiel was already pronouncing on their rank and social standing.

Joseph got painfully to his feet just as George Foster sprang lightly from the lead coach, followed by Sir William Cuthbert. The pair stood for a second, hands on hips, gazing at the spectacular mountain surroundings. Around them, servants began to throw down trunks and suitcases from the roof of the carriages.

After admiring the scenery, the two men strolled casually towards the main entrance of the *Gasthaus*. As they entered, George Foster turned towards the bakery and gave a cheery wave. Joseph chuckled as he pictured the embarrassed chaos the gesture would have caused inside the shop.

His amusement was short-lived as more villagers made their way towards the *Bäckerei*. He inwardly groaned as he realised that a substantial number of his friends and neighbours now stood between him and the most direct route to his home. His burned, wet trousers – and his painful gait – were bound to attract attention and, no doubt, ribald comment. Joseph was a proud man and had no intention of being the target of village amusement. He decided to creep as inconspicuously as possible along the track around the back of the village. The journey was further and would take him twice as long, but it would be worth it if he avoided being spotted.

He waited for the best time to make his move. The more villagers who were focusing on the new arrivals meant that fewer were likely to anywhere near the back path. He set off in an ungainly bow-legged scamper down the slope towards the path, wincing at every painful step. He made it to the edge of the village surprisingly quickly. Confident that his progress remained undetected, he paused, and conducted a swift reconnoitre of the path ahead. The next hundred metres were clear. The corner of Old Mother Norbert's cottage, where the track turned sharp right towards his home, was his next waypoint. He steeled himself against the pain and, with a determined expression fixed on his face, launched himself onward.

On the flat, he found that splaying his legs as wide as possible while avoiding bending his knees significantly alleviated the amount of chafing. Furthermore, increasing the length of his stride not only reduced his discomfort but also meant he could cover the ground more rapidly. He reached the corner and peered cautiously around. The back door of the family farmhouse, and sanctuary, was less than a hundred metres away.

Then he caught sight of Frau Norbet and his heart sank. She sat, still as a corpse, on a bench in the small veranda outside her kitchen window. Joseph ducked back behind the corner of the building and glanced nervously back along the path before taking another surreptitious peek.

Frau Norbert hadn't moved. She appeared to be dead to the world: her head tilted back, toothless mouth agape, some half-finished knitting lying in a tangled heap on her lap.

Joseph breathed a sigh of relief. A comatose Frau Norbert ought to present no obstacle. Her advanced years meant she spent much of her time in a state of torpor. Joseph snatched one further glance before breaking cover and continuing his splay-legged advance towards home and safety. He took extra care to waddle quietly so as not to awaken the old lady. Nevertheless, he kept a watchful eye on the sleeping form just in case. He successfully traversed the critical twenty metres that marked the boundary of Frau Norbert's garden. She remained motionless. Joseph increased his pace; certain he had gone unnoticed.

He was wrong. Frau Norbert opened one flinty eye and followed Joseph's progress until he disappeared behind his back door. Although she was ancient, her hearing and eyesight were as razor-sharp as those of an eighteen-year-old. Her slack, toothless mouth slowly formed a mischievous grin as her mind sprang to its own conclusion as to Joseph Breitner's affliction. She gave a hoarse cackle as she considered what to do with her intelligence. Then she levered herself to her feet and reached for her stick and coat. Her news had to be shared.

For the moment, Joseph had no idea that he had been spotted. He stumbled through his back door and swung it shut behind him, resting his head on the doorjamb in relief. Instinctively he threw the bolts, as if to make doubly sure he was safe. He drew in a series of deep breaths and considered his next move. He could now afford to relax and take his time. First things first. He needed to get his trousers off and inspect his injuries. He unbuckled his belt and was about to drop his trousers when a voice behind him rooted him to the spot.

"Are you all right, Papa?"

Joseph's surprise almost caused him to spin around in shock. He realised just in time that such a reaction would result in the evidence of his whole sorry predicament to be exposed. That would be bad enough if it were a friend or neighbour. The fact the enquirer as to his welfare was his daughter-in-law was too horrible to contemplate. Joseph found himself frozen: the upper half of his body turned towards his daughter-in-law, his lower half resolutely facing the door. He clutched his already undone trousers.

"I'm fine, Heidi, dear." Despite trying to sound nonchalant, his reply emerged as a strained squeak.

"You don't look all right. What's happened?" Heidi put down the infant she was carrying and made to advance towards him, a look of concern on her face.

She was brought up short by Joseph's panicked plea. "No, no, honestly, Heidi, sweetheart. I'm catching my breath. I'm fine. I just need some fresh air." His attempt to retreat outside only made his predicament worse. The door was locked. Like an idiot he had thrown the bolt. To release it would demand some dextrous manipulation if he was to avoid his trousers dropping to the floor.

His feigned casualness wasn't fooling Heidi. She put her hands on her hips and glared at him. "What's happened, Papa?" she said in a firm voice that indicated she wasn't going to be trifled with.

Joseph's mind raced as he desperately tried to think of a way out of the situation. He couldn't even conjure a way to stall for time or find some plausible excuse to send her out of the room. He was caught.

Heidi stood resolute.

Joseph's eyes flickered towards his daughter-in-law, but he couldn't look her in the eye. He was also aware that his young grandson was hanging on to his mother's skirts, thumb plugged into his mouth, staring at him with wide-eyed curiosity.

"I've had a bit of an accident," he muttered.

"What?"

"I said, I've had a bit of an accident," Joseph said, more loudly than he intended, startling his grandson, who shrank back behind his mother.

"What sort of accident?"

For Joseph's grandson, the word 'accident' had a particular meaning. His eyes widened even further in amazement, and he glanced up in astonishment at his mother. "Has Opa pooed his pants, Mama?"

"No, I haven't!" Joseph said sharply. "It's not that sort of accident, Sep," he said in a softer tone as he saw his grandchild's bottom lip start to droop. "It's only a little accident, Sep. Nothing to worry about."

"Then for goodness' sake stop prevaricating, Papa, and tell me what's happened."

Joseph sighed. He knew his options had run out. It was time to come clean. Slowly he turned around to reveal the scorched edges of the hole in his trousers and the beer stain.

Heidi's hand flew to her mouth. "What on earth have you done to yourself?"

Joseph looked resigned. "I dropped my pipe and set light to myself." He shook his head sadly, still unable to look at her. "Paraffin – an accident."

"Well, I would be surprised if you'd done it deliberately." Having recovered from her initial shock, Heidi was doing her best to stop herself from laughing. She clapped a hand over her mouth in an attempt to stifle her giggles.

Sep's eyes widened, his initial upset instantly forgotten.

Joseph noticed his daughter-in-law's suppressed mirth. "It's not funny, Heidi. I've burned myself."

Heidi became serious. "Where? How badly?"

Joseph nodded vaguely towards his crotch.

Sep was incredulous "Has Opa burned his willy, Mama?"

"No, no, darling," Heidi spluttered. "Nothing like that." She crouched down and kissed her son. "Why don't you go and play outside for a bit while I look after Opa?" She ushered him towards the door before he had time to protest. "You can see if Stephan is in and invite him round for tea if you like."

The prospect of play and his best friend joining them for food was enough to distract the toddler, and he scampered off before Joseph could intervene.

Heidi turned back to her father-in-law. He stood, head bowed, looking defeated. "For goodness' sake, Papa, I'm sure it's not that bad."

Joseph regarded her with a sad, resigned expression. "I think you'll find it is," he whispered.

As if on cue, Sep's shrill voice floated in through the kitchen window. He had found his best friend. "My opa's set light to his willy!" he shouted excitedly.

Joseph knew that message was sure to be spread around the village faster than if he had climbed the steeple of St Martin's church and made the pronouncement himself.

"Oh dear. Maybe that wasn't such a good idea." Heidi bowed her head so Joseph couldn't see her tears of silent laughter.

Joseph made to shuffle off and find some quiet, private refuge where he could sort himself out.

"Where are you going?"

"To find some clean trousers to change into," he replied irritably.

"You'll do no such thing. If you've burned yourself, you need to put some balm on it."

"For God's sake, Heidi, it's a tiny burn."

"Papa, I know you. You'll try and pretend it's something trivial and before you know it, it will get infected and go septic." She stood and barred the door. "Let me see what damage you've done. You might have to see a doctor."

"I don't need a doctor."

"Oh, so you're a medical expert, are you?"

"Heidi, I'm telling you, it's not serious."

"I'll be the judge of that. Now get your trousers off and let me see."

Joseph looked at her, horrified. "I'm not taking my trousers off in front of you."

"Oh, for goodness' sake, Papa."

"I don't want anyone looking at me – down there. It's not decent." Joseph tightened his grip on his belt.

"Papa, don't be foolish. If you've burned yourself, it must be treated. Don't worry. I'll get you a cloth so you can cover your … your … your privates." Despite her resolve, Heidi couldn't prevent herself from blushing. "It's better if a member of the family takes a look at you. It's either that or I take you to Doctor Rubenstein."

"I haven't got time to travel all the way to Achbrugge."

"Exactly! So, you don't have any choice, do you?" She fixed him with a steely gaze, daring him either to contradict her or push his way past her. "We have to be sensible, Papa. Judging by the size of the hole in your trousers, it must have been quite a fire."

Joseph raised his eyebrows and grimaced. "It's old age and a dead hand." He grinned ruefully.

Heidi knew she had succeeded in winning his cooperation. She opened a kitchen drawer and extracted a clean tea towel. "Cover yourself up with that. I'll go and find some balm." She left the kitchen. "Mind you, if it's serious you *are* going to Doctor Rubenstein," she said over her shoulder

She returned clutching a bottle of coal tar, a pair of clean trousers and a linen sheet, to find Joseph sitting on a kitchen chair, bent over, examining the wounds on his inner thigh. He held the tea towel strategically – and firmly – over his manhood.

"Let me see," she said firmly. She peered at the blistered skin for a few moments. "That's bad – but not too bad. You need to wash it with clean water and rub some of this on it." She waved the bottle of coal tar at him, then filled a kettle and banged it on the stove. She busied herself by preparing the family supper, chatting to her father-in-law as they waited for the kettle to boil.

Joseph looked forward to their chats, as did Heidi. He quickly overcame his awkwardness of sitting half-undressed in front of her. Their conversations tended to be serious rather than idle tittle-tattle. Heidi appreciated the fact her father-in-law was genuinely interested in her opinions and valued her insight. Joseph mentioned the arrivals at the Adler. "With a bit of luck, there might be some business coming to the village as a result of the return of George Foster and his master."

Heidi looked surprised. "They are back so soon."

"No reason to hang around. The sale of the land and lease of hunting rights has been agreed by the Farmers' Council, and signed off by the Landesmann last month. I expect Sir William has arrived to see what his money has bought."

Their conversation was interrupted by a thump on the back door. Someone was trying to get in, and obviously hadn't expected the door to be bolted. The noise made them jump.

"Oh, that's Fritz. Wait a second!" Heidi called out, rushing to release the lock.

Fritz bowled into the kitchen as soon as the door swung open and gazed in bewilderment at the bolts. Nobody locked their doors in

Dopplegau. Bolts were only fitted as an ornament – if they were fitted at all. "What's with the locked— Oh, I see." Fritz's consternation evaporated when he caught sight of his hapless father still sitting half-naked, clutching the tea towel. "So, it's true then?"

"What's true?" Joseph decided that sounding belligerent from the outset might allow him to assume control of the conversation. After all, it had worked throughout most of Fritz's childhood. There was an outside chance it might work now even though he was addressing a twenty-five-year-old man with the solidly muscled frame and ruddy weather-beaten complexion of an Alpine farmer.

Fritz grinned broadly and stood with his hands on the ceiling beam, towering over his parent. "Well, according to everyone I have met since walking back from the top barn to here, my highly respected and normally sane father has deliberately set light to his todger."

"Fritz!" Heidi shrieked, catching sight of Sep, who had chosen to make his reappearance at the precise moment the deliciously naughty-sounding word 'todger' was uttered. Although he didn't know what it meant, he knew that his mother's panicked reaction meant that it was a rude word.

"So, what's the story then?" Fritz peered at the blisters on his father's legs.

Joseph drew a deep breath and prepared for the second time to relate his tale of woe. He had hardly started when the kitchen door was thrown open. There stood their next-door neighbour Suzanne Wachter, little Stephan in tow. "I heard what happened and came as quick as I could," she said breathlessly.

Joseph groaned. "To do what, exactly?"

"To see if I could help." Suzanne appeared to have no qualms about seeing her neighbour in a partial state of undress. She barged past Fritz in her eagerness to examine the extent of Joseph's injury.

Joseph had no chance to escape, and sat passively, gazing at the ceiling as Frau Wachter and young Stephan inspected the damage.

"Ooo, that looks nasty," she announced after a thorough examination. "I've got just the thing for burns." She reached into her apron pocket and produced a small green-ribbed glass bottle.

"What's that, Suzie?" Heidi stepped in before her neighbour had a chance to lever the cork out. As far as Heidi was concerned, if anyone was going to administer any remedies in the Breitner household, it was going to be her.

"It's new medicine, Heidi. I got it from Doctor Rubenstein only two weeks ago. It's called disinfectant." Frau Wachter looked around, as if expecting a round of applause. "It's the latest treatment,

35

according to Doctor Rubenstein. It stops wounds from putrefying. He says it kills the germs that cause infection. It's like coal tar – but better. He uses it all the time." She rummaged around in her apron pocket and produced a small crumpled piece of paper and thrust it towards Heidi. "Here – read it yourself."

"I'm not being used as an experiment for dodgy remedies."

"Shush, Papa." Heidi brushed aside Joseph's protestation as she unfolded the paper and carefully read the neatly typed text.

Sep decided to join Stephan while his mother was preoccupied, and together they gazed in wonder at Joseph's raw blisters. Joseph tried to ignore the inspection of his thighs by the two toddlers. He was attempting to work out at what point his attempt to keep his misfortune confidential had started to unravel. "I'm not having any stuff applied to my body if it stings," he said to the room in general.

His plea was instantly dismissed by Heidi. "Shush, Papa." She waved her hand in his direction as she studied the leaflet. Behind them, the kettle belched steam and began to rattle on the stove. "This looks like proper medicine," she said eventually, turning over the paper a few times to ensure she hadn't missed anything important. She gave the beaming Suzanne a cautious look. "From Doctor Rubenstein, you say?"

Suzanne nodded enthusiastically.

"In that case, we should give it a go," Heidi announced.

"Not if it hurts!" Joseph cried.

His daughter-in-law remained unsympathetic. "Shush, Papa – don't be such a baby." She became business-like. "It says the wounds should be thoroughly washed with sterile water before applying. Fritz, can you pour some boiling water into that?" She pointed to a white porcelain bowl that hung from its hook at the end of the dresser.

"I'm not having boiling water poured over me." Joseph knew before he opened his mouth that his plea would fall on deaf ears. He was right. He resigned himself to his fate. He had become a spectator at his own operation.

The two youngsters continued to stare at Joseph's blisters, round-eyed, occasionally peering into his face to see whether he was in pain. Sep secretly admired his Opa. The blisters looked painful, yet Opa wasn't crying, and young Sep could only imagine how much having a burned todger must hurt.

Finally, when the women judged the water had cooled sufficiently, the two toddlers were shooed away. Joseph couldn't help feeling there was something inappropriate about two young women being in such close proximity to the most private parts of his

36

anatomy. He gripped the tea towel more tightly as the treatment was applied.

It was this vision that greeted Bürgermeister Peter Ansbacher, as he entered the kitchen after a cursory tap on the door. He grasped Fritz warmly by the hand, bowed his head politely at the two women, and ruffled the toddlers' hair before regarding Joseph solemnly.

"I'm sorry to learn of your ailment, Jo," he said slowly, shaking his head mournfully to emphasise his sorrow. "It comes to us all eventually." He laid a sympathetic hand on Joseph's shoulder.

Joseph looked perplexed. "It was an accident, Peter."

His friend nodded sadly. "I understand, really I do. It comes to us all eventually. It's nothing to be ashamed of."

Joseph looked around at the others in the room, who gazed at Peter in confusion. Joseph was relieved. At least he wasn't the only person who was struggling to understand.

"Has something happened that I don't know about?" Joseph enquired.

Peter expelled a tired sigh and shook his head. "Oh dear. I expect the shock of it has blanked much of the detail from your mind." He peered around at the others.

"He's not in shock." Heidi gave Joseph a closer look to satisfy herself she hadn't missed any tell-tale signs of concussion or trauma. "He's been lucid since he arrived."

Peter steepled his hands and raised his eyes heavenwards. "That at least is a blessing. The body might start to fail, but it is infinitely worse when one starts losing one's mental faculties."

"What the hell are you talking about?" Joseph said indignantly.

Peter appeared oblivious to Joseph's sharp tone and gazed sympathetically at his friend for a few seconds before responding. "It's no longer such a big issue, Jo. Plenty of people – especially those of advanced years – have had to cope. It's a price we all have to pay as we get older. You can get treatment, you know. And special … um …. garments. Doctor Rubenstein will know what's best."

"Peter Ansbacher, what on earth are you talking about?" Heidi looked at him askance.

For the first time, he looked confused. "Frau Hagspiel told me you'd had an accident."

"I have had an accident. It's not serious. I'm not at death's door, as you can see." Joseph didn't bother to hide his exasperation.

Heidi's antennae were activated as soon as Frau Hagspiel's name was mentioned. She advanced towards Peter. "What sort of accident did Frau Hagspiel think Joseph had?"

Peter instinctively shrank back as Heidi advanced. She could be intimidating when she chose to be. Now he thought about it, he realised he should have been less ready to accept intelligence from such an unreliable source. "She said Joseph had been – you know. He had been seen. She was told by Frau Norbert that … um."

"For God's sake stop shilly-shallying. Spit it out, man," Fritz said in exasperation.

Nervously, Peter cleared his throat. "She said – that is, Frau Norbert said you had passed her house in some distress. The way you walked – she said you were waddling, or squelching. She said she'd seen you had wet yourself." Peter looked around for some understanding. How could any reasonable person not come to a similar conclusion? "Naturally, she assumed … Given your age, Jo …"

"Jesus Christ! So, thanks to Frau Norbert and the actions of the village gossiper-in-chief, the entire village thinks I'm deranged and incontinent?" Joseph glared accusingly at Peter.

"Well, yes, I suppose they do."

"And you hot-footed up here to see how senile and decrepit I'd become, to add further fuel to the fire?"

"No, no, I was coming here anyway. Frau Hagspiel caught me as I was leaving the Adler."

"Well, for your information I am not suffering from senility or incontinence," Joseph said angrily.

"Honestly, Peter. Why did you trust Frau Hagspiel, of all people?" Heidi looked at him incredulously.

"It wasn't just her. Everyone was talking about it." Peter looked around, an expression of desperation in his eyes. "If it had only been Gertie – well, I would have taken it with a pinch of salt." He found nobody was listening to him. Heidi and Suzanne had returned to administering antiseptic to Joseph's legs.

Peter edged nearer for a closer look. "So, if you're not suffering from incontinence, what sort of accident have you had?"

"He set fire to his todger," Sep announced in his shrill voice.

"Oh. Right." Peter nodded. That seemed a reasonable explanation in the circumstances.

Fritz thought now was a good time to remove Sep and Stephan from the kitchen before either had the chance to utter any further comments.

For a few minutes, silence enveloped the room as the two women focused on wrapping gauze bandages around Joseph's wounds. Joseph's thoughts had already moved on to his social standing among his peers, and the village in general, and how it would be affected. In less than three hours, half the community believed he had degenerated into an incontinent wreck. He could see endless opportunities for amusement and ridicule at his expense. He eyed the guilty-looking Peter. "So, if you weren't on your way to check on my welfare, why were you coming here?"

The question prompted Peter out of his musings. "Oh, Herr Foster has returned to the village. He has asked me to contact you and invite you to meet him this evening at the Adler. He has a business proposition he would like to discuss with you."

The following day passed quickly for Sep. The ophthalmologist arrived and, after re-examining Sep's damaged eye, declared the patch could be removed. To Sep's relief his vision, although blurry, seemed to be reasonable. Later a thoroughly irritable Doctor Forsythe appeared at his bedside, accompanied by two nurses Sep didn't recognise. They removed the swaddling around his stump. For the first time Sep steeled himself to face the reality of his loss. Even though he had prepared himself, the absence of his lower leg and the sight of the blood-congealed stitches shocked him. The stump wasn't even a healthy-looking pink. It was a mottled swamp-like dark blue and green. To Sep's eyes it looked dead. He found himself gawping at the gory half-limb in speechless horror. Images of a butcher's shop flashed across his mind. As usual, Doctor Forsythe acted with professional detachment and apparent indifference to the distress of his patient.

"It's healing well, Mr Breitner. I'm pleased with your progress."

Sep reeled from the smell of alcohol on the doctor's breath. He flicked his eyes towards the clock. Eleven o'clock in the morning and the man was half-cut. Sep said nothing but cast his eyes towards one of the nurses. She gave him a tight-lipped grimace.

The doctor abruptly turned and made his way unsteadily towards the door. He didn't bother to turn around. "Can you get Mr Breitner, you know … mobile?"

The nurses' demeanour changed with the doctor's departure. It was as if a pressure valve had been released. They fussed and chatted with Sep as they changed his bandages, becoming relaxed and more animated. It was only when one left the room and returned pushing a wheelchair that he realised they were being cheery partly in anticipation of his reaction. The nurse parked the chair in front of him as if giving him a Christmas present. Once they'd helped him into it, they stood grinning at his obvious pleasure.

When they left, he propelled himself towards the window and gazed out. He didn't care that it was a dull, overcast day with the view obscured by a fine, persistent drizzle; it was his first view of the outside world in weeks. From what he could see, he was on the ground floor of a large chateau. A broad grassy terrace stretched out in front of him, with a gravel pathway running in front of an ornate stone balustrade, in the centre of which was a flight of steps. He assumed they led to some kind of formal garden. He longed to get out. He stayed glued to the window. Occasionally a few figures rushed past, hunched up in the rain, clutching at flying coats or capes.

As dusk approached, he retreated to his bed and sifted through the magazines. Hidden among them was another edition of *Better Times,* which he decided to read after the evening meal. For the first time since he had arrived at the hospital, he felt in charge of his fate.

"Well, look who's on the road to recovery!" Nurse Jones' cheery voice broke into his concentration. She laughed. "I couldn't wait to see the look on your face."

He spread his hands out. "I have my own chariot."

She stood in front of him, drinking in his happiness. "I can't believe the progress you've made."

"It is mostly down to you, you realise."

"You men always say that. The fact is, healing has much more to do with the amazing powers of the human body to repair itself. That, and a strong streak of self-survival and mental toughness." She pulled up a chair and sat down, smoothing her skirt beneath her as she did so, then leant towards him to examine his unbandaged eye. "That's mending nicely. How's your eyesight?"

He closed his good eye and squinted at her. "You have hazel eyes, some faint freckles on your nose and a small mole under your chin." He held her gaze for a second. "And you're blushing."

She looked flustered. "I am not."

He laughed. "Today is turning out to be a good day for me."

"No pain?"

"Not as much. I think I can manage with a lower dosage."

She looked unconvinced. "Would you like to go for a trundle?"

"A trundle?"

She nodded towards the door. "A trip. I'll push you. You've been cooped up in here for too long. Added to that you'll be doing me a favour. Pushing patients is part of nursing duties. It'll look as if I'm working."

"You are here in your free time?"

"Yes. I wanted to talk to you about your story."

"Did you like it?"

She raised her eyebrows and looked accusingly at him. "You were right. It's a very silly story, *and* it's a bit fruity, isn't it?"

"Fruity?" He looked at her, confused.

"Risqué … a bit near the knuckle."

"I don't understand."

She leant closer towards him and lowered her voice. "You know – writing about … you know." She glanced towards his crotch.

Sep's face fell as her meaning sank in. "Mein Gott! I hope I haven't offended you."

"I loved it." She giggled as she relived the memory. "Reading it felt a bit like sampling forbidden fruit. Did it really happen?"

"Of course. Naturally, I only learned the full story when I got older. But it is now part of our village history. It gets told over and over again. I filled in the missing bits." He glanced sideways at her. "I was only a small boy when it happened."

"A very mischievous boy." She looked at him, her eyes dancing. "I can imagine you shouting out rude words at the wrong moment." She got to her feet. "Come on, I'll take you for a walk. We can talk as we go." She pulled a blanket from the bed and wrapped it around him.

They set off.

Sep was amazed by the size of the hospital. Every part of the chateau had been put to use. The enormous ballroom, dining room and day rooms had been converted into wards. Iron beds lined the walls. The air was thick with the smell of disinfectant, carbolic soap and cigarette smoke. Gathered around were scores of bandaged men. He looked on, overwhelmed by the scale of their injuries. Men with heads swathed in dressings so large they looked like turbans. Men missing arms, legs, hands. Some lying staring sightlessly at the ceiling, others bent over in chairs, still as corpses. They passed yet more of the injured, swinging their way across the wards or along the corridors on crutches. Everywhere there was a constant low buzz of noise. Men gathered in small groups chatting, smoking, playing cards, writing letters, reading. Every now and then the ward was lit up by a sudden burst of ribald laughter as jokes were shared.

The men glanced across with mild curiosity as they passed, and nodded friendly acknowledgement to Sep. Many shouted greetings to Nurse Jones. It was evident that she was a popular figure. She batted them all off with good-humoured replies delivered with practised ease. Sep noticed she seemed to know them all by name and rank. He also noted the respect she commanded.

"How many men are here?" he asked

"About two thousand. It used to be double that, but we've repatriated all the patients in the top-floor wards, most of the officers, and of course all the German casualties."

"Am I the only enemy left?"

"You're the only Austrian." She clipped him gently on the top of his head. "And you're no longer an enemy."

To his delight, she wheeled him into a large room that had been converted into a canteen and parked his chair beside a trestle table. "Would you like something to drink? Tea? Coffee?"

42

He nodded. "I have become a tea drinker."

He glanced around as she went to the serving hatch. The canteen was busy. He spotted Nurse Mandy spoon-feeding a soldier who was missing both hands. Sep watched her and marvelled at her gentleness. He didn't want to think about what the future held for the injured man and resolved never to feel sorry for himself. Living without hands! The idea filled him with despair. He switched his attention to a group of injured soldiers at the far end of the room, chatting.

"Officers," Nurse Jones said, following his gaze. "The top floor of the chateau is reserved for commissioned ranks." She placed cups of tea on the table before sitting opposite him. "In theory, as a lieutenant, you could move in with them if you want."

"No. I told you, Susan, I'm not really a soldier. In any case, I much prefer it where I am."

She shuffled uneasily on the bench.

"Are you all right?"

She looked embarrassed and lowered her voice to a whisper. "I don't want to be rude, but when I'm in uniform would you mind not calling me by my Christian name?"

He looked puzzled.

"It's an etiquette thing. We're supposed to keep some distance between us and our patients."

"Oh. I see."

"It's OK when we're alone. Or when I'm out of uniform, off duty." She lowered her eyes and looked flustered. "I'm sorry. It's a bit awkward."

"Hey, don't worry. Nurse Jones it is – until it is not." He laughed.

"So, Mr Breitner, how can you not only speak English but write it so well?"

"I owe it to Mr Foster and Fraulein Rubenstein."

"Who are they?" She held up her hands. "No, don't tell me. I want you to tell me in writing, along with everything else that happened in your village."

He laughed, pleased. "You are asking me to write a book?"

"Well, why not?"

He considered the idea. "I'm not sure what I could write about. Being a farmer's son isn't that exciting, you know, and not a lot happens in a small village."

"What do you mean?" She sounded exasperated. She retrieved his story from the pocket of her uniform and smoothed the papers on the table before stabbing her finger at various passages. "I'd like to know what this disconcerting letter is all about, what these two English chaps are doing in your village, and who is this Frau Hagspiel, the village gossip. I like the sound of your mother, and I want to know more about her, and your father – and you." She looked intently at him. "I'd like to know how you learned English, and how you ended up hundreds of miles away from your village in Austria and your comrades in Italy, in an English field hospital in Northern France."

"With one leg missing, drinking English tea, talking to a short-sighted English nurse."

She vibrated with half-suppressed laughter. "Exactly!"

He pondered the idea. "*If* I wrote about my life, there will be some dark episodes," he said eventually. "If you remember, that is not what you said you wanted to read."

"Well, no. But it can't be *all* bad. I mean, you said yourself, you had a happy childhood."

"Happy – but no different from most other children. It is hardly interesting. Eating dirt, falling out of trees, pulling legs off spiders, chasing the village girls. It is not what your William Shakespeare wrote about."

"Then write about the interesting things that happened to you." She sipped her tea. "I mean it – you write well." She looked at him over the rim of her cup and grinned. "Your story brightened my day."I've got to travel back and forth across the Channel over the next few weeks with the evacuees. It would be nice to have your story to read."

A stab of pain shot from his injured leg, making him wince.

She noticed his discomfort. "No more morphine unless you agree." She smiled evilly at him.

"You have a cruel, sinister side to your nature, Nurse Jones."

"So, we have a deal?"

"Of course." He winced again.

She stood up and became serious. "Come on, drink up. We need to get you back."

Sep couldn't hide his look of dismay. "No, please sit down." He reached out and grabbed her hand, gently pulling her back towards the table. "Susan – Nurse Jones. I have to deal with this. I am not having my life ruled by running off for morphine every time I feel uncomfortable." He looked at her with pleading eyes. "I was enjoying our conversation."

She sank uncertainly back into her chair. "You need to guard against pushing yourself too hard." A flicker of a smile flashed across her lips. "And you need to remember I'm the professional. That means I'm in charge. Ten minutes." She raised her eyebrows at him – a look he found endearing.

"Ten minutes," he agreed. "During which time I will stay silent while you tell me about yourself."

"That won't take *five* minutes. I haven't lived such an interesting life as you. Here and Skipton are the only two places I have lived." She slipped her hand out of his grasp and took a sip of tea.

"Skipton is where?'

"It's in the north of England – in the West Riding of Yorkshire. It was where I was born, baptised, went to school, grew up, and no doubt would have ended up getting married, having children and grandchildren and eventually dying and being buried – if I hadn't volunteered.

"And your family?"

"I'm the eldest of three sisters. We live in an old dilapidated rectory that's cold in winter, hot in summer and damp all year round. Father died two years ago, but my mother is still with us, bright as a button. Still bossing us all about."

"She must miss you."

"Yeah, I'm sure she does. But she was determined to send her girls out into the world to make something of themselves." She glanced across at him. "She suggested I join the Voluntary Aid Detachment as a nurse."

"A few thousand soldiers have a lot to thank her for then."

She looked at him with a curious expression of surprise mixed with pleasure. "You know, you do come out with such nice comments."

He chuckled "Will you return to Skipton when all this is finished?" He jerked his chin to indicate the hospital.

She sighed. "That's the big question. The idea of returning to a life of domestic drudgery or some boring job in a corner shop – or, worse, being a factory slave in the local mill – fills me with horror."

"You could get married."

She snorted. "And become a kept woman." She thought for a few seconds. "It wouldn't be so bad if there was a rich local lord of the manor." She ran her hand over her headscarf as if smoothing her hair. "The truth is, I don't know what the future holds, and it's beginning to worry me." Absently, she looked over at Mandy, who was still patiently spoon-feeding her patient. "There's not many options for women in England at the moment," she said wistfully.

"Kinder, Küche, Kirche."

"What?"

He repeated the phrase. "It is a saying we have in Austria. It sums up the role expected of women. Children, kitchen, church."

"It's pretty much the same in England – apart from the church bit."

"Things will change. Even in my small village life can never be the same."

She looked at him curiously. "Why and how? You can tell me all about it in your book."

Sep bent his head and studied the table top. She had given him an idea. Maybe he *should* write things down! God knows he had lost his bearings over the past four years. The world had changed. It needed to. Now, after the war, he had no idea what the future held. Revisiting the past might anchor him. "When is your next evacuation trip?"

"Next week. Assuming the UK hospitals and rehab centres have capacity," she answered, her thoughtful gaze fixed on him as if she was trying to read his mind.

"I can write something for you," he said confidently. "How long will you be away?"

"Two weeks. I'm taking a week's holiday."

He felt a ripple of disappointment.

"I'm catching a train to Skipton. We're having an early Christmas celebration."

"Does that mean you will be here for Christmas?"

She nodded sadly. "I got the short straw." She nodded towards Nurse Handsworth. "Mandy covers for me, and I cover for her."

"Well, I'm pleased, even if you're not." He looked happily at her. "Christmas with Nurse Jones. What a great present!"

She shook her head. "Sep Breitner, you are becoming such a flirt." She reached over and moved his cup out of his reach. "Come on. This time you are being sent to bed. You definitely need some rest."

The next day breakfast came early. Sep took the opportunity to chat to the affable orderly. It had taken Sep some time to attune his ears to his thick Glaswegian accent.

"Could I ask your advice, Corporal?"

"It's Sandy McPherson, sir. Everyone calls me Sandy. Ask whit ye like. Ah can always say no."

"I need to sort out a few things."

"Like what?"

"Money. Clothes – I assume my uniform has been destroyed. I need some crutches so I can find my way around the hospital."

By mid-morning, not only did Sep have a British Army uniform, but he also had a Salvation Army demob bag containing a

46

full set of civilian clothing and a Red Cross parcel of soap, toothbrushes, toothpaste, a flannel, chocolates, tins of condensed milk, other food items, two tins of tobacco and a packet of Woodbines. He also had four shillings advanced against a promissory note against his Imperial Army back-pay.

He eyed the crutches. "I would like to give them a go. Just to stand and get used to them," he added quickly as he saw McPherson about to protest. "Come on, give me a hand." He held out his arms expectantly.

The corporal glanced nervously towards the door. "I dinnae think we should."

Sep wasn't prepared for the wave of nausea or the intense pain that seared through his stump as his body was raised to a vertical position.

"No' as easy as ye expected, eh sir?" The corporal moved to take his weight.

It was all Sep could do to shake his head. "Keep me still for a minute or so. I'm sure it will reduce." Gradually the agony faded away. He felt the corporal progressively reduce his support until Sep was able to bear his own weight. He looked at the corporal in triumph. For five minutes he stood and gazed about. To his disappointment, he realised it would be impossible to take a step. His left leg was too weak, and he lacked the confidence to even try. "Every day we will practise," he said with grim determination. He glanced across at the orderly. "You will help me, Sandy?"

The corporal helped him back into the chair. "Aye. But ye gave me a direct order, ye ken?" He grinned at him. "Ah dinnae want tae get on the wrong side o' Nurse Jones."

As Corporal McPherson departed, clutching two Woodbines, Sep picked up the writing pad and pen. He grinned to himself. Through his writing, he would tell Nurse Jones so much – but not everything. Despite his initial enthusiasm his confidence quickly evaporated. He stared at the blank piece of paper in consternation. Why was writing about his life suddenly so difficult? He had so many memories. They tumbled into one another, vivid and vibrant. His mother, father, brothers and sister, friends, neighbours. He could see them all clearly; their laughter, arguments, jokes and upsets all etched in his mind. Right at the centre stood Sep Breitner: as a happy, carefree little boy, an awkward, bashful teenager, a confident, fit young man. Sep felt his throat constrict. A fit young man! And what was he now? He glanced down at his missing leg and answered his own question. A sad husk of his former self. A man broken in body – and in mind. A different Sep Breitner, living in a different world.

He shook his head and refocused his attention back on the empty page. It was no good. The pen refused to move across the paper. He threw it down in frustration. He knew what he wanted to write about. In his mind he was reliving the events that had shaped his childhood, developed his personality, underpinned his beliefs and made him into the person he was.

The thought came like a bolt out of the blue. *That* was the issue. His memories had made him what he was *then* – not what he was *now*. As soon as the realisation entered his head, Sep felt the black ball of terror emerge from the dark recesses of his mind.

He buried his head in his hands and inwardly wailed at what he had become. It was so obvious. His childhood memories appeared as the bright, sunny uplands of his life. Pure, unsullied, happy, untroubled. The Sep Breitner of those days was an innocent – a completely different person. An irrational logic took hold of him. Writing about his memories would destroy the only good part of his life. Making any connection would be an intrusion – no, it would be worse than that. It would be an insult, a pollution, an assault. He couldn't do it.

Sep eyed his crutches and felt his spirits plummet still further. What was he now? A man with a crippled body and a broken mind. He felt the familiar depression and despair start to build. He knew that, in this mood, he wouldn't be able to write anything. But he'd made Susan a promise. The task was simple – and his failure to complete it might mean she would think badly of him. The prospect forced him to pick up his pen. He was not going to be beaten. He wasn't going to let Susan Jones down. Despite his determination, he remained motionless as he wrestled with the dilemma. Eventually, a solution began to come to him. There was no point fighting it. The old Sep Breitner was a different person – not a stranger, but someone he used to know and looked upon with affection. It was best to leave *him* in his own world.

Father Wagner was troubled. From the vantage point of St Martin's church graveyard, he gazed across the valley. He didn't take in the natural beauty of his parish. The lush, vibrant green spring leaves that adorned the mountain ash trees, and the splendour of the snow-topped mountain crags made vivid by a piercing blue sky, hardly intruded into his consciousness. He was so lost in thought that he barely registered the arrival of the two carriages, and only glanced with mild curiosity at Herr Breitner scurrying along the back path.

He knew all about the newcomers, of course, and absently made a mental note to formally welcome the visitors in the next few days.

He glanced at the letter in his hand, and decided to reread it. The contents were so clear and precise. Someone possessing considerable skill had taken particular care in drafting it. The case was laid bare. The arguments cogently expressed. The moral and practical issues comprehensively dealt with, and the conclusions confidently stated. It was hard not to argue with the recommendations, even if he was minded to. Father Wagner shook his head to banish the ludicrous thought. The conclusions and recommendations brooked no dissent, and for that he ought to be grateful. The letter was deliberately devised to ensure he, and anyone else who read it, had to comply.

The 'recommendations' weren't anything of the sort. They were instructions – slyly crafted to appear at first glance to be reluctantly arrived at, benevolent, sympathetic, compassionate even. He pressed his lips into a grimace. These were orders, and he was expected to comply. He could see the logic. The missive let everyone off the hook: the bishop, the Diocesen Council, the abbess and of course himself. The letter was their release, their 'get out of jail' card. No wonder such care had been taken over its composition.

For a few seconds he felt uncomfortable. There was an undeniable deceit at work. It ought to play badly within his conscience – and his faith. The fact neither was troubled made him question what life as a priest was about. As for the victim? Well, he had only himself to blame. Victim? Victims, more like. Father Wagner shook his head as if to erase the need to consider them. They had been given a way out. It was up to them to take it.

Of all the parties, he was the subservient player in the matter. His role was to do as he was told. Besides, Dopplegau was his first parish, and it wouldn't do to cross the bishop when his career in the church had barely started. He knew any doubts and concerns on his part would count for nothing – assuming he was minded to express them. He would be branded an ungrateful troublemaker if he offered any opinion, let alone an objection.

Carefully he refolded the letter, sighed and turned towards the church. He decided an appeal to the Almighty for clemency and understanding would be more than enough to clear his conscience.

Joseph's progress that evening along the narrow gravel lane was a lot more comfortable than he had expected. Heidi and Suzanne had made sure he looked his best for his meeting with Herr Foster. After ninety minutes Joseph had found himself washed, shaved and decked out in his Sunday *tracht*: a clean white shirt and thin bootlace tie, a heavy loden jacket with subtle red piping, his best lederhosen, knee-length woollen socks and a pair of gleaming leather boots. Heidi handed him his fedora and walking stick. Joseph was required to parade up and down the kitchen to practise walking. It wouldn't do to enter the Adler in a bandy-legged waddle. As it was, the bandages round his injured thighs minimised any chafing and Joseph was able to adopt an almost dignified gait. At the appointed time he left the house.

Despite the lateness of the hour, residents along his route came out of their farms and cottages to watch his progress, scrutinise his comportment and assess his sanity. Joseph was pleased with the opportunity to scotch the rumours that by now had reached every corner of Dopplegau. He nodded politely and tipped his hat to acknowledge his friends and neighbours. Inevitably a few could not resist the opportunity to have some light-hearted fun at his expense. He tried to ignore the number of chamber pots that were waved at him, and declined the invitations to stop and use the privy. Nobody went too far. Herr Breitner commanded too much respect within the village. Besides, the news that he had been invited to a personal business meeting with Herr Foster had swept around the community. The canny Brandterwalders swiftly recognised that a good commercial deal could potentially benefit them all. It wouldn't do to get on the wrong side of Joseph Breitner now.

The *Gasthaus* was almost empty. It was midweek. The farmers would be busy bedding down their animals for the night. The only local present was a morose-looking Helmut Hagspiel, sitting alone nursing a beer that he planned to drink slowly, to delay returning home to his wife.

Joseph gave him a polite nod.

George Foster was the only guest present. He sat expectantly in the small alcove that was ideal for discreet conversations. When Joseph walked in, George rose to greet him with a warm, friendly handshake. "Joseph – it is so good to see you, and thank you for coming at such short notice." His greeting was delivered in impeccable Hochdeutsch.

Joseph was charmed by the young man, as he had been when they had met over two years previously when the Englishman had first arrived in the village. "The pleasure is all mine, Herr Foster. George. It has been a long time since your last visit – eight months, I think?"

"Far too long, as far as I'm concerned." George gestured towards the chair. "Can I get you a drink?"

"Something light if we are to discuss business."

His host chuckled. "Of course – a Pils?"

Joseph nodded and made himself comfortable. Foster beckoned the hovering Franz Zinnermann, the Adler's landlord, and placed their order. While they waited Joseph reacquainted himself with the young man sitting opposite.

George Foster was English, which was sufficient to win him a certain status within the village community. He attended church every Sunday – not because he was religious, but because it was the local custom. The gesture instantly endeared him to Father Wagner and almost all the women of the village. They were prepared to overlook his Protestantism on the basis that they would succeed in converting him to the one true faith in the fullness of time. More importantly, in the eyes of the community, he'd taken the trouble to learn German. Not only that, but he had made honest – albeit clumsy – attempts to modify his accent to incorporate the Brandterwalder dialect and idioms. Towards the end of his last visit, he had even felt confident enough to tell an English joke to an audience who politely slapped their thighs and laughed, though the majority had not understood the humour.

He dressed for the most part casually. However, for business meetings or the numerous festivals, civic events and Sunday services to which he was invited, he took the trouble to turn out in the English style in a three-piece suit with matching tie, and an impeccably folded handkerchief protruding from his top pocket. He was a well-built young man with a strong, athletic physique. His physical attractiveness and good manners, combined with his foreign mystique, drew admiring glances, especially from mothers with eligible daughters. So far he'd successfully avoided any entanglements. He was excellent company, and Joseph was looking forward to their discussion.

"I trust you are well, Joseph?" George moved the paraffin lamp to one side so he could see Joseph better.

Joseph shot him an irritated glance before realising the comment was made in innocence. Even Frau Hagspiel hadn't had sufficient time to draw Mr Foster into the rumour mill.

"Never better, thank you. You are looking in good spirits yourself."

"Indeed I am." He raised his glass. "Cheers."

"Zum voll."

Across the *Gasthaus*, Herr Zinnermann noted the exchange and smirked to himself. The signs looked positive.

Joseph took a generous swig of the Pils, smacked his lips appreciatively, settled himself comfortably in his chair and looked across at his friend. "So, George, what is this business matter you wish to discuss?"

"I have recommended you to Sir William."

Joseph managed to conceal his surprise. Long experience of negotiating business deals had taught him never to show emotion – especially in the early stages. "Recommended me as what?"

"The best builder and craftsman in this part of the Brandterwald."

"The best builder in all of Brandterwald," Joseph said, as if it were a fact. "However, there are better craftsmen."

George grinned. "Honest and modest at the same time. I have seen examples of your work. You built this *Gasthaus*, I understand."

"Rebuilt it. There has been an Adler on this site for over three hundred years."

"I've seen the house you built for Herr Bechter in Gau."

"House, forge and workshop. The Bechters are my daughter-in-law's family."

"Well designed, solidly built and incorporating some new technology and innovations."

"That's Herr Bechter's influence. He's very forward-thinking."

"Precisely the qualities Sir William is seeking."

"Forgive me, George, but exactly why did you recommend me to Sir William? I am assuming he requires something to be built – or renovated."

"Indeed." George leant forward in his chair as if about to say something confidential – then a short, thickset man dressed in smart tweed trousers and a smoking jacket, burst through the door that led to the reception area, and staircase to the guest bedrooms. George looked startled and leapt to his feet as the man approached.

"Sir William, I wasn't expecting you quite so early."

"Relax, George. I'm keen to get things done." He put his hands on his hips and gazed approvingly around the *Gasthaus*. "I can see why you like it here, George – very accommodating." He swivelled around and looked sternly at Joseph, who was slowly getting to his feet. "George, aren't you going to introduce me to your companion?"

"Of course. Sir William, this is Herr Breitner…" George waved his hand towards Joseph.

53

"Ah, the man who might be able to turn my dream into reality."

Joseph hadn't understood a word of the exchange. His brief exposure to the English language had convinced him that Anglo-Saxons spoke far too quickly, and had thousands of words for objects that only justified a single expression. He recognised his name however, deduced he was being introduced, and was happy to extend his hand. He winced as Sir William delivered a finger-crushing handshake while subjecting him to a fierce, unblinking stare. Joseph was immediately on the defensive – as Sir William intended. He quickly recovered and inwardly smiled. If Sir William meant to intimidate him, it was an error of judgement.

Outside the village, the man brought the pony and cart to a stop and stared along the street. The sun had long since dropped behind the mountain, and the valley was engulfed in twilight. Only a crescent moon and the yellow glow of the Adler's paraffin lamps shed a spectral light into the main street. The man could just make out the shape of two parked carriages. For several minutes he stood still, scanning the street and listening for any sign of movement. The Gasthaus worried him. Midweek, and at this time of night, no one should be out drinking, yet the lights were on. As if on cue, the main door of the Adler suddenly opened and briefly illuminated a sad-looking figure that slowly emerged and trudged unsteadily across the street until it disappeared into the gloom.

"Can we go on now?" a thin, timid voice pleaded.

The man wheeled around. "Keep quiet, you silly girl," he snarled. "Do you want everyone to hear us?"

The young woman on the cart shrank away from him, and clutched the tiny infant in her arms tightly as if to shield it from a physical assault.

"Do you want to advertise our presence, eh?" He spat the words out as if each one was wrapped in bile.

In the dark she shook her head, wept cold tears and waited in trembling silence.

He regretted his harsh words. He was exhausted and scared and shouldn't have taken his fear out on the girl. He would apologise later. Right now though, he had too much on his mind. He resumed his watch. He expected the Gasthaus lights to be extinguished, then their way would be clear. He waited with increasing irritation. In fact, instead of the lights being dimmed, it seemed that they had got brighter. The girl had a point: they couldn't stand here all night. It was already getting cold, and they needed to reach shelter. They had to make a move. His already black mood worsened as the infant started to whimper. He did his best to block out the sound.

He moved the pony on at a gentle walk, all the time scanning the road ahead. The soft crunching of the cart wheels on the gravel road seemed to him to be amplified. He was sure the whole village would be able to hear their approach. Behind him the infant continued to whinge, adding to his rage. An imagined movement behind one of the parked carriages caused him to stop dead. His heart beat hard and fast. He strained his eyes, desperately seeking out the threat. The baby's complaints increased.

"For Christ's sake, shut the kid up," he hissed.

The girl fumbled with her cloak in the darkness, trying not to drop the child. The thick layers of clothing defeated her. She briefly considered passing the increasingly distressed youngster to the man but stopped herself, fearful of what he might do. Eventually, her fingers found their way inside and she felt the baby's lips fasten onto her breast. She closed her eyes and prayed her thanks.

Satisfied that the movement had been an illusion and reassured by the silence, the man yanked on the reins and urged the pony on. It was better to make a dash. If anyone was on the street, it was too bad. They had to chance it. Although they didn't have far to go, it seemed as if the journey took forever. They drew level with the Adler and the two parked carriages. Nobody challenged them. The man breathed a sigh of relief when the lamps of the inn faded behind them. Darkness returned. The man stopped to allow his eyes to adjust to the gloom. From this point he had to navigate solely by the light of the stars and moon. Shelter lay five kilometres further on. He breathed in deeply and tried to calm himself. The worst was now over, he tried to convince himself. He jerked the reins to set them on their way. In less than a minute they passed the last inhabited building. They were on their own.

From the shadows of Herr Drössel's bakery, a black-cloaked figure stood and watched their lonely progress until the forest engulfed them. Even then, the figure continued to stare at the spot where the track disappeared into the trees, as if half-expecting them to reappear. Eventually, the figure turned and walked quickly and silently towards home.

Franz Zinnermann quietly positioned two additional oil lamps around the trio who were bent over the drawings, spread out across the dining table. George nodded his thanks before turning to Joseph, who moved one of the lamps to cast more light over a detailed set of graphics.

"Whoever designed this is a master architect. I've never seen such attention to detail." Joseph was genuinely impressed.

George translated.

"I employ the best, Herr Breitner. The point is, what do you think? Can it be built?" Sir William's manner was brusque. During their meeting Joseph occasionally wondered whether he was getting irritable. It was only George's conspiratorial wink after one such brisk comment that reassured Joseph this was just his master's manner. If Sir William was irked, it was perhaps only out of frustration at the need for the constant translation.

Joseph eased himself erect and clasped his hands behind his back while George delivered the latest interpretation. Joseph was getting tired. It was late and the disjointed conversation was beginning to exasperate him. He decided to set out his concerns. If it upset Sir William, well so be it.

"Of course, the building can be built. However, some elements of the design need to be amended. For example, the main structure." Joseph stabbed his forefinger down on the plans. "These pillars are far too thin. They will hold the roof up in the summer but won't take the weight of winter snow. You have to realise, Sir William, we can get two metres of snow overnight in this part of the Brandterwald." Joseph didn't wait for a reply but pressed on. "The plumbing system relies too much on standing water storage tanks that would freeze and burst. The proposed number, positioning and capacity of the *Kachelofens* are inadequate. As a consequence, the space allocated for wood fuel storage is too small. The isolation of the site means provision would need to be made to double the number of stables. This, in turn, means the size of the hayloft and carriage houses would need to be increased."

Joseph continued his critique; turning over each drawing, pointing out the problems and suggesting what needed to be done to make the building work.

For nearly an hour Sir William allowed Joseph to continue, uninterrupted. He listened intently to George's simultaneous translation, all the while watching Joseph with a stony expression.

Joseph finally came to the end of his analysis. "The building is beautiful, original, imaginative and basically well designed. However, it is clear that the architect has little experience of constructing buildings capable of withstanding the extreme weather conditions in Austria." He turned to face the aristocrat, half-expecting to be met with fury. He waited patiently until George completed the translation.

For a few seconds, the room was silent. Sir William continued to stare at Joseph.

Joseph drained his glass of beer and prepared to be dismissed. He was taken aback when Sir William advanced towards him, looking delighted. He grabbed Joseph's hand and shook it vigorously, simultaneously slapping him on the back.

"Congratulations, Herr Breitner. An excellent analysis, if I may say so." He looked at George. "By God, George, you've found a real expert here."

"I take it you wish to commission Herr Breitner to build the Lodge?"

"Build it, select and supervise all the trades, craftsmen and sub-contractors – the whole shooting match, George."

Joseph stood, looking perplexed. He hadn't followed the exchange, but guessed that Sir William was very happy, or perhaps he was amused at Joseph's audacity.

Sir William poked his finger into Joseph's chest. "I want this man to build my dream hunting lodge." He laughed and gave Joseph a friendly pat on the shoulder. "By God, he knows what he's talking about."

"We need to agree terms, Sir William – costs, timeframes."

Sir William waved his arm dismissively. "Yes, yes, George. I'll leave the details to you. You know my requirements."

So it was that Joseph Breitner arrived back home late that evening, having secured the largest, most prestigious and profitable building commission of his life.

t took Joseph two years to build the Lodge, as it became known, during which time the fortunes of the Breitners surpassed all his expectations. But Joseph didn't try to hoard all the benefits for himself. He generously distributed sub-contract works throughout the community.

Sir William frequently returned to monitor progress. Each time he brought with him a small entourage of his wealthy friends and business associates for two, sometimes three, weeks of mountaineering and hunting. As a consequence, the bounty spread to the younger men of the village, who used their knowledge of the mountains and the game that lived there to act as guides and beaters. The young women of the village bided their time, confident that, once the Lodge was complete, Sir William would need chambermaids, cooks, cleaners and housekeepers.

The village demonstrated their approval of the largesse that Joseph Breitner brought by electing him *Bürgermeister*. The honour ought to have cemented the Breitners' already considerable status within the community. However, something happened that bruised the standing of the family. The incident became Sep's second earliest childhood memory.

Raised voices drifted up the stairs into his bedroom. At first, the exchanges were mild and barely distracted him. Then the argument escalated. Each gust of disagreement grew stronger and louder as the storm developed. Sep heard his father's voice becoming deeper and more aggressive and his mother's responses became firmer and more resolute. The gusts quickly became angry, vicious squalls, and Sep's world rocked on its foundations.

His parents had argued before, of course, but their arguments were usually over in minutes. This was different. Sep went to the top of the stairs. He felt the bonds of his secure and certain existence begin to loosen. His new young brother sensed the disturbance in the atmosphere and, from the refuge of his cot, began to whimper. Sep was sure Klaus's crying would distract his mother and the squabble would end. However, the passion of the clash had obviously swamped her maternal antennae. She hurled another comment at her husband, only to receive a shouted reply that had Sep reeling in shock. He'd never heard his father speak to his mother in such a way. Sep covered his ears to try to shut out the sound, and tears streamed uncontrollably down his face. He desperately wanted to run to his mother, be engulfed in her arms, feel her warmth and her reassuring kisses on his cheek. But he remained rooted at the top of the stairs, terrified.

Klaus's whimpers intensified into a wail of distress. Still the argument raged. Sep buried his head in his arms and curled into a tight ball. The fury showed no signs of abating. The sound of an object being banged down on the range prompted him into a blind panic. He had to rescue his brother. He screamed and ran to Klaus's bedroom. Klaus stood; his tiny hands gripping the cot rail, his eyes wide, face contorted, beetroot-red and wet with tears, frantic for reassurance. Sep ran to the cot, climbed in, wrapped his baby brother in his arms and pulled the covers over them both. They clung to each other, sobbing.

The sound of the bedroom door slamming and the stifled cries of their offspring, jolted the warring couple out of their hostility. They were overcome with feelings of guilt and remorse. His mother flew upstairs.

Sep found his blanket cocoon being lifted. He and his brother were soothed, rocked, patted and calmed with soft words and cooing. Gradually the boys stopped crying. Sep risked a glance back towards the bedroom door. His father stood framed there, his head low, exhausted. All the fight had gone out of him.

Fritz glanced across and met his elder son's eye. For a few seconds father and son held each other's gaze, before Fritz crossed the room and sat next to his family. His big hands caressed his sons' heads before gently stroking his wife's cheek.

"We're stupid arguing like this," he muttered.

Heidi looked at him with tear-filled eyes. "Fritz, you know I'm right. It's not what we are as a family." Her voice was tired but firm.

Fritz held up his hand to forestall any further argument. "Don't," he said quietly. "*If* the rumours are true."

"They're not just rumours, Fritz. Frau Ansbacher told me. She's not a gossip like Gertie Hagspiel"

Fritz cupped his wife's face gently and stared into her eyes. He wanted an end to their hostilities. "We don't know the facts – and even if we did, what business is it of ours?"

"It's our business – because it's wrong."

"*Was* wrong. It happened a long time ago. We can't go spreading rumours or slander."

"OK, OK, let's not argue. We need – *I* need – to know the truth. You can call me irrational if you like, but I have to know." Heidi kissed Sep on the top of his head and handed him to his father before walking purposefully towards the door, carrying baby Klaus.

Fritz looked perplexed. "Where are you going?"

"To question Father Wagner directly." She swept out, leaving Sep and Fritz staring at each other.

Gradually a slow, grudging smile spread across Fritz's face.

Sep was reassured. Calm had been restored. He smiled back at his father.

Fritz ruffled his son's hair. "Women, eh?"

For the first time in his life, Sep felt a real connection to his father.

Whatever truth his mother managed to extract from Father Wagner, the impact was immediate. Heidi Breitner stopped attending Mass at St Martin's church. Her absence shook the community to its core. The church represented the village. It was its soul, its conscience and its heartbeat. Failure to support the church constituted a betrayal of everyone. Worse – by not attending, Heidi Breitner excluded herself from confession. In the eyes of the village, that represented a mortal sin and caused more disquiet.

Initial concern for Heidi's absence was quickly replaced by silent condemnation once it became evident that illness wasn't the cause. The mild disdain rapidly developed into sly hostility, malicious comments and deliberate shunning, stoked by Gertie Hagspiel, who gleefully assumed the role of village tormentor-in-chief. Her sense of betrayal following Joseph's election as *Bürgermeister* – a position that, in her mind, ought to have passed to her husband – now had a convenient outlet. She spread petty spite, falsehoods, half-truths and innuendo about the Breitners in general, and Heidi in particular. Most of the women of the village were happy to believe the gossip, or at least do little to counter the slanders.

For the most part, the men of the village chose to ignore the vendetta. The Breitners were too well regarded – even by Helmut Hagspiel who, despite his wife's ambitions, had never wanted to be *Bürgermeister* in the first place. The men gathered as they always did in the Adler after Sunday morning Mass to talk about their own cares, politics, the state of the pastures and the health of their animals.

Heidi wasn't without friends and support. Suzanne Wachter and a few others remained loyal, despite their ignorance of the real reason for Heidi's boycott.

No one within Dopplegau knew what had caused Heidi's self-imposed exile, apart from Fritz and Father Wagner, and they'd reached an uneasy agreement not to share their knowledge.

One other person found out by using his contacts and applying some rudimentary detective work. For the moment he kept

61

his findings to himself. Although they weren't to know it, his intelligence cost the women of Dopplegau dearly.

The simmering discord went on for weeks, then months.

It ended in the school playground.

It took some time before the poison worked its way to the childish world that Sep occupied. But, thanks to Gertie Hagspiel's vindictiveness the day wasn't long in coming. Gradually, Sep became aware that the previously warm welcomes his family received when they went shopping had become stiff, awkward and cool. Neighbours drifted off, rather than stay and engage in polite conversation. Frau Hagspiel made a point of looking the other way or crossing the street on the few occasions she and Heidi met in public. Sep's innocent mind failed to make any connection until Will Hagspiel's comment in the school playground.

"Your mama won't go to heaven," he said out of the blue.

Sep was taken aback, but tried to make sense of the statement. As far as he was concerned, his mother was fit and well. He knew she was expecting another baby – but only very sick or old people died. Of that Sep was sure. "Yes, she will," he replied, still bewildered by Will's assertion.

"No, she won't," Will said with childish certainty.

Sep found the comment disturbing. He stopped poking at the long-legged spiders they had been tormenting, and stared at Will in confusion. "Why are you saying that?"

" 'Cos God's punishing her."

Sep felt a wave of shock. Why would God be upset with his mama? She crossed herself every morning as she passed the family crucifix that gazed down on them all from the corner in the *Stube*. "No, he ain't," he said firmly.

"Is so." Will sensed he'd succeeded in upsetting Sep and, with the sly instinct of a bully, looked for the opportunity to press the torment further.

"What for? She ain't done nothing."

"My mama says she don't go to church – and that makes her heathen. Heathens don't go to heaven." Will smirked, bent down and picked up a spider and began to pull its legs off with casual cruelty.

Sep was astounded. He didn't know how to counter the apparent logic of his playmate's statement. It was true. His mama no longer went to church. Until now, he hadn't attached much importance to it. After all, his grandfather, father, younger brother and he still attended Mass.

Sep was speechless.

Fortunately, Stephan came to his aid. "That's not true. God loves everyone. You only don't go to heaven if you've been really bad – tell lies, murdering people – things like that."

"Being heathen is bad. My mama says." Will threw the small, legless corpse of the spider to the ground before stamping on it. He turned to square up to Sep. "Heathens don't believe in God." He spat the words into Sep's face.

"My mama believes in God – she prays. She makes me and my brother pray every day," Sep said, confident this fact would prove his argument. "We say grace and everything."

"You got to pray in church. Otherwise it don't count, stupid."

"'Course it counts. And you're the one that's stupid."

"You're stupid, and your mama is stupid as well. Stupid, stupid, stupid." Will emphasised each spite-filled taunt, thrusting his face closer to Sep's with each barb.

Sep's mind went cold. Nobody insulted his mama. He glared at the sneering face in front of him and planted his fist squarely on his tormentor's nose with such force that Will tumbled backwards, ending up in a sprawled heap.

For a few seconds Will lay still; shocked, his head spinning, unable to comprehend what had happened. Blood pouring from his nostrils panicked him back to reality. He screamed at the top of his voice.

Stephan scrambled to his feet. His instinct was to run away from the dreadful scene, but his loyalty to his friend rooted him to the spot.

Sep found the coldness hadn't left him. He sat and gazed dispassionately at Will, who was doing his best to increase the volume of his screaming, confident his distress would attract the attention of the other children and hopefully some avenging adults. Help wasn't long in coming.

Sep was vaguely aware of being propelled through the throng of bemused-looking children into the school building and into Father Wagner's office. He looked on with detachment as Father Wagner, tall, black and menacing, barked at Will to cease his noise, while he staunched the youngster's bleeding. Once calm had been established, the priest began his interrogation.

Sep allowed Will and Stephan to do the talking. His mind was blank. He knew he was in trouble, but was equally sure his action was justified. He couldn't imagine what the consequences might be and only held one thought in his mind: to tell the truth.

To Sep's surprise, the cross-examination was over much quicker than expected. Once the priest had established the facts, he seemed eager to deal with the matter as fast as possible.

Stephan was dismissed and ran back to his class, Father Wagner's praise for his honesty and loyalty to his friend ringing in his ears.

To his chagrin, Will found himself on the receiving end of one month's altar duty, and the awful prospect of a further interview with Father Wagner, this time with his parents present. He fled the priest's room and blubbed his way home.

Sep sat quietly and returned Father Wagner's silent, thoughtful gaze. Although he was confused, he was sufficiently attuned to adult behaviour to realise that something was troubling the man in front of him.

Eventually, the priest made up his mind. "This has gone too far," he muttered. "Come, Master Breitner, I think it's time we went to see your mother." He grabbed his hat and cloak, and the pair made their way down the hill towards the Breitners' farm.

Heidi was surprised to see her son home from school so early, and even more surprised to see the priest standing on her threshold.

"We need to talk, Frau Breitner." Father Wagner didn't wait for an invitation. He swept off his hat and entered the *Stube*.

Sep found himself ushered to his brother's room and invited to spend the rest of the afternoon playing with his younger sibling. He was called down, not for admonishment, but when his tea was ready. On entering the *Stube*, he was perplexed to see Father Wagner seated at the table enjoying coffee and cakes, and engaged in conversation with his parents.

Only briefly did the easy atmosphere dissipate when, as Father Wagner made to leave, he broached the subject of a punishment for the blow to Will's nose. "I feel maybe Sep ought to join Will on one month's altar duty?" he suggested. The way he wrung his black hat in his hands betrayed his embarrassment at raising the issue.

Out of the corner of his eye, Sep saw his mother tense and a look of anger flash across her face. She was about to respond when the firm, calm voice of his father cut across her.

"I think, Father Wagner, that having just agreed a way forward to correct one injustice, it would be a shame to sully the day by creating another."

Sep stared in confusion at his father, who was smiling thinly at the priest. "Rest assured I will have words with my son about his conduct."

They eyed each other: the priest, nervous and uncertain; Fritz Breitner, firm and intractable.

Father Wagner knew he didn't have the moral high ground. He gave a curt nod to break the impasse. "You're right, of course." He tipped his hat and departed.

Fritz slowly closed the door and turned to his son, a stern look on his face. "Well, son, what do you have to say for yourself?"

Sep glanced uncertainly at his mother, who looked unsmilingly back at him, her hands resting on her pregnant belly. "I hit Will Hagspiel because he said nasty things about you."

"Did he apologise?" his father asked gently.

Sep shook his head. "He said it again." He looked directly at his mother. Her eyes moistened and the flicker of a smile crossed her lips.

"And you're not sorry you hit him?"

Sep shook his head and looked at the floor before risking a brief glance towards his father.

His father grinned and nodded his head. "Good lad. Always stand up to bullies and people who insult our family." He ruffled Sep's hair. "You did right, my son. Your mama and I are proud of you."

Until the opening of Cuthbert's Lodge in 1903, Sep's childhood memories were of one-off incidents: his grandad's self-immolation, the first serious row between his parents, and the bloodying of Will Hagspiel's nose were etched into his memory. Now his world exploded into a myriad of events, strange new faces, fresh smells, sounds and spectacles. Everything appeared to run into everything else in a kaleidoscope of confusion. Some things made sense; others, no sense at all. Just as he thought he was beginning to understand the universe around him, something would happen that turned his world upside down. He was aware that the village was experiencing change as he listened to his parents' conversations, and read their reactions to the unfolding events.

Sir William's guests arrived with increased regularity to stay at the Lodge. Rich and cultured, speaking in strange tongues and wearing outlandish costumes, they gathered in the Adler like exotic, painted creatures from another planet.

While the locals stared openly at them in wonder, the aliens remained distant and, for the most part, kept their own company. They regarded the villagers surreptitiously out of the corner of their eye or, more often than not, with disdainful glances. There was no hostility, but there was a mutual recognition that two different worlds had rubbed up against each other. Only George Foster and Joseph Breitner moved easily between the groups.

The foreign women intrigued the Dopplegauers. Good manners, appearance, etiquette and, above all, status seemed to count for everything. Anyone breaking the guidelines was met with immediate social isolation. The effort of compliance was considerable and could not be sustained.

The villagers took to laying whispered wagers about when the dam of repression would break.

When it did, the transformation was remarkable. It was as if overnight the ley-lines had shifted, the phase of the moon and the influences of the forest spirits all coincided, compelling the women to break the bonds of their stifled existence – and live.

Immediately after breakfast they headed off into the mountains, equipped with picnic hampers groaning with sandwiches, cakes and pies from Drössel's *Bäckerei*, along with generous quantities of wine. They set off prim, proper and correct. By the time they returned late in the evening, they were creatures transformed. Their shrieking laugher preceded them as they made their unsteady way down the steep mountain path, hair unbound, skirts gathered above ankles and blouses unbuttoned. They fell stumbling into the

Adler where their high spirits continued well into the night. On such occasions it was not unknown for the two universes to come together, albeit briefly, and for conversations between villagers and gentry to break out.

Having sampled the sweet taste of freedom, it was inevitable that subsequent visits would demand repeat performances. Each time, boundaries were crossed, inhibitions discarded, barriers taken down, risks taken and life for the wealthy and indolent women became more exciting, colourful and daring.

Initially, the men were more predictable and dull - bankers, stockbrokers, industrialists. They were inclined to hunt, and hired the older men and younger boys, who could be spared from the farms, to help. The wily Dopplegauers quickly realised that most of the city dwellers were utterly incompetent at stalking any creature, unless it was tied down, no more than one hundred metres distant, or already dead. The cunning villagers took to tethering mountain goats and corralling a few deer in fixed locations before releasing them as the hunters approached. Even then, the amount of game they bagged was pitiful. As the effort required for hunting took its toll and interest waned, the visitors turned their attention to good food and wine. They drank often and heavily, becoming increasingly loud, aggressive and abusive.

In later years Sir William's guests were drawn from an entirely different social circle – artists, academics, philosophers and writers. They were flamboyant, radical, bohemian and scandalous. Rumours began to circulate of wild parties, indiscreet behaviour, bawdy antics and licentiousness. The young men rushed to hide in the woods surrounding the Lodge, hoping to catch a glimpse of the wickedness that lay within.

Two years after the opening of the Lodge the military arrived, and the village began to feel crowded. The soldiers came unexpectedly in the early spring and set up their tents in the meadow adjacent to the Adler. Children, teenage lads and young women were instantly attracted, moth-like, to the glamorous, charismatic men in uniform.

But the troops came armed; not with rifles, bayonets or grenades, but with theodolites, ranging gear, sighting poles and heavy measuring chains. The General Staff in Vienna had decided the track that ran through the high pass needed upgrading to enable the western border of the Empire to be quickly reinforced. Nobody could work out exactly which enemy the top brass had in mind, as the neighbouring Germans and Swiss spoke the same language, had similar cultures and had been peaceful for as long as anyone could remember.

No one complained about their arrival. Once it became clear the work would take months to complete, the villagers seized the opportunity to turn a profit. The soldiers were enticed to swap their cold canvas shelters for a warm straw bed in a cosy *Bauernhaus* billet, with regular hearty meals – and, if they were lucky, close attention from the farmer's wife and daughters. A sudden flash flood caused by a late spring storm swept away the camp and accelerated the soldiers' migration. Both parties were delighted with the new arrangements – none more so than Frau Hagspiel's daughter who, much to her mother's glee, managed to capture the affection of the platoon sergeant, who made up for his spectacular lack of good looks with an abundance of charm and kind-heartedness.

Eventually, the military contingent moved up the valley as their work took them further towards the high pass. No sooner had they departed than the men from the *Staatregierung* arrived. Their presence owed everything to Bürgermeister Joseph Breitner. He organised the Farmers' Collective Council, and cajoled, flattered and bribed the local politicians and officials with generous hospitality and large quantities of the local alcoholic brews. Above all, he shamelessly used his association with Sir William to elevate his status and authority.

As a consequence, a programme of public investment finally connected the villages to the outside world. By 1906 a post office – complete with telephone and telegraph apparatus – had been built. The installation of a sewage and mains water systems enabled a new *Volksschule* to be constructed. The River Ach's flood defences were upgraded, and the road to Achbrugge was widened, with new tunnels cut through the mountains in more hazardous parts of the route. There was even talk of extending the electricity grid up the valley from Achbrugge.

The comings and goings in the village were echoed in the Breitner household, but for altogether different reasons. The birth of Thomas Breitner gave Sep and Klaus another sibling. Before Tom's arrival, Sep considered the family home to be cavernous. Now it felt cluttered and small. The *Stube* and small veranda were permanently festooned with drying nappies, sheets and towels. Klaus and Sep were forced to share a bed to make room for Tom's cot. It seemed to Sep that no sooner was Thomas born than his mother had proudly announced they could all expect another arrival. Sep was intrigued: what exactly was causing this regular supply of brothers? He put it down to weather and the time of year. After all, most of the pigs, cattle and chickens seemed to be born when the sun shone and winter had passed.

Sep saw less and less of his grandfather, who was spending his days further up the valley, building the Lodge. He would arrive home after sunset, and collapse exhausted into the fireside chair, where he would sit smoking his pipe until Heidi called him to the table. As often as not, Joseph Breitner would leave again as soon as he had cleared his plate and downed his coffee, to attend meetings of the Farmers' Collective or the *Staatregierung,* or to meet George Foster.

As Joseph left, Sep's father would appear, looking equally drained. At least his day was done. After the cows had been milked and the animals fed, watered and bedded down, Fritz Breitner could stagger up the stairs to his bed. He would be up six hours later.

Father Wagner became a regular visitor. Regardless of the weather, he arrived on the first Monday of every month, his day off, early in the morning. He came wearing heavy boots and a thick leather coat, prepared for a day of hard walking. Only his dog collar and broad-rimmed black hat singled him out as a man of the cloth.

Sep knew when the priest was due: the night before his arrival his mother would set an extra place for breakfast and prepare a large parcel for him to take on his hike.

Sep would sit in uncomfortable silence, watching the priest eat.

His mother appeared to find Father Wagner's presence unsettling. Most guests to the Breitner house could expect a warm welcome, free-flowing conversation, jokes and banter as well as good food and drink. During Father Wagner's visits the atmosphere was chilly, and conversation became stilted and awkward. It was as if the clergyman was merely tolerated. Sep's father always had an urgent chore that needed his attention whenever the priest called. Later, when Sep entered his teenage years, Fritz Breitner didn't bother to hide the fact that he would much prefer it if the priest didn't visit at all.

Sep never warmed to Father Wagner. He was aware that almost all adults in the community treated him with deference, yet there didn't seem to be anything about him that justified such respect. Father Wagner tended no animals, harvested no crops and, as far as Sep could see, provided no service beyond overseeing the school. He had an elegant house next to the church, but was not married and had no family. It seemed to Sep that Father Wagner didn't belong in the village. He was an outsider. Added to that, Sep found the Latin church services utterly baffling, and Father Wagner's preaching boring and incomprehensible. Nevertheless, he attended Mass, sat yawning and fidgeting through Sunday school, and went

69

along with all the other events and ceremonies because his parents wished it, and the village expected it.

In contrast, all the Breitners looked forward to George Foster's visits. George appeared to enjoy their company. His calls became more frequent and of longer duration as the construction of the Lodge progressed.

George provided a window on a world that enthralled the entire household, especially Sep and his mother. They would often sit around the kitchen table drinking English tea that George had brought, listening to his tales of travels, places and people he had met, things he'd seen and the wonders of distant lands.

Everything about George intrigued Sep. Initially he appeared reserved and serious. But as his friendship with the Breitner household developed, his guard came down to reveal an entirely different character.

He readily accepted invitations for Sunday lunch after Mass. Heidi prided herself on her cooking prowess, and the Sunday meal was not to be missed. It was also a sacred time when the Breitner clan came together to gossip, exchange news, and hear important family announcements. When everyone had eaten their fill, Fritz would settle at the ancient pedal organ. This signalled the start of the traditional post-meal family entertainment. It was the highlight of Sep's week. Every member of the family took part, and Sep was always eager to get proceedings under way.

"Tell us a story, Grandad," he urged, bouncing in his chair in excitement.

His grandad always obliged. He seemed to have a bottomless well of tales – of witches, goblins, trolls, fairies, dragons, knights, kings, queens, princesses, heroes and villains. There would be poetry, card games or skittles as the mood took them. But there was always singing. The traditional country songs of the Alps lent themselves to two and three-part harmonies. To Sep, Sunday afternoons were pure magic – especially in the middle of winter when the pungent smell of wood smoke swirled around the *Stube* and the family gathered around the *Kachelofen*, snug and warm, as the winds howled around the eaves and blizzards battered the windows.

Sunday lunches also brought out the extrovert in George Foster. He could play the piano and belted out songs – hymns as well as classical pieces – on the family's small pedal organ. He was also an excellent singer. Sep especially enjoyed his renderings of British sea shanties. The *Stube* would be transformed into the quarterdeck of a battleship. George became their rabble-rousing captain, leading the family crew into a fantastical world of magic and adventure. They acted out hoisting sails, hauling on imaginary thick hemp ropes. They strained and pushed and heaved around the table capstan, bringing in the great iron anchor. They rolled about like drunkards on the storm-tossed deck or, best of all, fired the cannons at marauding pirates. In his mind, Sep could feel the wind, taste the salt, smell the powder. The more George urged them on, the louder their singing and more riotous their laughter. The first English words Sep learned were the lyrics to '*What Shall We Do with the Drunken Sailor?*'. Eventually, they would all collapse in a happy, laughing heap.

George took a shine to all the Breitner children. He often brought them gifts, and the day would end with him acting out a bedtime story, complete with sound effects that had the toddlers either gaping in wide-eyed bemusement, or sent them scurrying under the duvets in terror.

His return from his foreign trips was always keenly anticipated. He invariably came back laden with toys and books. It was the books that captured Sep's imagination. It didn't matter that almost all were in English. They were full of vivid pictures, brightly coloured illustrations and sepia photographs of an unfamiliar world Sep found fascinating. George seemed to instinctively know what publications would stimulate a child's curiosity. He bought books of fairy tales, illustrated encyclopaedias, adventure stories, and painting and colouring books. Before bedtime George would gather the children, and together they would select a book to be read or explained. During one such discussion, something happened that transformed Sep's life.

George had finished reading Klaus and Sep the story of the three little pigs in German. He closed the book and was about to leave when Sep piped up.

"Herr Foster is '*Die Drei Kleinen Schweine*' the same in English?"

George hesitated at the door to the bedroom. "Of course. It's exactly the same – only told in English."

"A *Schweine* is a pig?' Sep knew this from his previous trips around the farm with George.

"That's right. And *drei* is...?"

Sep thought for a moment. George had already taught the boys how to count to twelve in English. "Three," he said with childish certainty.

"Correct. And the English word for *kleinen* is little."

"Three, little, pigs." Sep nodded.

"Bravo, Master Sep." George clapped.

"Is it easy to learn English, Herr Foster?"

"Very easy. And it's a useful skill to have, I might add."

"Could you teach me English?"

"Of course. If you would like to learn, it will be my pleasure to teach you. Your mother wants to learn as well. So we could do it together."

Sep beamed. Being taught by Herr Foster with his mama sounded like fun.

"Shall we start now?"

Sep looked bewildered. Surely it was bedtime?

George gave Sep a low bow. "*Guten nacht, Sep. Schlaft gut.*"

Sep's response was automatic and tinged with disappointment. "*Guten nacht, Herr Foster. Schlaft gut.*"

"Goodnight, Sep. Sleep well."

Sep laughed as he realised it was a game.

"Goodnight, Herr Foster…"

"Sleep well," prompted George.

Together they repeated the phrase until George bowed low again, blew the candles out, and closed the door.

From then on, every visit by George included an English lesson for Sep and his mama. Each session was delivered to ensure maximum fun and laughter. They sang, acted out scenes from books, mimed and played party games – all in English. Only occasionally, or when he left to go on his travels, would George require them to adopt a more formal approach – by writing things down, committing specific grammar rules to memory, or setting them both tasks to learn from a language textbook.

They learned quickly. However, Sep's learning accelerated thanks to an event that, with hindsight, he wished had never happened to his mama.

The slamming of the *Stube* door, followed by the clatter of people running up and down the stairs, woke Sep. For a while he lay still, listening. He could hear low, urgent voices and people moving inside his parents' bedroom. He strained his ears and made out the voice of Frau Wachter. He sat up. Why was their neighbour visiting in the middle of the night, and what was she doing in his parents' bedroom?

He was wide awake now, and could tell from the adults' voices that something serious had happened. He heard his father say something, then his heavy footsteps on the stairs. The *Stube* door crashed shut as he left the house. The house fell silent. Sep strained his ears. Gradually he made out the faint sound of Frau Wachter and his mother in soft conversation, followed by a low whimpering groan. Something was wrong.

Sep slipped out of bed, leaving Klaus, fast asleep. He padded softly towards his parents' bedroom door and peered cautiously into the dim, lamp-lit room. Suzanne Wachter sat on the bed, her back towards him. She was sitting on the duvet, which had been pulled down. Sep could see his mother's feet, naked against the white linen. Frau Wachter half-turned and dipped a cloth into a bowl before wringing it out.

Sep felt his heart thud in his chest and a wave of pure terror seize him. The cloth was crimson with blood.

"Mama!" he cried in a choked voice.

Frau Wachter spun around in shock. She leapt up, throwing the duvet over Heidi, and swept Sep into her arms.

"Goodness me, Sep. You gave me such a start." She swivelled so he wasn't facing the bed and looked hard into Sep's face. "What's the matter, sweetie? Can't you sleep?"

Sep was having none of it. He craned his neck to see his mother. What he saw terrified him. His mother's face was pale, almost corpse-like. Her hair was dishevelled and her eyes sunken into two bruised pits. She grimaced and licked her lips as if searching for moisture. There was a damp sheen across her forehead. On the bedside table next to the flickering candle stood the blood-splattered bowl.

"It's all right, Sep, Mama's all right." Her voice was a dry rasp. She pulled up the duvet cover and smiled weakly.

Sep wriggled in Frau Wachter's arms. She dropped him gently to the floor, her arms encircling him. Sep felt her grip tighten and she looked directly at him, her face serious.

"Sep. Sep." She gave him a soft but firm shake to ensure she had his attention "Sep. Your mama's not well. It's nothing to worry about. Your papa's off to fetch the doctor to make her better."

"What's wrong with her?" Sep's eyes darted in half-suppressed panic.

"She's had a bit of a turn. These things happen now and again."

"Will she get better?"

"Of course." Suzanne continued to hold him firm. "Your grandad stayed at the Lodge, and I could do with your help. Will you help me?"

Sep nodded.

"Good boy. I want you to go to the kitchen, collect as many clean towels as you can find, and bring them here. Can you do that?"

Sep nodded. He knew the drawer where his mother kept the pile of pressed and folded towels. He set off purposefully down the stairs. When he returned, the bed looked tidier, the bowl had been removed, and his mother seemed more peaceful.

"Good lad." Suzanne took the towels from him. "Now, there's lots more to do, Sep. But you need to go and get washed and dressed first."

Sep cast an anxious glance towards his mother, nodded and ran out of the room to do Frau Wachter's bidding.

For the rest of the night, Frau Wachter kept him distracted until her husband arrived and took over, then Herr Wachter made sure Sep was kept busy. After breakfast he and Stephan were engrossed in feeding chickens, retrieving their eggs, cleaning the milking pails and raking out the straw bedding in the pig pens on Herr Wachter's farm. When they had completed those tasks, they did the same for the Breitners' animals.

Just before lunchtime, his father returned on horseback. He quickly dismounted and tied his horse to the rail. He was drenched in sweat and covered in dust. He went to the water trough, stripped off his shirt and plunged his head into the cold mountain water before dousing his chest and arms. He stood for a few seconds staring at nothing, as he dried himself off with his discarded shirt. He came out of his reverie as a small pony and trap clattered into the yard behind him.

Herr Wachter grabbed the reins while Sep's father helped a young woman down. She retrieved a large leather bag from the back of the trap and followed Fritz into the house. Nobody had said a word.

Sep stared after them. A feeling of dread welled up inside him.

A few minutes later Frau Wachter emerged; a bemused-looking Klaus clutching her hand and the infant Thomas in her other arm. The boys spent the rest of the day playing with Stephan and his sisters. But while the rest of the children charged about shrieking, tripping over each other, grazing their knees and bumping heads in innocent, carefree fun, Sep sat to one side. As each hour passed, he became more anxious.

Late that afternoon, an immaculately dressed elderly man with a goatee, silver hair and shiny round spectacles arrived on a pony and trap and disappeared into the farmhouse. By now, Sep had lost all interest in play, despite Frau Wachter's encouragement. He knelt on the bench, his nose pressed against the window, his eyes locked on the door of his home further down the track. Eventually, he saw his father emerge and start to make his way towards him. Sep didn't wait. In seconds he was off his perch and through the door, running as if pursued by demons into his father's outstretched arms. His father swept him up in his thick, muscled arms as if he was made of paper.

His father gave nothing away. "Let's fetch Klaus and Thomas, eh?"

With his brood hanging off his arms, Fritz Breitner returned home. He handed the infant Thomas to a young woman who was leaning on the *Kachelofen* warming her hands, and settled Klaus at the table.

Sep found himself being carried upstairs and into his parents' bedroom. The curtains were drawn and the candles lit. In the peaceful gloom, it felt to Sep like the small chapel inside St Martin's church. The room was filled with a strange astringent smell. In a corner, the bespectacled elderly man stuffed items into a large leather bag.

The bed had been freshly made up with starched white linen and a heavy blanket. Only his mother's head was visible. She looked less gaunt, and her hair had been neatly combed. She gazed at him, smiled weakly and held out her arms. Fritz gently laid his son next to her.

Sep immediately wrapped his arms around his mother's neck and buried his face in her cheek. He couldn't prevent big tears from rolling down his cheek. He'd never seen his mother looking so frail and vulnerable.

"Hey, little one, what's this crying for?" Her voice was soft and reassuring. He felt her gently stroking the back of his head.

Sep didn't answer but buried his face further in her neck. He felt her warmth and her hair brushing against his skin. He never wanted to leave. They lay together for a long time saying nothing, drawing comfort from each other.

"Will you get better, Mama?" he whispered, half-fearing her reply.

"Of course. Don't you worry about that. I need to rest for a bit."

"I can look after you."

He felt her smile. "I'd like that. Could you could look after Papa as well? He's going to be very busy and I'm sure he'll need some help."

Sep nodded. "I can feed the hens, and pigs, and I can collect the eggs, and change the straw and everything." He thought for a bit. "I can't cook, though."

"Helping with the animals would be really useful." His mother sighed. She sounded tired. "Frau Wachter has said she will help cook – until I get better."

Then his father came back in. "Time for bed, young man. Mama needs a good night's sleep. Give her a big kiss."

The following morning began like every other day. Sep awoke to the familiar sound of his father's footsteps crunching on the gravel path, and the gentle clanking of the milk pails as he made his way to the cattle stalls.

The bedroom door opened. Sep sat up expectantly but when Frau Wachter entered. Sep's heart sank. He was so sure that his mother would be back to normal after her good night's sleep.

Frau Wachter tiptoed across the room and pressed her finger to her lips. Mama was still sleeping and must not be disturbed, she whispered. Klaus and Sep dutifully washed and dressed in silence before creeping downstairs. Breakfast was already on the table. Hunger overwhelmed them, and they attacked the plate of wurst, eggs and cheese like starving fledglings. Frau Wachter settled herself at the end of the table and breast-fed their younger sibling.

The sound of creaking stair-boards again set Sep's heart racing. There was no one else in the house. It had to be his mama but once again his hopes were dashed. The door opened and the young woman entered. Sep stared open-mouthed at her, veering between disappointment and wonder. He'd never seen anyone so beautiful.

The young woman glanced across to Frau Wachter.

"She's had a good night. Sleep and rest are what she needs now," she said before turning to face the two brothers. "And who are these two fine-looking boys?" She stood with her hands on her hips and her head cocked to one side, a sunny smile on her face.

76

Sep felt his fears melt away. If she was so relaxed there could be nothing to worry about. He stared at the girl in awe until a gentle chastisement from Frau Wachter brought him back to earth.

"Sep, have you forgotten your manners?"

Blushing furiously, Sep dropped from his chair and approached the goddess with his hand outstretched, looking directly at the visitor as he had been taught. "Sep Breitner," he said in a confident voice that he was sure would have made his parents proud.

She knelt so her face was level with his. Her handshake was like silk. "Pleased to meet you, Sep Breitner. I'm Fraulein Rachel Rubenstein. And who is the other young gentleman?" She glanced sideways at Klaus.

"Klaus Breitner. He's my brother."

Klaus said nothing but stared at her in wide-eyed wonder.

Frau Wachter eased the contented Thomas from her breast, placed him in his cot and buttoned her blouse. "Sit yourself down, Rachel – you must be hungry and tired. I'm sure you would welcome a coffee."

"I'll have some coffee, but nothing to eat, thank you."

Rachel sat opposite Sep and glanced across at him. "I expect you're anxious about your mama?"

Sep nodded and said nothing.

She rested her arms on the table, clasped her hands together and looked grave.

Sep found himself gazing into the darkest, deepest brown eyes he'd ever seen. He was mesmerised. There was something exotic about Frau Rubenstein. Her skin was a flawless, creamy tan. Her lips were full and lush; her mouth had a pleasing little indentation under a turned-up nose. Her face was framed by thick, wavy tresses of hair so dark it was almost black, swept back from her face. She looked like none of the girls in the village, or anyone Sep had seen in his short life. Small golden earrings were just visible. A gold bangle hung round her right wrist and a bright, exotic-looking wristwatch decorated her left. Her blouse was crisp white with short sleeves, leaving her forearms bare. A small silver-star shaped pendant nestled at her throat.

She stared steadily at Sep for a few seconds, as if considering her words.

"At the moment your mama is asleep, Sep. She's very ill and needs a lot of rest if she is going to get better."

"She will get better though, won't she?" Sep asked in a small voice.

Rachel's grave expression didn't change. "She will, if we all look after her."

"I told her I would help." Sep's voice was eager. "I said I would help Papa as well."

Rachel blinked. "Yes, everybody will need to help."

"What's wrong with my mama?"

"Well – she was hoping to give you another baby brother or sister. But something went wrong." She continued to hold his gaze. "Because it went wrong it made your mama ill and upset."

"I don't want another brother if it makes Mama ill."

Rachel nodded. "I understand. But we need to help her get better, don't we?"

Sep nodded enthusiastically. "Can I see her?"

"Not yet. She's tired, and we don't want to wake her up, do we?" She smiled broadly at him, revealing a neat row of perfect teeth. "After school would be a better time. Which reminds me, can you take me to your school? I need to see Father Wagner."

A dismayed Frau Wachter spoke before Sep could reply. "Oh, Rachel, do you need to do that now? You've been up all night."

"It's best I do it straight away, Frau Wachter. Besides, I could do with some fresh air. The walk will do me good." She turned back to Sep. "So, young man, will you escort me to school?"

"I have to feed the animals first, and collect the eggs, and change the straw for the pigs." Sep made to get down from the table. The exciting prospect of walking with Fraulein Rachel to school – and his friends' reactions – was a powerful incentive.

And so Fraulein Rubenstein joined the Breitner household. Her stay, although brief in the overall scheme of things, was considerably longer than she, the family, or the village had expected. She wanted to meet Father Wagner to discuss her idea of opening a small clinic to provide the community with rudimentary healthcare. She assured Father Wagner that her initial focus would be on children – although she would treat anyone who sought her care. The clinic would only be available for a limited time – a few weeks, or until her nursing of Heidi Breitner was complete.

With Doctor Rubenstein's practice a half-day journey distant, even in good weather, and inaccessible during the winter snows, Fraulein Rachel might have expected her initiative to be welcomed. That wasn't the case.

From the outset she was regarded with suspicion. She was too young, for a start. How could someone not yet in her twenties possess any useful knowledge on things medical? She wasn't a proper doctor. Learning at her father's practice, good though Doctor Rubenstein was, cut no ice. Besides, the women of the village relied on their own homespun remedies and treatments involving pungent cocktails of herbs, infusions, liquors, extracts and potions, even animal parts and incantations, that had served the community well for generations.

As ever, Frau Hagspiel placed herself at the forefront of the opposition, stoking the fires of rejection and adding spite and prejudice into the mix. "Fraulein Rachel is too vain and pretty to be taken seriously," she announced. "but even worse, she's of the Jewish faith, and everyone knows what that means!" Nobody did – but none could be bothered to confront the prejudice.

But the worst thing, in Father Wagner's opinion, was that she was female. He knew of no medical university that accepted women students. Simple logic applied. If learned institutions barred women from the profession, they must have good reasons. After all, the Catholic Church barred women from becoming priests. Father Wagner could relate to that. He refused to bless Rachel's initiative, in the mistaken belief that Rachel's purpose in meeting him was not out of courtesy and respect, but to seek his consent.

In what he took as a deliberate act of defiance, Rachel ignored his rejection and opened the clinic in Frau Wachter's *Stube*.

The Breitner and Wachter children were the first to receive Fraulein Rachel's attention. She began her assault on ailments and vermin: hair lice, ringworm and threadworm were so common that no one considered them health hazards at all. Children happily coughed and sneezed over each other with abandon. People had a casual approach to dirt. They occasionally visited the water trough to remove obvious filth, but otherwise the children's skin quickly acquired a scaly brown sheen that was sufficient to mask day-to-day smears. Bathing was mostly confined to the summer months when the scorching sun drove youngsters into the Ach, more to cool down than from considerations of hygiene. People typically bathed once a month, even in the Breitner and Wachter households, which were more concerned with cleanliness than most.

Rachel set to with energy and enthusiasm combined with good humour to establish the clinics. Despite Frau Hagspiel's persistent efforts to oppose the venture, the younger mothers were quick to attend. The prospect of a good gossip over *Kaffee und Kuchen*, plus the chance to gawk at the attractive newcomer, was too hard to resist. The group grew and became established in the weekly social calendar. Word got around, and young women from neighbouring villages began to attend. Numbers could no longer be accommodated in Frau Wachter's *Stube.* In a move that further irked Father Wagner and reduced Frau Hagspiel to apoplexy, Rachel charmed Franz Zinnermann into allowing the clinic to be run from the Adler.

"Women in a *Gasthaus*! Without their husbands! Have you ever heard of such a thing?" Even though she was outraged, Frau Hagspiel found her following diminished. In a twist of exquisite irony, her husband became the first male in the village to seek treatment from Rachel. He fell heavily from his hayloft, badly dislocating his shoulder. He staggered in agony the short distance from his farm to the *Gasthaus* and burst into the circle of astounded young women. In no time, Rachel realigned Helmut's protruding bones in a simple, if painful, manipulation that was not far short of miraculous as far as her audience was concerned. From then on, the men of the village were not slow to discover ailments that required the urgent attention of the delectable Fraulein Rachel.

Rachel became indispensable to the Breitners and Wachters. Heidi's recovery took much longer than anyone expected. After two weeks she was well enough to leave her bed, but she was a pale shadow of her former self. She was tired and listless. Gradually her body recovered, and the trauma of her lost baby dimmed in her memory. But it was a painfully slow process. As a consequence, domestic chores fell to Suzanne Wachter and Rachel.

To Sep, the world now seemed to consist of endless washing, scrubbing, cleaning and ironing. Fraulein Rachel was obsessed with soap, water and a seven-day cleaning schedule. Sheets were washed, ironed and changed on a weekly basis. Dishcloths were boiled and pressed on the same frequency. Shirts, blouses and undergarments were included in her routine. Sep couldn't see the logic. Previously, items were cleaned when the dirt was clearly visible, and most things could last for weeks, if not months. according to his criteria.

Rachel's enthusiasm for cleanliness extended to the household. No one was permitted to sit at the table unless faces, arms, hands and fingers glowed a scrubbed-up pink, and fingernails were untroubled by residues from the farmyard. She introduced handkerchiefs as an alternative to the backs of hands, sleeves or a freestyle nasal blast into the gutter. Anyone could find themselves being temporarily banished from the *Stube* if they dared to cough or sneeze without taking appropriate protective action.

Rachel introduced the measures through education and good-natured tyranny. Nobody objected, as they could see both the logic and the benefits.

Of all the steps she introduced, the most eagerly anticipated among the Breitner and Wachter children was the Saturday evening bath. It was two hours of bliss-filled chaos. Rachel and Frau Wachter selected each child in turn to get in the large tin bath for a thorough scrub. It was like catching fish in a bucket. The *Stube* was full of flying water, soapsuds, screams, wriggles, giggles, splashes, laughter and wails as each youngster was caught and processed. Every now and then one of the children would be allowed to escape and flee naked out of the house, only to be pursued, recaptured and returned to the tub writhing and shrieking with joy. When the last of the children had been scoured, they were lined up along the bench seat wrapped in towels to await their victuals.

Sep never imagined that getting clean could be so much fun. The sight of his mother laughing uncontrollably for the first time in months would be forever etched in his memory. Sep was sure his life couldn't get any better.

One bath-night Sep's mother was settling him into bed. Fraulein Rachel was in the room too, retrieving scattered towels and dirty clothing to deposit in the now firmly established wash bag. A book fell out of one of the towels. Rachel picked it up and glanced at it.

"This is an English book." She looked across at Heidi in surprise.

Heidi nodded. "It's one of Sep's. Herr Foster brings them. Sep and I are learning English – although I have to admit I'm now well behind." She shook her head sadly.

Rachel turned the book over in her hands and read the cover. "Rumpelstiltskin?" She looked curiously at Heidi.

"It's for Sep, really. He can read well, can't you, my clever lad?" She ruffled Sep's hair with motherly affection.

Sep grinned and nodded. He felt extraordinarily proud of himself, and was delighted to have been praised in front of Fraulein Rachel, who Sep loved almost as much as he loved his mother.

Rachel went over to the small bookshelf and stooped to read the titles. "You can read all of these?" She looked sideways at Sep.

"Not all of them. Some are too hard. I'm waiting for Herr Foster's next visit."

"I don't think we need to wait that long."

"What do you mean, Rachel?" Heidi asked.

"I mean, I could help teach you. I love English books. I've got hundreds at home."

"I didn't know you could speak English."

Rachel grinned ruefully. "I don't get much chance to practise around here. My aunt and my governess taught me. Both were English. And my father was keen I should learn." She dropped her voice to mimic her father's gruff tone." 'If you want to become a doctor, Rachel, you must learn to read the best textbooks. And the best medical books are produced in London.' We should set aside an hour each day. What do you think?"

The completion of new buildings in the small community represented expansion, progress and confidence in the future. It was a cause for celebration. The Lodge was over six kilometres outside Dopplegau, but this didn't prevent the village from claiming it as part of their parish, and its opening an excuse for a party.

Almost the entire population of Dopplegau, dressed in their Sunday best, walked the six kilometres to the Lodge, laughing and chattering excitedly behind the village band. The children scurried between adults' legs, playing hide-and-seek up and down the length of the crocodile. Teenage girls bunched together, whispering, clucking and giggling among themselves and casting furtive glances at the young men who pushed and shoved one another and exchanged manly banter in an effort to gain the girls' attention.

Every now and then the column would move deferentially to the side of the track to allow carriages full of Sir Cuthbert's guests to pass. As each gleaming conveyance squeezed through, the more brazen and curious villagers craned their necks to catch a glimpse of the gilded passengers. False rumours were already circulating that at least two Royals were attending.

The cavalcade gathered on the turf outside the Lodge. It had been cut short and mown in pleasing stripes to represent an English lawn. Their eyes were drawn as much to the unfamiliar serving girls as to the feast that was already spread out on long white-clothed tables in front of them. A buzz went around the crowd. Who were they? Where did they come from? Answers had to wait until after the speeches.

Suddenly Sir William appeared on the veranda. He waited patiently until the last of the children had been shushed into silence.

"Ladies, gentlemen, friends and neighbours." He paused and leant over the balustrade, allowing his gaze to pass over all the upturned faces staring back at him. More than half his audience had no clue what he was talking about. Sep felt a small shiver run down his spine. He had recognised at least some of the words! He turned and beamed up at his mother, who smiled back at him in mutual understanding. For the first time, the English words in the books had wings.

To Sep's relief the speeches were brief.

The guests applauded, all the while stealing famished looks towards the piles of meats, pâtés, cheeses, pickles, salads, breads, cakes and buns that lay tantalisingly off-limits.

Finally, Father Wagner was invited to give the blessing. The final amen marked the starting gun. The guests fell on the food as if it was their last supper. Their initial anxiety that there wouldn't be enough to go around was quickly dispelled. Freshly restocked platters and bottles arrived with reassuring regularity, and everyone relaxed.

As the drink flowed, social constraints began to loosen. The band knew what the crowd expected, and the first couples were soon dancing. By mid-afternoon the party was in full swing, and the first cracks in the invisible barriers that had kept the villagers and the English guests apart began to appear.

As natural reserve and caution were put to one side within one section of the assembly, there was a slight rise in tension in another. The more forward of the village lads made tentative contact with the mysterious serving girls. This caused a ripple of disquiet among the young ladies of the village. They had formidable rivals. Counter-action was required. Eyelids were fluttered, hips swayed seductively, dancing became closer and more intimate, and their flirting held out the seductive promise of a diversion into the woods or hayloft on the trip home.

Sep, Klaus and Stephan sat cross-legged under one of the trestle tables, stuffing themselves with ham, eggs, cakes and buns piled on two large plates that lay in the centre of their circle. Each clutched a confection so unfamiliar and delicious that they had each returned for resupplies three times already. It was their first introduction to chocolate, and it would stay in their memory for a lifetime.

Sep made to set off for his fourth replenishment but found himself thwarted by the restraining hand of his mother on his shoulder. "No more, Sep. You'll make yourself ill."

His protestation was cut short by the arrival of George Foster. After greeting them both, he sat next to Heidi.

"You look well, Heidi."

"I am much better, thank you." She gazed around at the throng of guests. "It certainly lifts the spirits seeing so many people having fun and enjoying themselves. I assume this is all thanks to your organising skills, George?"

He chuckled. "No. Fortunately, my responsibilities don't extend to planning parties, or the domestic management of Sir Cuthbert's household."

"You weren't involved in the recruitment of his staff, then?" Heidi glanced deliberately towards the serving girls, now surrounded by a bevy of admiring males.

George followed her gaze. "Ah! I thought they might set a few tongues wagging."

"So, who are they?"

"They come from South Tyrol," he said easily, as if the matter was of little consequence. He fell silent, watching her reaction from the corner of his eye, deliberately teasing her.

"And?"

"And what?"

She flicked his arm with the back of her fingers. "Oh, honestly! George, come on. I'm curious."

George sighed and leant back in his chair. "They have been employed by Sir William's head housekeeper as maids."

Heidi looked surprised. "He's employed girls from South Tyrol to come here as domestic servants? Why not use the local girls?"

He thought for a moment before replying. "Because I advised him not to." He saw her shocked reaction and shrugged. "It was my sole contribution to the recruitment process."

She glanced around as if searching for the right words to express her disbelief. "Whatever possessed you to offer such advice? The local girls are hard-working, reliable – they live on the doorstep, for goodness' sake. Why recruit staff from two hundred kilometres away?" She stared at him, bewildered.

George studied her. "It's a matter of business practicalities. Sir William and his guests need staff on-site from six in the morning until one or two in the morning. Travelling backwards and forward to the village would not be practical, even if it is only six kilometres. It's better to have live-in staff."

Heidi's eyes narrowed. "That can't be the only reason."

George leant forward and spoke softly, as if he was concerned that their conversation be overheard. "No. There are two other reasons." He leant closer to Heidi's ear. "Some of Sir William's friends and acquaintances are … um … how can I put this? Very modern in their outlook. I suspect aspects of their behaviour would cause unnecessary upset and offence to the local community." He leant back and waited for Heidi's reaction.

Heidi looked shocked. "What sort of behaviour are we talking about, George?"

George chuckled. "The French have a phrase for it – *au naturel*. It means—"

"I know what it means, George." Heidi shook her head in disbelief. "You cannot be serious?"

"I'm afraid I am. That's why Sir William wanted a secluded site and staff who are … um … a little more open-minded."

"In other words, he wants employees with loose morals." Heidi sniffed.

"Or broad-mindedness – which is not an adjective I would use when describing most of the inhabitants of Dopplegau."

Heidi bristled. "We're not all village idiots, George."

George looked chastened. "Heidi, I do apologise. I meant no offence. My remarks were meant to embrace the community – present company excepted. Please accept my apologies."

"I should think so." She tossed her head. "Narrow-minded indeed. I thought you knew me better."

"I hold you in the highest esteem, Heidi, you know that. But there was another factor." He sat back in his chair and took a sip from his wine before using his glass to gesture towards Frau Hagspiel. "Some of Sir Cuthbert's business interests are extremely sensitive. He cannot afford to surround himself with people who are incapable of respecting confidentiality."

"George, do you believe all the women in the village are untrustworthy gossips?"

George was unfazed by her outburst. He nodded. "With the obvious exception of yourself. For example, you refused to divulge certain extremely sensitive and potentially damaging information to your neighbours and the wider community, despite considerable pressure, including the threat of social isolation. Am I not correct?"

She returned his look but not his smile. "You are a strange character, George."

He shrugged. "If you knew my secret, you'd understand why I am what I am." He raised his eyebrows conspiratorially. "Anyway, it's because you are quite unlike our village busybody over there…" – he nodded towards Frau Hagspiel, who was scowling her disapproval of the lads openly flirting with the serving girls – "that I have a business proposition for you."

Heidi looked puzzled. "What sort of business proposition?"

George edged his chair closer and lowered his voice. "Sir William is a major shareholder in the British Empire Bank based in London. The BEB has a majority stake in the Austrian-Hungarian Landesbank which, as you know, has a branch in Achbrugge."

"Go on."

"Sir William has a lot of business interests in this part of the world – Switzerland in particular – that he prefers to keep confidential. It also is important he can operate some of these from an Austrian, rather than London-based, address. At present, I handle these matters. However, now the Lodge is finished, I will be spending much less time in Dopplegau. But the business requirement is still there." He glanced at her. "Sir William has asked me to find someone to take over. Plus, the Lodge will require some basic administration, keeping tabs on the accounts, ensuring the needs of guests are looked after and so on."

"You want me to do that?"

"Yes."

She shook her head slowly and stared at him in disbelief. "George, I'm a farmer's wife, a mother of three young children. I have no background in business, let alone banking. Looking after the house and farm is a full-time job on its own. I'm totally unsuited to what you're suggesting."

"No, you're not." George's reply was almost fierce. "Heidi Breitner is bright, intelligent and burning to make more of her life. Yes, she's a loyal, loving wife, a marvellous mother, a wonderful homemaker. But I suspect you are these things because that's what is expected of you. You do it out of duty, loyalty, love – because that's the role all women are expected to play in this backwater. I am certain you want something more out of life – something that will challenge your intellect and abilities." He stared hard at her before continuing in a low, passionate voice. "I think you feel trapped to some extent – and, believe me, I know what that feels like." He looked at her intensely, his eyes burning into hers. "I am offering something extra, Heidi. Something that will enrich your life. Don't worry – it's not a full-time job, and I will be around to train you."

She laughed. "And what makes you so certain of all this, George? How many women take on this type of work?" She spotted Fraulein Rubenstein dancing with one of the village lads. "Look at poor Rachel. She would make a superb doctor – but women as doctors?" She left the question hanging in the air.

"Women have been able to become doctors in England for the past twenty years. I've spoken with her and her father, and she's applied to the London School of Medicine for Women. Hopefully, with her English and the training she's already received from her father, she'll be successful."

Heidi looked surprised. "I never knew. She never said anything."

"No, she didn't want to get her hopes up. But even if she fails in London, I'll wager she'll reapply, or try her luck in France." He placed his glass precisely on the table, as if to emphasise his argument. "Heidi, the world is changing. People – women like you – need to seize the opportunities. You're far too intelligent to waste your talents in a sleepy little village like Dopplegau. Look how quickly you picked up English."

"I like living here."

"And this opportunity will enable you to continue to do so – and achieve something more." He glanced across at Sep, who had been listening quietly to their conversation. "And this young man will go far. He's got his mother's curiosity. Providing he gets out into the world." George studied the youngster for a while before adding, "When you're old enough, I'll take you to England so you can get a taste of what the world has to offer." He grinned. "You and your brother. Would you like that?"

Sep nodded eagerly.

Heidi remained silent as she absorbed George's offer.

George left her to her thoughts for a bit before getting to his feet and holding out his hand. "Don't think about it, Heidi. Just do it." He smiled warmly at her. "In the meantime, would you do me the honour? It's a waltz."

***

High above on the ridgeline, the man stared at the forest below, where the Lodge nestled among the trees. Despite the distance, music and laughter drifted to him on the still mountain air. He lingered, a half-smile playing around his lips, as he heard the opening bars of a familiar tune. He closed his eyes and for a few moments was transported back to his youth, reliving a distant, fleeting memory of floating around a dance floor with … He couldn't recall her name. But he could remember the fun, laughter, shouts and banter, the taste of good food and beer, the smell of wood smoke.

His smile faded as he remembered the bitter years – and the names of the evil and corrupt. Those who had tried to destroy him. He would never forget, or forgive. He hated them. He relived their callous duplicity, cynical hypocrisy and cold indifference. He remembered them all – especially one.

Then he thought about his own role and a wave of self-loathing swept through him. Who was he to judge?

His heart grew cold. He opened his eyes, gathered the coarse skins around him, spat on the ground, turned and headed back over the ridge into the mountains. He was better off without them. God curse them all.*

The sound of the medicine trolley heralded the arrival of Corporal McPherson.

"Mornin', sir. How are ye today?"

Sep felt extraordinarily good. He'd slept deeply, and the constant throbbing in his legs had diminished. There were no pains in his chest, and his eyesight was almost clear. "I'm very well, Sandy."

"Ah'm right pleased to hear it. Ah've a proposition for ye."

"A proposition?"

"Aye. There's a few lads in that ward that play cards, ye ken. They want to know would ye like tae join them? As yer on yer lonesome."

Sep considered the offer. Although there had never been any sign of hostility since he was captured the thought of mixing with men who only a few weeks ago had been deadly foes was a worry. On the other hand, he realised that, although writing and reading magazines, papers and books had kept him busy, there were times when he was lonely and he missed male company. He made up his mind.

"Yes, Sandy. I'd like to join them."

The corporal grinned. "You'll have tae make it yersel'."

Sep looked uncertain. "How far?"

The corporal jerked his head towards the door and the direction of travel. "Fifty paces tae the ward."

"I can do that. What time?"

"After yer breakfast."

When he reached the ward, the men were gathered, heads bowed, staring intently at a jigsaw puzzle that was scattered on a table in front of them. There were four of them. One looked up as Sep approached.

"Ah, our Austrian friend. Come and join us." He nudged his comrade. "Move yer arse, Curly, and let the man park."

The men glanced up and nudged each other until a space was created. One completely bald man went off and returned with a chair. He placed it next to Sep.

"There you go, mate, sit yourself down." He held out his hand. "Curly Bennett." His handshake was warm and friendly. Sep immediately felt at ease.

One by one they introduced themselves. Sep couldn't help noticing their injuries. Bob Evans was a heavyset man who looked older than the rest. Steve Joyce, by contrast, was young and thin –

he looked like an emaciated schoolboy. Both men were missing their legs.

Curly Bennett's left shirt sleeve hung empty and flapping. There was an angry red scar running across the left-hand side of his skull, and a black patch covered his missing left eye.

Bert Fanshawe, who had been first to greet Sep, sat immobile from the waist down in his wheelchair. "Any good at puzzles, Sep?"

"It's a long time since I've done one."

"It's supposed to look like this." Bert reached behind him and retrieved the lid of the puzzle. He dropped it on Sep's lap. It was a picture of Constable's *The Hay Wain*.

"It is a difficult one."

"Well, we've got all the time in the world to finish it." Bert laughed.

"We have – he ain't." Steve jerked his chin towards Bob, who was sitting opposite. "Yer off home tomorrow, ain't ye?"

"I am that, bonnie lad. Home to the bosom of ma family."

"What'll be the first thing you'll do when you get home then, Bob?"

"Give his missus a good seeing-to." Steve gave a lewd cackle.

Bob rode out the banter and slowly shook his head. "Nay, lad! A couple o' bevvies of Newcastle Brown at the White Horse is top of ma list, then watch t' game at Roker Park, back t' White Hart for post-match analysis, stop off for some fish 'n' chips on the way home – and *then* look after the mlssus."

His friends chuckled good-naturedly.

"Aye, ye've got to get yer priorities right." Curly sighed. "What about ye, Sep? Have ye got plans?"

"Oh, I'll pick up where I left off. Look after the animals, prepare for the new arrivals. Spring is always a busy time of year."

"Ye're a farmer, then?"

Sep nodded. He reached out and positioned a piece of the jigsaw.

"It's good to have a job to go back to. Ye're a lucky man. There's a lot of us will be worrying about work when we get back." The comment was made without a hint of rancour or bitterness.

"Ye'll be right enough, Curly. Ye've got brains, lad." Bob glanced furtively down the ward. His gaze settled on a young soldier who sat, his eyes glazed, relentlessly rocking, obviously caught up in some private mental torment. "There's plenty here who ain't so fortunate," he muttered

"I'll tell you what I'm looking forward to," Steve said. He looked at each of them in turn to make sure of their full attention. "My mum's Sunday roast."

"Now yer talking, bonnie lad. Roast beef, roast potatoes, carrots, cabbage and thick, thick gravy."

"And Yorkshire pudding," Sep added.

They looked at him in surprise. "You know English Sunday roast then, Sep?"

"Oh, yes. We had an English friend. He introduced us to it. I have to say it is one of the best meals I have ever tasted." Sep could see the meal in front of him. "He cooked us Sunday roast and spotted dick with English sauce for pudding."

"Nay, nay, nay, lad. Not spotted dick. Yer proper pudding's apple pie and custard."

A debate over the merits of various puddings and meals was followed by an equally light-hearted discussion on the best way to spend a Sunday afternoon, including music hall acts and entertainment they had experienced. They talked about anything. The moment one topic was exhausted, someone would introduce another. The jigsaw gave way to cards: a sixpence maximum stake in a game of pontoon.

Sep found the lads readily accepted his company. There was no inquisitiveness about his time in the Imperial Army, his regiment, where he served or saw action or even how he came to be wounded. Gradually, it dawned on Sep that nobody had mentioned the war all day. It was as if they'd blanked the whole thing from their minds. He glanced around at the wounded soldiers and wondered how many of them suffered from terrors, like he did. They spent the rest of the afternoon laughing, joking and, as far as Sep was concerned, losing money. He didn't begrudge the loss. It was a long time since he had enjoyed himself so much.

He spotted her at the far end of the room. She and Nurse Mandy were working their way along the ward, stripping sheets and blankets from empty beds and tossing them into a large, wheeled laundry basket.

The closer she got the more his attention wandered from the cards, and the more money he lost. Inwardly he shook his head, trying to refocus on the game. But she was magnetic. His eyes kept returning to her. The two nurses had reduced the task of bed stripping to a smooth, practised routine. She and Mandy chatted as they moved along each side of the bed peeling off the blankets then folding them in an automatic sequence that appeared choreographed. They laid the blanket on top of a neat stack at the foot of the trolley before they repeated the sequence with the sheets, which they threw into the linen hopper on top of the cart. He watched her move. It was graceful, almost dance-like. As they finished each bed, they rolled the trolley on to the next, drawing ever closer to Sep.

Sep forced his eyes back to the hand he had been dealt.

"Stick," he said automatically before realising his error. His hand added up to thirteen. He resigned himself to losing another penny from his dwindling supply of cash. To his astonishment the others all bombed out, and he won.

Curly expressed his good-natured outrage when he saw Sep's hand. "Thirteen! You Austrian bandit."

Sep laughed. "Pure luck. Neither good judgement nor skill had anything to do with it." He raked the modest winnings towards his side of the table. At least his cash pile was partly replenished.

When he glanced up, Susan had paused and was looking directly at him. Neither looked away. She smiled at him, her eyes lighting up. The moment was fleeting. Nurse Mandy said something to her, and she returned to their task. Sep felt his heart constrict and a tightness grip his throat. What was it about her that he found so bewitching?

To his surprise and delight, she came to his room mid-way through the afternoon. He glanced up from reading *The Better Times* as she entered.

She looked happy, and he felt a pulse of pleasure pass through him.

"How much did you lose?" was her opening question.

"I broke even – more or less."

She went to the window and stood looking out. She placed her hands in the small of her back and stretched.

"Stripping beds is not good for the lower back."

"No, it is not! Fifty-six beds Mandy and I got through." She continued to gaze out. The light silhouetted her figure.

Sep traced her curves with his eyes.

She half-turned towards him. "Did you enjoy your day with the lads?"

"Very much. They made me feel welcome. Bob is going home tomorrow."

"Yes – he's on the convoy." She turned from the window and leant back, half sitting on the sill. "It's a shame. It will split the group. They all came in together, and they've become good pals."

"It is probably the only good thing about this war. You become close to your comrades."

She nodded and looked wistful, then looked over her shoulder at the garden. "It's a lovely afternoon. Would you like to go for a walk?"

"Of course." He searched around for his crutches.

She laughed. "Hold on – you'll need a coat. It's sunny but a bit chilly out there." She moved across the ward to retrieve his coat from the hook. When she turned around Sep was standing, swaying on his crutches.

She gave him a look, as if she was about to admonish him.

He anticipated her objection and moved to forestall her. "I need to practice, Susan … Nurse Jones. I managed to get to the ward and back with no trouble." His eyes pleaded. "We can take it one step at a time."

She shook her head in resignation and crossed the room, holding his coat open. "If you fall over I'll leave you where you are. That'll teach you." She stood in front of him and did up his coat buttons.

He was painfully aware of her proximity. He drew in everything about her: her scent, the faint freckles across the bridge of her nose, the smoothness of her skin, the gentle curve of her eyebrows, the hazel eyes which flicked towards his own.

"Where shall we go?" he asked, hoping his expression was neutral and his voice covered the tautness of his throat.

"Depends how far you can manage. Let's see if we can make a circuit around the gardens. It's more or less level paths all the way around."

She swept her cloak around her, and they set off.

Sep cautioned himself to stay within his limits. He felt less than confident, despite his initial bravado. Swinging forward on his crutches threatened to topple him face-down if he tried to force the pace. By the same token, if he failed to propel his body far enough forward, he risked collapsing onto his back. A steady, regular momentum was called for.

Susan hovered like an anxious bird with a chick taking its first flight. Several times she had to grab and steady him as he teetered.

Gradually, as his confidence grew, she began to relax, and they could both enjoy the beauty of the bright, fresh winter afternoon.

"Have you heard from your family yet?"

"No. I hope they will reply in the next few days. The post in Austria tends to be a bit slow."

There was a slight pause before her next question. "And nothing from the repatriation office?"

Sep realised he didn't care whether or not he heard from the Imperial Army. He shook his head. "They may have forgotten about me." He glanced at her. "I sorted out my pay, though, and I would very much like to treat you to tea and cakes at the end of our walk."

Her face lit up. "That will be something to look forward to."

They reached the far end of the path. He stopped, shuffled himself around and gazed back at the chateau. "This must have been an enormous hospital when it was full."

"It was. Very busy, especially in 1916 after the Somme offensive."

"How many casualties?"

"They haven't released official figures, but the lads who came through here reckon we lost over four hundred thousand." She looked at the ground. "We lost nearly sixty thousand in one day." She looked bleakly at him. "We had over ten thousand come through this place in four weeks."

Sep immediately felt his mind constrict and an internal alarm sound. The conversation was drifting towards an area he didn't want to go. He felt like a diver about to advance along the high board, but unwilling to jump off. He changed the subject. "What about the large grey-looking building?"

Her face fell and her voice became flat. "Ah, that's the isolation block."

He looked surprised. "I did not think you would have a problem with infectious diseases."

She paused before replying, as if steeling herself. "It's not because of diseases, Sep," she said quietly. "Men were isolated because of their injuries. Some of the lads had horrendous wounds: half their faces missing, loss of all limbs, stomachs ripped apart or terrible burns. It was felt it would be bad for morale if they were in regular wards."

Sep felt a pang of panic and his throat tighten. He was still in dangerous territory. "Did you have to work in such a place?" He coughed to disguise his disquiet.

She nodded. "We all did our bit. It was tough. Many of the patients in there pleaded for us to give them an overdose of morphine. They couldn't face returning home to their wives, sweethearts or parents. Some doctors and nurses were badly affected too, and had to be sent away to recover."

"*Scheisse.*"

She looked relieved. "It's over now. Thank God."

"I hope we learn from this." Once again, he tried to change the subject. "What are those buildings on the right? They look as if they don't belong. They look new."

"That's the nurses' quarters. I live on the top floor. See the third window from the corner?" She leant her head next to his and pointed. "That's my room. It has a fantastic view over the grounds and the valley. In spring and summer on days off, I sit with a book and pretend I'm on holiday."

"You have your own room?"

"I do now. I used to have to share with four other nurses, but they've headed back to Blighty."

"And the small white building?" He nodded towards a small structure that looked like a summerhouse.

"That's the hospital chapel. It used to be the coach house. It's been done out really well. It's worth a look." She glanced at his crutches. "If you think you can manage it?"

The chapel was small, intimate and, in Sep's eyes, charming in its simplicity and lack of adornments. There were none of the trappings he was used to in Catholic churches. A simple wooden cross framed by silver candlesticks stood on a white-clothed altar. Battered folding chairs were neatly arranged on either side of the aisle. In the right-hand corner in front of the congregation was an ancient-looking pedal organ. On the left-hand side a small raised dais and plain wooden lectern faced the congregation. A series of small windows set high in the wall ran either side of the building. The chapel could hold fifty or sixty people at best, Sep guessed. The ceiling was made of exposed rough timber joists and rafters. There appeared to be an empty jackdaw nest in one corner.

The place projected an aura of peace and quiet reflection.

They wandered slowly down the aisle, breathing in the musty air until they reached the altar.

"Are you religious?" Sep asked.

"No, not at all." She pondered for a few seconds. "I mean I believe in a God, but I don't follow any particular religion or belong to any denomination. How about you?"

"I'm supposed to be a Catholic. It's expected. The Catholic Church is dominant in Austria. But ever since I was a small boy I never felt it was for me. Even less so now." His eye fell on the organ. "We have one very similar in our *Stube*."

She followed his gaze. "Can you play?"

"Yes. But not well."

"Go on then." She nudged him gently towards the instrument.

He propped his crutches against the wall and sat down. "What would you like me to play?"

"Anything you like. The tunes you would play if you were back home."

He thought for a bit before turning to her. "I have a problem."

"What's the matter?"

"One foot. Two pedals."

"Oh!" She glanced around and pulled up a chair next to him. "I'll work the pedals." She glanced sideways at him. "Ready?"

She began to press, and the old instrument wheezed into life.

He let her keep pedalling before she realised he hadn't reached for the keyboard.

"Come on!" she urged him.

He grinned at her. "I thought I would let you get some practice in first."

She laughed and hit him playfully on the shoulder. "Get on with it, Sep Breitner."

He began to play. Instantly he was transported back to the Sunday afternoon family tradition. He played his father's favourite tune and, in his imagination could hear his fine baritone filling the *Stube*. Each tune drew another sweet memory and a broad smile to his lips. He remembered George and his love of British sea shanties. To Susan's delight, he started to sing *'Hearts of Oak',* rolling back and forth on his chair. She joined in, and soon they were singing a full medley of nautical songs. She put her arm around his shoulder to hold herself steady as they swayed.

Sep felt her touch as if it were a bolt of electricity. He forced himself to focus on hitting the right notes. He felt the warmth of her body, her breath on his cheek, the brush of her legs against his as she pressed rhythmically on the pedals. Her arm rested gently across his back, her fingers lightly gripping his shoulder. His entire body was aware of her. Her voice was filled with fun and happiness. He desperately wanted to stop playing and take her in his arms. But such madness would destroy the moment, and perhaps ruin everything.

Eventually, the day and fatigue caught up with them. She glanced at her watch. Sep's heart fell. He didn't want the afternoon to end.

"We have to get back." She sighed.

"Oh yes, I promised to treat you to tea."

"In that case we need to be quick. The canteen closes in an hour." She looked at him, her face pink from exertion and her eyes laughing. "One last tune?" She hadn't withdrawn her arm. It was as though they were in a private cocoon of their own – relaxed and revelling in each other's company.

He grinned broadly at her. "Which one? You choose."

"The lullaby one. The one you said was your mother's favourite."

He stroked the keys, trying to extract the maximum feeling from the lilting melody. As he played, she allowed her head to droop until it was resting on his shoulder. His smile grew broader. By the

96

last verse she had slowed her pedalling and was pretending to snore gently. He let the last few notes wheeze out of the organ, and the small chapel fell silent.

He bent over and gently kissed the top of her head through her scarf, as he would a small child. "Beaks under wings," he said softly.

For a few seconds, she didn't move. She seemed as reluctant as he was for their afternoon to end. "You play well. You have a nice touch," she murmured.

"One day I'd like to be able to buy a proper piano."

She sat up slowly, leant back and placed her hands in her lap, then turned to look at him, her face a picture of contentment. "Shall we go for *Kaffee und Kuchen*?"

The canteen was almost empty when they arrived. They ordered a pot of tea and two slices of fruit cake.

"Are you looking forward to tomorrow?" he asked, trying to keep his voice light and nonchalant.

"Yes and no." She took a bite of cake and caught the wayward crumbs that fell from her lips. "We have a lot of patients to look after on this trip, so it will be hard work. I doubt I'll get much sleep. Then I'm catching a train from Brighton to London, the tube to King's Cross, another train to Leeds and then a local train to Skipton." She looked across at him. "Those are the bits I'm not looking forward to."

"And the things you are excited about?"

"Apart from meeting my mum and sisters? I can't wait to go for a long hike across the moors."

"In winter?"

"Oh, it will be cold, wet and miserable. I'll get soaked through, no doubt. But it will be just me and the wild open countryside."

"You are a country girl, then?"

She nodded. "When I was younger and living in Skipton, I used to dream of living in a big city – London especially. As I've got older, I've changed my mind and prefer living closer to nature." She took another bite of cake and frowned. "Mind you, it has to be proper nature in the raw – you know; rivers, mountains, forests, lakes, wild weather. I wouldn't like to live around this part of France, for example. It's all flat and boring."

Sep took a sip of tea and tried to still his thumping heart. He dreaded his own questions. Each one seemed to be an acceptance of their inevitable separation, an acknowledgement that, far from their worlds coming closer together, their circumstances would drive them apart. He felt he was admitting defeat before he had even had the chance to engage. "Will you look for a job when you return finally to England?"

She grimaced.

"I'm sorry. Perhaps it is not a good question to ask."

"No, Sep, it's fine." She ran her index finger around the rim of her cup. "I honestly don't know what I want, that's my problem. And even if I did know what I want, there's always the issue of whether or not I'll be *allowed* to do it." She looked across at him. "Did you know that thousands of women are being made redundant back in Blighty? I know the lads need to return to their jobs. But we've worked damn hard for the last four years, and throwing us onto the scrapheap like that isn't fair."

"Is that what you think might happen to you?"

She spread out her palms. "There aren't many hospitals in the UK, and I don't want to end up as a junior nurse looking after old people."

"It would be a waste of your talent, for sure."

"And I want to see things as well." She sounded pained. Then she grinned at him. "Did you know that, before the war, over eighty per cent of British soldiers had never travelled more than fifty miles from the place of their birth? And I'm not much better."

"Do you want to continue nursing?"

"Not just to stand still. I'm a senior ward nurse. I know I could become a ward sister if there was a vacancy here. But we're closing down." She fell silent. "It's like being on a railway journey. Everyone gets off when the train reaches the terminus – but nobody knows where they want to go next." She flicked her eyes towards him before lowering her gaze. "How about you? What will you do when you get back to Austria?"

Miss you, was the thought that instantly flashed through his mind. However, he managed to mask his emotion. He shrugged. "I honestly do not know. My family will expect me to run the farm. My father is getting on a bit, and won't be able to continue for much longer." He sighed. "Everything has changed. I would like to be more adventurous. Maybe expand our business, use my English. I do not know. What time are you leaving tomorrow?"

"First thing. Six o'clock wake-up call, breakfast and then assemble the lads for boarding the transport at seven o'clock for departure at eight." She looked at him eagerly. "Do you have something for me to read?"

"Of course – and I will write some more while you are away."

"Maybe you'll become a famous author."

He laughed. "In that case, please do not throw my writing in the bin. You have the original copies. One day they will be worth a fortune."

She looked hurt. "Whatever makes you think I would throw them away? I intend to keep them all."

The sound of the wooden shutters of the serving hatch being closed startled them.

"Time to go, I'm afraid. I need to get ready for tomorrow and have an early night."

Sep reached for his crutches. "Stay here. I'll go and get my writing for you." He hobbled back to his ward and retrieved his manuscript. He paused, leaning on the bed. He felt the weight of depression building in his mind. She would only be away for two weeks. It wasn't as if she was travelling to the other side of the world! He couldn't understand why the prospect upset him so much. He shook his head and pulled himself together.

When he re-entered the canteen, she was sitting with her chin resting on her hands, looking deep in thought. She had removed her headscarf. She glanced sideways at him as he entered. Her hair cascaded around her face, framing it in a wreath of curls. To Sep she looked entrancing. Her eyes widened in surprise as she saw the papers in his hand.

"My word, you've been busy!"

"I am up to Chapter 10." He handed her the papers.

She stood and faced him, clasping her hands in front of her as if she was nervous or uncertain. Her eyes were downcast.

"Sep, I've had a lovely afternoon." She glanced shyly at him.

He smiled. "Yes – it was something special, wasn't it?"

She nodded. "And thank you for the *Kaffee und Kuchen*."

"I should thank you for your company. I won't forget today. Maybe I will include it in my book."

They stood, feeling awkward.

"I must go."

He held out his hand. "Of course. I wish you a good trip. I hope you have a wonderful time with your family, and I very much look forward to your return."

As they shook hands, he looked into her eyes. He was searching for something – anything that told him she might feel the same way about him as he did about her. What he saw confused him. Her eyes smiled, laughed, sparkled – she had genuinely enjoyed herself. Of that he was certain. But how did she feel about him? He could not tell.

As she was about to walk through the door she turned back. "I'll bring you something back from England."

The sound of trucks, the slamming of doors and the faint sound of voices woke him. He lay still for a moment listening, feeling comfortable and relaxed. It slowly dawned on him that for the first time he was almost totally pain-free and his feelings of sadness and hopelessness had become less frequent. He glanced at the clock. It was ten past seven. Pangs of hunger prompted him to get up. He reached for his crutches, swung himself out of bed and headed for the bathroom.

When he returned, the sounds had increased. Curiosity got the better of him. He struggled into his pants and shirt before picking up his crutches and making his way to the window.

Outside he could see the roofs of trucks and ambulances parked in a line at the end of the formal garden. Orderlies and nurses helped scores of soldiers make their way towards the vehicles. Their excited chatter, shouted jokes and laughter indicated that the men were in high spirits. They were heading for Blighty, and for once the assurance of being home for Christmas was no false promise.

At first glance the evacuation seemed chaotic, but Sep spotted the order behind it. The more seriously wounded and still stretcher-bound were moved first. Others appeared to be being assembled according to their injuries. Sep guessed they were being sent to specialist hospitals and recovery centres. There were dozens of men in wheelchairs, hobbling on crutches, or being supported by nurses and staff. The walking wounded milled around, exchanging parting words, shaking hands or sharing a final joke. A few officers stood to one side; smoking, observing the scene. A few – Sep assumed they were the more popular – shared a friendly wave or gentle ribbing with the wounded men as they passed. The atmosphere was akin to an excited bunch of children about to embark on a school outing.

In the midst of the crowd, Sep spotted her standing behind a long trestle table at the head of the steps. She held a clipboard. It quickly became clear she was the hub of the operation. A steady stream of officers, doctors, orderlies and nurses queued up, waiting to receive orders from her. Sep watched in growing admiration. Even from a distance it was obvious – from their body language and their attentiveness to her instructions – she commanded respect. Now and again an evacuee would shout out a comment to her. Sep guessed they were expressions of gratitude. Sep shook his head in admiration. She was unflappable.

Sep scanned the crowd and tried to assess how many patients were being sent home. It had to be well over two hundred. His eye fell on an officer standing to one side. He was particularly

100

smartly dressed. His polished leather boots and Sam Browne belt gleamed in the early morning sunlight. The pips on his shoulder indicated he was either a captain or a major. A captain, Sep decided, as he looked too young to be a major. He had a string of medal ribbons across his left breast pocket. Sep assumed from his high boots and flared breeches he must be a cavalryman. He stood, hands behind his back and his gaze fixed on Nurse Jones.

Sep felt his good humour start to fade. He watched the officer intently. The captain only averted his eyes once – to retrieve and light a cigarette from a silver case.

Sep continued to watch the young officer; all thoughts of breakfast banished from his mind.

Gradually the last of the evacuees were loaded into the transport and the non-travelling orderlies, doctors and nurses returned inside the chateau. The only person left was the young captain.

Nurse Jones reappeared. She was dressed in her travelling cape and held a small brown suitcase. Immediately the captain threw down his cigarette and ground the stub into the gravel path. He advanced towards her; his arms outstretched. She half-ran towards him, her face wreathed in a smile. The pair embraced. The captain scooped up her bag and, with his other arm circling her waist, they almost skipped down the steps.

Sep's eyes followed the couple. They clambered into a small olive-green staff car. In seconds they were gone.

Sep stared at the cloud of dust that marked their departure, trying to come to terms with the confusion in his mind. He felt numb, angry, depressed, foolish, upset, hurt – but above all, sad. The emotions swirled around his head all day. He tried to read, flicking through some magazines before giving up when he realised, he wasn't taking in the words. The same questions kept repeating themselves. Why hadn't she mentioned the captain? Who was he? What did he mean to her?

He filled in his own responses. *You didn't ask. Why should she tell you? What business is it of yours, in any case?* But the biggest answer brought him up short. A beautiful, intelligent, self-assured young woman like Nurse Jones is bound to have a string of admirers.

His naivety harried him. Naivety or vanity – or both? Either way, he felt stupid and embarrassed. He was glad now he hadn't revealed his true feelings for her. He glanced at his missing limb and inwardly laughed. Dashing, young, virile cavalry officer versus half-crippled Austrian farmer. No contest.

He felt his spirits rise as a new thought took hold. A farmer who might write something worthwhile. He realised that his writing wasn't just a pleasant diversion. It was doing him good – especially mentally. He hoped that Susan would enjoy reading his latest chapters.

Perhaps writing for a living was something he ought to think about. He glanced towards his crutches. Running a farm wasn't going to be easy with one leg. He might have to consider alternatives – or at least something to supplement his income. Right now, thinking about home would do him good. He comforted himself with the thought. Writing about Dopplegau, his family, the special moments etched on his memory, the good and not so good times. Yes, that would be therapeutic.

He glanced at the clock. It wasn't yet eight o'clock. He'd head to the canteen and cheer himself up with breakfast, then pick up his pen.

After her miscarriage, Heidi quickly fell pregnant again. The rest of the village greeted the news with resignation. After all, it was a woman's lot to bear children. Families with eight or nine offspring were not uncommon. The only person who was surprised – and distraught – was Rachel. Her dismay stemmed from her knowledge that large families, poor health and poverty invariably went hand in hand. She was also concerned about Heidi's well-being.

The Breitners and the Wachters were unusual in having relatively few offspring, although Sep often thought that the two families were like one big family, they were in and out of each other's houses so often. Their close relationship was reinforced by odd symmetries: the children were of similar ages. Stephan was the only boy with two sisters, Maria and Klara, while Josephine Breitner was the only girl among three brothers. However, the symbiosis did not extend to the children's temperaments.

Klaus Breitner was quiet, gentle, thoughtful and prone to prolonged periods of silence, as if he was observing the chaotic world around him with half-amused indifference.

By contrast, the youngest brother Thomas, was a handful. Headstrong and fearless almost from birth, he was determined never to be left out of anything. He was like a young bull, full of energy and daring.

Josey Breitner was a tomboy. She was strong-minded and assertive. Throughout her childhood, Josey frequently arrived home bearing the scars of exuberant play: a scratched face, grazed knees, bruises and the occasional broken bone, which often made her mother wonder whether any obvious feminine traits might emerge. She climbed trees and scaled the higher mountain crags and bluffs. Any activity, dare, challenge or risk the boys threw down, she embraced.

The eldest, Sep was seen as wise – and boring. The villagers relied on him to restrain his more exuberant siblings. As far as his brothers and sister were concerned, he was their leader and ultimate protector in the battlefields of their play and adventures.

Stephan Wachter was Sep's best friend. Slow, steady, reliable and loyal, Stephan lumbered along at his own pace. Never one to lead, he met life's challenges with studied consideration. No decision was quick, and no action rash. His steadfastness and constancy were in stark contrast to his two flighty sisters, who had many characteristics in common. They were both beautiful in face, figure and personality, and possessed the lush dark brown hair and sturdy frame that ran with the Wachter lineage.

Of the two, Maria, the eldest, had the warmest nature. She was kind-hearted, gentle, caring and fussy. In Maria's world everything and everyone required looking after.

Klara was vain – but she didn't see that as a problem. She enjoyed her beauty and invested heavily in it. She loved to be seen as pretty and she was universally regarded as the village princess. The rough and tumble of play would send her fleeing to a safe distance. There she would stand, looking horrified, safe from any prospect of being sullied by grubby hands, splashing mud or flying manure.

Heidi was at the centre of the Breitner clan. She provided her brood with unconditional love – even the wayward Thomas, whose recklessness occasionally reduced her to despairing tears. Her children wanted for nothing that was important in life. 'A warm bed, a full stomach, an active mind and a clear sense of right and wrong' was a mantra on motherhood Heidi was fond of repeating. She laid down the household rules before any of the children had the time or intellect to question them. Meals, bedtime, mornings and bath-times all adhered to a strict schedule. Meals were taken together, except during harvest or the twice-yearly cattle drives. Sunday afternoons were reserved for family bonding. She kept her family well dressed and was adept at making, mending and altering clothes.

By such means, Heidi ensured the Breitner household was a haven of efficient good order and happiness. But, despite her devotion to her family, there was a gap in Heidi's life. She came from Bechter stock that was outward-looking, entrepreneurial and successful. Being a homemaker, loving wife and mother were not enough for her. She was ambitious. She was educated and well read, and took an active interest in politics, current affairs and business – she railed against the barriers, prejudice and discrimination that barred her entrance to them all.

Fortunately, the opening of the Landesbank office came at just the right time. She quickly overcame her initial doubts about accepting George's offer to help manage the new branch, and took up the position. She soon demonstrated her ability and ensured the success of the enterprise. Most of the farmers and businesses in both villages used it. She became indispensable to George by looking after the accounts of the Lodge and Sir William's broader commercial dealings with his Swiss and German business associates.

If Heidi was the soft centre of the family, Fritz Breitner was the bedrock. Fritz was a conscientious farmer and businessman. He worked hard, to the point of permanent exhaustion. Throughout his life, Sep couldn't remember a time when his father's working day was anything less than fourteen hours. His one day of respite was Sunday, when he reserved the seven hours between the start of Mass and the evening milking to spend with his family. He was shy and almost awkward in unfamiliar company. Apart from his father-in-law and the Wachters, he had no close friends. He happily joined the rest of the farmers in the Adler after Sunday Mass and enjoyed a few beers in their company, but was uncomfortable with any hint of being the centre of attention and tended to stay out of the limelight.

By contrast, Joseph Breitner, the family patriarch, was a flamboyant, extrovert, larger-than-life character who loved being at the centre of everything important that happened in the village. He made up having for no formal education by being astute and cunning. As a consequence, by Dopplegauer standards, Joseph Breitner became a wealthy man. By common agreement, he was also the most effective Bürgermeister the village had ever elected.

For all their differences – or perhaps because of them – the Breitner and Wachter families rubbed along well together. In both households, the hub of activity was the *Stube* and kitchen. Both houses had creaking wooden floors worn smooth by countless boots; low, smoke-stained ceilings; half-completed knitting and darning scattered on the low, cushioned bench that wrapped itself around the *Kachelofen*. Both shared the all-pervasive smell of wood smoke and chopped pine logs, and the permanent sound of the common pot bubbling on the range. The families were frugal. Nothing was ever wasted. Vegetable peel, flakes of cheese, scrag ends, ham bones and chicken carcasses were all thrown into the common pot to produce a broth so flavoursome that the hint of its aroma drifting out of an open window was sufficient to ensnare the children and send them running home for sustenance. If they timed their run well, they could take their fill from the Breitner pot before scurrying around for second helpings from the Wachters.

The atmosphere in the *Stube* changed with the seasons. In summer, the windows and shutters were thrown open to let the soft Alpine air drift in, along with the distant sound of cow-bells from the cattle on the high pastures and the verdant musty smell of newly mown grass.

In winter, everything was sealed up and bolted down. The family would sit around the comforting heat of the *Kachelofen* feeling safe and snug as outside the ground became iron, winter storms battered the shutters, and the snow drifted so high that on occasions they had to dig themselves out.

Spring filled the house with the smells of the farmyard as the cows, pigs and chickens were freed from their winter quarters to gambol across the lush green meadows while the byres, sties and pens were mucked out. And autumn was the time of berries, fruits, herbs and vegetables;f the pungent salty odour of smoked hams; and sweet and sour perfumes from endless glass jars, stone pots and bottles filled with jams, preserves, pickles, vinegars and wines.

Throughout his life whenever he felt a wave of depression or despondency start to build, Sep would close his eyes and allow himself to imagine his family gathered in the warm comfort of the *Stube*. He'd picture himself sitting beside Fraulein Rachel, his head close to hers as they bent over the latest English novel. Or perhaps George would strike up on the pedal organ, or his grandad would tell one of his tall tales, or – best of all – he'd remember his mother ladling out broth into bowls set in front of Sep and his siblings. For a time it was an idyllic existence. It couldn't last – and it didn't.

Eighteen months after she arrived in the Breitner household, Fraulein Rachel announced that she was leaving. Sep initially thought the news was a joke. A young man in a smart uniform riding a sleek groomed horse, had galloped to the Breitner front door and presented Rachel with a piece of paper. The message had a dramatic effect. Rachel shrieked, threw up her arms and burst into tears. Sep reeled in shock. He'd never seen her so animated. Heidi flew into the *Stube*, fearful some disaster had occurred.

"I've been accepted!" Rachel's eyes glistened through her tears. She passed the telegram to Heidi, who read it before staring at Rachel in disbelief.

"Oh, Rachel, I am so happy for you," she said before she too burst into tears and held out her arms to embrace her friend. The two women stood in the middle of the *Stube* hugging, laughing and sobbing.

Sep watched the scene in bewilderment. He was unsure whether something good or bad had happened.

Rachel's shriek had alerted Suzanne Wachter, who bustled in, an anxious look on her face.

"What's happened?" she said breathlessly.

Wordlessly Rachel handed her the telegram.

It was Suzanne's turn to shriek and join the tearful huddle, further adding to Sep's bemusement.

Stephan followed his mother in and glanced in confusion at the women. "What's happened, mate?"

Sep shook his head. "Don't know. I think Fraulein Rachel has had some good news."

"When do you have to leave, Rachel?" his mother asked.

Rachel wiped the tears of joy from her eyes and considered the question. She looked uncertain. "I don't know. Soon though." She put her hand to her mouth to compose herself. "The course starts the first week of September. I need to sort out accommodation in London – plus travel." She gasped in shock. "I'll need to leave here next week, or the week after."

Sep didn't hear the rest of the conversation. His mind was whirling. He felt sick and desperately upset. Tears welled up as he stared at the chattering women he had trusted above all others in his life. How could they be happy? Why were they celebrating? This was a disaster. His world was shattered. He felt hurt and betrayed. He dropped from the bench and ran to his room, only just holding back his sobs until he had shut the door behind himself and flung himself onto his bed. Later, Rachel came to his room. She quietly shut the door and sat on the edge of the bed next to him. He lay still, his face buried in the pillow. He was exhausted from weeping. He felt her softly stroking the back of his head and wondered whether he would feel her gentle touch ever again.

"Do you want a cuddle?" she asked softly.

How could he refuse?

She opened her arms to him, and he went to her.

"I don't want you to go." He sniffed, trying not to start crying again.

"It's not easy for me, chicken." She rocked him gently. "But I have to go. You know I've always wanted to become a doctor – and now I have the chance." She pushed him carefully away so she could look directly into his face. "You have to take the chances life throws at you, Sep. Even though sometimes it's hard." Tenderly she cupped his face in her hands. "I thought you would be pleased for me."

Sep looked shocked. "I *am* pleased for you." He couldn't prevent tears filling his eyes. "It's just that I don't want you to go. I might never see you again."

"Well, that's silly, Sep. Of course, you'll see me again. Whatever makes you think I won't come back?" She gave him a reassuring hug. "One day I'll come back. After all, this is where I'm happiest. It's my home, and your ma and pa and your brothers and sister are my second family." She gave him another squeeze. "And you're my special friend. Or are you too upset to remain friends?"

"No – we'll be friends forever."

She smiled. "I know. And I want to ask you a favour when I move to London."

"What favour?"

She thought for a bit. "London is a big city – much bigger than Wien and Budapest combined. In fact, it's one of the biggest cities in the world. Did you know that?"

He did. He knew a lot about London from his annuals. It was the capital of the British Empire, it was reputedly the most populated city in the world, it had an underground railway, the King lived in a place called Buckingham Palace – and it was a long way from Dopplegau.

"I'm going to be by myself. I expect I'll be lonely and homesick – and I'll probably get upset at being so far away from my family, your mama, Frau Wachter and you."

Sep cottoned on straight away. "I could write to you."

"And keep me informed about everything that's going on here in Dopplegau. Every last detail, mind. Would you do that?"

Sep grasped the idea like a drowning man reaching for a rope. The thought of losing all contact with Rachel was too horrible to contemplate. "Of course. And you can tell me about London and what you're doing," he said enthusiastically. "I'll write every week."

She frowned. "That might be a little difficult for me to manage. I have to study hard. Once a month, perhaps?" She looked enquiringly at him.

He was sure he could manage that.

"You have to write to me in English – I don't want you neglecting your studies or forgetting everything you have learned."

For Sep it was slim pickings – but he was grateful for every crumb.

Rachel was as good as her word. At the end of the month, Sep would get increasingly excited as the letter day approached. He became a familiar visitor to the post office. A shake of the clerk's head meant disappointment and a slow trudge home. An upraised hand holding the precious letter meant a headlong, madcap, excited sprint. Sep leapt up the stairs two at a time, before throwing himself onto his bed. He carefully broke open the seal: even the envelope was precious. Then he took out the letter as if it was a sacred relic. Rachel always wrote to Sep as if he was an adult. She told him everything in vivid prose that made London and England come alive. Sometimes she would enclose a postcard or newspaper cutting she thought Sep might find interesting or informative. Sep kept every single one of her letters. All of her life was laid out. She spared Sep none of her emotions: her highs and lows, her anger and frustration at the prejudice and patronisation women faced, the anti-Semite bigotry she experienced. The absence of universal health care and the plight of the poor and downtrodden in the slums, all leapt from the page into Sep's imagination. He lived her successes with her. He was filled with joy when she graduated, then obtained her professorship. She explained the purpose of her research papers, and the awards and accolades she accumulated. She sent him articles she had published. It was only over time that Sep realised that Rachel's reputation and importance in the world of medicine meant it was unlikely she would ever return to Austria, let alone Dopplegau. In 1909 his hopes plummeted further when Rachel announced she had met someone very special – a fellow doctor and colleague. She was in love, she announced. Sep greeted the news with delight. He'd finally realised that he and Rachel would not marry. Nevertheless, in the darkest corner of his mind lurked a lingering regret that she had been born too early – or he too late.

Sep worked hard to make his letters as interesting as possible. He made notes of things that happened in the village that might amuse her and remind her of Dopplegau. He sent her copies of the local newspaper, underlining articles that demonstrated the progress that was slowly creeping across Austria. As he got older, he wrote about the books he had read and asked her opinion. She in turn would either send him books or recommend other authors. Sep was wrong about one thing though. Frau Rachel Weiss returned to Austria with her family in 1913 to take up a new post as Head of Women's Medicine at the Franz Josef Hospital in Vienna.

Sep's distress at Rachel's departure was echoed by the residents of both Gau and Dopplegau. The clinic had now become indispensable to the community, and the threat of its closure caused a ripple of alarm. Fears were allayed however, when it was revealed that Doctor Rubenstein himself would provide a weekly surgery, with a view to opening a permanent practice once his eldest son had qualified and was able to take over the family business.

Until the opening of the *Volksschule*, there was little distinction in the minds of the village children between work, education and play. They merged into one another. As soon as they were able, all offspring had to do their share of the family chores. It was an accepted part of village life – and family survival. It was simple: failure to work meant loss of earnings, and inability to earn meant being unable to eat. The need to stock up on sufficient fodder to tide the animals over the lean winter months meant that helping out on the farm took precedence. Attendance at the small village school fitted around farm work, and play time filled the remaining nooks and crannies.

Trouble started when the school opened its doors. From the start, the school ran to its own timetable. It had scant regard for the needs of the seasons, or agricultural schedules. Attendance was compulsory for all children aged from five to sixteen. At a stroke, the school deprived the village of nearly half the workforce it required to survive.The headmaster and teachers appointed were outsiders, who carried their professionalism with arrogance. They were deaf to the views of the community who, in their eyes, were illiterate and little better than their uneducated offspring. The Education Authority was also sly and knew how to undermine any opposition. The dominant influence at all levels of society was the Church. Ensure the clergy were on side, and the masses would follow. In Father Wagner, they found an obedient lapdog. The *Bildungsbehörde* had the explicit support of the bishop, and that was reason enough for the priest to align himself with the bureaucrats.

The villagers realised that relying on their parish priest to fight their corner was futile. He was evasive, avoided the issues, claimed he had no influence, agreed to consider their complaints and then did nothing, asserted that the villagers' concerns were trivial or, when boxed into a corner, made it clear that he could not help. The community had no experience of dealing with the faceless bureaucratic monster in their midst. They were baffled by the instinctively obstructive attitude of the officials. It quickly became apparent that the school would change their way of life forever, and ruin them all. Tensions mounted, before the villagers turned to the one man they knew was capable of dealing with the situation: *Bürgermeister* Joseph Breitner.

In short order, Joseph countered the *Bildungsbehörde* diktats with some of his own. He used political brutality, called in favours, provided a sympathetic local press with leads relating to the financial proprietary and peccadillos of certain officials within the

Bildungsbehörde. He threatened court action and hinted at the crippling damages arising from the farmers' loss of earnings. His assault was short, sharp, relentless and ultimately successful.

The authority caved in. School days, term times and holiday periods were all adjusted to reflect the needs of the community. Compulsory attendance was the one area where Joseph Breitner yielded ground. He was determined that no child should suffer from a lack of formal education, as he had.

The *Bildungsbehörde* took encouragement from his endorsement and hunted down children with the determination of rat catchers. The result was a testament to their efficiency. Every child from the two villages, and even the more remote hamlets and farmsteads, was caught in the dragnet.

To Sep's bemusement, the first week of the opening term passed in a chaotic blur of children of all shapes and sizes running, shouting, pushing, shoving, falling over, screaming, laughing, crying, cutting their fingers, grazing their knees, gathering in small groups or chasing each other in great waves. Everywhere there were new faces: diminutive children who looked as if they might be trampled underfoot, and giant teenagers - the boys full of blustering bravado, the girls haughty and mysterious.

Some he'd never seen but only heard about. They gathered, looking wretched and bewildered, at the back of the classes and loitered like spectres on the edge of the playground. It was if they already knew they were condemned. Children with lazy eyes, thick glasses; a tiny, thin girl with chalk-white skin and strange pink eyes; a couple of boys who seemed unable to control their limbs; and three hobbling on home-made crutches that marked them out as victims of polio.

They were easy targets. The bullies started the taunts, but were quickly joined by others, glad that someone else was being picked on. The outsiders found themselves surrounded: relentlessly poked, prodded, teased, their hair pulled, their ears twisted, their noses tweaked, their crutches kicked away, abused and humiliated. The afflicted children looked like cornered sheep. Most cringed, their heads held low, their eyes downcast. Some gazed bovine-like at their tormentors as if such abuse was familiar and expected. A few attempted to defend themselves but lacked quick wits and mental dexterity. Their lame attempts merely served to egg on the bullies.

Sep and Stephan watched from a distance, appalled at the spectacle but uncertain what to do. Sep scanned the playground, anxious that his brothers and sister were not swept up in the mob or tempted to join in. He spotted them, waved them over and looked around, expecting to see some authority figure step in and end the shame. But no help was forthcoming. It was as if – for the opening few weeks at least – the staff had decided the playground lay beyond the boundary of adult responsibility, and the children were to be left to sort out their own pecking order.

"We ought to do something, mate," Stephan said, as the crowd began to chant. A small crippled boy had been reduced to tears and, to the delight of his persecutors, had wet himself in terror.

Marie Wachter, and the unexpected action of a stocky, bald lad, made the decision for them. Marie spotted a group surrounding a frail-looking girl, who was staring at the sky as if oblivious to everything going on around her. Only her fingers, anxiously twisting her long blonde hair, betrayed her anxiety. Some older lads lifted her skirt, trying to get a reaction from her. Marie pushed the boys aside, before wrapping her arms around the girl and moving her away. The teenagers closed in, pleased they had a new target for their malice. Sep and Stephan instinctively ran to protect the girls. It was like a couple of puppies getting between a pack of hyena and their prey. The gang confronted the two eleven-year-olds.

"You kids keep out of it, if you know what's good for you," one snarled.

"She's my sister, and you'll leave her alone." Stephan squared up to the bully, even though his opponent was a thickset boy at least two years his senior.

Sep stood alongside his friend and prepared himself for an inevitable beating. He and Stephan were outnumbered, and the boys surrounding them looked like ogres.

The expected massacre didn't happen. Just as blows were about to be exchanged, a hushed silence fell across the playground. More immediate violence was on offer.

All eyes turned towards the bald boy who was standing nose to nose with Will Hagspiel. The crowd sensed blood. A circle quickly formed around the pair.

A chant went up: "Fight, fight, fight, fight…"

Will Hagspiel had expected the lad to wilt under his taunting. But the boy was not intimidated. Not only did he hold his ground, but he retaliated. He pushed his face directly into Will's.

"Dare you to say that again."

Will's sneer was replaced by a flicker of fear as he realised he was now under scrutiny by the crowd. The option of backing down had gone. He smirked uncertainly, hoping his bravado would carry the day.

"Bald-headed—"

It was as far as he got. The bald lad's fists crashed into Will's face. The mob were silenced. Blow after blow rained down on Will's head, body, stomach so fast and hard that Will stood no chance. He flung his arms over his head to protect himself, then doubled up as a fierce punch was driven into his kidneys.

Sep stepped in when Will crumpled in a heap, gasping for air, blood pouring from his nose and mouth. Although Sep had no respect for Will Hagspiel, he was a neighbour, and village honour suggested he ought to try and protect him from a further beating. He grabbed the bald lad's arms.

"Enough, mate. You've made your point."

The boy glanced at him, his eyes ablaze with anger and aggression. He dropped his fists and turned to face the crowd, who stared at him in awe. They'd witnessed scraps before, but they were typically over after one or two blows. The savage violence of this assault shocked them. "Anyone else feel like saying something to me?" He glared round; his head held high. Even the older lads stayed mute. "Nah – I thought not." He pushed his way through the throng, looking angry and sad. He went over to the low wall where Marie and the blonde girl stood. He bowed his head to recover his breath, rubbing his scratched and bleeding knuckles.

Marie stared at him before rummaging in her pocket for a reasonably clean-looking handkerchief. "Here," she said. "Use this."

The lad cocked his head and looked at her. "Thanks, but I don't want to ruin it."

She said nothing, but gently shook the hanky to indicate he should take it in any case. Although she didn't realise it, Marie had just met her future husband.

The Breitner and Wachter children gathered around, their interest divided between the mysterious blonde girl and the strange-looking lad.

The girl broke the awkward silence. "Where's my home?" She had a pronounced Brandterwalder accent and she sounded like a timid, bewildered infant. She stared vaguely into the middle distance; her eyes not focused on anything. "I can hear my Peter calling."

The bald lad didn't look up. "Your home's where it's always been, Freya, and it's time you headed back. You shouldn't be here."

There was no indication she'd heard him or was even listening. "I like birds," she said absently.

Sep examined her curiously. She was filthy. Her skin had a pale greenish, scaly sheen to it. Her fingernails, black with ingrained dirt, were bitten down to the quick. Her dress was flimsy and threadbare. She had the sour, earthy odour of someone who hadn't washed for a long time.

113

The bald lad stood in front of her, grabbed her shoulders and looked into her eyes. "Freya, you ought to go home," he said firmly.

His action jolted the girl into semi-reality. She looked unblinkingly at him. Gradually an expression of understanding washed across her face. She was gaunt. Sep guessed she hadn't eaten for days. Despite her emaciated appearance, she was extraordinarily pretty. "But I like it here." She tipped her head to one side and smiled at Marie. "I have a friend."

"You can come back tomorrow, if you like," the lad said as he gently turned her around so she faced the school gate. "Everyone is going home in any case, Freya. You go, and we'll see you tomorrow."

"Will my Peter be here?"

"I expect so. Off you go now."

The group watched in silence as Freya drifted out of the gate and made her way along the gravel path. Every now and again she would skip or twirl as if some random music had come into her head, prompting her to dance.

"Who is she?" Josey asked before turning abruptly to the bald lad. "And who are you? I'm Josey Breitner, and I'm seven."

The lad grinned. "I'm Norbert Haufmann. My dad knows your grandad well." He looked around at the group. "I take it you're all Breitners?"

Josey took it upon herself to do the introductions. "So, we've told you our names – you haven't told us how your dad knows our opa."

He chuckled. "My dad owns the sawmill and wood yard in Gau. Your opa has put a lot of business our way over the past few months."

Sep frowned. He'd heard his grandad talk of the Haufmanns, but never heard him mention the name Norbert, although he did recall a lot of other names of the Haufmann clan. Sep looked at Norbert curiously. "Strange he never mentioned you."

"Wingnut," Norbert said with a smile. "Everyone calls me Wingnut."

"Why?" Josey said.

Norbert laughed, squatted in front of Josey, put his index fingers behind his ears and pushed them forward. "It's because I look like a wingnut."

Josey looked baffled. At seven, she had no idea what a wingnut was.

Sep, Stephan, Thomas and Marie looked at each other in embarrassment. They saw the resemblance immediately. Sep grinned to himself. He recalled the name now, but had assumed Wingnut referred to a pet dog.

Josey wasn't going to allow her ignorance of metal fastenings stand in the way of her curiosity. "So, Wingnut, who is Freya?"

Wingnut looked towards the retreating figure. "She lives beyond the Nebelspitz. Her parents have a farmstead up there. Or perhaps a hovel would be a more accurate description."

"That place is ancient. I didn't think anyone lived there," Sep said. The Nebelspitz wasn't exactly off-limits, but it was difficult to get to, especially from Dopplegau, and parents discouraged their children from playing there. It was reputedly a place of child-eating trolls, malign spirits, tortured souls, spiteful wood elves and dark deeds. A more plausible rumour was that it was a plague village, and residues of the infection still lingered. It was enough to dissuade inquisitive children from visiting.

"I heard that the only buildings there are the old-fashioned kind, with turf roofs and stone walls."

"That's it exactly. Freya lives with her parents and her crippled brother in a place that's little better than a pig sty."

"You've seen it?" Marie asked.

Wingnut nodded sadly. "You wouldn't believe it if you saw it. Thing is, they're all – you know – like her. Mad. Her parents are odd to say the least, and her brother – well, he's little more than a cretin."

"How do they manage? I mean in winter the place must be completely cut off."

Wingnut shrugged. "Oh, they know how to farm. They have some animals, grow some vegetables – enough to survive. When Freya turns up, we give her some stuff, and I dare say a few others in Gau do the same." He turned to face Marie. "It was kind of you to rescue her."

Marie blushed.

The group became aware that the playground bedlam had grown subdued. The ferocity of Wingnut's assault on Will had shocked them all. The children found other activities to distract them. Some drifted off into small groups, looking shamefaced, as if embarrassed at their behaviour. A few talked to the children, who only minutes before had been the target of their malice and cruelty, as if to make amends.

Nobody helped Will Hagspiel, who clambered slowly and painfully to his feet. He stood for a second, swaying, before wiping his sleeve across his mouth and eyes, then examining the resulting streaks. The evidence of his humiliation appeared to focus his mind. He set off across the playground for the long path back to Dopplegau and the sanctuary of his home.

There was no repeat of that day's events. Perhaps the teachers had been smart after all, and realised some blood-letting had to be allowed to prepare the ground for the imposition of order on a more chastened and compliant population.

The school fell into a routine. The staff's modest objectives were driven by expediency rather than quality. Basic mathematics was taught with regimented efficiency. Hochdeutsch grammar was nailed into reluctant brains by article, gender, tense, verb and conjunctive. The correct form of writing was imposed, letter by letter, and with no allowances made for any child who had the misfortune to be left-handed.

Despite its high-minded ideals, the school rapidly abandoned any pretence of providing education for all. One by one the simple-minded, and those beyond discipline, were allowed to drift away. To teach them sapped the energy and patience of the staff. In any case, the school was an educational institution, not a poorhouse or centre for social care.

The exception to the expulsions was Freya, who drifted in and out of the school like a stray cat. In a rare demonstration of compassion, the staff indulged her random visits. Invariably she would seek out the one person who, to her addled mind, had shown her kindness. She skipped and danced along the corridors before entering the nearest classroom mid-lesson, to scan the grinning, half-embarrassed faces, seeking out her friend. In such circumstances the teacher would suspend the lesson, and stand patiently until Freya completed her scrutiny. If Marie was not to be found, Freya moved on to the next class until her quest was successful.

Once discovered, Marie was excused the rest of the class to accompany Freya wherever her flights of fancy took her – this was invariably the spot in the playground where she'd found safety and friendship.

In contrast to her first experience of the school, Freya now experienced a degree of tenderness. The children took to leaving her small gifts, something from their lunch box, cast-off clothing, ribbons, home-made jewellery or anything they thought she would find useful or which might delight her. She always appeared in a disgusting state, however, and Marie would steer her towards the wash-house for a scrub and disinfestation.

The school's failure to recognise or meet the needs of the disabled and disadvantaged was mirrored at the other end of the spectrum. Bright, gifted children or those with unusual talents or abilities were equally poorly served. Many children devoured the mathematics and Hochdeutsch curriculum and were hungry to progress. Their hopes remained unfulfilled.

There was no outlet for Klaus's outstanding artistic abilities. As a consequence, he detested the *Volksschule* more than anyone.

It represented everything he wasn't. For Klaus, entering the playground each day was like passing through the gates of a prison. The stress began to show, and he became silent and withdrawn, shunning the hustle of the playground. He took to standing by himself, willing the school day to end. He feigned illness or failed to turn up at all, instead spending the day wandering the paths and forests above the village.

Fortunately he was rescued by George, who arrived back in the Breitner fold bearing a trunk-full of gifts, following an extended trip back to England.

"I have something for you that I am confident you will use for your own and, dare I say it, everyone else's pleasure," he announced. Slowly, he took a large wooden box out of his travel trunk. Inside was a complete set of oil paints, the finest artists' brushes, a set of architectural pencils, charcoals and a palette. "I have a set of canvases and sketch books for you as well, but they're in another box."

For Klaus, it was if he had been handed the keys to his freedom. At a stroke, his world was transformed. From then on, he endured the *Volksschule* and focused on becoming an artist.

Sep also presented the school with a problem. His command of English, even though still far short of fluency, was higher than the modest standard the school set for even its most senior students. Sep had four times as many English books at home than the school had in its own library. His English proficiency came close to matching that of Frau Meusbruger, who was supposed to be teaching the language. She provided Sep with her own copy of a German–English dictionary, and a complete set of novels by Charles Dickens which, judging from their pristine condition, had never been opened, let alone read. These books, along with the history books, magazines, papers and letters sent by Fraulein Rachel and George, were his salvation.

Wingnut became part of the combined Breitner–Wachter family. Although the Haufmanns' home, sawmill and wood yard lay at the furthest end of Gau, he would regularly trudge the four kilometres between the two villages to join the other families. Adventure, fun and play were his primary motivation – although partaking in the feasts from the common pots always made the effort worthwhile.

It would be years before his friendship with Marie blossomed into love and marriage. But something happened before then that cemented Wingnut into the Breitner family forever.

He joined them at the breakfast table on what promised to be another hot Alpine summer day. He came equipped with a long steel chain scavenged from his father's timber yard, the purpose of which was already known to the grinning, fidgeting children.

They had hatched their plans over the past week. Engineering work on taming the Ach had recently been completed. The meandering channel had been straightened and great stone flood banks constructed on either side, along with two weirs to slow the waters. Above the top weir, the water had been allowed to back up to create a deep pond. The mature mountain ash, chestnut and oak trees there were left untouched – including an ancient chestnut with a bough ideally positioned to provide an anchor for a rope (or a steel chain) for the perfect swing.

The chain wrapped around Wingnut's body indicated that today was the day. The children already pictured in their minds the endless fun that awaited them. They gobbled breakfast in a race to get to the river. They hadn't considered how they would attach the chain to the tree; all that mattered was the vision of the completed job.

As expected, Klara declined to take part. To her mind, climbing trees, diving into water and swinging off metal chains was not decorous. She said that she might join them later.

The rest were like racehorses straining to be released from the starting gate. Josey was the keenest. She gobbled her food at such a pace that her mouth was quite unable to cope. The last of the bread was crammed into an already stuffed mouth, still awash from the previous ladle of broth. The resultant overflow dribbled slowly down her chin. She made to drop down from the bench to be first out of the kitchen.

Her mother's stern voice brought her up short. "Where do you think you are going, young lady?"

Josey gulped, swallowed hard, wiped the leaking broth residue from her mouth, and looked bewildered. She thought for a second, trying to guess where she might have transgressed, before a light of understanding went off in her brain. She rapidly climbed back up onto the bench seat. She had forgotten her manners, she reasoned. "Oh. Finished now. Please may I get down?" She indicated her empty plate.

"You may get down, Josey, but you are to stay here with me and Klara."

"What!" Josey's mouth fell open, revealing a mass of half-masticated bread. Her dismay at her mother's unreasonableness blotted out any rational response. "Why not? That's not fair! I want to go!" she blurted out, allowing a globule of half-consumed broth-saturated bread to drip onto her bright red shirt.

"You know very well why not, Josey." Her mother's tone was firm.

"But why?" Josey feigned ignorance. She'd hoped a combination of her speed out of the door and her mother's distraction would work. She'd even dressed in her red playshirt and lederhosen to make clear her intention to indulge in some serious fun and games.

"Josey, you know you can't swim," Tom said, exasperated. He knew this argument, if allowed to develop, would slow them all down. Worse, it might open up a discussion about alternative things they might do that didn't involve excluding his young sister.

"You know the rules, Josey. No one is allowed to go near the river unless they know how to swim properly." Heidi held up an admonishing finger, daring her youngest child to contradict her.

Josey looked as if she would explode. Her face began to match the colour of her shirt. For a second, she glared at her mother. Huge tears appeared in the corner of each eye. She leapt from her seat and flew out of the room, slamming the door behind her. Great thuds marked her ascent of the stairs: her progress punctuated by plaintive wails relating to the unreasonableness of parents, the fact that as the youngest she always missed out, and the unfairness of life.

Heidi pursed her lips, trying not to laugh. Play involving the river always bothered her, even though all the other youngsters were accomplished swimmers. She turned to the rest of the children, looking serious.

"I don't want you going anywhere near the weirs. They are dangerous, even if you do know how to swim. Do I make myself clear?"

They nodded, looking equally sober. They were well aware that Heidi Breitner treated any child who entered her house according to her rules. Any breach would result in the same sanction, regardless of who the miscreant's parents were.

Heidi nodded, satisfied the message had been received and understood. However, she decided extra reinforcement was necessary on this occasion. "Sep, you are the eldest and will be in charge. Is that understood by everyone? I'm talking to you, Thomas Breitner, in particular."

Tom gave his mother a look of astonished hurt at the injustice of being singled out.

Klaus rolled his eyes at the futility of the instruction and led the way out of the door.

Once outside, they sprinted towards the pond, Tom in the lead, with Marie, struggling to run in her smock dress, bringing up the rear. The tree with the convenient bough was on the far bank, so they had to follow the track further upstream where a gap in the bushes allowed access, and the water was shallow enough for them to wade across. They gathered at the base of the great tree and stared up at the tangled mass of boughs and branches.

"We should have brought a ladder," Sep said, looking at the lowest branch they would have to reach to gain access to the bough.

"I can stand on your shoulders." Tom was keen to start.

Klaus shook his head wearily at the obvious flaw in Tom's suggestion. "You're too short – you won't be able to reach."

Sep thought for a while. "We'll use the chain. Throw it round that branch." He pointed to a low-hanging branch. "I'll be able to climb up. After that, it should be easy to work my way over to the bough." He indicated his intended route.

"How will you get back down?" Stephan asked.

Wingnut slapped him playfully on the shoulder. "Don't worry about that, mate. Sep will work something out."

Soon Sep found himself edging along the bough, his heart racing. He suddenly realised how high up he was, and how far the drop was into the water. The task seemed to be a lot riskier and scarier than he'd anticipated. He glanced down at the upturned faces.

Only Marie seemed concerned for his safety. "Be careful, Sep." Her well-meant caution only served to remind Sep of his precarious position. He shuffled another half a metre forward. For the swing to have the maximum fun factor, it had to be secured at least another two metres beyond his outstretched hands. That way almost all of its arc would be over the water.

Beneath him, Tom had lost interest in watching his older brother. He stripped off and dived into the pool. Stephan soon followed, leaving Marie, Klaus and Wingnut to monitor Sep's progress and encourage him.

Sep nudged himself forward. The bough abruptly dropped under his weight. Sep felt a surge of panic and desperately locked his arms around the branch. He paused to catch his breath and steady his nerves. He was glad his friends were unable to see his fear. The fact was he was petrified. For a few minutes he lay frozen, terrified to make any move backwards or forwards. He pictured himself crashing from the branch into the water below.

Far below, Tom and Stephan swam back and forth, splashing each other, appearing disinterested in Sep.

Sep gradually beat his fear. He was close to the attachment point, and steeled himself to inch forward once more. He looped the chain twice round the bough, attached the hook through the last link, and breathed a sigh of relief. The chain was secure. He let it drop towards the water.

"Give it a tug," he shouted to the two lads beneath him. As soon as he said it, he knew it was a mistake. The two boys grabbed the chain and tried to climb up it together, setting the swing in motion. Their combined weight proved useful in testing the robustness of the hook fixing. It also sent the bough swaying and bucking. Sep was pitched forward, then sprung upwards, as the two boys fell from the chain back into the water.

"That's enough!" Sep yelled. "I need to get down."

His appeal fell on deaf ears. The swing was attached, therefore the fun could begin. Tom and Stephan hauled on the chain again.

Above them, Sep felt his grip begin to loosen. He wrapped his arms and legs around the heaving bough, shut his eyes and hung on.

"Get off the chain! I'm going to fall!" he shouted. The boys couldn't mistake the anger and fear in his voice. They let go of the chain and swam away, looking sheepishly up at Sep.

Sep let the swaying branch come to a stop before cautiously opening his eyes. What he saw threw him into a panic. On the opposite side of the pool, he saw a body slowly drifting downstream towards the weir. His initial shock turned to terror when he realised that the body was wearing a distinctive red play shirt.

"Josey!" he screamed.

The others looked up at him, perplexed.

Sep pointed towards Josey. It looked as if she was making an attempt to swim, as an arm flapped ineffectively against the water. She rolled over in the water, coughing and spluttering.

"Josey's in the water!" Sep shouted at the top of his voice, frantically pointing towards his sister.

Wingnut was the first to act. He spotted Josey. In a second he was off, running back through the shallow crossing point, then sprinting down the path to overtake the drowning youngster before she reached the weir.

Instinctively, Marie leapt up and followed.

Sep abandoned all caution. He had to get down from the tree, fast. He reached under the bough and lunged for the chain. He managed to get a partial grip – enough to allow him to swing beneath the branch. He lost his grip, and fell. The cold of the water shocked him. He felt himself sinking, and his wet clothes began to drag him down. Adrenalin kicked in, and he struck out for the surface with a surge of frantic energy.

Stephan waded back to help drag his friend out of the water.

Sep turned and desperately tried to locate his sister. He spotted her still struggling to stay afloat. Despite her efforts, she was being drawn inexorably towards the weir.

Ahead, Wingnut fought to find a way through the thick undergrowth that barred his way to the river. He stopped and scanned the water. He could see the inevitable. Even if he was able to force his way through the undergrowth, there wasn't enough time to rescue Josey. She was going to go over the weir. Wingnut scrambled out of the bushes and dashed down the path, discarding his clothes as he went. He had to get downstream of the waterfall.

Marie sped after him. Sep was not far behind. He screamed at Josey: "Keep swimming! Keep your head above water!"

Whether Josey heard him or not, she increased her desperate attempts to stay afloat. It was too late. The current had claimed her. Even the strongest of swimmers would be unable to break free of its grasp.

Downstream, Wingnut slid down the great granite blocks. Here the Ach waters were fast-flowing and tumbled over and between rocks. He scrambled over the boulders, ignoring the cuts and grazes they inflicted. He plunged into the foaming water and made his way towards the waterfall.

Marie now understood his plan. It was brave and reckless. And she realised Wingnut couldn't do it alone. She peeled off her dress, scrambled down the bank, and charged into the rapids.

Above the weir, Sep watched in horror as the current swallowed Josey up. With a forlorn wave of an arm she disappeared over the edge.

Wingnut caught a glimpse of the small figure above him before she was engulfed by the foaming, roaring deluge. It was enough. He dived under. The water battered his body. Deafened, he reached out blindly for Josey before she was sucked into the undertow. Something solid crashed into his arm. He snatched at it, grabbed a fistful of cloth, and heaved himself back towards the surface.

His head popped above the water and he sucked in great lungfuls of air. He glanced at the limp girl in his arms. Josey's eyes were closed. She was unresponsive.

Wingnut rolled onto his back and swam furiously to the bank. He was exhausted, but forced himself to keep going until he felt Marie's hands grab his shoulders. Together they waded and scrambled through the water and over the rocks, carrying the unconscious Josey.

Between them, they passed Josey to Sep at the top of the bank. Tom, Klaus and Stephan looked on, horrified.

Josey's face was white and her lips blue. She wasn't breathing.

Wingnut hauled himself over the top granite block. He flipped Josey face-up, pinched her nose, locked his mouth over hers and inflated her lungs. He watched her chest rise, then fall, then breathed into her again. He kept repeating. After every fourth inflation, he rolled Josey over and firmly pressed his hands down on her back

Sep felt numb and helpless. He was shaking with shock.

Marie hauled herself over the bank and knelt next to Wingnut. She grabbed Josey's hand.

"Come on, little one," she pleaded.

Sep felt powerless. "Keep talking to her," he suggested. It was all he could think of. He'd seen his pa use the same technique to coax life into new-born calves.

It worked for them – and it worked for Josey. She coughed, spluttered and vomited. She opened her eyes and stared with incomprehension at Wingnut, who loomed over her. She rolled onto her stomach, and puked and strained until all the water was expelled.

Wingnut sat back and studied her. His feet and legs were covered in blood from the cuts and grazes he'd suffered in his headlong dash over the rocks.

"That was close."

The five of them watched as Josey drew in great lungfuls of air.

Sep finally stopped shaking. He clapped his friend on the shoulder. "Well done, mate. Where did you learn to do that?"

Wingnut shrugged. "I saw a man in Gau being dragged out of the Ach last year. The rescuers did the same thing. It worked for him."

Marie put a consoling arm around Josey. "Are you all right?"

"We should get Mama," Klaus said.

The comment seemed to stimulate Josey into urgent recovery. "No! Please!" she spluttered. "Don't get Mama."

Her stomach convulsed and she coughed up more mucus and water. "Please don't," she croaked. "I'm fine now." She knelt on all fours, her chest heaving.

"Yes, yes, Josey. It's all right. Calm down." Marie glanced anxiously at Sep. "Let's get you sorted first. Then we'll decide what to do."

"Is Sep here?" Josey asked.

"Yes," Sep replied. His earlier terror had been replaced by an overwhelming feeling of relief – and anger. What the hell was Josey doing near the river?

"I'm in big trouble, aren't I?" Josey said between gulps of air.

"Yes."

Josey nodded. "I need to learn to swim."

Tom laughed, partly out of relief. "Josey, lesson one is easy. You don't go swimming with your clothes on."

Josey didn't share the laughter. "I need to learn to swim." She pulled herself into a kneeling position. She looked directly at Sep. "You have to teach me."

Sep looked at his sister in bewilderment. He had expected shock, hysteria, a flood of tears from the fright she'd endured. Instead, Josey appeared lucid and calm.

"Josey, what are you talking about? You nearly drowned!"

"I need to learn how to swim." Josey stood and started to undo the straps of her sodden lederhosen.

"Are you stupid or something?" Tom spluttered. "You want to go back in?"

Josey nodded. "I can't go home until I can swim."

Sep grew angrier. "Josey, what did you think you were doing coming down by yourself and diving into the river?"

Josey looked equally furious. "I didn't *dive* in! I fell in. It was an accident. I couldn't get out." She glared at Sep. "There's no point getting angry with me. Now I have to learn to swim, otherwise I'm in double trouble."

They all regarded her with bafflement.

Klaus finally worked out Josey's warped logic. "Because mama said you mustn't go near the river until you can swim."

Sep grabbed his sister by the shoulders and looked her in the face. "Josey, learning to swim won't stop you getting a thrashing from Pa. You have to face it. You're in big trouble."

Josey wriggled free. "I know that. I'm not stupid. But at least it will have been worth it." She peeled off the rest of her clothes and stared defiantly at Sep. "If I can't learn to swim, I can't go near the river. But I must go in the river to learn to swim." She glowered at him, daring him to deny her logic.

Sep scowled at her. "You can't go near the river without mama's permission."

"I'm already in trouble for that," she retorted.

Any other child would have been traumatised by what she'd experienced. Josey appeared to have already put the whole matter behind her.

"We might as well teach her to swim," Klaus said eventually. "She'll have to learn sooner or later."

"I'll teach you while the boys are playing on the swing," Marie suggested.

Josey stared at Sep. If she was going to get her way she needed Sep's approval. A slow smile spread across her face as she realised her elder brother was wavering.

Sep shook his head and sighed, signalling his consent. He picked up Josey's wet clothes. "We need to hang these on the bushes to dry."

Under Marie's tutelage, Josey learned to swim. The speed of her education was undoubtedly influenced by the anticipated mitigating effect it would have on the heavy punishment that awaited her. By early afternoon, she could swim across the pond and back. By late afternoon she and Marie gleefully joined in with the boys, swinging and in great arcs across the pond before crashing into the water with loud splashes and whoops of joy.

Eventually, hunger and fatigue got the better of them. Reluctantly, they dressed and headed for home and the reviving prospect of broth from the common pot.

Josey's pace began to slow as they approached the farm. Sep stopped to allow to catch up. It was like watching a condemned man mounting the scaffold. She took Sep's hand.

"What's up?" Sep asked gently.

For a minute she said nothing. She stared at the ground, rubbing her bare feet against each other.

Sep knelt in front of her. "It's best to get it over and done with," he said quietly.

She sniffed. "It's not that."

"So, what's the problem?"

She looked directly at him. For the first time, he saw fright in her eyes. "I was lucky, wasn't I?"

He nodded. "If Wingnut hadn't pulled you out …."

"You have to stop me doing things like that."

Sep laughed. "I can't promise that if I'm not around. But if I am, I'm better at telling you what the right thing to do is." He grinned at her. It was the first time they had felt the strong bond between them that would endure throughout their lives.

As they had expected, Josey received the biggest thrashing of her life from her father that evening. It reduced both parents to tears. It was also the last time she received such a punishment – although it didn't dent her determination to achieve anything she put her mind to.

n 1910, when Sep had just turned sixteen, death visited the village. Bereavements usually attracted little attention. Infant mortality was something almost all families had experienced, and the demise of the weak, frail and elderly, especially during the winter months, caused little comment – or grieving, for that matter. It was expected. Father Wagner provided the necessary requiem Mass, friends and neighbours delivered fitting eulogies, and the deceased joined the other corpses in the cold, dank earth of St Martin's graveyard. A small cross and perhaps a bunch of wilted flowers marked their passing. It was left to the remaining spouse and close family to mourn the loss in private.

However, these deaths were different. They were unexpected and violent. They also occurred within days of each other. This led some villagers to believe that a curse had been laid on the village. They happened in the spring.

As was the custom, farmers took advantage of the improving weather to ascend to the high plateaus to repair and stock up the mountain huts ahead of the arrival of their cattle a few weeks hence. Helmut Hagspiel's mountain pastures lay at the edge of the village parish, above the upper reaches of the pass beyond the Lodge. He set off before dawn, leading a pony laden with two large hessian bags containing enough provisions for several weeks. He passed through the village, nodding greetings to the other farmers preparing to embark on similar journeys. It was the last time he was seen alive.

The second night after Helmut had left, the Brandterwald was hit by an unexpected, unseasonal storm. The blizzard, howling gales and brutal sub-zero temperatures lasted three days and nights.

Afterwards, villagers emerged to snowdrifts that reached the eaves of their houses. Some sheds and smaller buildings were completely buried. As the villagers dug themselves out of their homes, a sense of foreboding swept around the community. The villagers gazed anxiously up at the peaks that surrounded them.

"East wind. That puts them west-facing slopes at risk." Konrad Wachter pointed at the snow-laden escarpments that gleamed in the late afternoon sun. Even from a distance, the wind-sculpted overhangs were visible. It was as if a vast ocean wave had been frozen at the point of breaking into a maelstrom of surf.

Fritz pursed his lips and shook his head knowingly. "Fresh snow falling on bare ground is bound to lead to trouble. There'll be avalanches for sure."

"Do you think the village is at risk?" Herr Zinnerman looked around. He was the only one present who was not a farmer, so he knew the least about avalanches and the factors that heightened the risk. What he did know was that he'd sunk his life savings into his *Gasthaus*, and taken out loans to finance its expansion. The last thing he wanted was to see his livelihood destroyed.

Herr Wachter sucked on his pipe and considered the question. "Difficult to be certain. That's the slope we need to worry about." He pointed at a rocky outcrop high above them. "If that goes, there's enough snow to break through the forest. Then we're in trouble."

Sep looked with apprehension at his father. It had never occurred to him that the village, and his home, could be destroyed.

Fritz sensed his son's anxiousness. He glanced down, gave a reassuring smile and ruffled Sep's hair. "Nothing to worry about, son."

Since they were in the Adler, they might as well enjoy a couple of beers. Contrary to his expectation, Sep wasn't sent home, but for the first time his father bought him a lemonade and allowed him to stay with the men.

They were on their second beer when they heard the distant rumble. Immediately the *Gasthaus* fell silent. The men tensed. The rumble developed into a savage growl that grew louder and louder until it was a mighty roar that reverberated around the valley: the sound of millions of tons of snow, ice, rocks, boulders and uprooted trees hurtling down the mountain.

The noise convinced Sep that the whole mountain must be collapsing. The air itself seemed to vibrate, and the fury to go on forever.

The men sat still, held their breath, gripped their tankards, glanced nervously at each other. They'd seen and heard avalanches before, but none had come close to the howling savagery and volume of this one. They tried to judge whether or not it was heading for them.

Konrad Wachter broke the silence. "That's up the pass," he said confidently.

The men didn't move. They prayed their friend was right. If he wasn't, they knew they probably only had seconds to live. There was no point running or seeking shelter. If the wall of snow came crashing down on top of them, there would be no escape. An avalanche that size would smash through the Adler, leaving nothing standing, killing anything living in its path, or entombing those unlucky enough to survive the initial impact. Unless they were rescued within minutes, slow suffocation was inevitable.

Then a shockwave hit the Adler, shaking the building and rattling the shutters.

"Jesus Christ." Herr Zinnermann looked around frantically.

Sep looked at the men. They stared at nothing, concentrating on the noise outside. Waiting. They were frightened, and their fear was transmitted to Sep. He glanced anxiously at his father. Fritz Breitner took a leisurely sip from his tankard, glanced at his son out of the corner of his eye, smiled and winked. Sep knew his pa really was a hero.

After more than ten minutes, which seemed like ten hours, the angry growling diminished until the valley finally fell silent.

Sep's pa let out a sigh of relief. "God help anyone caught in that."

"Who's up the pass?" someone asked.

"Helmut. He went two days ago."

None of the farmers seemed concerned, however. They knew the mountains – the forests, paths, rivers, peaks, hidden valleys, bogs and caves – as well as they knew the traces of veins on the backs of their hands. They also knew how to survive in the harshest weather: stay in the high mountain hut, don't venture out, hunker down, keep warm, dry and fed, and wait until the worst passes. They were confident that Helmut would turn up in a couple of days.

After seven days, they had begun to get concerned. The weather had turned again and a rapid thaw set in. On the tenth day, Fritz and Herr Wachter headed up the mountain to set up their own mountain huts. They took the high mountain track to Helmut's land so they could check on him. His hut stood empty. The valley route he would have taken to return to Dopplegau was impassable. The avalanche had followed the line of least resistance and had filled the valley with a glacier-like tumble of rock-strewn ice and snow that would take all summer to melt. Somewhere under the million tons of debris lay the body of Helmut Hagspiel.

Helmut's death also killed his widow – at least, in mind and spirit. Gertie lost her spite and vigour. She physically shrank and became a lost soul. She had no body to bid farewell to, no grave to weep over, and no mate to badger, bully – or love. She also had no shoulder to cry on and no friend to talk to about old times. Her daughter now lived in Innsbruck with her soldier husband and rarely visited her mother, who had shown her little affection.

The death of his father drove Will Hagspiel further along the road of bitterness and self-pity. He inherited the family farm, as was the custom, but he was far too young to take on such responsibility, and ran it badly. He took out his anger and frustration with the world by neglecting his livestock, and shunned the older farmers' well-meaning attempts to help him. A neighbouring farmer, distressed at the suffering of the animals, finally assumed control and ran the farm with the blessing of the Farmers' Council. The villagers hoped time would cure young Will of his grief and resentment.

Nearly nine months after the tragedy, Sep was leaning out of his bedroom window gazing at Mittelspitz, the high mountain that dominated the top end of the valley. Regardless of the time of year, it was always the first peak to catch the earliest rays of the sun. Its craggy summit was bathed in a dull ochre glow. Sep never tired of the spectacle.

Out of the corner of his eye, he caught a movement at the edge of the forest. A figure, dragging what looked like a tree trunk behind him, was approaching the village from the top pasture. He had a brown bear pelt draped across his shoulders. His hair was long and shaggy, and merged into the fur of the cloak.

To Sep, he looked like a troll. He watched the man's awkward progress. About two hundred metres away he stopped and stood still, as if waiting for something to happen.

Then Sep saw his father emerging from the milking shed.

"Papa, there's a strange-looking man standing in the top meadow," he shouted.

His father put the milk pails down and walked to the corner of the shed, where he had a line of sight to where his son was pointing.

The troll man spotted Fritz. He waved, pointed to the ground, then abruptly turned and walked rapidly back towards the trees. In seconds the forest had swallowed him.

Sep was intrigued. He rushed out of his room, down the stairs, out of the back door and caught up with his father as he made his way up to where the man had stood.

Strapped to a makeshift sledge was Helmut Hagspiel. He was the first dead person Sep had seen. Ice had preserved the corpse, but the force of the avalanche had shattered the body. The left arm was missing and the other limbs were twisted and broken. It was obvious that Helmut's spine was broken.

Fritz put his arm around Sep. "Look and learn, son," he said quietly. "This is what the mountains can do if you don't respect them."

The storm that had claimed Helmut Hagspiel took three others. In some ways the consequences were even more tragic – not because of the numbers killed, but because of what happened to the one survivor.

The day after the great storm, Freya was found collapsed outside the Haufmanns' farm. She was emaciated, barefoot, had severe frostbite in her toes, and her face and hair were black with dirt. The family took her in, warmed, scrubbed, fed and revived her. Once she had recovered, Freya began the disconnected ramblings she was known for.

It took several hours before Frau Haufmann realised there was a theme running through Freya's wild-eyed ranting. She began to question whether their initial assumption that the girl had merely got lost in the blizzard was correct.

As Freya regained her strength, she experienced fits of blind terror in which she would desperately beg for help. These suggested that something terrible had occurred. The family finally concluded that whatever had happened had taken place at the Nebelspitz, and it had to be investigated.

Gaining access to the Nebelspitz was not easy even in the dry summer season. Now, with the snowdrifts still deep, nobody was keen to venture beyond the village, especially while the avalanche risk remained. After three days it was deemed safe enough to try, and a group of men from Gau set out for Freya's home on skis and snow shoes.

At first it was difficult to see where the farmstead was. The building was buried and only the faint outline of the roof and chimney-stack hinted at its location. The men dug their way in. When the first shovel hit the stone lintel above the window, they began to see the full extent of the disaster. The stone was split and charred. The building had been gutted by fire. Only its stone construction had prevented it being razed to the ground. Nothing had escaped the inferno. Ash carpeted the floor, and the stench of smoke lingered in the air. At the back of the kitchen was an iron range upon which stood a few charred, buckled pots. The men also found some knives, forks, the frame of a hurricane lamp, two metal belt buckles and six neat piles of boot tacks. There was no trace of Freya's parents, her brother, or any of the animals.

The men guessed the family had built up their fire to keep warm in the storm. Maybe they had fallen asleep in the warm fug they had created. Perhaps a spark had leapt out of the grate, or a sap-filled pine log had exploded, setting light to something. With the doors and windows sealed, the family stood no chance. The men prayed that they had suffocated in the dense smoke. Being burned alive was too horrific to contemplate. Once a window had broken, or an external door been opened, the gale would have rushed in like an express train. In seconds the house would have become a crematorium. The men assumed Freya had fled through an open door or window – her escape may well have condemned her family to being burned alive.

There was little to be gained by staying, and nothing to be salvaged. The men left and headed back to Gau.

What would happen to Freya? She was incapable of looking after herself. She was homeless, destitute, orphaned, and – apart from her vague friendship with Wingnut and Marie – utterly alone in the world.

For a week the Haufmanns looked after her while the villagers discussed her future. The obvious option was to send her to the poorhouse in Achbrugge, but this was vehemently opposed by Frau Haufmann. Such an institution was no place for any child, let alone a vulnerable girl, she argued. Besides the poorhouse was little better than a prison. It would be cruel to send a free spirit like Freya to such a place.

Nobody knew if Freya had any other relations – or, if she did, where they lived. They decided to consult Frau Norbert. By now Frau Norbert was the oldest person in Dopplegau, if not in the Brandterwald. No one was sure exactly how old she was. She was a living encyclopaedia of every birth, death, marriage, affair, scandal and business deal of every family in the upper reaches of the Brandterwald.

Frau Haufmann; Father Zach, the elderly priest from Gau; Heidi; Father Wagner and Marie Wachter, who asked to attend out of concern for her friend, gathered in the old woman's *Stube*. Frau Norbert sat in her rocking chair, a pile of recently spun balls of wool nestled in her lap. She continued knitting while listening intently as Frau Haufmann related Freya's plight. Her hands manipulated the needles at a furious pace, and her eyes darted from face to face.

Her body may have been frail, but her mind remained as agile as her fingers.

Finally, Frau Haufmann reached the end of the tale.

Their faith in Frau Norbert's knowledge was not misplaced. However, far from resolving Freya's precarious situation, Frau Norbert's information only worsened the orphan's plight.

"Her grandma and grandad are both dead," Frau Norbert said confidently.

"Grandparents on both sides?" Frau Haufmann asked.

"Her grandma and grandad are both dead," Frau Norbert repeated. She sounded testy, as if her statement was somehow distasteful to her. "They're buried at the Nebelspitz."

There was an embarrassed silence. No one wished to contradict Frau Norbert or imply that she might be losing her faculties.

Frau Haufmann laid a gentle hand on Frau Norbert's arm. "Are you saying that neither set of grandparents are still alive, dear?" she asked tactfully.

"I know what I'm saying, and I know the truth of it. As do you, Father Zach." She directed a fierce glance at the elderly priest, who shuffled uneasily in his chair. "Thuller was their name, wasn't it?"

The priest looked at the ceiling as if searching his memory. "I'm not at all certain what you are talking about, Frau Norbert. I confess I don't recall the name."

"Pah! No, I expect you don't. I'll bet there are no records in the parish register, neither." Frau Norbert's laugh was humourless. "No one wants to remember."

"What are you talking about, Frau Norbert?" Heidi asked.

"Brother and sister they were." She pointed a knitting needle at Father Zach. "Aye, you can look shocked. But you know the truth of it. Brother and sister they were – unmarried, shunned by all, especially the Church. They had two children – at least, two that lived, a boy and girl." Frau Norbert looked around at the group. "The sins of the parents infected the children – at least, in the eyes of the Church they did, eh, Father?" She shook her head. "No chance of God's embrace for those poor mites. They never knew what it was to mix with anyone, other than themselves. Well, you can't blame them for what happened. What was good enough for the parents was good enough for their offspring."

The group looked at Frau Norbert in shocked silence, apart from a grim-faced Father Zach, who sat with his head bowed, stroking his chin. Marie, who hadn't grasped the significance or meaning of the statement, looked at Heidi, confused.

"Freya's parents were also siblings?" Frau Haufmann squeezed the words out in stunned disbelief.

"Certainly," Frau Norbert replied matter-of-factly. She recast a needle before adding, "Although I can't say for definite who was Freya's real father."

"You're making this up." Heidi glanced nervously at Marie. This was not the kind of conversation that should take place in front of a thirteen-year-old.

The old woman's reply was terse. "True as I'm sitting here. I'll swear it on the good book, and may God strike me down if I'm false." She gave Father Zach a scornful look. "He knows the truth of it. Refused to baptise any of them, or have their bodies buried in sacred ground, didn't you Father?"

"I'm afraid I don't recall. Perhaps it was before my time. I'll need to check the parish records."

Frau Norbert dropped her knitting into her lap and fixed her sharp, bright eyes on Father Zach. "Pah! Check the parish records, indeed. As if such a thing would be recorded. Out of sight, out of mind, out of conscience. And burned in the fires of hell, you say? A fitting end if ever there was one." Frau Norbert suddenly swung her attention towards Father Wagner. "You're very quiet, Father Wagner. Maybe you think such sins don't happen in this day and age, eh?"

Father Wagner looked shocked, before quickly recovering. He tried to change the subject – sounding, to Heidi at least, oily and insincere. "What's done is done. We can investigate the past at some future date if there is any merit in it. The issue we have before us, and to which we must bend our minds, is the consequences of the fact that the unfortunate child has no living relatives. Is that correct, Frau Norbert?"

"It is."

"So, we have a real problem on our hands," the priest continued smoothly. "The poorhouse appears to be the only option open to us." He held up his hand to thwart Frau Haufmann's protest. "Which, I am aware, is not likely to be supported by some in our community."

"She can't stay with us," Heidi said. "I'm sorry, but we have enough mouths to feed, and that goes for Suzanne Wachter as well." She gave Marie a meaningful look.

"Most families won't be willing to take on a girl with Freya's waywardness. Even less if they know her background." Frau Haufmann shook her head sadly. "There must be something better than the poorhouse for the poor mite."

The *Stube* fell quiet as they considered the dilemma. The only sound was the clicking of Frau Norbert's needles.

Father Wagner broke the silence. "I may have a solution – but I will need time to set the wheels in motion and consult with the appropriate people."

They looked at him expectantly.

"She might be able to be placed in the Convent of St Catherine in Littesau. They have taken in young women in the past who have, er … um … fallen on hard times."

"That's a good idea." Frau Haufmann couldn't hide her relief. "She would be safe, the nuns are good people, and the grounds of the convent would give Freya some freedom to wander."

Father Wagner lifted his hands. "Let's not get too far ahead of ourselves. This would need permission from the diocese and the abbess herself. Places are limited, and they are inclined to accommodate the … er … fallen girls from more local parishes. Gau is a long way from their normal catchment. Freya might not be eligible." He glanced around the group to ensure they understood the limitations of the proposal.

Frau Norbert listened intently.

"Also, it would mean that Freya would need to accept her life would not be her own. She would become a novice – devoted to God for the rest of her life." Father Wagner's eyes flicked towards the ceiling to indicate the sacredness of the calling.

"It would be yet another shock for the girl," Heidi said. "And Littesau is a long way from here."

"But the poorhouse would surely kill her. I'd rather she went to the convent. It would be for the best in the long run." Frau Haufmann looked at Heidi

"She might be prepared for the move, to make it less traumatic," Father Wagner suggested.

"What do you mean?"

"She could stay at the bishop's annexe under the supervision of Frau Weissman, my housekeeper, for the few weeks it will take me to speak to the bishop and the abbess. No doubt there will be other authorities and permissions." Father Wagner chuckled. "There is always paperwork." He rotated his hand. "Perhaps I could also introduce her to some basics of life within holy orders – you know, church routines, the power of prayer, some introduction to the scriptures, that sort of thing."

"Frau Weissman lives next door to St Martin's." Heidi thought about the idea. She was familiar with Frau Weissman. An honest, hard-working but simple-minded middle-aged woman, Frau Weissman had no malice in her. She was kind, a devout Catholic, and as quiet as a church mouse. She had provided domestic services for the St Martin's clergy since she was eighteen. She had been offered the position as an act of charity since her own intellect was that of a twelve-year-old – that had been her barrier to marriage. Heidi could see she might provide Freya with welcome companionship.

"And Marie would be just down the road. Freya would be among friends." Father Wagner leant forward and gave Marie a warm smile. "Perhaps you might help Freya move in, my child?"

"Of course, Father." Marie was delighted to be able to help.

The priest looked wistful. "Of course, if it doesn't work out, I'm afraid we must all accept that the poorhouse becomes the only option."

Frau Norbert shook her head, grimaced – but said nothing.

And so, Freya moved into the small suite of self-contained rooms attached to the *Pfarrhaus*. The annexe's sole purpose was to provide overnight accommodation for the bishop on his annual tour of his diocese, or for other church dignitaries who might pass through the village. It was warm, comfortable and private. A small, enclosed courtyard provided a space for quiet contemplation and reflection.

Freya was very taken with her new surroundings, especially the interior of St Martin's church, which was full of wonders as far as she was concerned. She would lie on her back and gaze up at Christ ascending to heaven, which was painted across the high ceiling, or stare for hours at the statues of St Martin and the Virgin Mary that stood on either side of the altar. The silver candlesticks and huge crucifix held a special fascination for her. She loved their sparkle and the way her distorted reflection danced as she circled around them. She would clap and skip in delight at the sound of the organ and the choir. Her greatest joy, however, was the magnificent stained-glass window. She would sit transfixed, her head to one side, watching the images and colours change as the sun traced its path across the sky.

It was clear to the villagers that Frau Weissman and Father Wagner were taking good care of her. Her appearance changed. Gone was the filthy, malnourished rag doll. She put on weight. A white flowing novice habit replaced her torn, thin dress. Her grimy skin shone with a healthy pink glow, and her blonde hair was tamed and fell neatly to her shoulders. She looked angelic.

The village praised the saintliness of Father Wagner, and his standing in the village increased. He was credited with Freya's metamorphosis. He was a true Christian – taking the poor waif into his own home. The results were there for all to see.

Heidi Breitner was expecting the knock on the kitchen door. She called out, "It's open, Father."

Sep stood up out of respect as Father Wagner entered, removing his long leather coat as he did so.

"You're late," Heidi observed.

Father Wagner shook Sep's proffered hand. "Bless you, my son," he said lightly, indicating the gesture held no particular sincerity. "Yes, I have to ensure the needs of my house guest are satisfied." He removed his wide-brimmed black hat and sat at the table. "It takes a bit of getting used to."

"How's she getting on?" Heidi placed a platter of cold meats, eggs and black bread in front of the priest.

Father Wagner let out a long sigh. "On the whole, she's doing well. But it's not been easy."

"She looks transformed," Heidi said.

"On the outside, in terms of her health, hygiene and general well-being, I would agree, Frau Breitner."

"But?"

He rubbed his forehead. "Her mental handicap and her … flights of fancy can be a problem. She lives in a fantasy world. Even Frau Weissman finds her trying."

Heidi laughed. "She's harmless, poor girl." She sat next to Sep and looked across at the priest. "I sometimes envy people like her – living in their own little world. She has such a sweet nature."

"You would think so, wouldn't you?"

Heidi looked surprised. "What? Are you saying she has a dark side?"

Father Wagner swallowed before replying, "No, no, no. Not a dark side as such. She had a problem separating reality from fantasy."

Heidi smiled. "That's probably more of a problem for us. For her, there probably is no difference between her world and ours. It's just one confusing, chaotic mystery. It can't do any harm, once people get used to her ways."

"Let's hope you're right, Frau Breitner," the priest said, although he didn't sound convinced.

"I'll ask Marie to call round to keep her company while you're on your walk, if you like."

Father Wagner looked up sharply. "Oh, today isn't a good day to visit. I've organised some small jobs for her. Frau Weissman is going to teach her how to do some domestic chores." He gave Heidi an exasperated look. "Somehow we have to get Freya used to looking after herself. The convent is disciplined in that regard."

"Oh, Marie could be a great help with that, Father."

"I'm sure she could – in time. But today I think a visit from Marie would be too much of a distraction – for Frau Weissman as well as Freya."

Heidi nodded and stood up. "One step at a time then." She looked around and spotted the package she'd prepared for the priest. She picked it up and laid it on the floor next to his coat. "It's a bit heavy this time, Father. I hope you don't mind?"

"Not at all."

"Ma, what's in it?" Sep asked.

"Old clothes, some food and other bits and pieces we don't need."

"Who's it for?"

His mother looked at him. "There are some people who live high in the mountains, way beyond the Lodge. They are very poor. It's for them."

"Like Freya's parents?" Sep asked.

"Yes, a bit like Freya's parents," Heidi said breezily. "Have you finished your breakfast? Because your father wanted you to give him a hand this morning."

Sep nodded and slipped down from the table.

Freya's move to the convent took longer than anyone expected. Father Wagner's monthly breakfast visits provided an opportunity to enquire about her progress. It soon became apparent that all was not going well.

Underneath her innocent exterior Freya had some character flaws, the priest informed Heidi the next time he visited. She had a sly, deceitful streak, Father Wagner claimed on his next visit. The following month he alleged she was prone to telling malicious lies. She accused Frau Weissmann of stealing for example. Naturally, he had investigated and found Frau Weissman beyond reproach.

By the following visit, Freya had become ungrateful and rebellious. She wasn't responding well to being taught even the most basic lessons; she refused to say her prayers; she had hit Frau Weissman. As a consequence, and reluctantly, he'd imposed some punishment. He was hoping an early date would be agreed with the abbess for Freya to move to the convent.

Marie was allowed to visit fairly regularly. However, Father Wagner always insisted that the timing of her visits was agreed in advance. Freya looked forward to seeing Marie. Her visits were a special treat, a reward for Freya's good behaviour, and therefore needed to be managed with care, he explained.

Marie's reports on Freya also that indicated things weren't going well. After her third visit she commented, "She's not her normal, happy-go-lucky self."

"What do you mean?" Heidi asked.

Marie pondered for a few seconds. "She's just not … you know, bubbly. There's no spark."

"It must be hard for her to cope with all the change."

Marie nodded. "She hates being cooped up."

"Don't you take her out for a walk or outside to play or something?"

"No, Father Wagner says we have to stay in the house – or in the courtyard. He says it's important Freya gets used to the idea of living in a convent-like environment."

"That's awful."

"Oh, he says he takes her out now and again. You know, when he goes on his walks. Into the woods, up the mountains."

"I've never seen him out with her," Tom said.

"Me neither," Klaus added.

139

Marie shrugged. "Well that's what he says."

Josey looked outraged. "It's cruel to stop Freya going out to play."

"Oh, she plays. But she has to stay inside most of the time."

"You should take her some of your toys, and you should invite her round here," Heidi said. "It would be a change for her."

Marie looked happy at the suggestion. "I'll do that."

But Freya never came around. There was always a reason that prevented her visiting. She had some domestic chores to do, or some prayers that needed to be learned, or she had transgressed and visits had been banned for a limited period. When Father Wagner did agree a date, it was cancelled at the last moment. He'd forgotten Freya was to help Frau Weissmann that day. Perhaps Marie wouldn't mind calling in the following day and seeing Freya – in the courtyard.

Five months after Freya moved into the annexe, Marie called round. Father Wagner met her at the front door of *Pfarrhaus*. He didn't look pleased to see her.

"Ah, Marie, my child. I'm afraid Freya is not herself today."

"Oh, is she ill, Father?"

The priest gave a wan smile. "I'm afraid Freya is always ill, my child. Her mind works in ways that are a mystery to us all."

"Can I see her?"

Father Wagner hesitated.

"I haven't seen her for over a month. Maybe she could do with cheering up." Marie didn't wait for an answer but walked down the corridor that led to the bishop's accommodation. She found Freya crouching in a corner of the courtyard. She was dressed in the white novice gown and was rocking backwards and forwards, her eyes glazed, as if in a complete trance.

"Freya." Marie touched her gently on the shoulder.

Freya jerked away as if she'd received an electric shock. She stared at Marie, her eyes full of hate and malice. "Leave me – I'll tell Peter."

Marie reeled back in shock. "Freya, it's me – Marie."

Freya glared at her until a small light of understanding dawned in her eyes. Her face softened and she threw her arms around Marie's neck. "Marie, Marie, Marie," she kept repeating, and held on so tightly that Marie thought she might suffocate.

Marie stroked her hair and gradually managed to extract herself from the embrace. "Freya, I have something for you." She held up her bag and waved it enticingly, then reached in and took out a toy. It was a rag doll Heidi had made for Josey when she was a toddler.

Freya's face lit up. "Peter?" She held out her hand expectantly.

Marie took out the toys one by one and delighted in watching Freya's joy as each one was revealed. Whatever had upset Freya she quickly forgot, as she and Marie settled down to play.

In the background, Father Wagner worked his way around the flower beds, apparently absorbed in weeding, pruning the roses and thinning the bedding plants.

Marie was kind and patient. Freya played as a small child might. Her attention was fixed to the point of obsession until it was randomly diverted by something new. Marie followed where Freya's mind took her. They sat cross-legged in the middle of the courtyard where the sun cast no shadow. Every now and again, Freya insisted that Marie move. At first Marie thought nothing of it, assuming Freya liked to be in the sunlight. Gradually she realised that wasn't the reason. Freya didn't want to be in the sun; she wanted to sit so she was always facing Father Wagner. Marie watched to see if she was right. It was uncanny. As the priest edged around the border, Freya moved with him. It was as if she didn't want him out of her sightline. Marie glanced over her shoulder. Father Wagner had almost completed the full circuit of the courtyard. The flower beds looked pristine. A muddy metal bucket full of weeds and offcuts stood in testament to his labours.

The faint sound of the *Pfarrhaus*'s doorbell drifted into the courtyard.

"Ah, that will be Frau Weissman." The priest stood up and rubbed the small of his back. "Marie, it's time for you to go, my child. Freya, say your goodbyes."

Freya leapt to her feet. "No! Marie stay, Marie stay, Marie stay." She looked at her friend in desperation. "Marie stay," she pleaded.

Father Wagner drew himself up and sighed wearily, as if he half-expected Freya's tantrum and had grown tired of the performance. He turned towards Freya, who stood wringing her hands, anxiously glancing between Marie and the priest. "Marie stay," she sobbed.

"Freya, I said to say your goodbyes." Father Wagner stabbed each word out in a menacing half-whisper. "Don't make me repeat myself."

Freya cringed and backed away. She looked terrified. In her fright she stumbled over the metal bucket. Marie rushed over and bent down to pick up the spilled contents. When she stood up, Freya was rooted to the spot, staring in horror at a muddy brown and green streak that had soiled her pristine white robe.

Father Wagner regarded her. His face was expressionless, his eyes cold. Slowly he raised his arm and pointed to the annexe. "Go to your room, remove that dress, and pray for God's mercy."

Freya wailed and fled.

Marie watched her flight in shock. The upset bucket was an accident; the stain on the dress was minor. She stared at the priest in dazed puzzlement. Surely, he could see that Freya was distressed? Wasn't that punishment enough for the poor girl?

Father Wagner glanced towards her and smiled. "Best you go home, my child." He sighed. "She is such a handful, that girl. I only hope the good sisters of St Catherine can succeed in taming her." He reached out and cupped Marie's face. "If only Freya could take you as an example." He put his hand on her shoulder and steered her gently, but firmly, towards the door.

Marie allowed herself to be propelled along the corridor. She felt his hand move casually down her back and over her waist to cup her behind. She found his touch repellent, and walked faster to break free from his contact.

Once out of the front door, she paused to collect her thoughts. She was confused – and, she realised, a bit frightened. She still felt the priest's hand on her. She shook her head. Why did the memory make her shudder? He'd rested his hands on her shoulder, stroked her hair, caressed her face, and it hadn't bothered her before. After all, Father Wagner did the same to all her friends. He was a naturally caring sort of person. The image of his cold, dispassionate face as he dismissed Freya, and his indifference to her distress, swam into Marie's mind. He hadn't acted like a compassionate, caring man then. Marie was sure of that. She turned and trudged towards home, deep in thought. Maybe her mother could make sense of it, she decided.

Suzanne Wachter grew increasingly serious as she listened to Marie's tale. As soon as Marie had reached the end, she grabbed her daughter's hand. "Come with me, Marie." They went next door. Suzanne wanted to talk to Heidi.

Once again Marie related her story. At the end Suzanne looked at her friend. "What do you think?"

Heidi didn't hesitate. "I think Father Wagner has some questions to answer."

"It's not that easy, Heidi." Suzanne glanced towards Marie. "It's Marie's word against his."

Marie looked aghast. "Ma, I'm telling the truth."

Suzanne clasped her daughter in a tight embrace. "Yes, I know that, dear. No one doubts you. But what if he denies your version of events? Who else witnessed it?"

"Freya," Josey said with childlike certainty.

"Who is not really reliable, is she?" Suzanne grimaced.

"I'm not bothered about what our Reverend Father has to say," Heidi said firmly. "It should be enough that he knows he's being watched."

Suzanne reached out and gently placed a restraining hand on her friend's arm. "It could cause problems, Heidi. Remember what happened last time you crossed swords with him? There will be many in the village who will take Father Wagner's side."

"I'm not worried about that." Heidi took off her apron as if she intended to march to the *Pfarrhaus* there and then.

Suzanne looked surprised. "You're not going now, are you?"

"No, I'll think about it first. I would like to see Freya – alone, if possible. Certainly not when Wagner is present."

But the meeting never took place. Freya disappeared. All the villagers knew was that Father Wagner returned to the village after dark. The following day he asked Frau Weissmann to clear Freya's room and to throw out a rag doll he found in the corner of the courtyard. Freya had joined the convent at St Catherine's.

It would be several years before Sep found out what had really happened to her.

"**M**ail for *Leutnant* Offizierstellvertreter Breitner of the Imperial Austro-Hungarian Army, 4th Tyrolean Kaiserjäger," Corporal McPherson announced, as he entered Sep's room and tossed a brown paper parcel onto the bed next to Sep.

Sep picked it up and examined the writing. He could tell from the neat italic script it was from Josey.

"Always good tae get mail. Good for the soul." The corporal handed Sep a knife to cut the string.

"It certainly is, Sandy." Sep's spirits soared. Carefully, he unwrapped the brown paper.

"Ah've got tae admire yer restraint, sir. Most lads just rip off the paper."

Sep grinned and handed back the knife. "Old habits, Sandy. We always recycle wrapping paper in our household."

"Very wise, if Ah may say so, sir." He turned to leave so Sep could examine the contents in private. "Oh, before Ah go, Ah suggest ye see Doctor Forsythe. He's being discharged at the end of the week. He's the one who will sign ye off."

Sep paused. "Dr Forsythe is going back to England?"

"Aye – and no' afore time. The man's no' well." The corporal leant on the door jamb. "Ah'll arrange an appointment with him this afternoon if ye like?" He left.

Sep opened the cardboard box. Lying on top was a letter. He was surprised to see his hands shake as he unfolded the paper.

Dearest, dearest Sep,

This is only a short letter to accompany the parcel. You will receive longer correspondence containing all our news from Mama and Papa in the next few days. But for now be assured that we are all well, and overjoyed to hear from you. We're so happy you are safe! I hope the English are looking after you, and you're on the road to recovery. It was sensible of you to write to me. Ma was convinced you were never coming home, and the arrival of a military letter would have probably killed her before she had the chance to read it. As it is, she hasn't stopped crying tears of joy ever since I broke the news to her.

When do you think you will be able to come home? I hope it won't be too long – maybe for Weinachtsfest*? Please write when you can. We all miss you and want you back so we can look after you.*
Your loving sister,
Josey

P.S. I hope the contents of the box will be useful.

Sep peered inside the box and extracted the contents one by one, savouring the excitement. His smile grew broader as he removed each item. Each was a little piece of home. Six small jars that he knew came from his mother's kitchen. Raspberry, strawberry, rhubarb jam. Some pickled ham, sauerkraut, home-made sweets and biscuits. A bar of home-made soap, a hairbrush and comb, two copies of the local *Brandterwalder Blatt* newspaper.

Sep laid them all out on the bed. He found himself weeping quietly as he stared at them. Suddenly he badly wanted to be back in Dopplegau with his family, sitting in front of his own hearth, breathing in the smell of the common pot and sipping a Pils.

Corporal McPherson popped his head around the door. "Everything OK, sir?"

Sep wiped his eyes. "Of course, Sandy. It's a bit overwhelming."

"Ah hope, in a good way?"

Sep looked at him and grinned. "Yes, in a very good way."

"Glad tae hear it, sir. It disnae always work out tha' way." He shook his head sadly. "Mail brings bad news sometimes that can kill a man."

"Dear John letters?"

"Aye, an' worse." The corporal picked up a jar of pickled ham. "Do yer family think we're starving ye?"

Sep laughed and reached for his crutches. "They would be surprised and delighted by how well I've been looked after."

"Ye'll be pleased to get home."

"Oh yes."

"Ye'll no' miss me?" Corporal McPherson held up both hands in a mock display of hurt feelings. "It's OK – ye can tell me the truth. Ah can take it."

Sep looked at the orderly. He composed himself. What he had to say came from the heart. "Seriously, Sandy, I can't begin to tell you how grateful I am for the care and attention you and Nurse Jones and Dr Forsythe – well, everybody – has given me."

"Ye'll miss us, then?"

"Of course."

"Especially Nurse Jones?"

Sep looked stunned. Were his feelings for Susan quite so obvious? "Especially Nurse Jones – although I suspect it won't be long before she returns to Skipton. I hope she finds a man who is worthy of her."

"Aye, she's a bonny lass. Heart of gold and a sharp head on her shoulders." The corporal seemed in no hurry to help Sep with his crutches, as he usually did. "Lots o' young chancers have tried their luck with her, only tae have their hopes dashed an' their hearts bust."

Sep struggled to his feet. "I'm surprised she isn't already married or engaged."

"Oh, she's too canny, sir. There's plenty o' youngsters made the pledge, only for their dreams tae be shattered in France." He replaced the jar of pickled ham on the bed. "Besides, once bitten twice shy."

Sep looked confused. "I don't know that phrase."

"She was engaged before. A young lieutenant like yersel'," he said quietly. "He fell in 1915."

Sep couldn't speak. He relived the unbearable pain of losing someone close. He pictured Susan's anguish at her loss. He knew the feeling. It was like having your soul torn out; it was burning, excruciating torture. The thought of her suffering upset him. "How did he die? Hopefully it was quick."

"Aye, it was quick, right enough. He didnae know a thing about it. Shot by a sniper. Bullet straight through the temple."

Sep reeled.

The corporal eyed him. "Aye, I thought you should know, sir."

Sep nodded. A wave of confused emotions swirled through his brain. He felt like a murderer. How many young dreams had he shattered? Any chance he had had with Susan was crushed. How could she consider someone like him as a friend, let alone as anything more? He shook his head. Dear God! She would hate him, and she'd be right to do so. He vaguely became aware that Sandy was still talking.

"…speaking out o' turn, but Ah think the young lady might have feelings for ye."

Sep looked confused. "I'm sorry Sandy, what did you say?"

"Ah said Ah hope ye'd forgive me if Ah was speaking out o' turn, but Ah think Nurse Jones may have some feelings for ye. Ah dinnae want ye putting yer foot in yer mouth, so to speak."

Sep stared at him in shock. He struggled to make sense of what he'd just heard and to square it away with his own thoughts and conclusions. "What about the captain?'

"What captain would that be?"

"I saw her depart with a young cavalry captain. They seemed to know each other very well."

"Sir, Nurse Susan is a catch. She has nae shortage of admirers. Ah know nae captain. But it'd nae surprise me if one fancied his chances." He shrugged and walked towards the door. "So

146

now ye know. Think on it, eh?" He paused. "Oh, yer appointment with Doctor Forsythe is at half two."

After he left, Sep stood deep in thought. His mind was in turmoil. The chime of the wall clock brought him back to his senses. It was two o'clock. He had to leave if he wasn't going to be late.

Doctor Forsythe glanced up as Sep entered the consulting room. The doctor was bent over an open travel trunk. A sheaf of papers was in one hand and a small textbook in the other. The room was chaotic. A filing cabinet stood with two of its drawers open. There was a pile of white gowns stacked neatly on the examining couch. More textbooks were strewn across the desk, apparently waiting to be sorted, packed or discarded.

"I'll come back if it's not convenient, Doctor."

"No, no, not at all," Doctor Forsythe said. "Please excuse the mess. I thought I would make a start on packing." He dropped the paper and textbook into the trunk before picking another book from the desk and throwing it in to join its companion. "One accumulates so much." He gestured to a chair.

Sep eased himself down and propped his crutches against the wall. He watched patiently as the doctor sifted through the files on his desk, before he found the one he was looking for.

Forsythe rifled through the pages, occasionally stopping to read some notes. Finally he snapped the file shut and looked directly at Sep. "So, Lieutenant, it appears that you have made an excellent recovery."

"For which I am extremely grateful to you and all the other staff."

The doctor waved his hands dismissively. "We had plenty of practice before we got to tackling you. I suppose you want to talk about being discharged?"

Sep nodded.

"Can you do the St Étienne run?"

Sep looked blank.

"Can you get to St Étienne and back on your crutches?"

"I've never been that far."

"Can you climb a flight of stairs – and I mean a serious flight of stairs, not a few steps?"

Sep shook his head. "I've not tried."

Forsythe looked exasperated. "My dear boy, if you can't walk to the next village and back, or climb a flight of stairs, how do you think you're going to cope with crossing the street in – where do you live?"

"Dopplegau, in Austria."

Forsythe shook his head. "Don't know it. Well, cross the street in Vienna, or whatever large city is close to your home. Think of railway stations, Lieutenant. Imagine yourself trying to cross a footbridge, force your way through rush-hour crowds, make your way up and down escalators on your own without anyone to help you." The doctor glared at him. "Could you manage it in your present condition?"

"I don't know," Sep replied honestly.

"Well, I seriously doubt it." The doctor pinched the bridge of his nose between his fingers as if he had a headache. He abruptly got up, crossed to the filing cabinet, opened the bottom drawer and extracted a bottle of brandy and a glass. "Care to join me?"

Sep was thrown by the abrupt change in subject, and nodded out of instinct rather than a desire to have a drink.

The doctor took out another glass, poured a generous shot into each, and handed one to Sep. "Cheers. Here's to peace."

They touched glasses.

The doctor slumped back into his chair. "Thing is, Lieutenant, if you want to discharge yourself, feel free to do so. Officially your status is that of a private patient. You're not a prisoner, you are not in the service of His Majesty the King. You are, in fact, a guest." He waved his glass around. "As such, you are perfectly free to leave, no matter what I, or anyone else, thinks about it."

"I would prefer to take your professional advice," Sep said.

"Sound move, my friend. And my advice is unless and until you can walk – unalded mind," the doctor raised a finger to emphasise the point, "to the next village and back, and ascend and descend the main flights of stairs in the chateau, top to bottom, you aren't fit to travel."

Forsythe drained his glass and immediately reached for the bottle again. He replenished his glass and settled himself back into his chair, then took another generous gulp before retrieving Sep's file. He studied it between sips.

Sep used the silence to look around the doctor's consulting room. It was cosy, almost domestic. Small ornaments and oil paintings had yet to be packed away. A set of six framed certificates hung in a neat line. To one side of the fireplace, the doctor's dress uniform and Sam Browne hung over a wingback chair. Above the fireplace, an ornate mirror reflected the bookcase on the opposite wall. On the mantelpiece was a photograph of a young Doctor Forsythe being presented with an award by a distinguished-looking man in flowing robes. Beside the photograph, three picture frames lay face-down. Sep frowned. From the dust on top of them, he guessed they'd been resting in that position for a considerable time.

148

"You've made a remarkable recovery, all things considered. Eyesight fine, ribs healed nicely. Any back problems, feelings of numbness?" Forsythe peered enquiringly at Sep.

Sep shook his head.

"Which leaves the ongoing issue with your leg and mobility." He snapped the file closed. "You are a good candidate for a prosthetic. Unfortunately, they are damned hard to come by, and they need to be fitted. I suggest, when you do finally make it to your home and your loved ones, you find out what might be done in that department." He gave Sep a serious look. "The St Étienne run and the stairs, my good man. Do them, and you're good to go."

"Thank you, Doctor, for this and for everything else. I'm forever in your debt."

Forsythe waved his hand dismissively. "Promise me one thing, Lieutenant."

"Of course."

"Don't get involved in any more bloody wars, eh?"

Sep drained his glass, grabbed his crutches, levered himself up and shook the doctor's hand.

"Goodbye, Doctor. Good luck to you – and thank you once again."

He stood for a second outside the consulting room door. Too much information flooded his mind. He needed a strong coffee. The convenient canteen made it an easy decision. He sat and stared for a long time at the cup. Gradually he became aware of a figure hovering next to him

"There sits a man who appears to have a lot on his mind."

Sep glanced up. "Oh, Nurse Mandy, please join me."

"Are you sure? You look deep in thought." She sat opposite him. "Something bothering you?"

"I've just seen Doctor Forsythe."

"Oh. Did you get him on a good day?"

Sep grinned. "He was forthright. Gave me a lot to consider."

"The village run and the stairs?"

He nodded. "Among other things."

She chuckled. "Yes, that brings a lot of patients back to earth." She peered sympathetically into his downcast face. "You can do it, you know."

"I'll have to do it. I don't have a choice." He glanced across at her and met her gaze. "How far is it to St Étienne?"

"A little over three miles."

Sep nodded. "I can do that."

"Not in one go, you won't. You take it one step at a – My God, I'm so sorry."

He laughed.

She stifled a giggle. "Anyway, don't try to do it all in one go. Try a mile at first and gradually build up." She glanced at the skylight. A sudden rain shower beat down on the glass. "And don't do it in this kind of weather. You'll fall over, and Susan will kill me for not looking after you properly."

"Susan?"

Nurse Mandy looked sheepish. "Yes, Susan. She left me strict instructions."

"I don't understand. I can look after myself."

"Oh, Sep." She regarded him in exasperation for a few seconds before getting to her feet. "Honestly, you men." She grinned at him. "I have to go. If I'm around and I'm not busy with real patients, *and* it's not tipping it down, I'll walk with you."

"I need to climb some stairs too, don't forget."

"I can help you with that as well," she said over her shoulder, departing with a cheery wave.

That evening Sep put the pot of his mother's strawberry jam in his coat pocket and hobbled to the nurses' quarters. He gazed in trepidation at the flight of stairs that seemed to go on forever. He remembered Nurse Jones's instruction. Sticks, then leg. He began the ascent. Thirty minutes later, he knocked gently on Nurse Mandy's room door on the third floor.

She opened it wearing a dressing gown, her head swathed in a white towel. "What on earth are you doing?" She glanced around nervously. "It's after curfew. This place is off-limits. You're not supposed to be here."

Without a word, Sep presented her with the pot of jam before turning to make the descent.

"You are bonkers, Sep. You do know that, don't you?"

At five minutes to midnight, Doctor Forsythe threw the empty cognac bottle into the bin. He stumbled around the room before managing to locate the mantelpiece. He leant on it for a few moments before turning over each of the picture frames. An attractive, smiling, dark-haired woman stared back at him. The other two frames held black-and-white photographs of two strikingly handsome young men: one in a Royal Navy Lieutenant Commander uniform, the other in the uniform of the Grenadier Guards. Doctor Forsythe drew himself upright and stared at himself in the mirror. For five minutes he stood swaying, his eyes unfocused. Then he slowly raised his Webley Service Revolver to his temple and blew his brains out.

The shock of Doctor Forsythe's suicide reverberated around the hospital. The wards fell silent. Nurses and orderlies wept in quiet corners or in the privacy of their rooms. Doctor Forsythe was the father of the hospital. He was widely respected, not just as a medical professional, but as a spiritual man who cared deeply about saving lives and looking after the welfare of his staff. They had lost their captain.

Sep heard the news from Nurse Mandy. She entered his room, closed the door behind her, sat next to Sep on the bed and broke down in tears.

"He was such a good man," she said. "It's such a waste. And just before Christmas as well."

Sep was numb with shock. He couldn't understand what would possess a man with so much talent and so much to live for to take his own life. But then he recalled his own darkest moments, when he'd been very close to ending it all. "I suppose his world was destroyed when his sons were killed."

"It's so unfair."

The door opened and Corporal McPherson entered. He held out his arms to Nurse Mandy. They leant on each other and wept unashamedly.

Outside, the cold December rain battered against the window. A grey start to a miserable day, Sep thought.

Later he joined Curly, Bert and Steve for a game of cards. But the usual banter was missing, the jokes half-hearted, and the normally ebullient Curly was subdued.

Sep returned to his room and sat down. An image of Nurse Jones came into his mind. He tried to blot her out. There was little point in dwelling on her. They had no future. He would return to Dopplegau, and she to Skipton, and that would be that. Once again, the black ball of dread and despondency started to fill his mind. He surprised himself by how quickly he was able to crush it. It was time he stopped feeling so sorry for himself. After all, he had a lot going for him. Corporal McPherson's words edged into his thoughts. "Ah think the young lady might have some feelings for ye." What had he meant? He mentally kicked himself for not interrogating the orderly more thoroughly. Corporal McPherson was probably mistaken. Sep tried to be rational. Susan was a good friend, he reasoned. Friends looked after one another. The least he could do was think about how to comfort her. She liked his writing and seemed to look forward to receiving it. Maybe he ought to compose something for her?

151

He reached for his paper and pen. He paused, considering what to write about. His eye fell on Josey's letter. He had his inspiration.

Almost overnight, what was considered acceptable behaviour in the community changed. The traditional, relaxed ways that had served the village perfectly well since time immemorial now became unacceptable. The combined forces of the Church and the *Bildungsbehörde* deemed that social interaction, especially between the sexes, needed to be controlled – in the name of education, progress and Christian morality. Physical contact between males and females became governed by the strictures of the one true faith. Any contact that fell outside the rules was a sign of loose morals. Outwith the sanctity of marriage, the sexes were segregated.

Father Wagner was behind the new policy. He dictated that contact between the sexes should be restricted at every opportunity. Within the *Volksschule*, mixed-sex classes were abandoned, boys and girls ate lunch separately, play was restricted to designated playgrounds, sports and recreational activities were divided. Girls and boys were expected to walk to and from school at different times. The priest pursued his crusade with ruthless determination. His sermons promised eternal damnation for anyone who might be minded to question his authority, and the power of the Church.

Despite some private irritation at the priest's high-handedness, few people openly objected and none actively opposed him. He was, after all, a good man. Plus, they were well aware of the cost of being ostracised in the village. It was God's will and a sign of progress, they reasoned. Perhaps it was true; they lacked the sophistication demanded by the modern world.

For Sep and his friends, who had been brought up in altogether freer and more liberal households, the new rules smacked of dogma, snobbery, hypocrisy and false morality. Josey, in particular, found the regime impossible to accept. It was bad enough that her natural tomboy instincts, thrill-seeking inquisitiveness and thirst for adventure were suppressed. The new approach also aimed to further curtail any feminist ambitions outside that of a life of domestic servitude.

For Josey, each new rule existed for one purpose: to be broken. She frequently scaled the wall that divided the two play zones so she could join the boys in playing football in summer, skiing and sledging in winter. She loitered outside the school gates to walk home with her brothers and Stephan, and nothing would stop her from going swimming.

As far as Father Wagner was concerned, Josey was the devil incarnate. She was wild, uncontrollable, a bad example and a disruptive influence. Not that Josey was bothered. She refused to enter St Martin's, let alone the confessional. Despite her defiance, Father Wagner baulked at summoning Heidi or Fritz Breitner for an interview. Wagner was no match for Heidi's intellect, or the political power wielded by the Breitner family.

Eventually, Josey curbed her wild ways. However, the person responsible for her change in attitude was herself.

Wingnut had a ratter called Alfie. He should have been named Psycho, as he had a split personality. Usually he was an adorable, loyal and well-behaved family pet. He was affectionate, and loved company. The sound of visitors arriving at the Haufmanns' home would send Alfie into paroxysms of tail wagging that involved his entire body in a sinewy, wriggling, squirming ecstasy. He took a particular liking to Josey and would roll on his back, all four paws in the air, waiting for his tummy to be tickled. Whenever Josey visited Wingnut's home, Alfie would follow her around in an excited twitching dance, and wait for her to settle. Once she was seated, Alfie would flop down in front of her, roll over and await the blissful massage.

However, should Alfie spot anything small and furry, he became a demented ball of unbridled fury. In less than a week he had cleared the Haufmanns' home, wood yard and farm of every squirrel, rabbit, cat, mouse, marmoset and rat.

The Haufmann family supplemented their income by offering a local pest control service. Exterminating rats was their speciality. In Alfie, they had the perfect tool for the job.

In the spring of 1911, the village of Dopplegau was overrun by rodents. The expansion of the village meant that more domestic rubbish was generated, which in turn encouraged the rats to breed. Privies also became redundant as households took advantage of the new sewer system and built indoor toilets. The rats quickly took over the vacant sheds as comfortable nesting sites. There was so many that the farm cats became fat and indolent. Catching and devouring the odd rat didn't require much stalking – or, indeed, any effort at all on the cat's part. All the local feline population had to do was loiter near any barn or privy, and breakfast would present itself.

A rat extermination week was declared. Every farm in the village was required to cooperate. Having been lectured by Frau Rachel on the number of diseases and health hazards that were associated with vermin, the Breitners and Wachters were more motivated than most to do something about the infestation.

The operation was planned with military precision. The village farm cats were rounded up and starved for four days to remind them of their hunting instincts. Nets and traps were set, and killing zones based on known runs and nesting sites.

On the Breitner and Wachter farms, the troops consisted of Fritz and his neighbour equipped with shotguns, plus Wingnut and the fearsome Alfie. Alfie would flush the rats out into the line of waiting guns. Any unfortunate rodent that survived being blasted would run into the path of catapults fired by Stephan and Sep. Behind them, Tom, Klaus, Marie and Josey wielded shovels and clubs. For the rats, escape was almost impossible. Fritz and Konrad had chosen the ground carefully. The rodents would find themselves fleeing into sealed barns that were now almost empty of winter hay. Few were expected to survive.

On the appointed day, Wingnut arrived with an already agitated Alfie. The dog had sensed blood, and was straining at the leash. The initial target for the morning was Konrad Wachter's barn, on the basis that any rats that escaped would seek sanctuary on the adjoining Breitner farm, little realising that they would be attacked again that afternoon.

Wingnut took the snarling Alfie to the rear of the building and waited for the start command. Fritz and Konrad loaded both barrels of their shotguns. Konrad nodded to show he was ready.

"Let him go, Wingnut!" Fritz shouted.

For a few minutes the only sound was grunting, snarling and growling as Alfie snuffled out and fell upon the nests. Then the rats began to bolt. One or two shot out to be blasted by the guns. Very quickly the numbers fleeing exceeded the ability of Fritz and Konrad to reload fast enough, and Stefan and Sep tried to pick them off using catapults. Tom, Klaus, Marie and Josey descended upon the dazed animals with upraised clubs and shovels. They showed no mercy.

After an hour and a half, an exhausted, bloodied Alfie emerged, his tail wagging furiously. Two rats clung to his face, their teeth locked on his lips. Wingnut despatched them and the group looked around. Over forty rats lay scattered around them.

They caught their breath while Tom collected the corpses and threw them on a pyre. Then they moved to the Breitner farm for phase two. The youngsters were breathless and excited.

"How many did you get, Sep?" Klaus asked.

"None. I winged a couple."

"I got five," Tom said, holding one up by the tail as proof.

"I got five as well," Josey said proudly, taking up position. It was always important to her to prove she was as good as the boys.

At Fritz's signal, Alfie was released. Whether the rats had some means of communicating, or they instinctively knew that safety relied on numbers, it was impossible to say, but they emerged en-masse. It wasn't an infestation; it was a plague. For over an hour the Breitner barn was a battleground as fleeing rats scuttled and dodged, being shot or bludgeoned to death. The shovels and clubs rained down. As soon as one creature was dealt with, another appeared. The air was thick with the sound of squealing rodents, the crash of shotguns and the thudding of clubs. Gradually the number of vermin diminished.

Josey had cornered a particularly combative rat. She brought down her shovel on it, hoping to finish the contest, but the rat dodged. She raised the shovel again and succeeded in reducing her adversary to an inert heap. She swung her weapon over her head to deliver the coup de grâce, only to strike Stephan – who was standing behind her – squarely on the head. Stephan crumpled to the ground, unconscious. Blood flowed from the gash in his skull.

Josey dropped to the ground and cradled Stephan's head. "Pa, I've killed Stephan!" she shrieked.

Fritz spun around. Stephan's hair was already drenched with blood. Fritz immediately picked him up and ran towards the kitchen door, the rest of the group following.

"Sep, go and get Doctor Rubenstein!" he shouted, kicking the kitchen door open.

Sep sprinted off. By the time he returned with the ageing doctor, Stephan had regained consciousness. He sat, looking dazed and confused, with his head swathed in blood-soaked bandages, cradled by his distraught mother.

Everyone watched in silence as Doctor Rubenstein rapidly got to work. The only sound was Suzanne quietly sobbing and Doctor Rubenstein chatting non-stop to Stephan. "How did it happen, Stephan? Were you rat-catching? Did you catch many? Who was with you, Stephan?"

Stephan stared vacantly, oblivious to the doctor's endless questions. Finally, the doctor succeeded in breaking through. "Who hit you, Stephan?"

"Josey … Josey hit me with a shovel. Josey did it … But she didn't mean to. It was an accident."

Sep glanced at Josey. Throughout, she had sat and stared at Stephan. She looked as shocked as her unintended victim. Even Alfie had failed to divert her attention.

"We know, Stephan." Doctor Rubenstein whetted a cut-throat razor and proceeded to shave Stephan's hair around the wound. "Gashes to the head always look a lot worse than they are," the doctor said to the room in general. "The blood vessels are near the surface of the skin, you see. They bleed like the river of Jordan." He cleaned the wound and prepared a suture. "This is going to hurt a bit, young man. Try to keep your head still. Maybe, Frau Wachter, if you don't mind."

Suzanne nodded and cradled her son's head as Doctor Rubenstein inserted eight stitches. Stephan couldn't help himself, he cried out in pain.

Quietly, Josey slipped off her chair and disappeared up to her room.

Finally, the bleeding was staunched, the wound sealed and Stephan appeared to be more coherent. The doctor passed his fingers in front of the patient's eyes before pronouncing his prognosis. "He has mild concussion and will require some quiet and rest for the next few days. It's likely he will have a headache. Call me immediately if his condition deteriorates. Otherwise, he'll be fine in a day or so."

Immediately after helping his Pa with the morning milking, Sep went round to check on Stephan. He found him propped up in bed looking alert and in good spirits. Perched on his head was a bright yellow woolly hat.

"What on earth is that?" Sep laughed.

"It's good, isn't it?"

"I wouldn't describe it as good." Sep snatched the hat off and examined it. "Where did you find it?"

"I didn't find it. Josey made it for me."

Sep looked at his friend in open-mouthed amazement. "My sister made this?"

"She came around this morning. Said she was sorry. I don't know what for. It was an accident, after all. Gave me a kiss and presented me with that." Stephan nodded towards the yellow object.

"She knitted this herself?"

Stephan nodded. "So she says. I think it's pretty good. "

"It's unbelievable! Since when has Josey ever taken an interest in knitting or sewing, or anything girly?"

"Maybe she's changed." Stephan held his hand out for the hat.

Josey *had* changed. When Sep returned home and got ready for school, he found that Josey had already left with the Wachter sisters. Whether it was the shock of the injury she had caused, or the fact that it happened to coincide with the beginning of her transition from child to adult, from that day forward she was a different person. It was as if the reckless, rebellious demons within her had thrown up their hands and declared, "It's OK, we're going. We know when our time is up."

157

She lost none of her single-minded determination or self-belief. But her spontaneity was replaced by a quieter, more cautious approach. Perhaps she had discovered that facing the world head-on could be bruising, or maybe she had realised she could find fulfilment by adopting a softer, more thoughtful approach.

She applied herself to her schoolwork with such dedication that she secured top marks in every subject and matched her elder brother's command of English. In Rachel, Josey had a patron who was both supportive and a conduit to broader knowledge and liberal ideas – especially the burgeoning ideas of women's rights and suffrage. Father Wagner did his best to undermine her. However, his efforts increasingly exposed his prejudices and lack of intellect as Josey's knowledge and self-confidence grew. With her mother's and Rachel's encouragement, she became the first Breitner to go to university.

nitially, the boys were baffled by Josey's change of allegiance, and even more perplexed by the collective madness that suddenly seemed to grip both Wachter girls.

"I've got to get out," Stephan said as he barged into the Breitner *Stube* one morning.

Heidi looked up in surprise at the unexpected visitor. "What's the matter, Stephan dear?"

"Nothing with me, Frau Breitner. I'm fine. It's that lot back there." He jerked his head in the direction of the Wachter house.

"Has something happened?"

"Something's always happening." Stephan stomped to the table, sat down and held his head in his hands. "One minute they're all laughing, happy, smiling and all. The next minute they're in floods of tears, or squabbling, or running off into their room in a huff about God knows what."

"They – I assume – being your sisters?" Heidi said gently.

Stephan nodded. "I don't know what's the matter with them." He glanced at Josey. "Do you know what's got them all het up?"

Josey shook her head. "Maybe you upset them."

Stephan looked outraged. "Me? What have I done?"

"I don't know. Did you say anything, or do anything?"

"When?"

"This morning."

"No. I just told Klara she had a spot on her forehead. Next thing I know, she's in floods of tears and runs upstairs, Ma accuses me of being insensitive, and Marie gives me a clip round the ear." Stephan looked hurt and confused.

"Seems a bit harsh," Klaus said sagely.

"Harsh? It's unfair. She *has* got a spot on her forehead – a really big one. You can't miss it. I'm telling the truth." He looked at each of his audience in turn, to ensure they fully understood the extent of his grievance and sense of injustice. "I gave Marie a clip back – 'cos she hit me first for no good reason, and guess what? I'm in trouble with my ma for hitting Marie." Stephan shook his head sadly. "It ain't the first time. It's like they're ganging up on me."

"I'm sure that's not the case, Stephan." Heidi came and sat next to him. "They're growing up, and sometimes girls find it all very confusing."

"It's confusing all right, Frau Breitner," Stephan spluttered. "Yesterday we were sitting around the *Stube* and Klara starts crying." Stephan looked up at Heidi, his eyes wide with astonishment. "Nothing has happened. She starts crying for no reason at all."

159

"*That's* not normal," Tom said. "Maybe she's ill or something."

Heidi frowned at her youngest son. "It's perfectly normal, Thomas Breitner. You boys are going to have to get used to the fact that there comes a time when girls start to mature into young women."

The boys all swung their eyes towards Josey, as if expecting her to morph there and then. Bafflingly, apart from blushing furiously, she looked exactly the same as she had yesterday, and the day before that.

Heidi put a comforting arm around Stephan. "You have a whole house full of sisters who are starting to go through this change." She gave him an affectionate squeeze. "Maybe it would be good if you spent a bit more time around here with Sep, Klaus and Tom."

Stephan nodded. "At least they are all sensible."

"Of course they are." Heidi's sarcastic tone was lost on the boys.

It wasn't as if the boys were ignorant about adolescence – or sex. The act of copulation was an everyday occurrence in a farming community. It was while helping introduce Gaston, the Breitners' prize boar, to Gertrude, a sow who had come into season, that his father casually remarked, "I expect you are wondering how humans make babies, Sep?"

Actually, Sep was wondering what his mother was preparing for tea. However, since his father had introduced the subject, Sep was happy to go along with it.

His father then proceeded to describe the process of sexual intercourse, with Gaston providing enthusiastic, practical illustration. "See – that's the sperm." Fritz pointed with unnecessary precision as Gaston reached the porcine equivalent of ecstasy. "Hopefully it's on its way to fertilise the egg – or eggs." His father glanced at his eldest son. "Any questions, lad?"

At the time Sep only had one.

No, his father told him, the eggs inside a woman were considerably smaller than a hen's egg. This came as a relief to Sep, as he was sure it must be quite uncomfortable for a woman to have to run around with an object that size inside her.

The rest of Sep's sex education was a mixture of lurid, mostly exaggerated tales from the older lads, and furtive romps in the forest or haylofts with the village girls, who seemed to be much more worldly wise and confident about such matters.

Sep was seventeen years old when Klara became his mentor. She grabbed his hand on the way home from the *Volksschule* and led him into the forest.

160

"Do you think I'm pretty, Sep?" she asked, once they had reached a suitably secluded spot.

"You know you are, Klara," Sep replied, still wondering why she'd taken him nearly halfway up the mountain.

"What do you like about me most?" She sat and looked at him with big, innocent eyes.

Since she was staring at him, Sep agreed that her eyes were indeed very attractive.

She smiled and then pouted. "What about my lips?"

Sep actually did think Klara's lips were attractive.

"Would you like to kiss them?"

Sep looked startled. "Yes, that would be nice." He found the experience more pleasant than he expected.

What Klara did next got Sep seriously interested. She slowly undid her blouse, then removed it. "Would you like to see my breasts?" Her voice had become warm, thick and strangely inviting. Suddenly Sep wanted to see Klara's breasts very much indeed.

Klara lay back, rested her head on a languid arm and looked at him through heavy-lidded eyes. "You have to take your shirt off. It's only fair."

Sep was happy to oblige.

For the next two hours they carefully examined each part of the other's anatomy, commenting on how different they were, how pretty or ugly certain features were: how soft, smooth or rough their skin, and the obvious differences that seemed so mysterious and fascinating.

Just as Sep thought his head would explode with unfamiliar and overwhelming feelings of lust, Klara got up and started to put her clothes back on.

Sep watched her get dressed. He felt confused and bewildered. He thought back to his father's advice on female behaviour.

"Gertrude lets us know when she's ready. All females are the same. It's a matter of reading the signs and respecting their needs."

Sep was pretty sure that putting her clothes back on was a sign that matters were not to proceed further on this occasion. He followed Klara's example and together they made their way home. As it happened, there was no future occasion with Klara. She turned her attention to a strapping lad from Gau – presumably to get a second opinion on the attractiveness of her attributes.

While the episode proved highly instructive in terms of the mechanics involved, neither the event itself or his father's terse observation about 'reading the signs' really threw much light on what exactly Sep ought to look out for.

161

Nevertheless, having had a tantalising glimpse of what was on offer, hardly a day passed when Sep didn't avidly study the girls at school for the elusive signals. It soon became apparent he wasn't alone. One by one Stephan, Klaus and Wingnut reported similar encounters. Notes were compared: who did it with who, when, where and how far did the experience extend?

Not to be left out, Tom barged into the discussions. Once he understood the matters being analysed, he applied himself to winning similar assignations with an enthusiasm and vigour that would have concerned his mother, had she been aware of what was going on.

Father Wagner would have been dismayed at the extent to which his segregation not only failed, but actually fanned the flames of adolescent passions. The fruits were obviously forbidden, and the illicit nature of the liaisons added a delicious frisson.

Fortunately, hormonal girls and fiery, testosterone-driven boys was something the villagers were used to dealing with.

The Breitner and Wachter boys, along with all the other lads suffering from sexual frustration and excess energy, were sent to the high Alpine pasture, ostensibly to look after the cattle. In reality it was a rite of passage. Chopping down trees, splitting logs, building or repairing the mountain huts, clearing rivers, digging drainage ditches, re-laying mountain tracks, learning to hunt, trap, track, shoot, bleed, skin and butcher deer, ibex and, if they were lucky, elusive brown bear, left the lads exhausted. They learned about the mountains, the fickleness of the local climate, how to read the clouds to anticipate storms. They discovered how the temperature differences between north- and south-facing slopes affected the ability to grow crops; where the best grazing was; how to orientate buildings to work with nature. They also read the dangers of the mountains and learned to be wary of slopes and scree fields that were prone to rock falls, landslides and avalanches.

Within the circle of male camaraderie, individuality was encouraged and self-confidence nurtured. Each lad tended towards a skill or characteristic that the elders encouraged. Decades of experience had taught the community leaders the importance of interdependence, and the value of friendships. Although not a natural outdoors type Klaus found his niche among the men. His skill as an artist was admired, and it was not long before everyone had their own pencil portrait. Sep discovered he had outstanding skill as a marksman. Under the tutelage of his father, he quickly learned how to strip, fire and maintain a rifle. He developed his fieldcraft and stalking abilities, and gained status for his hunting prowess as a consequence.

Despite the hardships, every boy in the village yearned for the time when they were invited to join the company of men. They learned to drink, smoke and chew tobacco – and they also learned about camaraderie, mutual support, trust, and codes of behaviour, respect and values from their fathers, grandpas, uncles and friends.

However, the one topic that defeated even the oldest, most experienced and wisest of men was how to interpret a woman's mind. 'Just read the signs' was about as close as anyone got to solving the conundrum.

At the same time as the boys bonded with their fathers, the girls received a similar introduction to adult society with their mothers, grandmothers and aunts. By the end of the summer they knew what was expected from them. It was a sobering experience for those like Josey, who had ambitions and aspirations that could only be fulfilled beyond the valley. But for the most part, daughters drew closer to their mothers, and their knowledge grew. They became more self-assured, wily and able to wield the limited power they had. They also understood men completely and marvelled at their simplicity.

Sep came away convinced that one summer spent with his pa among the high peaks above the village was worth five years of dry, rote-driven, theory-based education at the *Volksschule*. During his third summer in the Alpine meadows, his education was broadened by an unexpected encounter. One mid-morning, Sep spotted a familiar figure, bent double due to the weight of a knapsack on her back, trudging up to the small hut that served as the Breitner mountain home. He ran down the slope to greet her.

"Hi, Josey. What are you doing here? Is everything all right at home?"

Josey gave a tired smile. "Everything is fine, Sep." She slumped down on her back, threw her hands back beyond her head and closed her eyes. "Let me catch my breath." After a few minutes, she opened one eye and grinned at him. "You're as brown as a nut."

"We all are. The sun up here is fierce." He nudged the bag. "So, what brings you all the way up here?"

She eased herself into a sitting position. "Three things. First and most important; Klaus needs to come back down."

"What? Straight away?"

She nodded. "If Pa agrees. George has come back. He's secured a painting commission for Klaus. Apparently, some wealthy people staying at the Lodge want their portraits painted – and also there are some famous artist friends of Sir William's staying. George thinks it will be a great opportunity for Klaus to meet them."

163

"Pa's in the hut. What are the other two things?"

Josey was momentarily distracted when a small furry ball streaked over the meadow towards her, scattering cattle as it approached. Having leapt into her lap and wriggled himself to doggy heaven, Alfie flopped on his back in front of her and awaited his reward.

Sep waited patiently as Josey indulged him. Eventually she informed Alfie that he'd had enough, and returned to Sep's question. She nodded towards the knapsack. "Father Wagner has been called to Brandt for an important meeting with the bishop. Ma's anxious that the package gets delivered to that family – you know, the ones who live beyond the Mittelspitz. She asked if you can deliver it."

"To where? I don't know where they live. I've never been beyond the Mittelspitz."

"Pa can tell you the way." She held up her hand. "Yes, Pa could deliver it, but Ma thinks he's getting on a bit. Apparently, it's not an easy track. She'd rather somebody fit, young and agile does it." She grinned at her brother. "Unfortunately, I'm otherwise engaged – so you're the next best thing."

Sep grunted. "It's a day's trip at least, from here."

"I know, which is why I brought some extra food for you and everyone."

Sep picked up the bag. "Jesus, Josey! This bag weighs about thirty kilos."

"Which is why I'm exhausted." She glanced around the meadow, taking in the herd of cattle grazing peacefully in the warm summer sun. The only sound was the gentle melodic chimes of their cowbells. "Is Stephan around? I have some stuff for him as well."

Sep laughed. "I'm surprised you haven't spotted him already. You can't miss him in that yellow hat of yours. Come on. Let's get you to the hut for some food and drink." He held out his hands and pulled her to her feet.

Sep set out early next morning, leaving plenty of time to get there and back before nightfall. Besides, an early start was no hardship. It meant he could savour a sight that always made his spirits soar: the sun rising over the Alpine peaks that stretched as far as the eye could see.

The first part of his journey was over familiar tracks, and enabled rapid progress. He felt unbelievably strong, fit and healthy: he almost ran up the steepest slopes, and barely noticed the knapsack on his back. In less than two hours he'd reached the high escarpment that commanded the Dopplegau valley. He spotted smoke rising from the Lodge and the tiny figures of guests sitting on the sun-dappled front lawn waiting to be served breakfast. Another five kilometres and he would be further up the pass than he had ever been. He took a swig of elderflower-flavoured water his ma had packed for him, and pressed on, anxious to break the back of the journey.

He reached his first objective, and stared up at the escarpment. It was so steep; it was almost a cliff. The path zigzagged across the face and required caution. A false move could be fatal – the slope was still in shade and the rocks would be slippery with morning dew. He took his time, planting each foot cautiously and firmly. It took him an hour to reach the top. Before him stretched a lush Alpine meadow – and no sign of a path.

"Go straight across, keeping the peak of the Mittelspitz to the right. The slope will gently fall away until you hit the treeline," his pa had said. If he was on track, he should see a distinctive hat-shaped rock. Fifty metres to the left of that a narrow path entered the forest. He was to follow the track until it crossed a mountain stream, before entering another forest on the opposite bank. The trail would then climb steeply through the trees until it broke out into a meadow. At that point, according to his pa's instructions, he should see a small mountain hut in front of him. That was where he was to deliver the package.

The small mountain hut proved to be nothing of the sort. It was a substantial stone-built dwelling with a flat turf roof and a large timber extension that served as a hay barn and chicken coop. A wisp of smoke curled from a stone chimney.

Outside a young woman, maybe thirty years old, was splitting logs into kindling. She was small, and struggled to wield the axe. Her face was pleasant, rather than striking. Her skin had the dark reddish tan of someone who spent a lot of time outdoors under the Alpine sun. At Sep's shouted greeting, she glanced over. For a few seconds she stared warily at him, before putting down the axe, rubbing her hands on a dirty apron and sauntering towards him. She looked at him, her head cocked as if assessing him. "What do you want? Are you lost?" she said in a voice that was neither aggressive nor friendly.

"I have something for..." Sep suddenly realised he'd no idea who the parcel was meant for. He could hardly say it was for the troll man. "I have something for you." He swung the knapsack from his shoulders. Sep looked startled as the troll man himself emerged from the door.

"What is it, Petra? Oh, who are you?" The man swung his great shaggy head in Sep's direction.

"I'm Sep Breitner, Fritz Breitner's son. I have a parcel for you from Father Wagner." Sep couldn't help feeling nervous. The man was enormous. He was bare-chested, and his muscles rippled under his dark, almost teak-coloured skin. A thick black mat of hair on his chest merged with his long beard and moustache. He held a pewter flagon that looked like a thimble in his fist. He drained the mug and strode towards Sep.

Instinctively, he took a step backwards, convinced the giant was about to flatten him. In seconds the man was towering over Sep. "Father Wagner, eh? What's happened to the Holy Spirit then, Sep Breitner?" His voice matched his physique: big, powerful and overwhelming. "Fallen over a cliff, I hope."

"The Holy Spirit? Oh, you mean Father Wagner. Apparently, he's been called to a meeting in Brandt."

"Hopefully to be excommunicated, eh?"

Sep found an arm like a tree trunk wrapped around his shoulder. "You best come in, Sep Breitner. I expect you're hungry and thirsty, eh?" He steered Sep towards the front door. A fair-haired girl slightly younger than Sep peered round the door and watched them approach.

"Tara, don't just stand there gawping, girl. Rustle up some grub for our young friend." The giant led Sep to a felled tree trunk that had been crudely shaped into a rudimentary bench seat. "Sit yourself down, young man."

As soon as Sep was seated, the man swung an equally rough and ready timber table in front of him, and sat opposite. He turned to the woman who had resumed chopping kindling. "Petra, sweetheart, leave that. Come and sit with us. No doubt you want to hear what's been going on in the civilised world." The man swivelled his gaze towards Sep and leant forward; his bright, sharp eyes burning into Sep's. "Now, Master Breitner, how are your father and mother? Both well and in good spirits, I hope?"

"They are very well … um." Sep felt overwhelmed and intimidated. "I'm sorry, but I don't know your name, sir."

The man bellowed out a booming laugh. "Sir, is it? Hey, Petra, I'm a sir." His laugh increased. "That makes you a lady." He banged the table with his fist as he enjoyed the idea of being a member of the British aristocracy. Eventually, his humour eased. He held out his hand and beamed. "I'm Gregor."

Sep shook Gregor's hand. "I'm pleased to meet you, Herr … Gregor."

"And that's Petra, who is my …" He peered round at Petra. "What are you, Petra? My wife? My mistress? My lover?" Once again his laugh boomed out.

Petra ignored him and held out her hand towards Sep. "I'm his wife," she said seriously.

"In that case, this is my daughter, Tara." Gregor leant back and swept his arm back to welcome the approach of the young girl. She was carrying a plate of cold meats, black bread and pickles. She had the same deep bronze complexion as her mother. She was slim and moved with an easy grace. Sep recognised her dress as one of Klara's cast-offs. A home-made leather necklace of stones added to her wild, rustic look. Sep instantly found her attractive.

The girl shook her head in exasperation at Gregor, then grinned at Sep. "Ignore him, Sep. He's had a good day." She sat next to him, nudging him with her hip to make him shift along.

"So, Master Sep, tell us all the news."

Sep looked flummoxed. "Where do you want me to start? What would you like to know?"

Petra placed her hands on the table, as if contemplating the feast of gossip to come. "Start with your family. Your ma and pa are well – we know that. How's Klaus getting on with his painting? Has Josey calmed down? What about Master Tom?"

"You know about my family?"

Petra looked at him in surprise. "Of course. Your pa visits us – what?" She glanced at Gregor. "Every six weeks or so – more in the summer." She smiled across at Sep. "He's very proud of you all. Tells us everything about you."

"Say something in English," Tara said

"How…. my goodness, Pa really does tell you everything."

Tara nudged him. "Go on then. Say…" – she gazed about, looking for inspiration – "'It's a beautiful day, and I can hear the cry of the eagles.'"

Sep obliged.

Tara clapped in delight. "Say—"

"No, no, no." Gregor banged his fist on the table. "We're not going to spend the rest of the day asking Sep to act like a circus performer. Come on now, let's get back to important things."

Sep would remember this day for the rest of his life. It was a day of joy and gut-wrenching sadness; of making new friends and learning about the treachery of man; of startling revelations; of songs and laughter – lots of laughter. It was also the day Sep got so drunk that he awoke the following morning to the worst hangover he was ever to experience.

The afternoon started off with Sep fielding endless questions about every member of his family. They then moved on to the Wachter family, the Ansbachers, the Hagspiels, the Drössels, the Haufmanns...

"Wingnut will marry Marie," Tara declared out of the blue with a certainty that startled Sep.

"Are you sure?"

"I'm absolutely sure of it. The way you describe their relationship, the way they are always together."

"She's ... what's the word? Psychic," Petra said proudly, nodding towards her daughter.

Sep laughed. "Oh? And who will I marry?"

Tara didn't laugh. She twirled her leather and stone necklace in her fingers as she studied Sep intently. "I'm not sure. I can't see a face."

"No, no, no." Gregor banged his fist on the table – as he was prone to do, Sep realised, if the conversation began to deviate from the proper topic at hand.

By early evening a second stone flagon had been produced, and the subject had moved on to Sir William, George Foster and the Lodge.

"George has visited us, you know," Tara said.

"I didn't know that." Sep was genuinely surprised. It was a long, arduous trek the way he had come. Walking from the Lodge would be twice as daunting.

She nodded. "He came up here with his boyfriend."

"His boyfriend?" Sep's response was of shocked disbelief.

"Tara..."

Sep couldn't fail to hear the warning tone in Petra's voice.

"What?" Tara looked bemused.

"We don't talk of such things."

"Why not? Just because it's a problem for them down there." Tara waved clumsily in the general direction of the valley. "We don't have to live by their rules." She looked at her mother. "We're not ... hippo ... hippos." She giggled. "I can't get the word out."

168

"Hypocrites?" Sep suggested.

"That's the word!" Tara gave a triumphant smile.

"Tara, your ma's right. And you're right as well. We need to be careful what we say." Gregor belched loudly. "You have to realise George could get into a lot of trouble if his … inclinations became public knowledge, especially in a village like Dopplegau." He began to laugh. "I can't begin to imagine what they would make of some of the parties they hold in the Lodge."

Petra looked anxiously at Sep. "Gregor, you need to watch your tongue as well."

Sep tried to reassure Petra. "It's all right, Petra. I've heard the rumours."

"Rumours? Rumours? Ha, ha, ha. They're not rumours. They're true. I've seen sights that would make a sailor blush."

"Well, I'm sure Sep can use his imagination," Petra said, in a voice that was the equivalent of her husband's table-pounding fists.

Gregor looked at his wife sheepishly. "You're right, of course, sweetheart." He stood up and staggered towards the door, re-emerging a minute later with another stone jar hanging from his finger.

"George is a good man." He topped up each glass before refilling his own. "Bit like your pa and your ma, Sep. Good people."

"Certainly saved our skins in the early days," Petra said.

"How did you come to be living here?" Sep asked. "Were you always farmers?"

"Your ma and pa never told you?" Petra looked surprised.

"No, never. I knew Ma used to make up a parcel every month for Father Wagner to deliver."

"God damn his eyes," Gregor muttered.

"Gregor! Watch your language." Petra glared at him.

The big man waved a hand dismissively. He leant back and studied Sep for a minute, took a swig from his tankard and wiped his lips with the back of his hand before waving his forefinger in the air. "I trust this young man. There's a lot of his mother in him. Maybe it would do him some good to learn the truth. How old are you, Sep?"

"I'm eighteen."

Gregor pursed his lips. "You'd have been two years old when we passed through your village like thieves in the night."

"Were you in trouble?"

"Oh yes, lad. We were in big trouble." Gregor took another generous swig as if preparing himself for a serious discussion. Gregor swung his face in front of Sep's. "What do you think I might have been before taking up farming and hunting?"

"I have no idea." Sep looked at the size and strength of the man. His physique was that of a wrestler. Even his age was difficult to assess under the shaggy locks of hair. Maybe forty, Sep guessed. "Perhaps an engineer or a forester? but I really haven't a clue."

"I was a priest."

Sep looked stunned.

Gregor chuckled. His face then fell as he turned serious and launched into his story.

"I was a priest with a large parish on the outskirts of Brandt, in the poor quarter. Lots of down-and-outs, refugees, homeless people, beggars. Lots of work for me, but I was young, keen, and had bags of energy and ambition. To start with, very few people attended Mass, or came to pray at all; but, with hard work and the support of a lot of good people, we managed to turn things around. The bishop was pleased, and I got promoted. Initially, my work was to help other priests build up their parishes. I did well, and more promotions followed. I was happy, the bishop was happy, the people I served were happy. I was promoted again, and there was talk of me being sent to St Peter's. I was seen as a high flyer within the Church. I was given a desk job responsible for the administration of the diocese accounts, business dealings and troubleshooting."

Gregor paused, looking thoughtful. He took another swig as if to fortify himself, and continued.

"That's when my problems started. All of a sudden, I had an insight into exactly how the church was run. I saw how the clergy behaved, and it horrified me." Gregor took another generous gulp of his drink and glanced at Sep. "I hope you are broadminded, young man, because some of the priests' behaviour was truly appalling. It certainly wasn't in accordance with the Holy Scriptures, or the Ten Commandments for that matter."

"What are you talking about?" Sep was intrigued.

"You name it." Gregor held up his hands. "Don't misunderstand me. Most clergy were decent Christians, and above reproach. However, a minority were very bad apples."

"In what way?"

"Well, I would process receipts where the goods or services received were unclear. When I investigated, it transpired they were for meals at high-class restaurants, or for cases of wine and expensive trips abroad staying in top hotels and spas. Naturally, I brought these matters to the attention of the senior clergy, including the bishop. Shockingly, I was instructed to cover it all up." Gregor paused and looked pained. "To my shame, I did exactly that. Looking back, it was clear my appointment was a test – to see where my loyalties lay, and if I could be relied upon to protect the church." He sighed wearily. "I was promoted again, of course, as a reward for my lack of moral backbone. However, what I'd uncovered was just the tip of the iceberg. I was ordered to cover up all sorts of corruption and depravities using bribes, threats of violence, excommunication – anything. The message was clear: nothing and nobody was allowed to sully the Church's reputation." He squeezed his eyes shut and shook his head as if the memories were too excruciating and his guilt too shameful. "I dealt with a senior archdeacon who was a regular customer of the biggest brothel in Brandt; allegations of priests who were abusing altar boys – almost all of which were true; priests having affairs; nuns using novices as virtual slaves..."

Sep's heart went cold. "Did that include the nuns at St Catherine's convent?"

"*Especially* the nuns at St Catherine's convent. The abbess was an evil, sadistic monster. Hopefully she is long gone." Gregor stopped abruptly and looked hard at Sep. "Why do you ask?"

"I knew someone who was sent there – some time back."

"Then God help her."

Sep suppressed the memory of Freya. He would find out what had happened to her once he was back in the village. "So how did you get out of the situation?"

Gregor took a long draught from his tankard. He belched again and wiped his lips. "I visited the church in my old parish. I was disgusted with myself. I had no shame or integrity. I'd lost my way, morally and spiritually. I was suicidal with self-loathing." He glanced at Sep. "I hope you never experience that." He leant back and sighed. "Then a miracle happened. I was leaving late at night when a young orphan girl stopped me in the street. It turned out she was pregnant. She had been raped by a priest. She was thirteen years old." Gregor looked directly at Sep to let the information sink in. "God really does work in mysterious ways. I knew, sooner or later, the matter would end up on my desk, and I would be expected to make the case 'disappear'. The girl would be sent to a convent, a poorhouse, or maybe even sent to an overseas mission, or left to roam the streets. The baby – if it survived the birth – would be left on the cold slab or in the snow to perish. If it managed to survive that, it would be separated from its mother, sent to an orphanage, or put up for adoption. And I would be part of the atrocity."

Sep watched Gregor's expression turn from pain to anger.

Petra sat with her head bowed. Tara rested her chin in her hands. She looked sad. Neither said a word.

Gregor took a deep breath and blew a steady stream of air from the corner of his mouth. "I decided to take a stand. I discovered the name of the priest. The trouble was I couldn't prove it. The girl hadn't seen who had attacked her clearly enough to positively identify him, and nobody was going to take the word of a thirteen-year-old." He thumped the table. His growing anger made his words tumble out as he relived the treachery. "But *I* knew who it was. The rape was an outrage that even the bishop would not be able to ignore – or so I believed. I failed to understand how embedded the need for self-preservation was within the Church. I found myself threatened with exactly the same tactics I'd used against many others. Even worse, the charges were manipulated. *I* was accused of the rape. After all, the orphanage was in my parish, and I was a frequent visitor. They said my allegations were a cynical and wicked attempt to divert attention on to an innocent man. Not only did I now face excommunication, but I was also threatened with a very public prosecution. David versus Goliath – only this time Goliath was certain to win."

Gregor paused to catch his breath. "Fortunately, one of the good people in my former parish was a lawyer. Together he and I mounted a defence. It was desperate, based on bluff, half-truths and counter-threats. We let it be known that I had kept records of every single investigation and cover-up I'd conducted over the past five years. I'd release these to the press unless the charges against me were dropped. The bishop capitulated on condition I resigned from the Church and moved outside his diocese." Gregor reached out and gently took Petra's hand. "The thirteen-year-old girl gave birth to a baby girl on the morning of 22nd April 1896. Two days later we left Brandt to travel here. This land falls outside the diocese of Brandt."

"And the priest?" Sep already guessed the answer.

"Lives in Dopplegau."

Sep was outraged. The image of Father Wagner, the sanctimonious man of God, swam into his consciousness. "But he visits you every month. He delivers my ma's parcel!"

"You mean he delivers *his* parcel. The note he leaves never mentions who the real donors are. He leaves it at the foot of the big escarpment for me to collect. He wouldn't dare set foot on this land." Gregor laughed bitterly. "It's ironic. He knows I'm just up the valley looking over his shoulder, pricking his conscience every day."

"Do my parents know about all this?"

Gregor gazed at the sun, which was beginning its descent behind the Mittelspitz. "Your ma suspected something. The good people who helped with Petra's birth were friends of Doctor Rubenstein. When we left, they guessed where we would be heading and were concerned for our welfare. They contacted Doctor Rubenstein, who in turn asked Frau Ansbacher to keep an eye out for us as we travelled. She must have told your ma."

"Did she know that Father Wagner was the … rapist?"

Gregor shook his head. "No. When she confronted Father Wagner, he didn't bat an eyelid. He just brazened it out and lied. He admitted a priest had been involved and said that the diocese had taken appropriate action. He claimed he didn't know exactly what punishment had been meted out. It was an internal matter that the Church had dealt with. So it never occurred to your ma that Father Wagner was the rapist. Her refusal to attend Mass was a protest about the Church's complicity in the crime. "I never told her at the time. I couldn't. Without proof it was just an allegation – an outrageous slander. Your father knows, because I told him when your sister was ten or eleven years old. Father Wagner has a liking for young girls. I wanted to warn your pa never to leave Josey alone with him."

Sep felt a cold fury build inside him. What had Father Wagner done to poor, defenceless Freya? Who else in the village might have suffered at his hands? It now made sense why his father refused to be in the presence of the priest, and always checked where Josey, Marie and Klara were whenever the priest was due to call.

"It must have been hard for you when you moved here by yourselves. You're all alone."

Petra laughed. "Alone? We aren't alone here, Sep. There are lots of people living up here. Doctors, teachers, reformed priests: good people looking for a simpler life. They're scattered around." She placed her hand gently on Sep's wrist and leant towards him. "Mind you, it was extremely hard for the first year. Fortunately, we had all summer to get the house wind and weather-proof, and stock up on wood."

"We ought to change the subject," Tara said brightly. "What happened, happened. The main thing is we're happy now. Let's not spoil things by dwelling on dark times."

"Well said, sweetheart. Enough of this doom and gloom, and me prattling on. Sep, I hear you are a good singer."

Petra drummed the table top with her fingers. "Oh, come on, sing us a song or two. It's ages since we had a party."

Sep was happy to oblige. He chose songs that would be familiar to anyone who lived in the Brandterwald. They all joined in.

Another stone flagon appeared, followed by another, and another. They were soon on their feet dancing, laughing and tripping over each other as the alcohol took effect.

The songs tumbled out. As one finished, they would jostle to sing a particular favourite.

"Let's sing '*Lustig is das Zigeunerleben*'."

"No, we've sung it twice already. How about '*Wanderlust*'?"

173

"I know, I know," Tara slurred excitedly. *"Let's sing 'Mein Hut, der hat drei Ecken'."*

"Oh yes – that's fun."

And off they would go - singing and miming and collapsing in shrieks of laughter.

Sep had no idea when or how he found his way into the hay barn. He remembered them all standing with their arms around each other for mutual support, staring in awe at the millions of stars. He had a vague recollection of being half-carried to the barn and Tara lying beside him before falling into unconsciousness.

He woke up – and wanted to die. He was sure his head was split open and his brain was going to explode. His tongue had become too big for his mouth. It felt dry and numb. He rolled over and felt sick. He was shaking, and his body felt clammy.

He became aware of a soft clucking sound and opened one eye to see a chicken staring back at him. He lay as still as a corpse and whimpered. He'd never felt so wretched in his life. Over the soft clucking of the hens came the sound of a fast-flowing stream. Suddenly every fibre of his being wanted to be submerged in clear, cold water. He tried to stand up – and failed. He recalled Tara's presence, and looked around. She was gone. Maybe she hadn't been there in the first place. He abandoned the idea of standing, and crawled on all fours out of the barn, wincing as the searing sun rendered him blind. He homed in on the sound of the stream and made his way towards it. He reached the bank, where he saw a small waterfall.

Underneath it – fully clothed, her long bedraggled hair plastered over her bowed head – was Tara. She peered with bloodshot eyes in Sep's vague direction. Gradually her eyes focused on the figure looking at her like a dejected lizard. Without a word, she waved a tired arm at him to join her.

Sep slithered down and eased himself onto the rock beside her, allowing the cool mountain water to cascade over him. The pair of them sat in abject misery, their arms round each other's shoulders, allowing the ice-cold water to ease their hangover.

That was how Gregor found them. He stood on the bank, towering over them, with his great fists on his hips, as he cried with laughter.

"Hey Petra, Petra, come and look at this!"

His mirth was infectious. First Tara began to giggle.

Then Petra's face appeared over the bank. She too collapsed in hysterical laughter.

Sep daren't laugh or move. He was convinced he was about to die.

174

"Tara, love. You have to come inside. You'll catch your death." Petra reached down and tried to haul up her drenched daughter. The weight of Tara's water-saturated dress made the task impossible. Gregor stepped in and, with one hand grasping Tara's arm, he landed his bedraggled daughter on the bank as if she were a fish. Gregor offered his hand to Sep.

Sep shook his head. "Please, just leave me," he whimpered. "I'll be fine by tomorrow."

It wasn't until mid-afternoon that Sep felt sufficiently recovered to make an appearance. He entered the farmhouse to find Tara cooking. She glanced at him and smiled weakly. "How are you feeling?"

"Delicate. How about you?" He eased himself carefully onto the bench seat that surrounded two sides of the great stone fireplace.

"Fragile." She gave a light laugh. "It was a great day though, wasn't it?"

"Yeah – one of the best days of my life."

"So far. You'll have a lot of great days." She gave him a penetrating look. "You're a lucky person. More things will go your way than will go against you."

"You really are psychic?"

"Oh yes."

Sep laughed.

"Don't you believe me?" she said, without rancour.

"Yes, I do. I was admiring your certainty."

"I've made some herb tea." She waved at a pot.

"Love one – if you'll join me."

She sat opposite him, and they looked happily at each other.

"Yes, I like you too," she said matter-of-factly.

He laughed.

Halfway down the escarpment he met his father, slowly making his way up.

He stopped and waited for Sep to reach him. "I was worried. I thought you might have fallen."

Sep was touched by his father's concern. "Pa, you should have sent Klaus or Tom. You're getting too old to be shinning up these cliffs."

His father made to give him a clip round the ear. "Cheek of it," he muttered. "Did you meet Gregor?"

"I met them all. We had such a day … and night."

"Ah. Suffering a bit, are we?"

175

Sep sat on a rock beside the path and gestured for his father to do the same.

"I'll just rest my weary old bones," his father said, settling next to his son.

"Gregor told me everything, Pa."

Herr Breitner nodded. "I hoped he would."

"Why didn't you tell me?"

His father gazed out over the valley and was silent. "It's not my place to talk about something like that. If Gregor wanted his story to be shared with others besides me, that's a decision for him and Petra." He glanced sideways at Sep. "It takes a lot of courage for a woman to talk about rape. It's the ultimate crime, lad, especially when committed against one so innocent."

"Why didn't you report Father Wagner to the authorities, Pa?"

His father grunted. "I'd no more proof than Gregor. Added to that, if I'd reported the matter the *Kriminalpolitzei* would have arrested Gregor. Don't forget, lad, as far as the Church was concerned, Gregor was the one they'd accuse."

"Has he ... you know ... raped anyone else?"

"Not that anyone knows of. Certainly no one in the village. What he gets up to in his visits down the valley..." He let his words tail off.

"What about Freya?"

"I don't know. Gregor never knew about Freya. He only revealed Father Wagner's identity to me long after Freya was sent to the convent." His father was angry. "It was a bad decision made in all innocence to allow the girl to enter the *Pfarrhaus*. I suspect the worst. People like Wagner are clever and devious. They prey on the young and vulnerable. Think about it, lad. Suppose he did molest Freya. Without definite proof, who would believe the evidence of someone with her mental capacity?"

"We need to check on Freya, though."

"It's been done, lad."

Sep looked shocked. "Who checked? Is she OK?"

"Doctor Rubenstein checked – or tried to check. According to the abbess at St Catherine's, Freya ran away from the convent three weeks after she was admitted. She hasn't been seen since. The matter was placed in the hands of the *Kriminalpolitzei*."

"She's missing?"

"God only knows, son."

The Christmas decorations were going up, and the gloom and despondency that had pervaded the wards following Doctor Forsythe's death began to lift. Despite his resolve to banish her from his thoughts, Sep found himself thinking about Nurse Jones. What would she be doing now? What might she be wearing? Who would she be with? The image of the young cavalry officer intruded. She would be with him of course, walking hand in hand, laughing and smiling – or maybe in bed. That image jerked him back into reality. He needed to find something else to occupy his mind. Fortunately, a solution presented itself. Sep spent the morning with Curly, Bert and Steve making paper chains.

"By heck, this takes me back. Last time I did this, I must have been nine years old," Curly said.

"Christmas is always good when you're a nipper." Bert stopped colouring his strips of decoration and pondered. "You know, when I think back, the less we had, the more we enjoyed ourselves." He glanced around at his friends. "We were happy with the smallest of presents."

"Well, I'm glad to hear it, lad, cos you ain't getting nowt from me, so you should be in seventh heaven." Steve laughed.

"What kind of Christmas do you have in Austria then, Sep?" Curly asked.

"Going to church on Christmas Eve is the highlight. It's when all the community come together. Christmas Day isn't really celebrated. We don't give presents. My mother would bake hard sweet biscuits, make a stollen cake and we'd have a special meal. Lots of singing." He grinned. "Bert is right. The simpler, the better."

"It's nice to get something, though," Steve said wistfully. "It's symbolic – gifts from the three kings represent love and friendship."

Curly nodded. "I agree. But I'm telling ye now, lad, yer getting two ciggies from me. You can give two ciggies to Sep, he can give two to Bert, and Bert can give me two. That way we're all happy." He looked around at them and beamed at the logic of his suggestion. "Men are easy to give presents to."

"Unlike women."

"Ah, don't get me started, Bert."

But start they did. They spent the rest of the morning discussing the treacherous subject of selecting appropriate gifts for the fairer sex, and the tragic consequences of getting it wrong – as inevitably happened.

177

By early afternoon the rain finally stopped, the wind eased, and Sep decided to attempt the three-mile walk to St Étienne. He set off at a cautious, measured pace. It proved to be painfully slow. He forced his mind into a trance: one step at a time. He counted out each swinging stride.

Again, she slipped unbidden into his mind. He sensed her walking anxiously next to him; ready to provide a steadying hand, words of encouragement, or express exasperation at his determination and stubbornness. He smiled at the image and gave up trying to banish her from his thoughts. Why should he? He loved everything about her – he ought to be treasuring every memory.

He reached the village two and a half hours later. It felt as if his shoulders had come out of their sockets. Nevertheless, being outside in the fresh French countryside made the effort worthwhile. With dismay he realised he had not thought about what he would do once at his destination, other than turn back. Having come so far, he decided it would be a shame not to at least have a wander around.

To Sep's eyes, the village looked run-down and scruffy. Parts of the cement render on the low houses that lined the street had fallen off, and the paintwork was bare and weatherworn. Many of the timber shutters were askew, the pavement was cracked and the kerbstones uneven. Despite its ramshackle appearance, Sep found himself smiling. Compared to the pristine, sanitised hospital, the village felt unkempt, charming and very human. Apart from the occasional passing military truck and ambulance, there were scarcely anyone about. He exchanged nods with the few English people – soldiers, orderlies and nurses – he passed. He presumed they were taking the opportunity to escape the hospital until, rounding a corner and entering a small square, he spotted the café.

The enticing aroma of freshly baked bread and ground coffee drifted towards him. It was clear from the number of uniformed customers that the establishment was popular with the British. He was about to enter when he realised he had no French francs – or any money at all on him. He moved on, promising to treat himself next time. Maybe he'd invite Susan. On the opposite side of the square was a small shop. The door triggered a welcoming bell as he entered.

A middle-aged woman, who looked as dusty as the goods that surrounded her, greeted him. "Bonjour, monsieur."

"Bonjour, madam."

"You are looking for something?"

"No, I am looking around." He shrugged apologetically. "I have no money on me. I'm sorry."

The woman's previously welcoming expression froze as the prospect of a sale dissipated. "Please, look around." She looked sour and waved a dismissive hand.

The shop had clearly made a game attempt to serve the various needs of the community and the British field hospital. It was chaotic. Vegetables were piled beneath shelves containing tins and jars of preserves and pickles. A range of cheeses and pats of butter sat in folded paper napkins under a small glass counter, behind which a line of smoked sausages dangled. Sep leafed through a rack of postcards of French country scenes, patriotic slogans and some sepia photographs of scantily clad mademoiselles. Towards the back of the shop, bolts of cloth lay alongside shelves filled with pots, pans, small enamel milk churns and mixing bowls. A carriage clock rested on top of a pile of dusty books. A small glass display cabinet housed a small collection of religious artefacts.

He peered into the cabinet. At the back a small silver crucifix hung from a brass hook. Sep opened the cupboard, took it out and examined it. It was exquisite in its craftsmanship and simplicity. He imagined it hanging around Susan's neck, nestling against her soft, smooth skin. He pictured her delight.

The woman was immediately at his shoulder. "You like it, monsieur?"

"I do."

"For yourself?"

"No, for a ... friend."

"A girlfriend, a sweetheart, perhaps?" The woman's smile reminded Sep of a crocodile.

"A special friend."

"Ah."

"How much is it?"

"One hundred francs." She looked at Sep's confused expression "Four English pounds. It is pure silver."

Sep shook his head instinctively. He was fairly sure the price was inflated. He moved to replace the necklace on its hook. "I'll think about it."

She moved quickly to recover the item. "I put it to one side for you. You come back tomorrow."

He left the shop and contemplated the walk back with dread. His armpits ached from the constant pressure of the crutches. Three miles now felt like a very long way indeed. He set off and managed just over a mile before his arms gave out. He sank onto the verge and glanced at his watch. It had taken him ninety minutes to get this far, and the light was fading fast. He glanced up and down the road. There was no one about. In fact, now he thought about it, he hadn't

179

passed anyone since leaving St Étienne. It seemed that nobody – apart from a stupid Austrian farmer – ventured out at this time of day. There was nothing for it; he needed to press on. He struggled to his feet.

Half an hour later it was dark, and he was almost crying with pain. He scolded himself for his stupidity. What on earth had possessed him to try and walk so far? He glanced up as two tiny pinpricks of light appeared on the road ahead. A truck was approaching, driving towards St Étienne. Sep glanced back towards the village. Surely there would be some vehicle heading in his direction. He stared forlornly at the truck as it passed, then gritted his teeth and forced himself forward. Behind him, the lorry slowed, slewed across the road and completed a three-point turn. Sep looked up in relief as it drew alongside him.

A furious Nurse Handsworth peered at him from the passenger window. "I should make you walk back, Lieutenant Breitner, for the trouble you've caused." She opened the door and climbed down to confront him. "What did I tell you?"

Sep stood like a naughty schoolboy. English nurses could be fierce when they wanted to be, he thought.

"I said to do one mile, not six miles, didn't I?"

Sep nodded.

"I said I would walk with you, didn't I?"

Sep nodded again and looked shamefaced.

"Get in the back, Sep." She grasped his elbow firmly and steered him towards the rear of the truck. The driver had already got out and lowered the tailgate. "I am really cross with you," she said angrily, as she and the driver helped him into the back of the truck.

"I'm sorry. It will not happen again."

Sep was sure that on the way back Nurse Mandy instructed the driver to drive over every pothole and bump to increase his misery. The only thought that gave him relief was that Mandy had picked him up. If it had been Susan, he was certain she wouldn't have hesitated to box his ears.

"Who's been a naughty lieutenant?" Corporal McPherson grinned at him next morning. "Ye're nae Nurse Mandy's favourite soldier today."

"I was foolish," Sep agreed.

"How far did ye get?"

"There and nearly halfway back."

"That's nae bad for a first attempt." The orderly eyed him. "Was it worth it?"

Sep rubbed his aching shoulders and armpits. "Let's just say it taught me a few lessons."

"Not tae get on the wrong side o' Nurse Mandy being the most important."

Sep nodded his agreement. "I'll have to apologise." He swung his leg out of the bed and reached for his crutches. "I need to return to the village, though."

"Ye're nae going tae do tha' today, though," the orderly said firmly.

"I need to get a present. The shopkeeper's put it to one side for me."

"Ye canna walk it, man."

"Maybe not. Perhaps I can persuade someone to let me ride with them?"

"Cadge a lift?" The corporal scratched his head. He held a brown envelope. "Oh, this came for ye. It looks official." He handed the letter over. "Read this an' Ah'll find out if anyone is running to St Étienne today."

Sep shouted a thanks as Corporal McPherson disappeared out the door.

He flipped the envelope over. It was addressed to *Leutnant Offizierstellvertreter* Breitner. The crest of the Two Kingdoms was stamped on the letterhead. He ripped the seal and unfolded the letter. It was his summons home for discharge. He lay back and stared at the ceiling. He was now faced with some difficult choices.

He reread the letter. The orders were clear: once declared fit to travel, he was to make his way to Brandt via Brussels, Cologne and Stuttgart. A travel warrant was included. In Brandt, he was to report to the High Command for the disbanding of the 4th Tyrolean Kaiserjäger, receive his back pay and discharge papers, then return to civilian life.

He lay for some time wondering at his reaction. The letter was not unexpected, yet it came as a shock. He ought to feel a sense of euphoria. It marked the end of his life as a soldier. He should be positive and confident about the future, but he felt only trepidation. It was the feeling of foreboding that confused him the most. He knew what was causing the dread, and kept batting it away. It was the end of his hope of winning Susan's heart.

What was he thinking of? Their relationship was nowhere near that level of intimacy. She hadn't given him any hint of her feelings towards him – no matter what Corporal McPherson and Nurse Mandy might think. He hadn't made his feelings clear to her. Besides, her warm embrace of the mystery captain suggested that she had a fiancé, or at least an admirer. She probably had lots of admirers.

"Two-thirty, sir."

"What?" Sep glanced across at Corporal McPherson.

"Two-thirty. The mail truck is leaving on its rounds. The driver will drop you off in the village and pick you up again on his way back."

"OK. Thank you, Sandy."

"Good news?" The corporal nodded towards the brown envelope.

"Probably."

"Ah've some better news for ye."

"What's that?"

"The steamer's sailed from Dover. She'll be back tomorrow." The corporal winked and disappeared, leaving Sep feeling mildly panic-stricken. He had set himself a writing target – and he was still a couple of chapters short.

I n the early spring of 1914, the boys stood and gazed out across the Bodensee.

"Do you think the real sea is the same as this?" Tom asked.

"I expect it's just as wet," Wingnut replied sagely. "Maybe a touch wetter."

"Piss off, I'm being serious."

Wingnut ruffled Tom's hair. 'I suggest you join the Imperial Kriegsmarine to find out.'

"Have we got a navy?" Klaus asked.

"Course we've got a navy. We've bought a great big battleship from the English."

"Are you lads ready?" George appeared, waving a wad of tickets.

They walked up the gangplank of the pleasure steamer and immediately headed for the panorama deck, where they unpacked the lunches their mothers had prepared.

"I can't believe this. I've spent all my life in Dopplegau, and now in one day I'm travelling to three countries," Stephan said.

Klaus threw his arms out to embrace the still blue waters of the lake. "Come to Brandt and see the world – or at least a small town in Switzerland and an even smaller town in Germany."

They commandeered a table and watched in fascination as the steamer's great paddle wheels churned the ship away from the quay for the trip around the Bodensee. It had been a day of adventure and wonder, and much more was still to come. They had left Dopplegau at half past four in the morning and travelled to Achbrugge to catch the first steam train to Brandt. It was the first time the boys had seen the wonders of technology close up. The narrow-gauge steam engine that hauled its six tiny carriages down the valley into Brandt seemed to Sep to be a fire-breathing monster. It was only when they pulled into the central railway station that Sep truly appreciated the power and majesty of a full-size main-line locomotive.

Klaus, George and Sep had checked in their bags for the overnight sleeper, before they made their way into the city centre to be overwhelmed by the sights, sounds and smells of the modern world.

They saw their first motorcars – dozens of them, weaving around the horse-drawn carriages, whose drivers cracked their whips and cursed them as they passed. The air was thick with the smell of petrol fumes and horse dung. Buildings towered above them on either side of the street as they pushed and jostled their way through crowds of people dressed in slick suits, colourful summer dresses and smart uniforms. Even the children looked pressed and ironed. They caught a trolley bus for no reason other than the novelty of travelling by electric motor. At each turn there was a new sight to excite, amuse, or prompt disbelief. There were shops selling clothes ready-made off the peg; furniture that looked like it belonged in a palace, an emporium selling only hats, gloves and handbags. And there were *Bäckereis* with shelves piled high with chocolate and cream cakes that made the boys drool, and a shop that only sold flowers. How could anyone make a living out of selling only flowers?

George planned their itinerary well. Within an hour of arriving in Brandt he had already exceeded his ambitions, and their expectations – and for Sep and Klaus this was just a prelude. He had made good on his promise to take the Breitner children out into the modern world of commerce, business, arts, culture, politics and fashion.

Thanks to George's introductions, Klaus had already built up a small following of wealthy clients from the guests at the Lodge, who saw him as an up-and-coming artist. George – with Sir William's support – had arranged for Klaus to spend six months working at the Royal Academy of Arts in London, learning from the foremost painters in England.

He had arranged for Sep to work at the London headquarters of the British Empire Bank learning about business planning, investment banking, trade and commerce. He was to work from the Austro-Hungarian desk, acting as liaison and translator/interpreter.

The two brothers were excited – yet their excitement was tempered by doubt and trepidation. For Sep the highlight of the trip was that he would be staying with Rachel and her family.

"What will you do when you get to London?" Stephan asked as the steamer left the harbour.

Sep leant against the ship's guard rail. "Apart from visiting Rachel, George suggested that I visit the Science Museum and Klaus goes to the National Portrait Gallery. If it's sunny, then we'll head for the Tower of London and Buckingham Palace."

"I envy you, mate."

"You'll travel as well, Stephan," George said, "and don't forget this isn't a holiday. Sep and Klaus are going to have to work while they're in England."

"It's hardly work." Tom laughed. "Klaus painting pictures and Sep translating English into German."

184

"While you find out what *real* work is, helping pa run the farm." Klaus ruffled Tom's hair. "You'll be begging us to come home within the week."

"Well, I hope you both have a great time. But I will miss you." Wingnut sounded subdued.

Sep was moved. "Ah, thanks mate. We'll miss you as well. I'm sure the six months will fly by."

"It had better not be more than six months." Wingnut made the statement sound like an ultimatum. They looked at him curiously.

"Why not?"

Wingnut shuffled uncomfortably. "Well, I didn't want to say anything. Nothing is certain – and I don't want to tempt fate. It's not, you know, official yet. But hopefully things will turn out all right."

Sep was exasperated. He'd been aware for weeks that Wingnut appeared to be troubled. It was as if his mind was permanently on other things. "What are you talking about, man?"

Wingnut looked at Stephan. "Well, I have a meeting with your pa tomorrow evening."

"What for?" Stephan sounded perplexed. "I don't know anything about this. What are you meeting my pa for?"

"Well, it's, um … I'm going to ask for permission to marry Marie."

The news was greeted by stunned silence until Sep let out a whoop of joy. "Congratulations, mate." He clapped his friend heartily on the back. "You old dog, you."

"When did you ask her?"

"Last week."

"She said yes, I assume?"

"She needed a day to think about it. She thought she might be too young."

"She's eighteen. Bit young, I grant you."

"When's the big day?"

"We've not decided. I haven't got her pa's permission."

"Oh, he'll agree."

"This calls for champagne," George announced and disappeared towards the bar.

"What's with the six-month business? Why's that so important?" Sep finally managed to get his question in.

"That's when we plan the official engagement – and we want you to be present. We timed it so you'll both be back."

"We'll be back." Klaus laughed. "Even if It's only for the day."

"I was hoping you'd do me the honour of being best man." Wingnut said to Sep.

185

"Me, do you the honour? I think you'll find it's the other way round. Of course! It's a privilege – and I'm flattered to be asked."

George reappeared, followed by a waiter holding a tray which held an ice bucket and six champagne flutes. "Come on, lads, let's toast the lucky man. It's Sekt –far superior to the French stuff, and much more appropriate in the circumstances."

The waiter charged their glasses.

Sep stepped forward. "First duty of the best man. Gentlemen, raise your glasses to our dear friends, Wingnut and Marie."

Around them, other passengers who had overheard the conversation broke into spontaneous applause.

It was a perfect beginning to Sep's first trip abroad.

If Brandt was the appetiser, London was the full banquet. Sep and Klaus were overwhelmed by the scale, vibrancy and sheer energy of the city. George ensured they experienced everything the hub of the British Empire had to offer. On the first four days they visited the bastions of wealth, power and privilege. They dined at the Dorchester, attended the opera, visited the palaces of Westminster and Hampton Court. They watched the Trooping of the Colour, and stood open-mouthed on Tower Bridge and gazed in amazement at the activity on the river. They were unable to count the number of ships, barges and lighters they could see.

Then George took them on a tour of the East End.

Sep had never seen so much poverty and squalor. He was appalled at the mean, back-to-back hovels that housed families of eight or nine. Everywhere they went, barefoot, ragged urchins chased them, begging for change. At times the overpowering stench of raw sewage made them retch, and the thick soot-laden air caught in their throats.

They returned to Rachel's comfortable home in the leafy suburb of Hampstead, chastened by their experience and convinced they were infested by vermin.

That evening after dinner they made themselves comfortable over a glass of wine and reviewed the day.

George sat back and looked at Sep and Klaus. "So, you've seen the best and worse that London has to offer. What do you think?"

"Are all the British cities and towns like London?" Klaus asked.

"In terms of differences between the rich and the poor?"

Klaus nodded.

"Almost all of them. Some – like Glasgow, for example – are much worse. Others are affluent. The university towns of Oxford and

Cambridge tend to have fewer areas of deprivation, but it's still there in little pockets."

"How can people live like that?" Images of the wretched hovels swam into his imagination.

"They have little choice." Rachel nodded her thanks as George refilled her wine glass. "The working classes suffer from little or no education, poor health, and only have access to the worst paid jobs. They have no power – they don't own any land, or have much hope of making much money."

"They are little better than slaves. Why don't they revolt?" Klaus asked.

"They probably will someday. The trouble is, they can't get organised. As soon as there is the slightest hint of unrest, the bosses sack the troublemakers."

"It's an appalling way to live."

"Much worse if you are a woman," Rachel said. "Think about it. You have to live in insanitary conditions. If you are lucky enough to work, you're paid a pittance. Worse still, there's no contraception so you have a child every year, adding to the household burden that you're expected to manage, and damaging your health in the process." She looked at Sep. "It should be compulsory for every man to come and visit my hospital and see the appalling results of a lack of proper healthcare and contraceptive advice for women and girls. And when a woman tries to better herself, escape from poverty, get qualifications, secure a better-paid job, what is she confronted with? Barriers, prejudice and discrimination – and she can do nothing to change the situation."

Sep had never seen Rachel so animated. If she was so angry about the system, then he knew it must be wrong. He listened intently as Rachel continued her tirade.

"Did you know there is only one place in the British Empire where women have the right to both vote and stand for election?"

Sep shook his head, ashamed that his knowledge of the world was so limited and that he had never yet considered the plight of women. He glanced at Klaus, who also looked embarrassed.

"New Zealand." Rachel threw her hands up in exasperation and sat back in her chair. "It's a disgrace that this situation is allowed in the richest, most powerful Empire this planet has ever seen. This is 1914, for goodness' sake." She grinned sheepishly. "I'm ranting, aren't I?"

"It's not a rant, Rachel. It's an education in institutional inequality," George said softly. He didn't look at either of the boys. He didn't have to. He knew they wouldn't ignore this lesson.

Apart from the pleasure of staying with Rachel and her family, Sep didn't enjoy London. After two weeks, the novelty of the bustling metropolis started to wear off. He realised city life wasn't for him. It felt claustrophobic, and people's willingness to work day in, day out, in a soulless office building where fresh air and daylight barely penetrated, dismayed him.

Nevertheless, he applied himself diligently to his internship and received praise for his hard work and interpreting skills. He learned a great deal, especially about business planning and risk management, and could already see areas where the family farm and his home village would benefit from fresh thinking, investment and new ventures.

Klaus, on the other hand, found London to his liking. He was well received within artistic circles. He was naturally gifted, both technically and creatively, and found that his services as a painting tutor were as much in demand as his commissions.

But their time in England inevitably came to an end.

George travelled with them on the train ferry as far as Dover. He was as ebullient, considerate, generous and courteous as ever. Sep and Klaus saw him as a benevolent uncle, and Rachel as their feisty, outspoken elder sister. Their dockside parting was emotional.

"I hope you will continue to be a credit to your parents," George said. "You are both blessed with considerable talents. I am confident you will use these to benefit your family, as well as those less fortunate than yourselves."

"You are our inspiration," Sep said. "I'm not sure we can meet your expectations, and I'm certain we cannot match your generosity."

His brother added his own gratitude. "We can't thank you enough. I'm not sure we can ever repay you." Klaus was close to tears.

George was similarly affected. "You ought to go. It won't do to have a bunch of grown men blubbing like babies in public." They embraced and walked up the gangway.

George stood on the dockside, hat in hand, waving a final salute.

They would never see him again.

CHAPTER 20 – WINGNUT AND MARIE'S WEDDING

"So, what do you think?" Wingnut turned from the mirror and looked expectantly at Sep.

"Are you being serious?"

"Of course."

"I thought not having hair didn't bother you?"

"Course it bothered me. The trouble was, in the past there wasn't much I could do about it." Wingnut admired himself in the mirror. "I wasn't sure of the colour. In the end, black seemed to be OK." He looked at his friend. "So, what do you think?"

The truth was, the wig was hideous – but Sep wasn't about to hurt his friend's feelings.

"Where did you get it?"

"In Brandt, when you went to England. After you, Klaus and George left on the sleeper, I dived into that gentlemen's outfitters shop."

"Does Marie know about this?"

"No, I thought I'd surprise her."

"You'll surprise her all right." Sep scratched his head. He was struggling to get his mind around what possessed Wingnut to buy the … thing. It didn't even look real. It had obviously been designed for use on a mannequin.

Wingnut explained his logic. "I thought I ought to make an effort. Marie was keen to hire a photographer, and I want to look my best."

"But you didn't discuss it with her?"

"No, I told you I wanted it to be a surprise." He glanced anxiously at Sep. "Do you think I should have?"

"Definitely, it's her wedding as well. You don't want any surprises on the day."

Wingnut studied himself in the mirror, and adjusted the toupee. It was unnecessary: the object was grotesque from whatever angle. "It makes me look … more mature, more virile." He grinned happily at Sep. "Marie will love it."

"Well, you'd best make sure of that before the big day." Sep glanced at his watch. "We need to get going."

Wingnut carefully replaced the wig in its box, and the two friends walked towards St Stephen's church for the wedding rehearsal.

The ever-loyal Alfie spotted them leave. Not wishing to be left out, he scampered up the path to join them.

"What's Father Haphold like?" Sep asked. as they strolled the short distance to St Stephens church.

"He comes from the village. I've known him more or less all my life. Everyone in Gau was delighted when he took over from that old crook, Father Zach. Speaking of crooks, how did Father Wagner take the news?"

189

"Badly. He was disappointed that Marie had chosen to turn her back on her own parish and community traditions. He wasn't upset for himself, you understand."

"The man's a bastard." Wingnut spat the words out.

Sep looked grim. "An *alleged* bastard."

"Well, I hope he realises we're on to him and he has trouble sleeping. Come Judgement Day, he really will find himself thrown into the fires of hell." Wingnut bent down and scratched Alfie affectionately behind the ear.

"I don't think he can be in any doubt. Attendance at Mass has dropped. I understand quite a few people now worship at St Stephen's." Sep nodded towards the white-robed figure of Father Haphold, who was standing outside his church ready to greet them.

"Welcome, Wingnut, and you too, Herr Breitner." The young clergyman offered his hand. "Marie and Josey are already inside."

Alfie had already sensed Josey's presence and had bolted inside the church. This time he was disappointed. Alfie found himself evicted, and the rehearsal began.

On the day itself, St Stephen's was packed. Sep scanned the congregation. There was a danger that not everyone would fit into the church. The choirboys, under Tom and Stephan's supervision, were doing an excellent job of ushering the guests to the appropriate side of the aisle. Everything was going smoothly, and everyone appeared relaxed – apart from Wingnut.

"How long?" he asked anxiously.

Sep glanced at his watch. "Ten minutes to go. The guests are still arriving." He patted his friend on the back. "Calm down, mate. Enjoy the day."

Wingnut peered round at his proud parents and sisters seated behind him. They smiled their encouragement, but this only increased Wingnut's agitation.

"What do you think she'll look like?"

"Who?" Sep replied absently, his attention on people shuffling into the back of the church. It seemed that there weren't going to be enough chairs.

"Marie, of course."

"She'll look absolutely gorgeous."

"Have you seen the dress?"

"What? No, of course not! Josey said it looks magnificent, though." Sep found himself getting distracted. Tom and Stephan were frantically moving seats to accommodate the guests, who now were waiting outside the church.

"We might have to ask people to stand down each side," he said.

Hearing no reply he turned around, to find Wingnut had disappeared.

"Where's he gone?" Sep looked anxiously at Wingnut's parents.

"I don't know. He just ran out the side door." Frau Haufmann looked concerned. "You don't think he'd got cold feet, do you?"

Sep was already at the side door. In the distance, he saw Wingnut sprinting towards the village. He was about to shout out before realising the effort would be futile. Wingnut had already reached his house and disappeared inside. Sep dithered. Should he run after the fleeing Wingnut? Or stay and look after the guests? In the distance the open carriage carrying the bridal party hove into view. Marie had already left Dopplegau. In less than five minutes she would be at the church. He cursed inwardly. Christ, how was the disappearance of the groom going to be explained? He ducked back inside the church and tried to think. Stephan and Tom's help was required. He walked fast up the aisle, smiling and nodding greetings to the expectant guests, trying to look relaxed.

Tom stood, his hands in his pockets, watching Stephan settle the last of the guests into their seats. He glanced up as Sep approached.

"What's up? You look stressed."

Sep pulled Tom behind a pillar and beckoned to Stephan to join them. He lowered his voice to a whisper. "Wingnut's done a runner."

"What?" Tom exclaimed.

"Shush! Keep your voice down and listen to me. We've got to keep calm. I need one of you – Tom, you're the fastest – to run to Wingnut's house and find the sod. Stephan, I need you to get up the road and tell Marie and her pa to go round the village. Say we're having trouble fitting everyone in the church."

"Where shall I send them?"

"Send them anywhere. I need time to find out what's going on."

"What about if any more guests arrive?"

"Leave it to the choirboys to sort out."

Stephan and Tom made to dash off.

Sep grabbed Tom before he had a chance to depart. "Not that way. Go out through the side door – it's quicker. Come with me, and act normal." The pair of them sauntered back down the aisle, rictus grins etched across their faces. Sep tried to look as if he was casually opening the side door for some fresh air. He caught Herr and Frau Haufmann looking at him in wild-eyed panic. He gave them a reassuring smile as Tom disappeared out of the door, only to reappear almost instantly.

"It's OK, he's on his way back," he whispered as he closed the door behind him.

Sep let out a long sigh of relief. "Thank God."

Tom grinned. "Probably a call of nature – nerves and all that."

Sep nodded. "You'd best let Stephan know, then take your place." Sep mopped his brow and resumed his station next to Father Haphold.

The priest leant forward. "Is everything OK?"

Sep nodded. "Last-minute nerves."

They waited patiently for Wingnut to reappear.

After two minutes they were still waiting. Sep glanced at his watch. Four minutes had passed, and there was still no sign of Wingnut. His heart was pounding. There was a commotion at the back of the church as latecomers were shown to their seats. Sep couldn't allow himself to be distracted. After six minutes, he knew something had gone wrong. He glanced at Tom, who shrugged his shoulders, looking nonplussed. A slight murmur rippled through the congregation. Most of them had attended weddings before, and they were pretty sure the groom ought to be standing alongside the best man.

Outside the church, Wingnut had found the side door shut and had gone to the main entrance. Pausing for a second to adjust his wig, he entered the church to be confronted by a conscientious choirboy.

"Bride or groom?" the youngster demanded.

"Groom," Wingnut said, confidently.

"You need to sit there." The young lad pointed to a chair next to the last pillar. He delivered his instruction with such authority that Wingnut took it as an order and meekly sat down. The boy gave Wingnut an inquisitive look. He couldn't place the man with the distinctive head of thick black hair. Perhaps it was one of Wingnut's friends from Dopplegau. He wouldn't see much of the ceremony from where he was sitting. But that was his fault for being so late.

At the altar, Sep was sweating. He glanced again at Tom.

"Do you want me to go and look?" Tom mouthed silently.

Sep was about to agree when the main entrance door darkened. It was Stephan, who gave him a thumbs-up. Sep glanced at his watch and desperately considered what he ought to do. Wingnut had a few more minutes to make an appearance. Sep decided to wait before asking Father Haphold to pause the proceedings.

192

At the back of the church, Stephan looked puzzled. He could see Sep and the priest standing by the altar – but no groom. He scratched his head. Tom had told him Wingnut had been found. He glanced over his shoulder to see the bridal party's carriage swing into the small churchyard. He looked again at the altar. Maybe Wingnut was hidden from view. He walked across to the other pillar to get a better angle. It made no difference. He couldn't see the groom.

The carriage had stopped, and Herr Wachter was already helping Marie alight. Stephan felt a growing panic. He tore his eyes off the bridal party and jumped up and down to catch Sep's attention.

Sep spotted Stephan's desperate signals. Inwardly he groaned. There was nothing for it. They'd somehow have to stop Marie from entering the church until they had found Wingnut.

Wingnut sat intrigued by Stephan's bizarre dance. "You all right, mate?"

Stephan spun around. For a few seconds he stared in confusion at the strange black-haired man grinning back at him. Gradually it dawned on him that under the thatch lay Wingnut.

"What are you doing back here?" Stephan screeched in a strangled whisper.

Wingnut looked bemused. "I was told to sit here."

Stephan dragged him to his feet and propelled him towards the aisle. "Get yourself down the front."

Wingnut's walk to the altar would become part of village folklore. He strode along with a new confidence, beaming at his friends and neighbours, who watched his progress with open-mouthed astonishment. Most didn't recognise the hirsute young man and assumed, like the choirboy, that he was a late guest who seemed a bit full of himself. The beaming Wingnut took his place beside a stricken-looking Sep and Father Haphold, whose eyes locked on to the black object on Wingnut's head.

Before anyone could react, the organist took the arrival of the groom as his cue to start the ceremony. The strains of Wagner's 'Bridal Chorus' filled the church. Everyone stood and watched Marie's progress. She looked stunning. In an instant, everyone forgot about the unfamiliar man. A gasp of amazement swept around the church. Someone clapped. It had a ripple effect – everyone took up the applause. Konrad Wachter glanced at his daughter, unable to prevent tears from flowing down his cheeks. It was the proudest day of his life. Sep glanced at Suzanne Wachter, who held one hand over her mouth as if dumbstruck by the vision. In her other hand she held a lace handkerchief that was already damp with her tears.

While everyone focused on Marie, Sep frantically considered how he might whip the wig off Wingnut's head without anyone

193

noticing. He had a microsecond to react. He was too late. As Marie drew close, the opportunity passed.

Wingnut stepped forward, his face wreathed in happiness. He was totally smitten by Marie.

Josey, as chief bridesmaid, was the first to notice. Her expression changed from shock to horror. She glanced at her brother in wide-eyed dismay. Sep shrugged and shook his head to signal his helplessness. In the next few seconds, Marie would realise that the man beside her was not a church elder, an unexpected guest or a tailor's dummy, but the person she was about to commit to spend the rest of her life with. Sep closed his eyes and awaited the explosion. He imagined the shrieks, the flood of tears, the pandemonium, the outraged parents, Josey's fury, the sound of the bridal party fleeing the scene, the consternation of the congregation and the inevitable recriminations focused on him: the best man, who was supposed to make sure everything ran like clockwork. What he hadn't expected was the bride's reaction.

Marie stopped dead. She lifted her veil and peered at the grinning man alongside her. The church went silent. She abruptly covered her face with her hands. Her shoulders started to shake. Josey immediately put her arms around the quivering bride and shot her elder brother a withering look.

Sep wanted to die on the spot.

The church was suddenly filled by shrieks of laughter. Marie could hardly breathe. Her gales of mirth were infectious. She pointed at Wingnut's head and collapsed before she could get any words out. The congregation began to laugh. It was impossible not to.

Wingnut glanced around in bewilderment. His expression set Marie off again. She turned and held on to Josey, who was struggling to stop her own giggles.

Sep risked a quick glance at Fritz and Suzanne Wachter. To his relief, he saw that they had also managed to see the funny side of the situation.

Gradually the mirth subsided, although Marie's occasional sideways glances at Wingnut were enough to trigger a fresh bout of hysterics.

Eventually, Sep thought the moment was right to lean towards Father Haphold's ear. "I think it would be a good idea if the bride, groom and their escorts were to join you in the vestry to get us back on track."

The priest managed to get himself under control and nodded his agreement. He didn't trust himself to speak. He gestured for Marie, Wingnut, Konrad, Josey and Sep to follow him. Once inside the ante-room Marie sat, wiped the tears from her eyes and gave

Wingnut an exasperated look. "What on earth possessed you to buy that … thing?" It was no good. She couldn't help herself from collapsing once again into peals of laughter.

Wingnut blinked. "I wanted to look my best, Marie, for you. Well, for everyone, really."

Marie got up and cradled her future husband's face in her hands. "Wingnut, I love you just the way you are. I always have done, and always will." She raised herself up on tiptoe and kissed him on the lips. "It was a nice thought." Once again a fit of the giggles consumed her. "But I'm not sure I can get through the ceremony without laughing."

"Maybe if we start again, with your entrance?" Father Haphold suggested. "You and the bridesmaids look an absolute picture. I'm sure everyone will want a repeat performance."

The second time they tried, the wedding of Marie Wachter and Norbert (Wingnut) Haufmann went off without a hitch.

As soon as the ceremony was over, everyone climbed into the waiting wagons and headed to the Adler for the reception. Already they had agreed that the wedding was the best they had been to – and the prospect of good food, wine and dancing still lay before them.

Sep sat in the cart surrounded by the excited bridesmaids. While they dissected the female guests' dresses, hats, gloves, jewellery, posies and any other fashion accessories with forensic thoroughness, he offered a silent prayer of thanks to the Almighty. He thanked God for Marie's sense of fun, which had snatched victory from disaster. Somehow even Alfie had secured his reward. He'd hitched a ride and lay at the girls' feet being petted. Sep reached down and gave the terrier an affectionate pat on the stomach.

"I can't believe you didn't know." Klara poked Sep in the chest. "He always had a daft side to him. I'm glad we've got him as a brother-in-law. He'll brighten up the family." She laughed. "What on earth made him think he'd look more handsome with that thing on his head?"

"It wasn't your idea of a joke?" Josey gave her brother a hard look.

"Honestly, Josey, I'd nothing to do with it."

"Just you make damn sure he gets rid of it." She grinned. "In fact, you ought to throw it in the *Kachelofen* in case he's tempted to wear it again."

"Don't worry, its days are numbered." Sep stood up as the cart drew to a halt outside the Adler. The rest of the Doppelgauer villagers, including a sour-looking Father Wagner, surrounded the square to catch a glimpse of the bride and groom and watch the bridal party throwing sweets to the children. Franz Zinnerman had arranged for a large, flower-bedecked marquee to be erected on the meadow behind the *Gasthaus.* Inside, the village band played a jaunty polka, and the first guests swayed to the music. Marie, looking radiant, and a beaming Wingnut welcomed everyone as they passed under a floral arch. Sep was the last to enter. Marie wrapped her arms around his neck and gave him a kiss on the cheek. "I'm so happy," she whispered in his ear. He then found himself engulfed in a bear hug from Wingnut. "Thanks, mate – for everything."

Sep felt himself welling up: whether it was because he was caught up with the emotion of the day, or relief that the day had gone so well, he couldn't tell. He felt as if a huge burden had been lifted from his shoulders. He could relax and enjoy the wine and dancing. The three of them turned to join the throng who were already attacking the buffet.

"I hope you've got rid of the wig. Josey has given me strict instructions to burn it."

Wingnut reached into his pocket. "It cost me a lot of money, you know."

Sep stopped and looked sternly at his friend. "Wingnut, I don't care if it costs you everything you own. Get rid of it."

Wingnut looked sadly at the hairy heap in his hand. "I suppose you're right." He glanced sideways at his bride. "You don't mind?"

Marie laughed and kissed him on the cheek. "You don't need it, sweetheart."

Wingnut grinned "Yeah – you're right." Without a thought, he cast the wig aside.

Alfie moved so fast, the object didn't even reach the ground. As far as his canine brain was concerned, a large rat had invaded the proceedings, and it didn't deserve to live. The snarling ball of fury snatched the intruder in mid-air. It stood no chance. The demented terrier shook, tore and shredded the wig into oblivion.

It was a wedding that nobody would forget.

Sep glanced around nervously. The nurses' quarters were strictly off-limits. He moved as quickly as possible up the last flight until he stood in front of her door. Uncertainty washed over him. Was this the right door? He mapped out the building in his mind. Top floor, windows overlooking the chapel. He was in the right place. He propped his crutches against the wall and retrieved the envelope from his mouth, silently laughing at himself. A missing limb made even the simplest task awkward. All he had to do was stuff the envelope under the door. Easier said than done. He levered himself down the wall until he was sitting beside the door. Fortunately, the gap was wide enough, and his latest chapters slipped through easily. Now he had to get back up. It took him several undignified attempts before he managed to stand. He must practise, he reminded himself.

At two-thirty Sep was in the passenger seat of the mail truck as it bounced and lurched towards St Étienne. The single windscreen wiper fought a losing battle against the squally rain and, no matter how he tried to adjust his seating position, Sep endured a constant drip of ice-cold water down the back of his neck. The vehicle reared up as it mounted the grass verge. The young driver desperately spun the steering wheel to avoid ending up in the ditch.

"Don't worry, sir, I'll get you there." He laughed.

He was as good as his word, and Sep was soon being dropped off outside the shop, with a promise of a pick-up an hour later.

The woman looked up as he entered. Her expression transformed in stages: from a grimace to surprise as Sep shut the door behind him against the swirling wind, and then to a sly smirk as she realised that, once inside the cosy refuge of the shop the young man would be in no hurry to leave. She moved across the shop as a spider might approach a trapped fly.

"Bonjour, monsieur."

Sep eyed her warily. He was sure she licked her lips as she offered her welcome. He was well aware of his vulnerability, and prepared himself for battle. "Bonjour, madame."

The crucifix was her opening gambit. It was placed in his eye-line, but behind the counter and beyond his reach.

"Perhaps some perfume for the mademoiselle?"

"I'm afraid I don't know the young lady well enough to know her tastes," Sep countered. "Such things are personal, are they not?" He smiled sweetly.

197

"Of course, but silk-embroidered handkerchiefs are always appreciated by young ladies." She blew the dust off the box before presenting it for his inspection.

"They are beautiful, but not practical. She has limited space."

"Some finest French bonbons?"

"Chocolate makes her feel unwell."

"Perhaps a bottle of vintage wine, and maybe some cheese to share?"

"She doesn't drink, and I don't like cheese."

Sep had to admire her tenacity as she worked her way around the shop.

No, he didn't want a statue of the Madonna and child; he was an atheist. The book was undoubtedly a classic and antique, but it was in French, and neither he or Mademoiselle could read the language. They had nowhere to hang the grimy oil painting, even if it was by Rocheau. No doubt someone else would appreciate it.

Sep noticed the woman's tone become harder as her patter failed to land any sales.

For over an hour Sep held out. He knew he had secured victory when the woman attempted to sell him an assortment of vegetables. It was her last throw of the dice.

Sep heard the truck horn like a punch-drunk boxer welcomes the sound of the bell – although it was the woman who looked defeated. He decided to offer her a consolation prize.

"Madam, I will take the silk-embroidered handkerchiefs and the bottle of wine – with the crucifix." He smiled at her. "If the price is right."

"Of course, monsieur. One hundred and fifty francs."

"One hundred francs," Sep said firmly.

She hauled up the white flag.

The clock on the wall crawled towards five o'clock. Since returning from his skirmish with the shopkeeper, he had watched the hands creep their way around the dial with the speed of a glacier. He spent the afternoon glancing anxiously out of the window for any sign of activity, and wrestling with his emotions. By six o'clock, he had to conclude that he was no further forward than when he started. The weather mirrored his mental turmoil. He had never experienced such conflicting passions. Periods of calm were abruptly shattered by gusts of uncertainty. A burst of bright sunshine was abruptly erased by clouds of despondency and despair. Once again he lay back on his bed, tried to calm his mind and be rational. He was attracted to her. That was a fact. No matter what happened, that would always be the case. But his feelings were much more than mere attraction. He loved everything about her: the way she smiled, her grace, her sense of humour, her confidence, her hazel eyes, her freckles, the smoothness of her skin, her fragrance, her seriousness, her …

He gave up. This was getting him nowhere. He was only making himself agitated – and for what? He groaned, got up, grabbed his crutches and swung himself towards the window.

Outside, sheets of rain whipped up by the squall lashed against the glass. He peered through the gloom but could see nothing. No trucks drawing up, or anyone waiting expectantly for their return. It was hardly surprising. Nobody in their right mind would choose to travel in such weather. The roads would be flooded, for a start. Maybe the ship hadn't sailed. Maybe it had. Maybe it had sunk. The image grabbed his mind. For a second, it wasn't a fantasy; it was reality. Ships did sink. Maybe the captain had set sail, eager to get his passengers back on dry land before Christmas. In a moment of madness, he'd navigated his ship into the maelstrom – and had caused a tragedy.

Sep cursed, then immediately looked guiltily towards the door, hoping no one had heard his outburst.

Yet again, he thought about the time they had spent together, trying to be realistic and rational. There was no doubt about it – they did seem to enjoy each other's company. There was a spark between them; they were good together. They were like brother and sister – or patient and nurse. His spirits fell. Patient and nurse! That summed it up. He had to face the facts. She was a professional. Her job was all about having empathy with her charges. Look at the way the men treated her. They all loved her. He was no different. And yet?

"Lieutenant Breitner?"

Sep spun round to see a young corporal standing at the door.

"Yes, that is me."

"Some mail for you, sir. Arrived yesterday." The NCO shrugged. "I'm afraid we're short-staffed. I'll pop it on the bed for you."

Sep stared at the package. He saw from the stamps that it was from Austria. Maybe it was an omen, calling him home. He eased himself across the room, sat down and ripped off the brown paper. He recognised his mother's handwriting.

My dearest, dearest son,
Words cannot begin to describe the joy and relief we fell when Josey gave us your letter. We are sorry to hear about your injury, but that does not matter. You are alive! We hope the English are treating you well. They may have been our enemy, but we know they are not a

cruel or uncaring people, if George is any example. Please come home as soon as you can. We miss you and want you back. This war has been a terrible mistake that has ruined our lives. We just want to get back together as a family and live a peaceful life.

We are all well. But I am sorry to have to tell you that we have had sorrow in our family, as well as joy. I hate to upset you at a time when you have your own worries, but you should know the sad news before you return. Opa passed away five weeks ago. He just fell asleep and never woke up. We count it as a blessing that he knew you had survived the war before he passed away. You were always the apple of his eye. You will be pleased to know that so many people attended his funeral, St Martin's was overflowing. We were overwhelmed and humbled.

Thankfully, we also have some good news. We thought about not telling you until you got home, but Josey insisted we tell you. You will see why from what follows.

Stephan has proposed to Josey. We had no idea of their feelings for one another. However, apparently, they have been quietly courting for some years. They wanted to ask for your pa's permission, but decided not to until the war was over. That shows their good sense, given the circumstances. We have given our consent, but Josey wants your blessing as well. She said you will know why. I hope you will agree, as Stephan is already like a son to us and he has suffered greatly in the war. Everyone deserves to be happy, and I'm sure you will not deny Josey and Stephan their future together.

We hope you might be able to return before Weinachts, but I understand that your recovery may take some time. Come home as soon as you can. Pa wants you to know that everything is well with the farm – but he looks forward to you taking the reins.

Please come home soon.

Your loving parents

P.S. Please write to Josey and Stephan with your decision.

Sep put the letter down and wept. Irrationally, he had imagined his grandfather to be indestructible and immortal. He couldn't imagine how the family was going to cope without him. Joseph Breitner was more than the head of the family. He was the foundation – and not just of the Breitner clan. The whole village would mourn its loss.

His father was now the patriarch. Sep tried to imagine how he felt. Probably alone, and worried about the weight of expectation on his shoulders.

He didn't need to read between the lines of his mother's comment that Stephan had suffered in the war. He knew exactly what his best friend had been through.

Sep felt as if a deep pit had opened up in front of him. He grieved for his family as well as for himself. His grief triggered the release of the black ball of terror, and he found himself despairing. His eye fell on the bell. Before he realised it, it was in his hand. A dose of morphine would be welcome right now. He stopped himself, appalled. What was he thinking of? He hadn't needed the painkiller for days and he now knew how to get rid of his demons. He grabbed his crutches and headed for the canteen at a brisk pace. He needed to get a grip.

He treated himself to afternoon tea, to give him time to pull himself together and cheer himself up. It worked. He ignored the fact that the bread was stale, and the cake was a pale imitation of the confection he remembered from Drössel's *Bäckerei*. Nevertheless, a pot of tea could always be relied upon to raise the spirits. A few familiar faces stopped by for a friendly chat, and the Christmas decorations reminded him that this was supposed to be the season of joy.

At twenty past eight the doors of the canteen swung open, and a group of wet, exhausted doctors and nurses entered, followed moments later by an equally bedraggled company of orderlies and drivers. They fell on the counter. In an instant, every sandwich, cake and confection had been cleared from the shelves.

Sep scanned each nurse. There was no sign of Susan. He began to grow anxious. Had she decided to stay in England? Twenty minutes after everyone else, she came in. Sep's heart soared, only for it to come crashing down in an instant. It was apparent that something was wrong. She marched across to join her colleagues. Angrily, she discarded her wet cloak and threw it over a chair. Her colleagues leant towards her and listened intently as she spoke. A nurse pushed a plate of food in front of her, while another poured her a cup of tea. Sep watched the group. Whatever had upset Susan had clearly bothered them all.

She was angry; there was little doubt about that. However, he saw that her fury was tempered by control. In spite of her obvious rage, she was on top of the situation, and seemed to be finding a way out of it. Her colleagues listened to her intently, nodding. She selected individuals and appeared to give them instructions, or offer a suggestion. She, in turn, listened patiently to their response. Slowly the dynamic of the group changed. The tension began to ease as her colleagues bought into whatever plan she had proposed. The anger was replaced by humour. Someone cracked a joke; another immediately added a rejoinder, and a wave of laughter filled the canteen.

Sep felt like an intruder. He desperately wanted to go to her – and do what? He wanted to be with her: to talk, to help ease whatever had upset her. But now was not the right time. It was evident that she didn't need his support. She exuded confidence and authority. Sep studied the group. There were a couple of doctors and a young Royal Engineer officer, along with an older officer who Sep assumed, from the pips on his shoulders, must be a captain. They all deferred to her, even though they were senior.

Sep leant back in his chair and watched her delegate. It was clear she could command. *Mein Gott, she could probably lead an entire army corps.* Sep found himself smiling at the thought. His smile faded as he realised what it meant for her. *So much ability, yet so little recognition, reward – or opportunity, for that matter. It was no surprise she was worried and frustrated about the future.* He imagined how she must feel. *Angry, for sure – maybe even bitter. And what could he offer her? Kinder, Küche, Kirche. What a pathetic prospect.*

She was back, and safe. For now, that was all that mattered. Whatever the crisis she was busy resolving, he would find out about in due course if she was minded to tell him. His best move would be to make a quiet, discreet exit. He reached for his crutches, got to his feet and glanced towards her. She was looking straight at him.

She muttered something to her colleagues. The captain sitting next to her said something and patted her shoulder as she got up. Sep caught a few congratulatory words.

She picked up her cloak and walked across the canteen towards him. She looked dishevelled and exhausted.

"I'm glad you're back," he said.

She nodded and looked sideways at the floor, as if avoiding his gaze. "It's been a rough trip."

"I gathered something was up when you walked in."

"That obvious, eh?"

He nodded. "Looks like you've sorted it, though."

She looked up.

Sep was shocked. He realised she was only just holding herself together. She was close to tears and still obviously upset. Instinctively, he reached out and caressed her shoulder. "Hey, what's happened?"

"I can't tell you right now, Sep. I'm dog-tired. I've had a bloody awful trip back. I just want to go to bed. I'm sorry. I'll try and see you tomorrow." She squeezed his hand, turned and left.

Sep watched her go. He glanced over at the table where her colleagues still sat. They too watched her leave, concern for her etched on their faces.

Sep hardly slept that night. He gave up trying to make sense of the confusion in his head. She was back. They would talk. He also felt a sliver of shame. Although he was dealing much better with his bouts of depression, he was still prone to self-pity. He vowed to deal with his bouts of terror and depression, using Susan as an example. If she could rise above her setbacks and inspire others around her at the same time, then he was damn sure he could.

At two o'clock in the morning, he wrote a long, positive letter to his parents. At ten past three, he wrote to Josey and Stephan. His smile broadened as he imagined them together. He chuckled to himself. How had they managed to keep their courtship so secret? At quarter to four, he sealed both envelopes, lay on his bed and fell into a deep sleep.

"Mornin', sir."

Sep opened one eye and regarded Corporal MacPherson, who was standing over him, a razor in his right hand and a shaving bowl in his left. "Good morning, Sandy. And how's the weather?"

Sandy gave him with an appraising look. "Ye ken ye're gettin' more British by the day?"

Sep grinned. "Why? Because I'm asking about the weather?"

"Aye, that, an' ye're partial to the full Scottish." He handed over the shaving equipment. "Ye need to look yer best for the Christmas party."

"You'll miss all the fun."

"Why's that?"

"Aren't you heading back to Blighty for Christmas?"

"Nae, sir. Ah'm stopping here."

Sep looked surprised. "I thought you and Nurse Mandy were heading back?"

"She is, right enough. But no' me." Sandy laughed.

"What will you do now the war's over?"

"Ask Nurse Mandy to wed me – an' head for Australia, or New Zealand, or Canada. Wherever she wants tae go."

Sep stopped shaving and stared in surprise at the orderly. "Have you asked her?"

"No' yet. Ah'll wait until she's about tae leave." He grinned. "It's ma big surprise, ye ken. It'll give her summat tae think about over the festive season." He winked. "Ye have tae take yer chances while they're there. You dinnae get a second chance." He looked

203

long and hard at Sep. "An' tae answer yer original question, it's stopped stoating an' baffin'. It's a bonnie day." He handed Sep a towel. "Aye, it's the sort o' day tae take a lassie for a turn around the park, or maybe to a wee café…" He raised his eyebrows and looked meaningfully at Sep.

Sep stared back until the penny dropped. "I'd need transport."

"It's arranged. Half past twelve."

"I've not asked her."

"Well, ye'd better get yer skates on, cos if ye're nae asking her, there's plenty who will."

"She'll be working."

"It's her day off."

Thirty minutes later Sep stood at the foot of the staircase of the nurses' quarters and stared up. *Why did she have to live on the top floor?* he thought. He started his ascent. His heart thumped, and it wasn't because of the effort of climbing. He stopped on the second landing to catch his breath. It occurred to him that he'd never actually asked a girl on a date. In Austria, it was only when a couple had decided to become serious that the boy asked the girl to step out with him – and even then, he had to get permission from the girl's father. Prior to that, every contact had to be at communal festivities, when everyone mixed and danced with everyone else. The English way seemed to be much more daunting. *What if she refuses? Well, at least I'll know where I stand.* He stopped. *She might be affronted – or embarrassed.* But it was too late for second thoughts. He raised his hand, feeling like a nervous schoolboy. His throat went dry, and he couldn't remember the words he had been practising all morning.

He knocked.

"Who is it?"

"Sep."

There was a thump.

She opened the door and looked at him in astonishment. "What are you doing here? It's supposed to be off-limits." She glanced behind him to check they were alone.

"I know – but I want to ask you something."

"What?"

"I'd like to take you to St Étienne for lunch."

"What time?"

"Half past twelve."

"I'd love to."

"What?"

"I said, I'd love to."

"Right."

She beamed at him. "See you at half past twelve. Now go, before I call the guards." She closed the door.

Sep stood for several seconds contemplating the door. *I much prefer the English way,* he thought.

Out of uniform, she looked even more alluring. It was as if the hard edges of her profession had been blunted. She seemed softer, more graceful and feminine. Sep studied her as she squinted at the menu, her head bent, her right hand playing absently with her earring.

"You forgot your glasses?"

She half-smiled. "I didn't, actually." She retrieved her handbag and extracted her spectacles. "I try to get by without them."

He gave her a 'that's not a very sensible approach' look.

She put them on.

"They suit you. They make you look studious."

"Or prissy – like an old maid." She grinned at him and picked up the menu.

Sep watched her in silence. She had pulled back her hair so it framed her face. Her white brocade blouse was plain with an understated lace front and puffed sleeves. Her ankle-length skirt was made from a heavy material he assumed was linen or cotton. There was a subtle pattern woven into it. She looked elegant and sophisticated in a subdued way. Apart from small silver earrings, her only other adornments were a plain gold signet ring on her right hand and a silver watch on her left wrist. Sep was relieved he couldn't see any sign of a necklace. The crucifix would not have any competition, and he hoped it would match her taste and style.

"Have you decided?"

"I'll have the bisque and the duck," she said firmly.

"And some wine?"

She sat back, looking relaxed. "I'm not working." She took her glasses off and replaced them in her bag.

"You're looking a lot better than you did yesterday evening," Sep said after he'd placed their order.

"Yesterday was the day from hell. In fact, the whole trip back was a nightmare." She grimaced. "That's what you get when a complete idiot is put in charge of the hospital."

"So, what happened?"

She blew out slowly. "To be fair, I was already tired, having travelled from Skipton. I joined the team at Dover. That's when I heard about Doctor Forsythe – which upset me a great deal. Even worse, I found out that Major Peters is his replacement."

Sep frowned. The name was familiar. He didn't interrupt her, however.

"We found out that Major Peters' first decision is to send the Starboard crew back to Blighty – permanently!"

Sep looked confused. "I don't understand."

"We have two teams of nurses, orderlies, drivers and attached doctors. A Port team and a Starboard team. Each is responsible for organising the repatriation of patients back to England. Port team does one month, the Starboard does the next month and so on. Repatriation is a complex operation, involving transport, shipping, liaison with hospitals and rehabilitation and specialist centres across the UK. Plus, everyone needs to be looked after. We need supplies of food, water, petrol for the vehicles. Under Doctor Forsythe, we've developed the system over a long period of time, and it works like clockwork. You take one team out without any notice, and the burden falls straight on to the remaining team."

"Who are already exhausted, and looking forward to some rest and recuperation."

"Exactly. What's worse, the weather at Dover was appalling delaying our departure. When we put to sea, we were held for twelve hours outside Boulogne." The more she told him, the more animated she became. She threw out her hands. "And when we do finally get back, Major Peters thinks that's a good time to tell – or rather, order – me and the rest of the team to immediately prepare for the next batch of repatriation. The fact that it's Christmas and New Year, and everything is closing down and everyone going home, seems to have escaped him."

Sep was appalled. "You have to go back?"

"Yes. On the twenty-seventh. Sorry, I don't want to spoil our lunch by taking out my annoyance on you."

He laughed. "I'm glad you did. I hated seeing you so upset last night. I wanted to support you – but couldn't."

She looked at him intently, as if trying to read his face.

Her look discomforted him. He felt he might have said something wrong. "What?"

She smiled and gently shook her head. "Don't worry. Your story cheered me up this morning." She grinned at him. "I read it in bed. Your sister sounds like a bundle of fun."

"She's a handful all right. Or rather, she was a handful. She's slowed down a bit now she's grown up. We get on well."

"Kindred spirits, eh?"

He chuckled. "Not really. She's determined, headstrong, and can be a bit stubborn..." He stopped mid-sentence and frowned at

Susan who had closed her eyes and was shaking her head sadly. "What?"

She gave him an exasperated look. "Honestly, Sep."

The waiter arrived and held out the wine bottle for Sep's inspection. He glanced at her. "I have no idea about French wine. Do you know whether this is a good or a bad choice?"

She laughed. "That's what I like about you, Sep. You're so open. If you were English, you would study that bottle carefully, probably purse your lips and agree that it is acceptable, even though you hadn't a clue if it was good, bad or indifferent."

"In that case, let's take a chance." Sep looked at the waiter. "If it's bad, we'll let you know."

"Of course, monsieur." He poured the wine.

Sep waited until the waiter had withdrawn before raising his glass. "I want to propose a toast."

"OK – to what?"

"To you."

"For what?"

Sep looked serious. "I mean this, Susan. You have been wonderful to me. You've looked after me, you've been patient, you're professional." He looked deeply into her warm hazel eyes. "You're extraordinary, Susan. A special person."

"Sep, stop it!" She blushed.

"Why? I mean it."

She bowed her head, ran her fingers across her forehead and looked flustered. "You don't really know me, Sep."

"I know, but I would like to get to know you better." He took a sip from his glass and tried to appear relaxed, although he felt uncertain and nervous. "That is, if it doesn't make you feel uncomfortable."

She looked at him curiously. "Why would it make me feel uncomfortable?"

Despite his attempt to stay sanguine, he was conscious he'd begun to sweat. He felt that he was treading on eggshells in his attempt to fumble his way into a deeper relationship with her. One false move, inappropriate question, or an intrusion too far would throw up a barrier. He decided to take the plunge.

"I suppose I mean I wouldn't want to overstep the mark, or intrude into your privacy, or ask inappropriate questions." He took a quick sip of wine and pretended to study the wine bottle label to mask his disquiet.

She was already ahead of him. She grinned. "Is this your way of asking me if I am in a relationship?"

Sep knew his embarrassment must be obvious, not only to her, but to everyone in the café. "Um … well … I…" He glanced up to find her grinning at him, her eyebrows arched.

"Well?"

He took a deep breath and decided to come clean. "Well, yes, if I'm being honest."

If he thought his candour would let him off the hook, he was mistaken.

"And why would you think I might be in a relationship?"

"Oh come on, Susan. You are a highly attractive, intelligent, professional woman. It's clear that your colleagues, and the patients you look after, love and respect you. You have a whole army of admirers." He took another hasty sip of wine. "I couldn't help notice you were escorted by a young cavalry officer, for example."

She frowned before realising who Sep was referring to. "Oh, the dashing Captain Beverley."

"I don't know his name."

"Captain Beverley, Military Cross and bar, hero of the second battle of the Somme. Field-promoted twice."

"Really?" Sep's question sounded flat.

She nodded. "Yes, really. He's single, extremely wealthy, or at least his family are. Obviously very brave. He went to Harrow – a well-known public school in England."

"Is that so?"

She nodded, trying to stifle the grin that continued to play around her lips. "He lives not far from Skipton. He's known my family – and me – most of my life."

"Has he?"

She took a long sip from her glass, her eyes sparkling as she watched him over the rim. "Yes. He's quite a catch."

"Well, that's what I mean, Susan. I wouldn't want to upset such a relationship."

"But my sister isn't here to be upset."

Sep looked at her blankly.

She burst out laughing and reached out for his hand. "I'm teasing you, Sep. Captain Beverley is hoping to get engaged to my older sister. He travelled home with me. He's a close family friend."

Sep immediately felt relieved – and foolish. "Well, you get my point."

"I could ask you the same question." She gave him an intense look, which he found enchanting.

"No, I don't have any kind of relationship with Captain Beverley either."

Their laughter filled the café, until they realised they were drawing attention to themselves. Sep gazed out of the window, while Susan found an urgent need to adjust her hair.

Once they had regained their composure, she glanced sideways at him and grinned. "So, are you?" she said quietly.

He shook his head.

"Well, in that case, we can relax and get to know one another."

The gate had been opened. For the next three hours they talked. Their conversation was unhurried and unforced. One topic flowed easily into the next. They smiled, joked, teased each other, matched each other's wit, shared confidences and inner feelings. Mid-way through the conversation, Sep felt he was talking to someone he'd known all his life.

It was during a brief lull in their conversation that they noticed the surrounding silence. All the other patrons had left. Susan looked at her watch and looked aghast. "Do you know what time it is? Nearly four o'clock."

A feeling of horror seized Sep. Corporal McPherson had sorted out the transport to the café, but Sep hadn't considered how they would make the return trip. There was nothing for it; they would have to walk. He looked at Susan in dismay. "Susan, I am terribly sorry…"

"You forgot to arrange the return trip." She completed his sentence. "Fortunately, Sandy can be relied on." She swept her cloak around her shoulders before helping him find his crutches. "How's that for role reversal? Come on, Sandy is waiting."

Outside, Sandy sat in the driver's seat of the commandeered staff car, reading a newspaper and smoking a cigarette. He leapt out and opened the rear doors for them.

"Sandy, I owe you for this," Sep said. "How did you get hold of the car?"

"Ye dinnae want tae ask, sir," he replied as he closed the door.

Susan grabbed Sep's arm as the car lurched around the square and headed back. Sep wanted to remember everything about the journey: the closeness and warmth of her body as she nestled into him, the proximity of her, the feel of her hand in his, the rustle of her dress as she crossed her legs, the faint tickle of her hair on his cheek, the sound of her breathing. He was disappointed that the journey was so short – although he was aware that Corporal McPherson appeared to be driving unusually slowly.

The orderly dropped them off outside the nurses' quarters. Despite their afternoon of cosiness and intimacy, they found themselves standing in awkward silence, each wondering how to say goodbye. Emboldened by the wine, Sep decided he ought to take the initiative.

"Susan, thank you for coming. I've loved every minute." He intended to give her a kiss on the cheek. Any further demonstration of his affection might have crossed a threshold. It was, after all, their first date. Even his modest intention was thwarted, however, as he realised that to offer such an embrace would involve a lot of awkward repositioning of his crutches.

She sensed his predicament and came to his rescue. "Sep, I've had a wonderful time." She reached up towards him.

They turned simultaneously to kiss each other on the cheek. As they did, their lips briefly touched.

For Sep, the effect was electric.

It seemed to be the same for her. They held each other for longer than decorum allowed.

"Perhaps I could ask you out again?" He tried to keep his voice light, but the tension in his throat made the question come out in a squeak. He winced, embarrassed.

She nodded. "I'd love that. Maybe we might do something over Christmas?" She suddenly put her hand to her mouth. "Oh – I forgot! I have something for you from England. Two things, actually."

"And I have something for you." He grinned. "In Austria, we give gifts on Christmas Eve. Shall we do it then? It's only two days to wait."

He watched her climb the stairs. At the second landing, she stopped and waved. "I'll read the rest of your chapters tonight."

He followed her with his eyes until she reached the top, then turned to leave. As he did so, he heard a door open on the top floor, and the excited voice of Nurse Mandy drift towards him.

"Well, how did it go?"

He didn't catch Susan's reply.

The contrast between the highs and lows of life intrigued Sep for most of the following day. He couldn't get to grips with the euphoria he'd felt since yesterday afternoon and his previous moments when the swamp of suffocating despair had threatened to swallowed him up. He didn't even try to get her out of his mind. His instinct was to try and find her, simply to discover if she felt the same. Maybe they had got carried away with the moment? They had, after all, consumed a bottle of wine, plus a port for her and a large brandy for him. Maybe she had come to regret their intimacy. Then he dismissed his pessimism. Their cuddling in the car, their embrace – that kiss. They were all real enough.

Nurse Mandy eradicated his doubts. She entered the room dressed in her nurse's cape, ready for her trip back to England.

"You're looking on top of the world this morning," she said in a knowing voice.

"And you're looking radiant yourself, Nurse Mandy."

She laughed, her cheeks looking even more rosy than usual.

Sep assumed she had received Corporal McPherson's proposal, but he thought it prudent not to enquire. "When are you off?"

"In the next hour. We're just waiting for transport. Apparently, Major Peters' staff car has broken down." She looked at him, a mischievous glint in her eye. "If it's not fixed in the next hour, we'll either have to leave without him or he's going to have to slum it in a truck."

"He's going home for Christmas?"

"Oh, you can bet he's going home. He makes sure he doesn't miss out on anything – even if it means someone else has to pay, or suffer."

Sep changed the subject. "I have a small gift for you, Nurse Mandy." He levered himself up on his crutches and swung towards his bedside cabinet. "I understand a few days back some bone-headed lieutenant caused you a lot of trouble and inconvenience. In fact, I was informed that he reduced you to tears of rage."

Mandy's eyes widened. "Whoever told you such nonsense?"

Sep held his free hand up. "That is irrelevant, Mandy. The point is the lieutenant was out of order, is thoroughly ashamed of himself, and wants to make up for his behaviour." He reached in the drawer and retrieved the box of silk handkerchiefs, which he'd carefully wrapped in tissue paper. He turned serious. "I would also like to tell you how much I appreciate everything you have done for me. I can't thank you enough." He presented her with the small package. "Happy Christmas."

She surprised Sep by bursting into tears, throwing her arms around his neck and planting a kiss on his cheek. "I can't thank you enough either, Sep. You're a fighter, a bloody stubborn fighter, and I love you to bits."

Before Sep could recover, the sound of a truck horn drifted in through the window.

"Oh – I have to go. That's our assembly call." She kissed him again. "Have a happy Christmas, Sep – I'm sure the pair of you will. I'll see you in the new year."

And then she was gone.

It was evident from the organised chaos in the canteen that preparations for the Christmas party had been under way for some time. The main ward had been cleared of beds and had reverted to its original use as a ballroom. A small team of orderlies, nurses and able-bodied patients arranged trestle tables and chairs around the edge of the dance floor, laid tablecloths, set out cutlery, hung more decorations and made paper hats. At one end of the cavernous room, a space was prepared for the band; while at the other, an area was cleared for those who were still bedridden. Nobody was going to be left out of the last Christmas party of the British Army's 13th General Field Hospital.

In the canteen, cooks bustled around, banging pans on stoves, chopping, shredding, crushing, mixing and stirring ingredients while shouting instructions and exchanging banter.

The air was drenched with the smell of roast chicken and stuffing – mixed with the sweet bouquet of Christmas pudding.

Sep sat at a large trestle table with half a dozen other lads. He'd volunteered to top and tail what seemed like a never-ending pile of runner beans.

"How many are we supposed to be catering for?"

Curly paused in his task of dropping nettles and lentils into a large iron cauldron. "With the last batch heading for Blighty, I reckon around four hundred of us are left, maybe four hundred and fifty all told, if you include the doctors, nurses and orderlies." He waved his wooden spoon. "Oh, and of course we'll be feeding the band."

"We should feed the band first. Make sure they're up for a good time," Bert said sagely. "It's always a good idea to look after the entertainment – it's the key for a good party and a singsong."

Curly looked appalled. "You're not going to *sing*, are you?"

"The members of the Shipley Working Men's Club would be happy to testify to my singing prowess, I'll have you know." Curly winked at Sep. "Once I've had a few bevvies to get me in the mood, you can expect to hear my rich baritone reverberating off the rafters."

"In tune? Or is that too much to hope for?"

"Bert, I shall personally serenade you. You will think a nightingale has lost its way."

"A crow, more like."

"What've we got to wet our whistles?" Steve craned around, looking for any evidence of beer and wine.

"There'll be plenty of booze, lad. Don't you worry. Since when has Sandy McPherson ever let us down?" Bert said. "Besides I've got a bottle of whisky we can crack open."

By six o'clock the ballroom was filled with the buzz of chatter, the clink of glasses and the occasional sound of raised voices and ribald laughter as a joke was cracked or anecdotes shared. A haze of tobacco smoke filled the air. A lone piper heralded the procession of cooks bearing steaming cauldrons of nettle and lentil soup. They positioned themselves at the head of each trestle table and waited until the skirl of the pipes had died away and the room fell silent. The hospital chaplain walked to the centre of the dance floor. He beamed at everyone.

"Ladies and gentlemen, I shall be brief."

A cheer went up.

"Before we say grace, I have two things to say." His eyes swept around the room. "First, even when we are celebrating this day, let us have in our hearts our fallen comrades. May they all rest in peace."

There was a low rumble of muttered amens.

"Second, on behalf of us all, and before you get too inebriated, please show your appreciation for the nurses, doctors, orderlies, drivers, cooks and the other staff who have worked hard to prepare this Christmas party – and who have also looked after you."

A great roar of applause echoed around the hall. The chaplain waited patiently.

"Finally, I will be conducting a short service to celebrate the coming of our Lord Jesus Christ in the chapel. Service starts at eleven thirty. I hope many of you will attend. All faiths and creeds are more than welcome."

Sep glanced around after the last amen. The cooks started to ladle out soup. But where was Nurse Jones? He soon spotted her fussing around one of the bedridden patients. Once again she was in the thick of things, organising, encouraging, directing. She had time for everyone. He watched her move along the trestle tables, checking everything was in order, stopping for a chat, waving a light-hearted finger at someone's banter, laughing at another's joke.

The band struck up with some popular tunes. Quickly the revellers picked up the song. The band knew what they were doing. Familiar songs gradually made way for the real favourites. Before long, the first couples were on the dance floor. Sep was not surprised to see Susan among the first to be whirled around. With one nurse for every twenty able-bodied soldiers, every woman had a small queue of hopeful partners as each dance finished. For them it would be a long, exhausting night.

Sep felt a pang of regret. He cursed his missing limb. How he would love to take Susan in his arms and feel her body snug against his as they swayed and pirouetted. His disappointment increased as he watched her. She had a sense of rhythm and timing that spoke of a love of dance. He refilled his glass before cautioning himself not to over-indulge.

The band moved on. *'Tiger Rag'*, *'Rock-a-Bye Your Baby With a Dixie Melody'*, followed by *'Hail, Hail, the Gang's All Here'* had everyone roaring out the familiar choruses. Sep had no idea of the words, but thumped the table with the best of them. Soon he, Curly, Bert and Steve had linked up and rolled in unison to 'Goodbye' and the one song that Sep did know the words of, *'It's a Long, Long Way to Tipperary'*.

At the end of the chorus the four of them collapsed, laughing and slapping each other on the back.

"A toast, lads," Curly slurred. "Bert, where's that bottle of whisky you said you had?"

Bert bent down and presented the bottle as if revealing a holy icon. "It's a malt, lads. I hope you appreciate the sacrifice I'm making."

"It's appreciated all right – now drop a dram into here," Curly said, thrusting forward his glass. "Come on, lads. Not you, Steve, you're far too young."

"What?" Steve looked outraged. "I'd drink an old codger like you under the table any time."

Bert ignored the instruction, and the four of them held up their glasses.

Curly adopted the exaggerated seriousness of a man on the cusp of inebriation. "To us, lads. I hope good fortune lies in front of us all. Cheers."

They all downed the glass in one, apart from Sep.

"You're supposed to drink it, Sep, not watch it ferment," Curly said.

"It's a malt, Curly. It's the king of whiskies. It's to be savoured."

Curly considered the argument before nodding in agreement. "Well said, that man." He thrust his glass in front of Bert. "Refill us, Bert, if you may. I need to savour this one."

Sep glanced across the dance floor. Susan was watching him. Everything else ceased to exist. They held each other's gaze. She lowered her head and a coquettish half-smile played across her lips. He smiled back at her, transfixed. Slowly he raised his glass. She did the same. The moment was fleeting, but would forever be etched into Sep's memory. A soldier broke into their intimacy by asking Susan for a dance. Once again she was off, being swept around the floor. Sep watched them, his heartache replaced by delight as he saw the fun she was having. They would meet later. She had promised, after all.

She was true to her word. She arrived looking flushed, and still pursued by men eager to book a turn round the dance floor with her. She shooed them away good-naturedly. She'd danced all evening, she said. She needed a rest.

"I need to break up your party, I'm afraid," she said to the group, taking Sep's arm and helping him to his feet.

"Where are we heading?" Sep said

She led him back towards his ward, turning and walking backwards in front of him. She seemed excited. Sep assumed she was still in high spirits from all the dancing she had been doing.

"I told you I had something from England for you." Her eyes gleamed. "I wasn't going to give it to you until tomorrow, but I can't wait."

They entered his room. On the bed was a large package wrapped in brown paper.

"It's not really a present. I've got something else for you which is more personal – you know, from me to you. You can have that tomorrow." She looked flustered. "But I wanted you to have this as soon as possible." She gestured towards the parcel.

Sep sat on the bed. She stood in front of him, her hands clasped. "Don't rip the paper – there's a shortage." She looked embarrassed. "Sorry."

Sep laughed. "Susan, relax. You're like a chicken with fleas. Whatever it is, I'm sure I'm going to like it."

He deliberately unwrapped the parcel with exaggerated care and slowness.

"Oh, for goodness' sake, Sep." She hit him playfully on the head.

Sep peeled away the last of the paper and stared at the object. He found himself almost moved to tears.

She sat next to him and peered anxiously into his face. "What do you think? I haven't offended you, have I?"

Sep put his arm around her. "Susan, you are the most kind and considerate person I have ever known." He kissed her on the cheek.

"I wanted to get – you know, a proper one, but they're too difficult to get hold of."

"Susan, I don't care. This is … I don't know what to say." He picked up the prosthetic leg. He laughed. "It's got to be the strangest present I've ever had." He glanced at her. "Can I try it on?"

"I knew you were going to say that." She laughed. "No, not just now. It needs a lot of adjusting, and let me warn you right now, it will be extremely painful when you first try and stand on it." She

215

beamed at him. "Maybe tomorrow. I'll see if the fitter can spare you an hour or so, assuming he's sober."

"Tomorrow is Christmas Day."

"The hospital still keeps working – although I'm not, thankfully." She bent down and rubbed her ankles. "I'm exhausted, and these uniforms are not designed for dancing."

A shock of panic swept through him. "You're not going to your room, are you? I've hardly seen you all evening."

"Well, no." She turned bashful. "I thought maybe we could go to the church service. I know neither of us are religious, but I was hoping we might find a way to have some time together."

Sep breathed a sigh of relief. "That would be perfect. But I'd like to come back here afterwards. I have a present for you. It's traditional in Austria that we give gifts on Christmas Eve."

She looked sideways at him and nudged him in the ribs. "It *is* Christmas Eve."

He gave her a long, grave look. "Have you been good?"

She nodded her head eagerly.

"Well, since you have given me a wooden leg, I suppose I might be persuaded." He opened the bedside cabinet and retrieved the small tissue-wrapped package. A large label was attached to it. He considered what to say. He had to keep himself in check. What he wanted to say was 'I love you, Susan Jones', but that might seem too forward, and he didn't want to risk frightening her off by appearing over-eager or pushy. On the other hand, he was terrified of coming across as too frivolous. He'd spent an hour worrying about what to write on the label. He knew how he felt. It was simple. He loved Susan Jones.

She interrupted his thoughts. "It's awkward, isn't it?" she said gently.

He glanced at her in surprise. "What?"

"Putting into words what you really feel."

His head swam. "You too?"

She nodded and looked at him tenderly. "It's obvious we have feelings for one another."

"I never knew – never dared to hope."

She laughed. "I know. It's all too quick. It's like I'm on an express train." She looked at him steadily. "So, what *do* you feel?"

Suddenly, it felt perfectly natural to express his true feelings. "I'm falling in love with you." They were speaking in hushed tones. It felt as though they were in a secret, private refuge. His room felt like a sanctuary for them. He was only vaguely aware of the distant sounds of the party.

"How about you?"

"The same." She lowered her eyes. "It's as if I'm possessed. It's hard to describe." She swept a nervous hand across her forehead.

"We hardly know each other."

"I know. It's madness."

They sat for several seconds drinking each other in, scarcely believing what had passed between them. Sep had never felt so certain, yet so confused, at the same time. His world had shrunk to his room and the woman sitting beside him. He had a fixed grin on his face, but he was incapable of doing anything about it. He doubted he would ever feel happier.

Susan laughed. "It's great, isn't it?" She wiped a tear from her eye. "So what did you write?" She nodded towards the small package that he still held.

He grinned ruefully. "It seems so inadequate now. It took me over an hour to write, as well." He looked embarrassed. "I wanted to get it just right."

He handed the gift over.

She read the label in silence.

To my dearest Susan, Neither words, nor this gift, can begin to express the way I feel about you. You have more than my gratitude; you have my heart and soul. My most fervent wish is for your happiness, this festive season and forever.

With all my love, Sep

She was overcome. "Oh, Sep." She wiped away another tear and peeled back the tissue paper. Her eyes widened as she extracted the crucifix. "Sep, it's beautiful. It looks antique." She held it out. "Help me put it on." She lowered her head and lifted her hair out of the way.

He looped the delicate chain around her neck and did up the clasp.

"It doesn't go with this uniform." She undid the top buttons of her starched nurse's blouse and the crucifix nestled into her open neckline. She looked at him. Their faces were inches apart.

He studied every detail and drank in the new small discoveries. The tiny laughter lines at the corner of her eyes, the smoothness of her skin, the delightful dusting of freckles across her nose, the moist enticement of her lips. He was completely smitten.

Their eyes locked. Neither said a word. He felt her breath as slowly they leant towards each other. There was no need for haste. They both knew it was going to happen, and they revelled in the exquisite agony of anticipation. Their first contact was feather-light.

Sep felt a wave of confused and unfamiliar emotions wash through him. In an instant, years of pent up tension, suppressed horrors and denial seemed to evaporate. He had forgotten the joy of human touch and the pleasure of holding a girl in his arms.

Their tentative, uncertain contact began to disintegrate as they responded to each gentle caress. He felt her relax as if for her there was also some kind of liberation. Maybe it was the effect of the glasses of wine but her guard came down. Gone were the professional boundaries, to be replaced by a woman hungry for love and affection. She pressed herself against him. Their kisses became more urgent as their passion increased. The thrill of their disclosure threatened to consume them

"Sep, this is madness," she gasped, but her lips on his betrayed her. She pressed herself against his chest, her fingers slipping inside his shirt.

Time seemed to stand still as they teetered on the brink of abandon. They knew that somehow, they needed to wrest back control.

"We need to stop," she pleaded, her voice thick with passion.

"I know." Sep buried his face in her hair. "I know." He gritted his teeth and squeezed his eyes shut, fighting for control. In his mind, he had them undressed and wild in their craving for one another. She closed her eyes and pressed her forehead against his. He felt the rise and fall of her chest. Her rapid breathing revealed her hunger for him.

Slowly they forced themselves to stop. They lay alongside each other, aching with desire. For a long time they were content to gaze into each other's eyes.

He stroked back the strands of her hair, still damp from her passion. "I am desperate to make love with you," Sep whispered.

She giggled. "We will – one day." She leant forward and kissed him softly on the tip of his nose. "It'll be worth the wait." She giggled again. "Imagine if we had – and got caught."

He glanced towards the door. "It would look pretty bad if we got caught now."

She sighed. "You're right." She sat up and smoothed her crumpled uniform and did up her blouse buttons.

He lay and watched her, marvelling at her beauty. A host of dark thoughts tumbled into his mind. *She still doesn't know I was a sniper. How will she react? And I haven't told her about my mother's letter. Sooner or later I'll be discharged – and then what?*

"Susan, we need to have a serious chat."

She went still. "I know, Sep, but not tonight. Let's not spoil the moment." She glanced at him. "Maybe tomorrow? If we're going to get to the chapel we need to get going."

Time and time again Sep replayed the day in his imagination, as he lay in bed the following morning. The first touch of their lips. That had to be the most intense, the most uplifting, the most sublime moment of his life. He quietly laughed to himself as he recalled his euphoria. Or maybe the moment she revealed her true feelings? Or the hidden promise as he had run his hands over her body. The touch of her fingers as they crept inside his shirt. Their lingering kiss at the foot of the stairs to her room. Their secret interlocking of hands during the chapel service, or their shared look of affection across the dance floor. He shook his head. He was in danger of being submerged in thoughts of her. He wondered what she was doing now. *Maybe lying in bed, or soaking in a warm bath thinking similar thoughts.* The image of her naked in the bath swam into his imagination. *Oh, how he longed to make love to her.* He laughed out loud. He was like a besotted schoolboy.

This would never do. They had to talk. He sat up and swung his body to the edge of the bed, put his hands on his thighs, bowed his head and forced his attention onto the practical problems. How on earth were they going to develop their relationship? He glanced at the clock. It was a stark reminder that time was against them.

He considered his condition. *His physical wounds were almost all healed. He managed the stairs, and it would probably take little more than two weeks, maybe less, before he could walk to the village and back.* He eyed the prosthetic leg propped against the bedside chair. *How long would it take for him to learn to walk without crutches? He had no idea. And as for his mental condition? Well, his bouts of despair were less frequent, less intense, and he was dealing with them better.*

His thoughts were interrupted by Corporal McPherson bowling into the room.

"Morning, sir. An' a very happy Christmas tae ye." He shook Sep warmly by the hand. "Ah've a head like a jack-hammer's inside it."

Sep grinned. "It was a good night."

"Och aye. T'was grand crack." He eyed Sep. "An' how did ye get on with the lassie?"

Sep didn't answer. His grin told the orderly all he needed to know.

The corporal picked up the prosthetic. "This'll bring ye back tae life."

219

"It needs to be fitted and adjusted according to Sus— Nurse Jones."

"Aye. There's a skill tae it." He clapped a friendly hand on Sep's shoulder. "Ye'll be the master o' it in a jiffy."

Sep hoisted himself up and retrieved the bottle of wine from the bedside cabinet. "I've got you a present, Sandy."

"Och, ye shouldnae, sir."

"Yes, I should. You've been a great friend to me, as well as a fantastic support." He held the bottle out. "I hope it's a good vintage. I've no way of knowing."

"Ah'll soon let you know, sir." He became business-like. "Now, if ye're going tae get the leg fitted, ye need to be dressed proper."

"Will the fitter be working today?"

"Aye. It may be Christmas, but there's nae much tae do – so most of us keep working. Get dressed an Ah'll take ye tae his workshop straight after breakfast."

Slowly Sep released his weight. He winced as the raw nerve ends of his amputation protested at the unfamiliar pressure. Sep tried to ignore the pain. He felt his right arm go into spasm.

"Don't fight it, man. Your stump is going to have to get used to the idea. Go on, man, keep going. You're doing well."

Sep suddenly realised that his arms no longer supported him. He was standing on his own two feet! He felt euphoric, despite the excruciating pain.

"Hold yourself there. Don't try to move." The fitter darted around and examined Sep from every angle. "That's perfect," he said after a while. "Your gait is fine and you've got a good stance. How do you feel about trying a few steps?"

Sep nodded eagerly. For the next twenty minutes, he tripped, stumbled, crashed and lurched between the two parallel bars. By the end, he was drenched in sweat and almost crying in agony. Eventually, exhaustion forced him to stop.

The fitter sat at his desk and jotted down some notes. "You've done well, lad. Eight weeks since your operation! Normally we don't expect patients with your condition to start with a prosthetic much before twelve weeks. I'll give you an exercise regime to follow. You need to build up muscle tone in your stump," he said as he scribbled. "The nerve ends will get used to the idea soon enough, and the pain will reduce." He glanced across at Sep. "You follow my instructions to the letter, and you'll be walking just fine in a month or so. The trick is little and often. Thirty minutes for the first day, then forty minutes second day, and so on. Build yourself up slowly. Do you understand, Lieutenant?"

"Of course."

The fitter looked sceptical. "Aye, I hope you do. I've heard you've a tendency to try to run before you can walk." He flicked his pen towards a door. "There's a shower in there, if you want to use it. We need to see how you look in your uniform. You might need to get your trousers adjusted."

Sep emerged from the shower feeling mentally and physically refreshed. His spirits rose further as he struggled into his tunic and stood in front of the mirror. Bracing himself, he cautiously let go of the crutch and pulled himself erect. For a full minute he gazed at his reflection. He looked like a soldier. He looked normal. He shook his head and grinned. *No. I look like Joseph Breitner, son of Heidi and Fritz Breitner,* he thought. *And right now, I feel euphoric.*

His musings were interrupted by a conversation outside. He heard her laugh, and the deeper voice of the fitter. She laughed again.

He grabbed his crutch and emerged from the cubicle.

"Ah, the man himself." The fitter waved at Sep. "Already raring to go."

Susan looked at him, her eyes glistening with happiness.

Sep couldn't stop staring at her. He hardly noticed the fitter fussing around his uniform, muttering about the need to adjust the waist here or let out the seam there.

"You're free to go, Lieutenant," the fitter said firmly as if it was the second time he had issued the instruction – which was, in fact, the case.

"What? Oh yes." Sep forced his attention away from Susan. "I'm sorry."

The fitter shook his head and glanced at his watch. "I'll leave you to grab your things. I'll send my instructions later." He looked hard at Sep. "To the letter, Lieutenant. Little and often." He held out his hand. "Come back if you have any problems. We can fine-tune the adjustments if necessary."

Sep shook him warmly by the hand. "I'm grateful."

"All part of the service, Lieutenant."

Sep returned his gaze towards Susan.

She began to move towards him.

"No – wait."

She looked startled.

Sep propped his crutch against the wall and stood on his own two feet, swaying. Once he was stable, he slowly opened his arms.

She moved into his embrace.

He crushed her to him. For the first time he felt free to show how much he loved her. He wanted to wrap her up, absorb her, merge into her.

He felt her squeeze him as she buried her face in his shoulder. He covered her neck with kisses, gradually working his way around to her cheek and her lips.

She held his face, and their embrace became deeper, fiercer, as their passion increased.

He ran his hands down her back, over her hips. He wanted to touch every part of her. Her response was equally intense. It was if they wanted to merge into each other.

It was too much. He began to topple over backwards.

They shrieked – Susan, as she realised what was happening, and Sep, because of the excruciating pain. Just in time, she grabbed him and pulled him upright.

Once he'd recovered, they stood holding on to each other, laughing.

She gazed at him, then kissed him gently on the lips. "Happy Christmas, Sep."

He kissed her equally tenderly. "*Frohe Weihnachte*, Susan."

"I have a present for you."

"Another one?"

She nodded. "This one's a special one – from me to you. With all my love." She kissed him again before breaking away. "Come on, get that prosthetic off before it kills you." She handed him his crutches.

"Where are we going?"

"You'll see."

He followed her lead. They climbed the stairs to the upper floor, and made their way through empty echoing rooms. A musty smell hung in the air as they passed halls that only a few weeks earlier had resounded to the sound of hundreds of injured officers.

Finally, Susan opened the door to a room. A roaring coal fire greeted them. The room was large, comfortable, oak panelled. A group of sofas surrounded the fire. In two corners, wingback chairs stood around a low coffee table. In a third corner stood an elegant mahogany writing desk. A large picture, depicting British cavalry charging at some hapless enemy, provided a suitably martial ambience. The room reminded Sep of one of the gentlemen's clubs George had taken them to during their visit to England.

"This used to be part of the Officers' Mess," Susan explained.

Sep looked around anxiously. "Are we supposed to be here?"

She squeezed his arm. "Sep, you are an officer. You're entitled to be here. I'm your guest, and I'm not in uniform. It's my day off." She stepped in front of him and gave a twirl. "We won't be disturbed."

"Are you sure?"

She nodded. "I can't be a hundred per cent sure, but it's not likely." She glanced across at him. "I've pulled a few strings." She nodded towards some plates of sandwiches, cakes and a bottle of open red wine arranged on the coffee table between the sofas.

Sep grinned. "Is this my Christmas present?"

She laughed. "No. It's my treat – although Mandy donated the bottle of wine."

"Susan, you shouldn't have gone to some much trouble. You've got enough pressures."

"And this is my way of relaxing with someone special." She reached into the pocket of her dress and pulled out a small package wrapped in blue tissue paper with a white ribbon tied around it. "This is your present." She sat and patted the space beside her. "Come on, let's enjoy our Christmas." She placed the package on the table and looked at him expectantly.

Sep sat down, picked up the gift and examined it. "This is from England?"

She giggled in anticipation. "Oh yes, I can guarantee that. One hundred per cent English."

He peeled off the tissue paper to reveal a small, decorated box. He opened it. Inside was a heavy silver locket on a chain. Sep carefully pulled it out.

She placed her hands on his shoulder and peered at the object. "The locket opens."

Immediately he was aware of her closeness. His fingers fumbled at the delicate catch. Finally, he eased the locket open. Inside was a small photograph of Susan. She looked stunning. Sep stared, transfixed. On the other side of the locket was a lock of fair hair.

She leant forward and whispered in his ear, "It's a symbol of my love, Sep. Whatever happens to us. I never want you to forget me."

The phrase set alarm bells ringing in his head. Sep turned towards her. "What do you mean, whatever happens to us?"

She rested her chin on his shoulder and looked at him. Her eyes spoke of inner sadness. "You know what I mean, Sep."

Sep felt as if a great hand had seized his heart and was slowly crushing it. Of course he knew what she meant. The issue kept intruding into his thoughts like an uninvited guest. Each time, he'd succeeded in slamming the door in its face. Not this time, though. The matter-of-fact way she had introduced the problem threw him. What could he say? She was right. The trouble was, he was unprepared – and felt vulnerable as a consequence. He gazed at her portrait, searching for inspiration.

"Susan, you know how I feel about you." He moved to face her.

She reached over and cupped his face in her hands. Her eyes bore into his. "Sep, I love you. I can't help myself. I find myself thinking about you all the time." Her eyes scanned his face, looking for understanding. "I'm sure you feel the same way about me."

"Of course I do," he said fiercely. "I find you … beguiling, beautiful…. You're so…" He struggled to find words that would capture at least some of his love for her. "You're intelligent, caring. You're intoxicating. I've never met anyone who comes close to comparing to you."

She smiled. "Not even the free-spirited Tara? Or Klara's breasts?"

"Susan, I'm being serious."

She put a finger to his lips. "I know. I'm sorry. I'm struggling to know how to deal with our circumstances. Believe me, Sep, I feel the same way about you. But what will happen to us?" She held his gaze. "We've got some big decisions to make – or at least I have. There's no dodging it."

She was right. He couldn't avoid it. They had to deal with it.

"Sep, in a few weeks' time you'll be discharged. You have no choice. You have to go home. And what will happen to me?' She paused to let her words sink in. "I don't want us to get too far ahead of ourselves."

"Come with me, Susan."

"To what?" She searched his face. "I can't speak the language. Apart from you, I'll not know a soul. I'd be hundreds of miles away from my family. And what would I do? You said it yourself – a woman's lot in Austria is *Kinder, Kirche* and—"

"*Küche.*"

"Exactly." She pressed her forehead against his and closed her eyes. "That's not me, Sep. Children maybe, one day. But I need more than that. You understand, don't you?"

He stared for some time at the locket in his hand, trying to get his thoughts in order. She had a point. "I wouldn't want you to be unhappy. That's the last thing I want." His eyes burned into hers. "I also don't want to lose you, Susan."

"Or I you."

"It's not like it was – Austria, I mean. Things are changing. They have to change." He caressed her photograph with his thumb. "I understand what you're saying, Susan. My sister is like you in

224

many ways – and my mother, come to think of it. Angry, frustrated at the unfairness of the world and the way women are treated. Maybe I'm asking too much from you. I can understand it if you don't want our relationship to go any further."

She backed away from him, looking hurt. "I didn't say that."

"But that's what you're driving at."

"No, I'm not." She shook her head in disbelief. "I'm just saying … we've got to … I've got to..." She stopped and composed her thoughts. "We have to be practical and honest with each other."

Honest with each other! Sep closed his eyes as the other issue came to his mind. She had to know. He buried his head in his hands. This would be the killer.

She mistook his despair. "I'm sorry, Sep. I don't want to hurt you."

"It's not that."

She looked at him curiously.

"You don't know everything about me."

She caressed his head. "I know, Sep. And you don't know me. We need time to get to know each other."

"No, I mean … There's something you ought to know about me. About my time as a soldier."

Her face fell. "You weren't involved in anything bad, were you?"

He looked at her bleakly. "Some might consider it bad."

The colour drained from her face. "What are you talking about, Sep?"

There was no point ducking the issue. "I was a sniper." He found he couldn't look her in the eye.

She looked at him impassively.

"I know," she said, matter-of-factly.

He stared at her in confusion. "But doesn't that change things? Doesn't it matter?"

"We had snipers as well, Sep. All armies used snipers."

"But I-I was told you had..." Sep couldn't continue.

"I had a close, dear friend who was killed by a sniper." She spoke the terrible words for him.

He glanced at her to find her gazing coolly back at him. "That's what you were told?"

He nodded.

Her body tensed. She turned away from him. She crossed her arms, and leant forward, her expression grim. "Well, it's true. We were fond of each other. He was my first love. I think I was his first true girlfriend. We were young … and naïve. Life was so simple then. He was so sure he wouldn't get hurt, and that the war would be over

225

in a few weeks. Maybe, if he had survived, things would have turned out differently. Maybe you and I would have never met or fallen in love. Maybe, maybe, maybe." She spat the words out. "Maybe if we all lived in a perfect world we wouldn't have to deal with all this crap." Her words tumbled out. "Maybe we could all live normal lives and not be faced with horrible decisions." Her face crumpled and tears trickled down her cheek. "Maybe I could wave a magic wand ... and ..." She couldn't continue.

Sep was appalled at the distress he had caused her. Instinctively, he wrapped her in his arms. She collapsed into his embrace. "Hey, Susan, I'm sorry. I'm so sorry." He held her tightly as sobs of anger, frustration and sorrow racked her.

A battalion of emotions surged through him. Over four years of war had erased all certainties. Hopes and dreams had been crushed. Good people had been killed while the dregs of humanity had been spared. He knew her pain. His resolve teetered as his memories threatened to engulf him. He pulled himself together. Both of them sobbing helplessly wasn't going to help.

He tried to think of ways out of their dilemma, but could see no way forward. He glanced once again at the locket and forced his mind back to the problem. It couldn't end like this. They had to find a solution. The trouble was he had no idea what the future held. He didn't even know what awaited him at home. Rumours were rife about food shortages in Germany, strikes and riots in towns and cities, and even revolution following the rise of the Bolsheviks in Russia. Perhaps sleepy little Dopplegau had been affected.

He couldn't even offer her certainty about anything. No wonder she had doubts. Then again, what did England offer her? It was familiar, and her family were there. But would she find a fulfilling job? One that would make the best use of her talents? Sep stroked her hair and felt her grow still.

"Are you OK?"

She wiped tears from her face. "I'm sorry. I was trying so hard to hold myself together." She gave him a rueful look. "I was determined to be the strong, sensible one – and look at me."

He stroked her cheek. "It's best not to hold things back. It only makes matters worse." He kissed her softly on the lips. "We can't help falling in love – even if it is inconvenient."

"At least we know a bit more about each other now."

He leant back and regarded her. "You are remarkable. You know that, don't you?"

"'Fragile' is the adjective I'd use right now." She wiped the last of her tears away and regained her composure. "Since we're being honest with each other, I can tell you that you never actually get over losing someone close to you. But it can ruin your life if you don't learn to grieve." She looked hard at him. "I'll admit your arrival did reawaken old wounds, but I soon got over it."

"How did you know? Who told you?"

"Nobody. I read the despatches from the German liaison office, remember? That, and the nature of your eye wound, told me all I needed to know."

He looked at her questioningly.

"The shell-blast drove the telescopic sight into your eye. Doctor Forsythe said he reckoned he could read the word *Zeiss* imprinted on your eyelid." She rubbed her hands across her face. "Thanks to your writing, I know a lot about Sep Breitner – but not everything. You still have to tell me how you ended up in my life. I know you were awarded medals for bravery."

Sep felt a wave of disquiet. Talking about his war still made him nervous. Their conversation was turning back towards the past. It would serve no purpose. They had to focus on their future.

"I was awarded a prize for stupidity in the line of duty." He put an arm around her shoulder and pulled her towards him. She nestled against him. For several minutes they sat in companionable silence.

"We ought to work out a future we both want," Sep said softly.

"What do you mean?"

He pursed his lips. "I mean, it should be down to us to create the world we want to live in. *Kinder, Küche, Kirche* would never be enough for you." He glanced at her. "I've seen you in action. You come alive when you're in the thick of a challenge. I saw it when you came back from your last trip. You were tired, angry, upset about being dropped in it by – whatshisname?"

"Major Peters."

He grunted. "Yeah. But you also thrived on organising the solution. You enjoyed managing people and getting things done. I watched you sorting out the repatriation trip, the Christmas party – even arranging this." He waved his free hand to embrace the room, the sandwiches and wine, and the fire.

"What's your point, Sep?"

"The war changes everything. For you, the closing of the hospital takes away opportunities." He became more animated. "New ones might emerge – in England, or with me in Austria. But you can't be sure. All you can be certain of is that you need something – or lots of things – that will use your intellect, experience and energy."

She shook her head in exasperation. "I know that, Sep. It's been whirling around in my head for weeks. It's not getting me anywhere."

Sep continued, "I know I will recover, but when I get back to Dopplegau, things will also have changed. I don't know exactly how. But life can never be the same. I don't know, for example, whether or not our family farm, or my grandfather's businesses, can remain viable or whether I will be fit and able to cope. Maybe I will need to sell up and start again, or invent a new business. Like you, I can't go back to nothing. There has to be something I find interesting and worthwhile, that will keep me motivated." He glanced at her. "I can speak English. I could start something in England."

She turned to face him, astonished. "You can't do that, Sep."

"Why not? I've worked in England before: for the Empire Bank, where I learnt economics and commerce." He held her gaze. "Susan, my point is we can shape our future. We don't have to be passive. We can be in charge of our own destiny. We don't have to hope something will turn up."

She looked at him quizzically. "What are you suggesting?"

He considered the question. What was he suggesting? He didn't know what he wanted. The assumption had always been that he would inherit the farm and take responsibility for running it. That's the way things were done in Austria. "We need to take our time," he said. "We need to think about what we want for ourselves, and each other. Don't worry about other people. We need to be selfish. We need to write it all down." He grinned at her. "It will probably be good for us since we seem to have fallen in love a lot quicker than most. Maybe we'll discover some dark secrets about each other?"

"We can do that while I'm on the next trip to Blighty," she said, her voice enthusiastic.

He nodded. "When you're back, we'll compare notes. We'll then have something we can work with." He leant forward, an earnest expression on his face. "I'm not going to lose you, Susan. Not without a fight." He kissed her gently on the lips. "Together we can come up with something we both want."

She responded, "I can't write down everything I want." She brushed the tip of her tongue across his lips to make her meaning clear.

Sep gulped. Her briefest touch ignited an erotic fire within him.

Desire arced between them.

Now that they had agreed a way forward the world no longer felt confusing and hostile. The room wrapped them up in its cosiness. It felt warm, welcoming and safe. They could afford to relax and take their time. Their journey was unhurried and natural. Kisses and soft caresses became longer and more intimate. Before they knew it, they were lost in each other, oblivious to their surroundings or the world outside. Their desires urged them onwards. A delicious frisson developed. Each step on their journey felt so wrong and yet they were unable to hold themselves in check. Total abandonment threatened to overwhelm them as they became ever more passionate.

Suddenly, she froze. Her eyes opened in panic. "My God! Someone is coming!" She rolled off him and desperately did up her blouse.

Outside, the unmistakable sound of heavy boots echoed along the empty wards. Sep tucked his shirt back in, while simultaneously attempting to do up the buttons.

The footsteps halted outside the door. For a few precious seconds the room fell silent. Then a heavy knock almost shook the door off its hinges.

In an inspired move, Sep reached across her and grabbed the bottle of wine. He glanced at Susan. She looked reasonably composed. "Come in," he called.

The tableau that greeted Corporal McPherson as he entered was of Sep caught in the act of pouring Susan a glass of finest Bordeaux.

The corporal appeared to find the space one foot above Sep's head to be of especial interest. "Sorry to disturb you, sir, an yersel', Nurse Jones, but Ah have some urgent news, and ye need to know immediately."

"What is it, Sandy?"

Sep suppressed a grin at Susan's sangfroid.

She passed Sep a mischievous look as she held out her glass expectantly. "Yes please, Lieutenant."

"Major Peters is awa' back. His ship left Dover an hour ago."

Susan looked perplexed. "Why is that important, Sandy?"

The corporal now considered it safe to look them both in the eye – although he couldn't fail to notice that Sep's shirt buttons were misaligned and his belt buckle was inexplicably undone.

"Sorry to let you know, Miss Jones, but he's sent orders that he wants tae see you immediately on his return. Ah thought ye should ken the lie o' the land in case ye had any plans for later tonight – Ah mean today."

Susan placed her glass on the table, bristling with indignation. "It's my day off, Sandy. Major Peters will have to wait until I'm back on duty tomorrow morning. My shift starts at eight o'clock."

The orderly coughed In embarrassment! "Ye ken that and Ah ken that, Miss Jones, but Ah also ken that Major Peters rides roughshod over such conventions when it suits him." He paused, looking pained. "Apparently he's in a foul mood. Disnae like being ordered back."

"Honestly, that man!" She clenched her fists in anger before glancing at the orderly and softening. "Sandy, you're a real friend. Thank you for letting me know."

Sep raised the bottle. "Since you're here, won't you stop for a glass?"

"Nae, nae, sir. Yer very kind, but Ah've an engagement, and ye've got a lot tae talk about. Ah'll nae bother ye further." He looked meaningfully at them in turn. "Have a merry Christmas and make sure it's a happy New Year, eh?"

They waited until Sandy's footsteps had receded before breaking out in laughter.

"My God, Sep, another minute and we'd have been caught." She threw up her hands to cover her face. "Imagine the embarrassment."

He chuckled. "Corporal McPherson would have stared at the ceiling and discussed the weather, or the state of the canteen." He buried his head in his hands before looking across at her with a pained expression. "They ought to give medals out for unbelievable frustration."

She reflected his anguish. "We will manage it one day. And when we do…" She let his imagination fill in the void.

"We have to find a way forward first," he muttered.

She was determined to stay upbeat, despite their thwarted ardour. "Hey, come on. We've agreed a plan. Together we'll chart our future." She pushed his empty glass across the table towards him. "Come on, let's enjoy every minute we have together." She poured his wine and put the bottle down before raising her glass. "To us, Sep. We will make a great couple."

They turned their attention to the food and wine. The alcohol, the glow of the flickering fire, and their closeness left them feeling warm and cosy. Sep stretched out on the sofa, his head in her lap. He fingered the locket beneath his shirt. It felt as if he had part of her permanently with him. She weaved her fingers through his hair. He closed his eyes and revelled in her closeness.

She interrupted his musing. "Sep, can I ask you something?"

"Of course."

"What happened to you? In the war, I mean?"

He tensed.

"Don't answer if you don't want to."

He lay still. What had happened to him in the war? A lot. Too much. Memories flooded his mind – everything he'd tried to suppress. His throat tightened and he struggled to catch his breath.

He fought desperately not to be overwhelmed by panic. He flailed around for something – anything – to hold back the nightmares. He had done it before and was confident of winning the battle. He forced himself to slow his breathing, release the tension and force the demons back.

Susan seemed to sense his inner turmoil. Gently, she massaged his temples. "Take your time," she whispered.

Eventually Sep trusted himself to reply. "Why do you want to know?"

She was silent.

He stretched his head back to look at her.

She smiled and continued her gentle caress. "Whatever happened, you ought to write it down."

"I was just a soldier. I was called up, did my duty, and I hope never to see another conflict."

Her fingers worked their magic. Sep closed his eyes and felt the last of his tension melt away.

"You need to deal with it, Sep." Her voice was almost a whisper. "Something isn't right. You can't move forward until we deal with it."

He pondered her words. It was as if she could read his mind. "How do you know?"

Her fingers continued their work. "You told me."

He opened his eyes and frowned.

Her look was full of love and sympathy. "Right from the start you wrote about yourself in the third person. It's as if you're telling a story about someone else, another Sep Breitner." She bent and kissed his forehead.

He gazed at her. "You should be a detective."

Her expression became serious. "You need to write it all down, Sep. It will help you cope."

He found himself both disarmed and unsure. Her encouragement made the task seem less daunting. If he could bare his soul, he would rather do so with her. She was concerned for him.

"Besides, Sep Breitner, you promised to tell me your life story when we first met." She looked meaningfully towards the writing desk. "There's a pad and pens over there going to waste."

He recalled his promise and grunted. A chapter, maybe two – he could manage that.

Susan sighed and got up. "I need to go. I have an early start in the morning."

"Will I see you tomorrow?"

She shook her head. "Unlikely. I've a feeling Major Peters will invent a schedule of pointless tasks that the team will have to ignore so we can get on with the real job. Don't overdo it, sweetheart." Their kiss was long and tender. "Parting is such sweet sorrow."

He held her tight. "Remember to write down what you really want, Susan. Everything."

She nodded. "We'll work something out."

With that, she left.

Sep stood listening to her retreating footsteps until they faded away. He drained the last of the wine and put more coal on the fire before making his way towards the writing desk. For thirty minutes he stared at the blank sheet of paper. He cleared his mind and prepared to meet his demons head-on. When he was ready, he picked up the pen and began to write.

The man appeared from the hole in the ground, his face wreathed in smiles. *"Ci arrendiamo. Ci arrendiamo!"* he shouted, frantically waving a white rag. *"Nicht schiessen. Wir geben auf."*

Sep glanced anxiously towards his platoon sergeant.

"Hold your fire, lads." The sergeant advanced towards the Italian soldier and jerked his rifle, indicating the man should advance towards him.

"Ce ne sono quaranta." The man gestured towards the mud- and snow-covered trench.

The sergeant half-turned his head towards Sep while keeping a steady eye on the soldier. "What's he saying, Breitner?"

Sep was taken aback. "I speak English, Sarge, not Italian, but I think he's saying there are four of them."

Sergeant Havel was tense. His platoon was in open ground and vulnerable. He risked a nervous sweep of the landscape around them before shaking his head in exasperation. "Well, tell him to get them all out with their hands on their heads."

Sep was equally fearful. This was the first time he had been involved in an assault, and he had no idea what to expect. There was the distant rattle of rifle and machine-gun fire and the dull crump of artillery and mortar shells. Yet the area around them had fallen silent as soon as their platoon had been ordered over the top.

Sep advanced towards the Italian who stood with one hand on his hip and the other waving the stick with the white rag attached as if it was a fly swat. He looked relaxed and grinned at Sep. *"Non vogliamo combattere."*

Sep struggled to think of a phrase the man might understand. *"Amici fuori."*

"Si, si, signore." He raised his fingers to his lips and whistled. Immediately dozens of Italian soldiers emerged from the trench. They gathered around Sep and the bemused sergeant, laughing and chatting. Several lit up cigarettes and one man passed round a bottle of wine.

Sergeant Havel slung his rifle over his shoulder. "You better take this lot back to our lines." He turned and bawled across the snow- and mud-covered landscape that had been churned up into a moonscape by the previous six hours of bombardment. "Jägers Wingnut and Schwarze! Escort duty!"

Thirty metres to the right, Wingnut and Gunter Schwarze, a conscripted policeman from Brandt who Wingnut and Sep had befriended at training camp, emerged from a shell hole and slithered over the semi-frozen ground to join them.

"Have they surrendered, Sarge?"

The sergeant rolled his eyes. "No, Jäger Wingnut, they've invited you to join them for some coffee. Of course they've fucking surrendered. You two and Professor Breitner here can escort them back."

"Who do we hand them over to, Sarge?" Sep asked.

"The first *Feld Politzei* officer you find. They can sort this lot out. I want you three back here by nightfall."

The capture of the Italians was Sep's first taste of warfare – and he was amazed. He hadn't fired a shot. The enemy had capitulated immediately. It was a pattern that was repeated all along the front. As Sep, Gunter and Wingnut escorted the prisoners, it became apparent why. The Italian soldiers were mostly uneducated peasants. Their uniforms were inadequate, their kit rudimentary, their rifles ancient and each soldier's ammunition pouch held a dozen bullets, at most. They were also badly led. The officers had been the first to run, the soldiers explained as they chatted happily with their escorts. As they reached the Austrian trenches, the Italian troops burst into song. Being a prisoner of war was clearly a much better proposition than serving their country. In other parts of the front whole Italian regiments had surrendered en masse.

"This war will be over in no time if this is the best the Itis can throw at us," Gunter said as the three of them made their way back to rejoin their platoon.

Over the next six months, the Austrian soldiers encountered the odd pocket of resistance, but for the most part, the Italians were eager to surrender.

It couldn't last.

Gunter, Wingnut and Sep had spent all day digging trenches on high ground overlooking a small snow-filled valley high in the Dolomites. Less than four hundred metres away they could see the Italian soldiers doing the same.

Then Sergeant Havel arrived to inspect their work. He was in a grim mood. He didn't say a word as he passed along the trench, then spent a full five minutes scanning the enemy lines through binoculars. "You three, come over here," he called. They lined up behind him and waited as the sergeant continued to scan the distant fortifications.

"Notice anything today? Anything unusual?"

The men looked at each other. They had been so engrossed in trench digging that they hadn't spent any time observing what the enemy might be up to.

"No, Sarge. It's been quiet," Gunter said.

"Nothing from the *Ities* at all?"

The friends continued to look bewildered. Now the sergeant had mentioned it, they realised there had been none of the exchange of insults and banter that frequently occurred when they were so close to the enemy.

"Not a peep, Sarge."

Sergeant Havel grunted and slid from the parapet. "Dig deep, lads – and I mean deep."

"We're down three metres already, Sarge," Sep said.

"Dig down to the rock, Breitner, then build a bomb shelter, deeper than that. Pile everything on top."

"Something up, Sarge?"

The sergeant looked at each of them. "Something's brewing. The whole Italian line has gone quiet. The intelligence guys reckon the *Ities* have a new commander who has imposed some harsh discipline."

"You think they'll give us more of a hard time next time we attack?" Sep asked.

"No, Breitner. I'm expecting *them* to attack us. So get digging if you want to survive." He turned and made his way further along the trench. "Make sure you sort out your sight lines and fire steps. I'll be back to inspect later." He disappeared around the zigzag corner.

The three looked at each other. They had never been ordered to dig a defensive trench before. The prospect of an attack by the ragtag peasant army was so ludicrous that it was laughable.

The attack came five days later. It was three o'clock in the morning. Sep was coming to the end of his guard duty when the whole of the night sky was lit up by what he thought was lightning. Ten seconds later, artillery shells flew overhead, then exploded among the Austrian support lines. Sep stood, bemused, as the shellfire made the ground shake. The whistling merged into a continuous scream as the bombardment intensified. Still Sep stood fixed to the spot. It felt unreal. Either the Italians had deliberately targeted the logistical support lines, or they had not got their range. None of the front-line trenches were being hit. Sep watched as the light of dawn merged with the orange-red of fires and explosions. Plumes of thick smoke drifted over the ridge and began to merge into the clouds.

A sudden bright flash of a detonation less than two hundred metres distant shocked Sep into action. "Take cover!" he shouted, realising too late the futility of the warning. A second and third explosion, then a fourth and fifth, followed. The Italians were using a sweeping barrage.

Sep spotted Sergeant Havel, head down, running along the trench towards him, clutching his steel helmet. Havel grabbed Sep as he passed and forced him along the duckboards. "Get yourself under cover, you imbecile!" he screamed. Sep was flung inside the shelter. The sergeant piled in after him as another shell burst less than fiftty metres from the trench, causing part of the rampart to collapse.

A couple of soldiers dropped the wooden planks across the entrance and began to pile snow and soil behind it to form a makeshift blast screen.

Sep felt rough hands bundle him along until he came to rest beside Wingnut. A flash of an explosion lit up the shelter as the two soldiers desperately fixed the last of the planks in position. The walls were lined with soldiers, their eyes wide with fear.

"Helmets on, keep away from the entrance, and have your trenching tools at the ready!" Sergeant Havel roared. "We're safe enough unless we get a direct hit."

Suddenly, the ground heaved. The timber reinforcement around the entrance was sucked out as if made of matchsticks as an enormous explosion blasted the trench. Sep felt the air being sucked from his lungs. He gasped for oxygen. For what seemed like an eternity there was none until, with a rush, a cloud of thick, sooty smoke rushed back into the refuge. The men gasped, then coughed and choked as they inhaled the smoke.

"Seal it up!" Sergeant Havel bellowed before grabbing two soldiers and pushing them towards the entrance. The three of them worked like demons flinging wood, dirt, snow, kit bags, anything, to block the opening.

Then there was another explosion. And another. The sides of the shelter bulged, and troops were hurled into the middle. Part of the wall and roof collapsed on top of them. Terror at being buried alive sent a couple of the soldiers into panic. They screamed and lashed out as further explosions sent more debris down, entombing them in mud.

For a second Sep was frozen in absolute fear. Then the flailing hand of a buried comrade jerked him out of his paralysis. He fell on the pile of muddy slag and desperately dug, scrabbled and heaved to free his trapped comrades. The smell of shit, cordite, piss and vomit swam into his nostrils. Another explosion blew the shelter entrance defences in again. Sep was vaguely aware of Sergeant

Havel immediately moving to plug the gap. One soldier, his glazed eyes wide open in terror, his mouth agape, screamed, a damp stain of urine spreading down his trousers. Sep watched as Wingnut leant across to slap the soldier hard across the face several times. "Get a grip!" Wingnut yelled.

The soldier next to him sat, his head bowed, passing a rosary through his shaking fingers. Sep just made out the repetitive incantation. "Sweet mother of Jesus. Sweet mother of Jesus."

The ground continued to reverberate as the barrage moved across the line. For three hours the platoon sat impotently, waiting for oblivion. It was if the Italian gunners were playing with them. The shells crashed above their shelter, then slowly drifted away, before returning to torment the terrified troops. Time and again the waves of the bombardment swept the ground around them.

Sep imagined the spite of the enemy gunners. "This time we'll get you. No, no, not just yet … wait a moment. Maybe this one." He blanked out the sound of his comrades weeping and the endless muttering of the soldier next to him. "Sweet mother of God, sweet mother of God, sweet mother of God."

Finally, the sound and fury diminished. For a few moments hope washed through the platoon.

"It'll end soon."

The statement sounded like a plea. Sep recognised Gunter's voice. He had spoken too soon. Yet again the gunfire returned. The Italian artillery had learned their craft.

Sergeant Havel tried to rally his troops. "Keep steady, lads. We know what to expect. We can survive this."

Back came the bombardment like a vulture, determined to pick the last remnants of flesh from the corpse of the Austrian army.

Sep sat back and closed his eyes. If death came, he'd rather be at peace with himself. His concentrated on the sounds he could hear. The shells' screams were different, he realised. Far away they sounded like melodic whistles. Close by they were more ragged, like cardboard being ripped. He assumed he wouldn't hear the one that signalled a direct hit.

The sergeant had succeeded in instilling an uneasy calm among the men.

Despite his attempts to stay composed, Sep felt sweat drip steadily down his body. The sound of soldiers whimpering, calling softly for their mother or for God, threatened to undermine his resolve. The stench of fear In the shelter was overpowering.

Another huge explosion rocked the shelter and half-buried the soldiers. This time there was no panic. It gave them something to focus on. They set to and dug their mates out. Sep began to believe that they would survive the onslaught.

"Missed. You bastards."

Sep laughed at Wingnut's sardonic humour.

The shells passed over them, to claim victims within the rear echelons.

Sep breathed a sigh of relief and closed his eyes as the reverberations gradually diminished. He was close to tears as relief at having survived washed through him. He strained to listen. The dull thuds drifted like departing thunder. He pitied the support troops and imagined the carnage. They had no time to construct deep shelters and would have been decimated. He leant back and realised his whole body was shaking. He reached down to his groin – and felt relieved. At least he hadn't pissed himself. Gradually a new sound floated into his awareness. He frowned. The noise was vague, indistinct, as if a long way off. Sep removed his helmet and concentrated. The penny dropped.

"Sarge, infantry. We're under attack!" he bawled.

Havel didn't hesitate. "Everyone out. Take your positions." He pushed each man roughly out of the shelter, urging them on. "Fix bayonets!"

No one had time to think.

Sep emerged from the dugout and into the dull grey light of early morning. The sound that had intrigued him was now a wall of shouting, screaming, cheering men. He levered himself onto the fire step and risked a quick glance over the parapet. No man's land crawled with Italian troops. Their khaki uniforms stood out against the mud-splattered snow as they advanced with a plodding relentless momentum. The shell-pocked, semi-frozen ground made them stumble, slip and slide, yet they picked themselves up and continued like automatons. Sep was transfixed. He picked out the officers scurrying and slithering behind the lines, urging the troops onwards, chasing the laggards, picking up those who had fallen. A few marched at the front, holding their pistols high. Occasionally they turned to encourage their men forward. So far they were unopposed. They had made it over halfway across no man's land, and the absence of any Austrian resistance had clearly fed their courage. Their baying voices increased in volume.

Sergeant Havel barged in alongside Sep.

"Get your helmet on, Breitner, and fall in your position and— *Sheisse*." The sergeant's sentence was cut short as he took in the swarm of enemy soldiers now less than two hundred metres away. "Fix your bayonet and make every shot count." He clapped Sep on the back, then dropped into the trench and ran down the line, yelling as he went. "Space yourselves, lads! Pick your targets! Hold your nerve!"

Sep watched him reach the Skoda machine-gun crew, who were struggling to fix the heavy gun barrel onto its mount.

Sep felt numb. He glanced again at the advancing troops. His brain couldn't compute that the tiny figures represented death. His death. They looked so harmless. He fixed his bayonet, not knowing exactly why. His hands were steady. It was as if he was back at home, sliding the harness pin into the hay wagon. He opened the breech and rammed the clip into its housing. He was ready to fire. He glanced across and saw Wingnut watching him, ten metres along the trench.

Wingnut grinned and winked. "A hundred metres!" he shouted. "We can't miss."

Sep nodded and swung the rifle over the parapet. Hundreds of Italian troops were spread out in front of him.

The sound of a rifle salvo, followed by the staccato rhythm of machine guns, signalled that the Austrians had opened fire further along the line. The noise intensified as more soldiers joined in and fired. Sep picked his target. A lumbering Italian soldier, for whom the four-hundred-metre journey between the two front lines was probably the limit of his endurance. Sep couldn't miss. The man stopped and bent over to catch his breath. He stood up as if offering Sep a bigger target. Sep squeezed the trigger and watched the soldier topple backwards. For a second, Sep gazed at the empty spot where the man had stood. Either side of the space he saw the enemy start to fall. Some sank into the ground as if too tired to continue, while others were flung back by the force of the bullets. One soldier's helmet flew off as a bullet smashed through his face.

The air became filled with the screams, shrieks and shouts of men, the deafening crackle and rattle of the guns, the smoke and smell of cordite. It was as if the air was on fire.

Sep slammed in another clip. There were too many targets. It was like trying to halt a flood. Each shot was a kill. But for every man down, two or three more emerged through the smoke. The enemy infantry closed in. A figure dropped and aimed his rifle directly at Sep, who heard the bullet fly past his head like an angry wasp.

The enemy soldier had failed, and knew he was helpless. Frantically, he opened his ammunition pouch, his fingers scrambling for his next bullet. It was a futile last throw of the dice. He glanced up with terrified eyes as Sep's bullet found its mark.

Sep had no time to dwell on his victim. The Italians were now less than fifty metres away. He selected his next target.

A tremendous hammering ripped through the air as the Skoda team entered the fray. The machine gun scythed through the enemy, hurling them back, cutting them in half, blowing heads and limbs off. Yet the Italians kept coming. They bent over like exhausted old men. A second Skoda opened up from the left. The Austrians took encouragement as the enemy lines evaporated against the onslaught.

The noise was overpowering.

To his left, Sep caught sight of a group of Italian soldiers about a hundred metres distant. They were more organised. Not for them a slow trudge towards death. They advanced in a coordinated wave of three ranks. One rank fired a salvo that allowed the rearmost formation to rush forward and dive for cover. As soon as they hit the ground, the second rank rose and fired a salvo before they rushed forward. It was effective. In minutes they had closed the gap and had reached the Austrians.

Sep had no time to dwell on their progress. In front of him, a dozen more Italians emerged through the smoke. An officer led the charge, his pistol held high above his head, bellowing encouragement. The feather stuck in his helmet seemed like a futile gesture of defiance. Sep couldn't help but admire his courage. It was inevitable that he would be cut down. The Skoda zeroed in and reduced the hero to a bloody quivering carcass as the heavy calibre bullets shredded his flesh.

Sep lost touch with where or what he was. He aimed, fired, killed as if he was an automaton. Time meant nothing. He was vaguely aware of bullets showering his face with snow, mud and ice. He barely noticed the buzz of shots flying past his head, or the heavy blow as one ricocheted off his helmet. He concentrated on steadily loading clip after clip as he dealt out oblivion to someone's husband, brother, son, lover. He found himself praying for the enemy to stop their madness. This wasn't war. It was a massacre. And they kept coming.

He caught a movement out of the corner of his eye. An Austrian soldier fell by the trench dog-leg. Another body fell backwards on top of him, pinned down by the boot of an enemy soldier. The Italian plunged his bayonet into his helpless victim. The soldier screamed as he tried to stop the blade with his hands. Having made the kill, the Italian soldier trampled over him and rushed along the trench, thrusting and stabbing at other Austrians caught unawares on their fire steps. Two more Italians appeared behind their colleague, firing as they went. Sep took aim and fired, bringing down the initial attacker.

Three more appeared on the other side of the trench, running along and shooting down at the helpless Austrians. Sep swung his rifle towards the three. The lead soldier had a grenade and had already pulled the pin. Instinctively, Sep fired. The man dropped and the grenade spun uncontrollably into the mud. His two comrades immediately turned their attention towards Sep.

Sep aimed his rifle and squeezed the trigger. There was a click. He had run out of bullets! He felt a surge of fear, then adrenalin took over. He hurled his rifle, javelin-like, towards his attackers. It was enough to make them duck and shift their aim. He was about to launch himself at them when the grenade at their feet detonated.

Sep was thrown back against the trench wall. Wingnut charged along the trench, followed by several others. They fell upon the Italians, using anything that came to hand. This was no battle. It was fear-driven, primeval, hand-to-hand thuggery. Men bit, gouged, stabbed, strangled and bludgeoned each other. Trenching tools, timber props, knives, bayonets, steel helmets and boots were all used as weapons. Eyes were gouged out, ears bitten off, throats cut, men were suffocated in the mud.

Wingnut and Sergeant Havel were in the thick of it. They used their speed, aggression and strength to overwhelm their opponents. None of the enemy withstood the onslaught.

Sep sprang out of the trench, recovered his rifle and retook his position. The main Italian attack faltered. The Skodas had done their work: the enemy had turned and were running back towards their own lines. Once again Sep began to bring down as many of the retreating men as possible. As far as he was concerned, they were no longer men. Anyone capable of such savagery did not deserve to be considered human.

In the trench, the Italians were driven back until they were corralled. Only then did the handful of survivors throw up their arms and surrender.

Still the slaughter continued. The Austrian artillery bombarded the retreating enemy even as they sought the shelter of their trenches. Many of the shells landed in no man's land, showering the ground with body parts or burying the wounded alive.

After four hours the heavy guns finally fell silent. Only the occasional rattle of the machine guns and the sharp crack of snipers' rifles punctuated the still air.

Sep allowed himself to relax. He bowed his head and, for the first time, genuinely prayed to whatever God there was. Despite the fact he felt desperately tired, weak and lethargic, he was alive – and thankful. He slid from the fire step and squatted in the bottom of the trench, where he stared dumbly at the mud and let the bottled-up terror seep out of him. He had no idea how long he sat there. Eventually, he took off his helmet and ran his fingers along the scrape the bullet had gouged through the steel.

"So close."

His dice with death made him think about what had happened to his brother and best friend. He cast his mind back to late 1914 and the day the enlistment letters had started to arrive.

Wingnut received his call-up first. Two weeks later, Sep and Stephan received theirs, followed a week later by Klaus. After their basic training Sep found himself attached to 2nd Platoon, where he joined Wingnut.   Klaus and Stephan had been assigned to 5th Platoon. The 5th had been deployed to the left of Sep's position, and they would have taken the full force of the Italian assault.

A wave of panic threatened to consume him. He had to know if they were OK. He eased himself to his feet just as Sergeant Havel and Wingnut appeared around the trench dog-leg. The sergeant's head was close to Wingnut's. He had his hand on Wingnut's shoulder and spoke intently, as if imparting some vital information. They picked their way carefully over the dead bodies strewn along the trench floor. Behind them, parties of stretcher-bearers, medics and a priest tended the wounded and dying. All along the trench surviving soldiers stood or sat, shocked and exhausted. Nobody spoke. Each was in their own world. Some lay prone on the parapet, their heads resting on their arms as if asleep. Other sat and stared into space. A few lay in the foetal position, their arms locked around their knees. Others paced up and down as if in a trance.

Sergeant Havel and Wingnut drew level with Sep.

The sergeant glanced sideways at Sep before clambering onto the fire step. He sat down, lit a cigarette and gestured for Sep to join him. Sep looked at Wingnut.

His friend couldn't meet his eyes. His attention was fixed on a recovery detail dragging bodies over the parapet.

Sergeant Havel inhaled deeply before offering the cigarette to Sep. Sep shook his head. He'd never smoked and had no intention of starting now.

Havel took a deep drag and blew out the smoke in a long steady stream. "Shit day."

Sep nodded.

"5th Platoon got hit bad. Sep."

Sep closed his eyes. He knew what was coming.

"Your brother's gone, Sep." The sergeant's words were delivered in a soft whisper.

Sep's world caved in. He felt every emotion that was good, noble and hopeful drain away, and an overwhelming sense of indescribable sorrow rush in. He was crushed, and made no attempt to stem his tears. He doubled up in agony. He wanted to disappear inside himself: to find a dark place to curl up and die. His throat was so tight he could hardly breathe, and his head felt as if it would burst. He bent over and sobbed uncontrollably. He didn't care – about anything.

He felt the sergeant's hand on his shoulder.

"Klaus wouldn't have known anything, lad. The shelter took a direct hit."

Sep hardly took the information in. Klaus was gone. The reality was all-consuming. He took off his helmet and shook his head angrily. He was seized by the urge to lash out.

"Take your time, lad."

Sep struggled to control himself. "What about Stephan? Did they all…?"

Wingnut's voice seemed to come from far away. "Stephan's injured. But he's alive."

Sep took in the news. "How bad?"

"Very bad. He's completely out of it. Didn't recognise me … or anyone. Kept asking for his mama. He was buried alive. They only just managed to dig him out. *Sheisse*." Wingnut threw his hands over his head and wept.

"Can I see him, Sarge?" Sep forced the words out.

"He's been taken to the FAP."

"No … I meant my brother."

Sergeant Havel bowed his head. "There's nothing to see, Sep. It was a direct hit."

Sep nodded.

Sergeant Havel slipped from the fire step, bent down and started to brush the mud off his uniform. He stopped when he realised his uniform was smeared in blood. For a few seconds he stared at the stains, before straightening up. "Shit, shit day, lads. I need you two. You both did well today. Steady. Didn't panic." He looked Sep straight in the eye. "Get some rest, Korporal Breitner. You too, Korporal Wingnut. Report to me first light tomorrow for orders."

The Italians attacked again three weeks later. It was a pointless waste of thousands of lives. The Austrians had learned their lesson. Their bomb shelters were twice as deep. Three times as many machine-gun nests were in place. Barbed-wire entanglements, booby traps and mines had been laid. A second line of trenches had been constructed a hundred metres back from the front line, along with a series of fortified bunkers to provide multiple crossfire. Replacement troops, including specialist mortar teams, had been drafted in. The Italians were doomed before they even left their trenches. They were scythed down on an industrial scale. Sep watched the massacre, his mind in suspense. The scene was horrific. Desperate enemy soldiers flung themselves onto the razor wire in an effort to break through, only to be picked off by the Austrians. They rushed towards any gaps in the wire, and the Skoda teams mowed them down by the dozen. Everywhere bewildered, panicked Italian troops ran in confusion trying to escape the maelstrom, or plodded with weary resignation towards certain death. Corpses hung all along the entanglements. Sep watched as young men – boys his own age – had their heads and limbs blown off, or were shredded and disembowelled by the Skodas. His initial revulsion began to be replaced by cold indifference. Why couldn't the enemy see the pointlessness of it? Why didn't they stop?

For three days and nights, the enemy poured troops into the assault. Not a centimetre of ground was won. Eventually, sheer exhaustion forced the attack to peter out.

Sep did an impromptu roll call. In his section, two men had been killed and three injured. They owed their survival to holding their nerve and maintaining discipline. The no man's land in front of their position was piled high with Italian dead and wounded. None of the enemy attacking their position had got closer than one hundred metres.

Wingnut joined Sep as the last of the sporadic rifle shots rang out across the battlefield.

"You OK?"

Sep nodded. They had got into the habit of checking on each other, to provide mutual support and reassurance.

"How are your boys?"

"We're doing all right. Lost a couple and six injured, two serious."

Sep shut his eyes and pinched his nose. He was dismayed by how quickly they had begun to lose their humanity. *How have we come to this? We talk of death in such a blasé manner.* He rubbed his temples and dismissed his black thoughts. They served no purpose. He gazed out into no man's land. His eye was drawn to an Italian soldier who was struggling to pull himself out of a shell hole. The steep sides, made slippery by the mud and slush, sapped his strength. Time and time again he slid back into the crater. He had attracted the attention of the Austrian troops who shouted encouragement, then cheered each time he lost his grip and slithered back into the slush.

"Do you think they'll attack again?"

Wingnut shrugged. "They can't go on losing so many men." He waved his hand towards the masses of dead bodies. "They must have lost four or five thousand on this section of front alone."

Sep continued to stare at no man's land. He could hear the pleas of the injured and dying: pleas for help, water, Jesus, Santa Marie or their mother merged into a low murmuring wail that floated across the battlefield. No help was forthcoming. The Austrians were too busy with their own casualties.

Next morning Sep woke to the sound of cheering. Intrigued, he joined the rest of his section who had lined up on the parapet and were watching something in no man's land. It was the trapped Italian soldier. Despite the freezing temperatures he had survived the night and was still trying to escape. A combination of ice-coated mud, exhaustion, and frozen fingers made his task impossible. After two hours he disappeared from view, presumably resigned to his fate.

Then someone took pity on the exhausted man. Sep saw Wingnut cautiously crawl towards the crater. Sep watched anxiously. Although Wingnut was nearly three hundred metres from the enemy trenches, there was always a chance a sniper would fancy his chances. Wingnut reached the edge, laid his rifle down beside him and bent down to grab the Italian's wrists. In a couple of seconds he hauled him out of his frozen tomb, to wild cheering from the Austrian lines. Sep laughed. At least his friend hadn't lost his humanity.

Wingnut gestured for the Italian to start heading for the Austrian trenches. As he bent down to pick up his rifle, the Italian drew his pistol and fired.

Wingnut's head exploded.

A shocked silence descended among the Austrians. Already the Italian was sprinting towards his own lines. The Austrian soldiers roared, then fired wildly in rage and haste. A hail of bullets chased the fleeing figure. The Italian ducked, dived and zigzagged in an effort to cheat death.

In his fury, Sep was only vaguely aware that Sergeant Havel had joined him. "What's happened, Breitner?"

Sep didn't reply. He was consumed by ice-cold hatred. He picked up his rifle and lay across the parapet.

Already the escapee had made it halfway across no man's land. Sep heard the Italian soldiers cheering him on as Austrian bullets whistled around his head and splattered the earth around his heels The man seemed to have a charmed life.

Sep got a bead on the soldier, but he threw himself to the left.

Italian troops lined the top of their parapets, urging their man onward.

Once again Sep caught the man in his sight – and again lost the target as he flung himself over the tangled wire and disappeared into a bomb crater. He emerged seconds later, twenty metres to the left. He was now less than a hundred metres from the Italian trenches. He put his head down and sprinted. Fifty metres from safety the man stopped. In a gesture of arrogant bravado he turned towards the Austrian trenches and raised his arms, pistol in one hand. He gave the Austrian lines a V-sign.

He stood still long enough for Sep to settle his sighting bead on him. Sep squeezed the trigger. Two seconds later the bullet smashed through the man's forehead. Sep watched him fall with cold indifference. He threw back the bolt, reloaded and selected another Italian, who was half-straddling the parapet, staring in shocked disbelief at his fallen comrade. Sep fired. The man catapulted backwards into his trench. It was enough. The line of previously cheering, jeering enemy troops fled for cover.

Sep swept the trench line, seeking out other victims. The lines fell silent. Sep turned to find Sergeant Havel staring at him in awe.

"Where did you learn to shoot like that, Breitner?"

Sep was hardly listening. He could feel the little human decency that remained within him draining away. He felt as if he was dead. Unfeeling. A machine. "My father taught me." He sounded disgusted. He stood up and made his way along the line. Two of Wingnut's section had already recovered the body. Sep stared at his friend. Gazing into Wingnut's glazed eyes, he couldn't cry or speak. Only one concept consumed him. He wanted to kill, maim, murder, wound every enemy.

Two days later Sergeant Havel presented Sep with a Stutzen long-barrelled sniper rifle with a telescopic sight, and ordered him to get to work.

Sep was assigned to a specialist sniper platoon, and sent anywhere along the front where his services might be required. He killed with casual contempt and callousness. He gained a reputation for professional efficiency. Morale was lifted wherever he was deployed. He could be relied on to take out entire enemy machine-gun crews, specific Italian officers, or pin down whole sections of the front. Promotion and awards for his effectiveness and bravery soon followed. Sep barely acknowledged the honours. He existed in an world of his own.

He was aware that his efforts were pitiful. The slaughter continued unabated. He also knew that further tragedy was inevitable. He learned from his mother's letters that George had been killed outside a town called Ypres in France. Sergeant Havel managed to survive until 1916, when an airburst shell exploded ten metres above his head.

Each piece of bad news drove Sep further into his own private world. There was no escape. It was just a matter of time before he would be killed. His one hope was that it would be quick and painless.

The ruthless imposition of draconian discipline within the Italian army – and the supply of modern weaponry from their British and French allies – turned the war in their favour. By the late summer of 1917, the Austrians were on the back foot.

The detonation of a massive mine signalled the latest Italian assault. Sep watched in resignation as the explosion blew apart an entire Austrian trench system. A second explosion took out another two hundred metres of defences. Even though the blasts were over a kilometre away, he was blown off his feet by the shock wave. Immediately the shrill sound of falling shells heralded a further bout of slaughter.

Sep, along with thousands of Austrian troops, found himself caught in the open ground between the front-line and second-line trenches. They had been advancing to reinforce the front line. The bombardment had targeted the forward fortifications and trenches. The soldiers turned back and tried to outrun the guns: it was a race they were bound to lose. They had to pick their way through their own barbed-wire entanglements. What began as an orderly rush quickly descended into panic, as the fleeing troops realised their vulnerability. The distance between the two lines was over three hundred metres, and already the leading edge of the bombardment had passed through the front line and crept relentlessly towards them.

Sep dropped to his haunches. Retreating was pointless – in fact, it was suicidal. He watched with calm detachment as the shellfire fell among the retreating ranks.

Desperate Austrian soldiers streamed past him. Some screamed hysterically. The gaps in the barbed wire became clogged as soldiers kicked, shoved and punched their comrades In a stampede of terror. Anyone who fell was trampled underfoot. Some threw away their rifles as they ran.

Sep stood up as four soldiers sprinted towards him, their heads down, their minds focused only on outpacing the approaching shells.

Sep raised his rifle and fired. "Stand fast, you men!"

The shock of confronting a sergeant pointing a rifle directly at them halted their flight.

Sep made a deliberate show of throwing the bolt and sliding another bullet into the breach. He swung the barrel round to each soldier in turn. "Stand fast, if you want to live."

The men looked at him in confusion.

Sep advanced towards them. "Lie down – *now!*" He grabbed the first soldier and forced him to his knees. "Lie flat. Make yourselves small."

The men meekly did as they were ordered. An explosion provided added incentive.

Sep fell in front of them – and pressed his face into each of the frightened soldiers in turn. "When I say run, you follow me and run. Do you understand?"

Another shell exploded less than thirty metres from their position, showering them with mud, rocks and grass.

Sep leapt to his feet, dragging the nearest soldier with him. "Run!" he roared. He sprinted towards the crater, hauling the staggering soldier along with him. They dived into the shallow hole. The other three soldiers piled in on top of them.

Sep forced the soldiers to listen to his words. "This is the only way we're going to survive. Get your heads down!" Another shell crashed down. Sep risked sticking his head over the crater rim. Another shell landed in front of him.

Behind them, the barrage fell among the support trenches.

Again Sep peered over the crater rim. Thick smoke obscured his vision. In a break in the smoke, he saw a Skoda team abandon the heavy machine gun and scrabble desperately through a gap in the barbed wire. They succeeded – only to be obliterated by an enormous explosion.

"Run!" Sep screamed. The soldiers needed no encouragement. Moving to the newest crater reduced their exposure and increased the odds in their favour. They ran like demons and fell, gasping and wheezing, into the still smouldering bomb hole. Around them lay pieces of the Skoda team. Shreds of ragged uniform, body parts, intestines, one soldier's head still in its helmet, flesh strewn around like offcuts in a butcher's shop.

Smoke billowed around them, giving them cover.

The ground shook as the bombardment worked its way beyond the secondary trenches. The screams of maimed, broken men filled the gaps between the explosions.

The five men huddled together and waited for the next shell.

"There's more falling behind us than in front, Sarge," one muttered, daring to hope.

They listened intently. A new sound drifted towards them: the noise of thousands of Italian infantry blaring their aggression as they fell on the obliterated Austrian front line.

Sep peered at the wall of smoke, waiting for it to break. He could hear the enemy but could not see them. What he could see was the abandoned Skoda. He grabbed the two nearest soldiers. "You two, come with me. You others, keep your heads down and don't move."

The three of them dragged the heavy machine gun and its ammunition boxes back, and set it on its mount.

The smoke cleared to reveal lines of Italian infantry swarming across open ground. The last thing they expected to see was an Austrian machine-gun team directly in their path.

The Skoda's bullets swept up and down their lines, killing and maiming hundreds of men. If any soldier tried to approach their position, Sep despatched him with sniper precision. It was murder – yet Sep felt nothing, as bodies were scythed down, sent spinning, or punched backwards by the heavy calibre rounds.

For thirty minutes Sep and the four soldiers swept the battlefield with methodical and relentless fire. They bought enough time for the Austrians to organise a counter-attack. It was effective, but ultimately a hollow victory. Elsewhere along the front, the Italians had swept through the lines and once again the Austrian army was forced to withdraw.

Sep's mind retreated with the army. A vision of Wingnut appeared in front of him, as clear as if he was really there. Sep didn't know what was real and what had been conjured up by his imagination. He couldn't remember where he'd been or what he'd done. He sweated, and heard voices. He vomited black bile. His moods swung widely from depression to an irrational elation, bordering on hysteria.

Learning of Tom's death pushed him over the edge. Gunter, who had spent two days looking for him, delivered the news. Sep was in denial. His mind just couldn't comprehend what he had been told. He stared with pinprick eyes into nothingness. It couldn't be true. Tom was only a kid. He was under conscription age. It wasn't possible. Someone had made a mistake. The dog tag with his name on it, the photographs of Heidi Breitner and Tara, the leather stone necklace that Gunter handed over – they were all fake.

Sep's mind shut down.

For how long, he had no idea. Suddenly he was no longer on the front line. He found himself taken to one first-aid post; then another; then somewhere else, where people asked him questions and shone lights in his eyes. Finally, he was escorted to a place where everything was peaceful and quiet and people spoke softly and kindly to him.

One day – Sep had no way of knowing exactly when – an officer with three gold embroidered stars on his epaulettes appeared in Sep's room. Automatically, Sep went to stand as the *Oberst* entered.

"At ease." The man's tone was friendly, almost gentle. "How are you feeling, Sergeant Breitner?"

Sep considered the question. He didn't know where he was, let alone how he felt. "Confused, sir."

The *Oberst* laughed lightly. "Understandable, given what you've been through." He pulled up a chair and sat opposite Sep.

Sep glanced around at his surroundings. It was the first time he had really done so since his breakdown. He was in a room lined with shelves crammed full of books. Faded oil paintings adorned the wall. An ancient grandfather clock stood by the door. A large window let in the bright sunlight.

"I'm told you're recovering well."

Sep nodded. He was in no position to contradict this. Gradually, it dawned on Sep that he knew the man talking to him. It was his commanding officer.

"I've got some good news for you, Sergeant Breitner." The CO smiled broadly. "You've been awarded the Silver Medal for Bravery, (First Class), and the Long Service Cross, *and* you have been recommended for a field promotion to *Leutnant*."

To Sep's ears, the news was meaningless, but he nodded and tried to look suitably appreciative. "Thank you, sir."

"That's not all, Sergeant." The Lieutenant Colonel pulled his chair closer as if what he was about to say was confidential.

"I understand you are fluent in English."

Sep nodded. "I can read, speak and write in English."

"Excellent. We are putting together a team which you will join as soon as you are discharged." The man grinned broadly. "I need a front-line observer, a man with excellent fieldcraft. No more fighting for you, *Leutnant* Breitner. You've done your bit."

Two weeks later Sep found himself heading for southern Belgium as part of an intelligence-gathering team. The Austrian High Command realised they had to adopt new tactics. The German troops sent to help reinforce the Austrians and secure the Italian front were better equipped, trained and motivated than their Austrian counterparts. New technology was being deployed by the British, French and Italians, including tanks, improved infantry weapons, wireless telephony and aircraft. The enemy were adapting. Artillery support and infantry tactics were now vastly superior to those of the Germans and Austrians. If Austria was going to survive the war, they needed to learn – and fast.

Sep didn't complain. Life as a intelligence gatherer, observer and aide de camp sounded infinitely better than life as a front line infantryman. And so it proved. For three months he peered through the telescopic sight of his rifle, noting English troop deployments, watching the re-supply convoys and the movement of the great steel tanks that the English no longer bothered to camouflage. Despite the number of targets, he wasn't required to kill anyone, and no one shot at him. Until that fateful day when he was spotted.

Sep sat back and examined the papers neatly stacked on the desk. It had taken all night, and he was exhausted, emotionally and physically. He massaged his face and was surprised when his hands came away damp. He didn't feel sad, but he had been crying silent tears as he wrote. Despite his weariness, he felt surprisingly good – as if a great weight had been lifted off his shoulders. The English had a word for it. He tried to remember it as he stretched out on the sofa to sleep. Cathartic – that was it.

It was after nine o'clock when he woke feeling reinvigorated – even more so by the time he'd washed, shaved and wolfed down a full English breakfast. Life suddenly seemed full of purpose and meaning. He sipped his tea and considered how to spend his day. An hour's practice with his new prosthetic, followed by another attempt at the St Étienne run, weather permitting. That should take him to lunchtime. Then he would consider his future with Susan as he walked to the village.

His musing were interrupted by a gentle cough. "Excuse me, sir. Your presence is required by the CO."

"What time, Sergeant?"

"Immediately, sir."

Sep drained his cup and followed the sergeant.

While Doctor Forsythe had been content to use a modest side room, Major Peters had commandeered the drawing room of the chateau as his office. He sat behind a large leather-topped mahogany desk upon which a brown file lay open. He didn't look up as Sep entered, but continued to read the papers. "It's customary in the British Army for officers to salute," he said without raising his head.

Sep took an instant dislike to the man. He *had* saluted. Major Peters had had his head bowed, and had missed – and neglected to return – the mark of respect.

Sep flicked his eyes towards the sergeant who stood at ease to one side of the desk. He failed to hide the look of disgust that flashed across his face.

Sep gave a slow, exaggerated salute and held it until Major Peters eventually glanced up and casually returned the courtesy.

"Why are you still here, Lieutenant Breitner?"

"Because you ordered me to attend, sir."

Peters shook his head in irritation. "I don't mean why are you in my office, man. I meant, why are you still malingering in this hospital?"

"Because I haven't been officially discharged, sir."

The major dropped the papers he had been studying into the file and flipped the folder shut. "Well, you have now." He stared belligerently at Sep, but addressed the sergeant. "Sergeant, arrange transport to take this man to the nearest German liaison office."

"That will be Cologne, sir." The sergeant glanced at Sep. "Earliest I can manage that will be tomorrow."

The major signed a paper, then rubber-stamped it. He pushed the document across the desk towards Sep.

"Tomorrow at 0900 hours sharp it is then. Make sure you're ready, Lieutenant. That's an order. As far as I'm concerned this is a military establishment and you are appearing in front of me as a serving soldier in uniform. I don't want to have to send for an escort, or waste any more resources on you." The major's smile was delivered with cold indifference. "That'll be all."

For a second Sep held the major's gaze. He felt shocked, but there was nothing he could say. He picked up his medical discharge, saluted and followed the sergeant out.

Once outside the sergeant looked at Sep sympathetically. "Will you need a hand packing, sir?"

Sep was confused. The abrupt nature of the encounter and its outcome had thrown him. "No ... no, thank you, Sergeant. I think Corporal McPherson will assist me. I need to thank him for all his care and attention."

The sergeant looked uncomfortable. "I'm sorry, sir, but Major Peters discharged Orderly McPherson first thing this morning, along with a dozen other nursing staff. They're probably already on their way to Boulogne."

Sep looked aghast. "Did he discharge Nurse Jones?"

"Good God! No, sir. The man's not that stupid," the sergeant exclaimed before realising the inappropriateness of his outburst. "Begging your pardon, sir."

"It's OK, Sergeant."

He made his way back to his room in a daze. He had to speak to Susan. He glanced at the clock. The convoy would have left around two hours ago. There was a chance that they would be held at Boulogne waiting embarkation. Maybe he could telephone the port. He grabbed his crutches, levered himself up and rushed out to find the hospital's communication centre. He discovered the main switchboard in the bowels of the chateau. It took him over half an

253

hour to reach it through a labyrinth of steep staircases and narrow corridors.

A clerk looked up as Sep approached. "Can I help you, sir?"

"I need to contact a senior member of staff on the convoy as a matter of urgency," Sep gasped and wiped the perspiration from his brow.

The corporal gave a thin smile. "Of course, sir. Can I see your authorisation?"

"What?" Sep looked perplexed.

"This is a restricted area, sir. You need a pass just to be here, and specific authorisation if you intend to send any wireless signals, telegraph messages or telephone calls." The corporal peered at Sep. "I assume you have the required permits?"

"What? No, I didn't realise. The matter is urgent."

"I'm sure it is, sir. However, without the permit I can't allow access."

"Who issues the permits?" Sep knew the answer even as he asked the question.

"That'll be Major Peters, sir."

Sep stood, his head bowed. *Of course they wouldn't allow access to the communications room.* What was he thinking? *And to make a private communication!* He shook his head in disbelief. How could he be so stupid? He glanced at the corporal, who sat watching him impassively. "I don't suppose you know where the nearest public telephone might be?"

"I believe there is one at the main post office in Arras, sir."

Sep nodded with weary resignation. Arras was over thirty kilometres away.

The corporal noticed Sep's despair and tried to be helpful. "You could send a signal, sir. If it's cleared by—"

"Major Peters." Sep gave the corporal a sad grin. "Thanks, Corporal. I'll have to think of something else."

Back in his room he ran through his options. *Arras was out of the question. He'd never get there and back in time, even if he could find someone to transport him. He could discharge himself, take a billet in St Étienne and wait for Susan to return.* For a few seconds the idea seemed good, until he realised Major Peters would regard it as disobeying his orders. He'd probably be arrested and escorted to Cologne under armed guard.

He glanced again at the clock. Time was slipping away. She'd be on the ship by now for sure, and even more inaccessible.

"*Scheisse,*" he swore loudly, not caring who might hear him. He pictured her in his mind. Right now he was sure she would be thinking of him – maybe reading his last chapters, or planning how they might spend their life together. She'd be happy – and completely unaware that the odious Major Peters had just ripped their lives apart.

Perhaps an appeal to Major Peters might work. A few more days – what difference would it make? Surely the man had some compassion? He snorted. *Compassion and Major Peters? Maybe he could follow her to England?* As soon as the thought entered his head, it died. *How could he cross the Channel with no passport, money or papers?* He was clutching at straws.

He realised he still held the discharge letter. He gazed at it for a few seconds. Most men would have received such a letter with joy. It was their release: their ticket home to their loved ones. Yet, to him, it felt like a death sentence. He screwed it up, hurled it across the room and swore again.

It couldn't end like this. He buried his face in his hands and mentally screamed his anger and frustration.

The only thing to do was write her a letter and hope she received it. *And send it where? If he left it under her door, or in the post-room, there was a chance she wouldn't receive it – especially if Major Peters discharged her before she got back. He would have to send it to her home address.* He racked his brains. *Where had she said she lived?* He squeezed his eyes shut and cast his mind back to their conversation. *It was an old rectory in a small town. What was the name of the town? Yorkshire? No, that was the province. North Riding – that was it. But the town?* He glanced around for inspiration and found none. He abandoned the task. What mattered was to write the letter. Hopefully the name of the town would come to him.

His pen hovered over the page. *How could he put down on paper the pain and anguish he felt? What if she didn't believe him? What if she thought this was just him hiding behind some words on a piece of paper in an effort to escape to Austria?* He lowered the pen. *Maybe he shouldn't even try to pursue her. The odds were against them. Enforced separation might be a blessing in disguise. Perhaps their relationship was a fleeting affair, born out of the stress of war and loneliness. Surely it would be kinder if they went their separate ways. She was an attractive, intelligent young woman who would never struggle to find a loving partner. Whereas he was a cripple.* He stared at the blank sheet in front of him. *What could he offer her? Love – that was about it. Was it enough?*

Negative thoughts tumbled around his brain. Before he realised it, he'd erected a fortress of reasons their relationship was doomed. *What was he thinking? He loved her. That trumped everything, crushed all objections and swept aside all doubts. She had to believe him. She just had to.*

He started writing. He wrote from the heart, letting his emotions pour on to the page. One sentence flowed into another. He didn't care whether it made sense or not. She had to know how he felt.

Mid-way through he paused. They had promised they would write down what they wanted. He now realised exactly what that was. He wanted her beside him for the rest of his life. Nothing else mattered. He'd give up everything for her. All she had to do was let him know she felt the same way about him and he would come – no matter where she was.

He glanced up at the clock as it chimed the hour. Two o'clock. In less than twenty hours he'd be on his way back home and out of Susan's life. The thought appalled him. His eye was drawn to the clockmaker's name emblazoned in the centre of the dial. *John Suggs, Clockmaker, Skipton, North Riding of Yorkshire.* Skipton – that was the name of the town. He smiled in relief. It had to be an omen.

Still he didn't take any chances. He wrote two more identical letters. Then he delivered one to the post-room. He slipped the second under the door of Susan's room along with his latest chapter, and posted the third to the Old Rectory, Skipton, North Riding, Yorkshire, England.

***

Hardly a day went by that Sep didn't think of Susan. He thought of her now as he cleaned out his grandfather's spring farm. He smiled to himself as he remembered telling her about Joseph Breitner's paraffin accident, and he relived her shocked delight at the tale, which had seemed so scandalous to her.

He wondered what she was doing right now. *Striding over the Yorkshire moors, perhaps. Better that, than being forced to work in some cotton or wool mill – or whatever sort of mill there was in Yorkshire.*

No, she wouldn't be cooped up inside, and even if she were in a factory, no doubt she would be running it. His grin grew broader as he pictured her bossing the bosses about. *Maybe she had got a job in a hospital after all. That was closer to her vocation – and her nature.* He sighed. Thinking about her was just too painful.

He swung the shutters open with more force than was strictly necessary. The crash of the heavy blinds against the wall helped jerk his mind back towards the task in hand. The spring farm had been neglected. With all three sons away at the front, it had been too much work for his parents. The loss of Klaus and Tom had crushed Fritz and Heidi Breitner.

Sep threw himself into the work. The loft was almost empty, and took little time to clear. The animal pens took longer. He'd grown used to the prosthetic, but its lack of flexibility made even the simplest of tasks irksome. He moved into the interior. Everything was covered in dust and cobwebs. It needed a complete clear-out. He glanced at his watch. He'd work for another couple of hours then take a break. He reached up to unhook the paraffin lamp from its hook, and froze, as once again memories of her flooded his mind. *Why hadn't she written? She must have received at least one of his letters. She could have telegrammed, or even phoned. People did these days.* Carefully, he unhooked a lamp and placed it on the table. The paraffin had long since evaporated. It would need refilling. He felt his mood improve. *Better to have good, happy memories than none at all.* At half past one, he'd broken the back of the clean. The remaining tasks were to restock the kitchen stores, get fodder for the animals, and trim the wicks and replenish the paraffin lamps.

He settled down on the front porch and imagined his grandfather doing the same all those years ago. In some ways, nothing had changed. And in others, everything had changed. He heard the post bus depart, belching diesel fumes as it headed back along the valley. Cars and lorries were now a common sight in the village. The Lodge lay empty and shuttered. Sir William had been forced to sell and the new owners had yet to decide what they wanted to do with the property. The lack of business travellers and tourists meant that the Adler only had half its rooms available. But the starkest difference was the absence of young men. The war had taken a generation. Over fifty lads from the two villages had been killed – over a third of the young men. The oldest had been thirty-one; the youngest, Tom Breitner, eighteen.

He opened the lunch Josey had made him. At least she was happy. He watched her making her way back home. For the past few weeks, she had been acting strangely. It seemed that she had a secret that she was bursting to reveal. Sep smiled to himself. He thought he could guess the reason for his sister's barely suppressed excitement. Two trips to Achbrugge over the past month – neither of which was on market day – suggested appointments with Doctor Rubenstein. Sep's smile grew broader. He liked the idea of being an uncle. Josey was the bedrock of her family, that was for sure. She had such plans. Their grandfather had left the family well off, and Josey was determined to make the best of her inheritance and her university education. No *Kinder, Küche, Kirche* for her. She'd already bought two large parcels of land at knockdown prices, and was building a textile finishing factory on one site and a dressmaking/soft furnishing business on the other. 'We have to be positive and plan for the future' had become her mantra.

Sep conceded she was right. There were reasons to be optimistic. A few tourists were beginning to trickle back. So far, they were Swiss, who had profited significantly from the war and found taking their leisure in neighbouring Austria a much cheaper alternative to their homeland. No doubt the Germans, and even the English, would return in time. As if to prove his point, a young couple emerged from the Adler, dressed for a leisurely afternoon stroll around the village. And earlier he'd watched a motorcar park outside the *Gasthaus* and disgorge a smartly dressed middle-aged businessman – which suggested at least some commercial traffic was starting to use the pass. Sep sighed. Yes, things could only get better.

He eased himself erect and scanned the valley and village of his birth, absorbing the beauty and tranquillity of the scene. He was lucky, he reminded himself. There were worse places to be on the planet. Besides, someone had once told him that more good things than bad would happen to him. It was a matter of time. His gaze settled on Drössel's *Bäckerei* in time to see the two visitors disappear inside.

He made a mental list of his remaining tasks. Hang the new curtains, make a list of supplies, and replenish the lamps. Then he would be done for the day. For the next couple of hours, he buried himself in work. He placed the recharged lamps in a neat row down the centre of the table and stared at them. *Six months! And still she held his heart captive.* He leant forward and rested his head in his hands. *Maybe he should write to her. No, no, there's no 'maybe' about it. He would write to her. If only to make sure she was OK. Perhaps she expected him to write?* He considered the question. *He should write for his own peace of mind – and to find out whether she had forgotten him. He'd write as soon as he got home.*

The faint aroma of freshly baked cakes drew him out of his musings. He raised his head and cautiously sniffed the air. From behind him came a voice.

"You should be careful with paraffin. It can cause nasty accidents."

He turned around.

She stood, framed in the doorway, a nervous smile playing across her face.

He stared at her in disbelief. "You came?"

She nodded. "We didn't finish our conversation."

"No. We didn't." He got up. "I was rudely interrupted."

"So I understand."

"You got my letter?"

"I got all three of your letters." She held them up. "You're a persistent man, Sep Breitner." She advanced towards him.

"You're a determined woman, Susan Jones." He held out his arms to embrace her.

For a few seconds they held back, as if they were strangers. The pause allowed doubts and insecurities to rush into Sep's mind. Sep realised that she must have been with the man who had entered the *Bäckerei*. *Who had she been with?* He answered his own question. *She'd met someone else. That explained the six months of silence, her nervousness and hesitancy.*

Their embrace was stiff and awkward, their kiss brief.

Sep felt swamped by unease and embarrassment. "I thought you had forgotten about me," he muttered. "I had hoped you'd write and let me know how…" His words trailed off.

Her blush betrayed her discomfort. "I know. I meant to … but I had so much going on … and so much to try to sort out." She glanced across at him. "I'm sorry."

"What did you need to sort out?"

She shook her head and looked flustered. "Oh – everything, What I wanted. My mum and family, a job, somewhere to live." She looked at him. "You and me … our future. Your letters. Everything."

"Did you come to any conclusions? Did you find a job?"

"Oh yes. A good one, I think."

Sep steadied himself before squeezing out his question. "A nursing job?"

She nodded. "It's with a GP. The senior partner is retiring and his son and daughter are taking over. They're both doctors and want to expand the practice." She sank down into the chair and placed the paper bag containing the cakes on the table. "It's a big challenge for me. I need to learn about general nursing, midwifery, child care … It's the biggest challenge – and opportunity – of my life."

"They've agreed to train you, then?" Sep did his best to keep his voice level despite the tightness in his throat. Slowly, he sat down opposite her.

She nodded. "And provide accommodation." Her gaze was so intense that Sep thought it would go straight through him. "I've not decided to take it. At least, not yet." She glanced across at him. "I wanted to talk to you first." She continued to hold his gaze. "I wanted to be sure you still felt the same way about me as I do about you." Her eyes darted across his face as if she was trying to read his thoughts. "I'll only take it if you haven't met someone else, and if you still love me."

Sep tried to unravel what she just said. If he loved her? Was she saying that she would take the job? It had no logic. He ran her sentence through his mind again and came to the same conclusion. It made no sense. He wondered whether he had heard her correctly and was about to ask for clarification when she spoke again.

His silence appeared to unsettle her. "Do you still love me, Sep?"

Her directness startled him.

"Good God, Susan. I think about you all the time. Every day. The lack of news from you was killing me." His anguished look illustrated his sincerity. "I love you, Susan, with all my heart." He reached over and took her hands in his. "But I want to see you happy. I won't stand in the way of your career. If this job is what you want, I understand." A picture of her male companion swept through his mind. "And I can also understand if you have met someone else. Six months – it's a long time."

She twined her fingers with his. An expression of mischievous delight spread across her face. "You don't know, do you?"

"Know what?"

She laughed. "Has Josey not said anything?"

"What are you talking about?"

260

She leant across and kissed him on the lips. This time her touch lingered and Sep felt dormant embers of desire flicker into life.

She eased herself back from him. Their faces were inches apart. Her eyes were alive and full of mischief and intrigue. She giggled and sat back in her chair. "I can't believe she hasn't said anything to you."

Sep threw his hands up in exasperation. "Susan! For God's sake. I'm baffled. What's Josey got to do with all this?"

She threw back her head and laughed. "I think I should tell you everything." She took a deep breath and began. She spoke slowly and deliberately, as if anxious not to leave anything out. "I got the first of your letters – the one you posted under my door – as soon as I got back from Blighty. I was desperately angry and upset. All sorts of things ran through my mind. I thought about resigning then and there and chasing you across Europe. I thought I could catch up with you." She grimaced. "I had lots of crazy ideas running through my head. I didn't sleep at all. Next morning the staff sergeant told me about your discharge meeting with Major Peters and the post orderly delivered your second letter. I was beside myself with anger and frustration. I knew I had to sort myself out. The hospital wasn't the right place for me. I was exhausted – not thinking straight. Morale was low: Major Peters was letting staff go much too early and discharging patients before they were fit to travel. It was only a matter of time before he got rid of me." She let out a wistful sigh. "So, I decided to resign once the next repatriation trip had been completed, then head for home."

She glanced at him and grinned. "Your third letter was waiting for me in Skipton. I went for a long walk across the moors – several, in fact – to think. I was in turmoil. I wanted to be with you, above everything else. But I also wanted to have a proper job – something that would challenge me, keep my brain active and enable me to be independent. I wanted to be with you here in Austria, but I didn't want to leave my family – especially my mum. You understand that, don't you?"

Sep nodded dumbly. He thought it best not to complicate matters by telling her he had no idea what was going on.

"My mother finally lost patience with me and threatened to kick me out of the house if I didn't pull myself together. 'Write to Rachel', she said."

Sep sat up, startled. "To Rachel? You don't know Rachel! You've never met!"

"Yes, I know. But she was the only woman I knew who had travelled, worked and studied in different countries, away from her family and loved ones. Also, she knows you – and Dopplegau. She could tell me what to expect if I chose to come and live here."

"How did you find out her address?"

"It was easy. Your writings told me she was in Vienna, and she's famous in the medical world." Susan waved her hand. "Anyway, I wrote her a long letter explaining everything about you and me, my dilemma, and about potential opportunities for finding work in my field. To be honest, I didn't think she would reply."

"Why didn't you write to me?"

Susan looked sheepish. "I wasn't ready, Sep. I still didn't know what I wanted. Plus, I was scared. I didn't know whether I dared to go through with it." She looked pained. "I didn't want to raise your hopes. Also, I began to believe that you might not love me anymore."

Sep looked hurt. "I've never stopped loving you."

"I know, sweetheart." She giggled. "Josey told me."

"Josey?" Sep spluttered in disbelief. "How have you been contacting her? Why don't I know anything about all this?"

Susan laughed and reached across the table to pat his arm. "Us women stick together." She grinned. "Roughly six weeks later I received two letters. A long, detailed letter from Rachel, which I won't go into now. Suffice to say, she was hugely encouraging. She urged me to follow my heart, and my profession. She asked me to write to her setting out my medical and nursing experience, references, and what sort of work I'd like to do. She also mentioned that she had written to Josey. She thought it would be good if we corresponded."

"I'm guessing the other letter was from my devious sister, then?"

"Absolutely. It was so charming. She told me all about you, how you were, how you were coping and … how much you were missing me."

"She doesn't always tell the truth, you know."

Susan playfully slapped him on the wrist. "Those letters made up my mind. I decided to come to Austria and take my chance."

Sep stared at here in wonder. "And leave your family?"

"My mother was close to evicting me. 'You go and follow your dreams, my girl,' she said. 'You've got what it takes'." Susan shook her head and looked both rueful and proud. "My mum is an inspiration."

"So, when did you set off?"

"Not straight away. I had to wait. The one thing my mum put her foot down on was the idea of me travelling alone across Europe. She wouldn't be shifted on the matter. Apparently, I need a chaperone." She rolled her eyes and looked at him, outraged. "Can you believe it? It's 1919, for goodness' sake. I can travel from Skipton to London on my own, but not from Dover to Dopplegau."

Sep nodded sagely and said nothing, although he secretly sided with Susan's mother. He'd seen some sights on his own trip back. Post-war Europe was chaotic and could be lawless.

Susan moved on. "While I was kicking my heels, *and* getting on my mother's nerves, I got another letter from Rachel. Her father, Doctor Rubenstein, wanted to retire, and her elder brother was going to take over and expand the practice. Rachel also said she would return and help as a co-partner. They needed a practice nurse, and asked if I would be interested."

Sep's mouth dropped open in astonishment. "Doctor Rubenstein's practice in Achbrugge?"

Susan clapped her hands in delight. "Yes. It's a dream come true." She covered her face with her hands before continuing. Her words tumbled out in her excitement. "I couldn't believe it. The job would be initially for six months. I could live in a small apartment above the practice, and Rachel would supervise my training plus teach me German. But she wanted me to come to Austria to meet her father and brother before I made up my mind."

She awaited his reaction, her face flushed with happiness.

He studied her face. Surely there was more to come. "It's a fabulous offer. So why didn't you accept straight away?"

She shook her head in exasperation. "Because of you! I wanted to be sure you felt the same way for me." She grasped his hands. "Imagine if you didn't love me anymore, then I popped up here six months later."

Sep grunted. She had a point, he conceded.

"I thought about writing to you – but two days after Rachel's letter I received another one, this time from Josey. She offered to get the apartment ready and sort out local travel if I could give her the dates." Susan squeezed his hands. "Oh yes, and she also said I should not delay as you were clearly still missing me. What was the phrase she used?" She looked intently at the table as if searching her memory. "Oh yes. He's moping around the farm like a lovesick puppy."

Sep was outraged. "Josey said that about me?" His expression softened as he recalled her recent clandestine trips to Achbrugge. "The sly minx. Here was I thinking her visits to Doctor Rubenstein were for something completely different."

A flicker of a smile flashed across Susan's lips. "Maybe."

He cast her a quizzical look before deciding not to pursue the subject.

263

"So, who escorted you all the way to Dopplegau?"

"Captain Beverley." She laughed. "My sister gave him an ultimatum. No marriage unless and until he delivered me here safe and sound." She looked at him expectantly. "So here I am. Ready for our big adventure."

Sep struggled to absorb all he had been told. A thousand questions tumbled around in his head. He gave up trying to select one. Instead he gazed at the woman he loved above everything else. She hadn't changed. In fact, she was more beautiful than he remembered. The smiling hazel eyes, the scattering of freckles, the tiny mole, the fair hair. He marvelled at her determination, passion and enthusiasm. Did she have any flaws? He would love to find out. He shook his head. "Is it OK if I ask you some questions?"

She arched her eyebrows.

"May I call on you, once you have established yourself in your apartment?"

"You may." She smiled.

"And might I introduce you to my parents?"

"I look forward to meeting them." Her smile widened.

He cleared his throat. "And would you be prepared to walk with me back to this little farmstead one evening in the summer, just as the sun is setting?"

She looked at him curiously. "What for?"

He grinned at her. "So I can ask you another question."

Her smile grew even broader. "I think that would be perfectly acceptable."

ACKNOWLEDGEMENTS

Writing a novel is not something that can be achieved without a considerable amount of help and encouragement from a lot of kind and generous people. In terms of encouragement, no one has provided more than my wife, Andrea. She was convinced from the outset that there was a book inside me screaming to get out. Not only that, but it would be a worldwide bestseller and immediately be snapped up by Hollywood, Sky Atlantic and HBO. The one thing that I am determined to do is try and get this book transferred into an audio format so she can experience for herself what she helped produce.

I am grateful for the critique undertaken by Alison May (https://alison-may.co.uk/about/). Her advice and guidance were invaluable especially in respect of developing the draft into something approaching a publishable work. Also, my thanks to professional editors and copywriter Jane Hammett (http://www.jane-hammett.co.uk) who managed to eliminate all the basic errors of punctuation, grammar, word repetitions and other howlers that littered the original text.

I would also like to thank two established authors Jules Wake and Louise Ross who were so generous with their time in providing advice and especially encouragement when the book was still little more than a series of chaotic ideas and concepts

I am also indebted to the independent reviewers who gave up their time to read through the pre-production drafts and provide me with honest, objective feedback – all of which was taken on-board. Jackie Rawlings, Clare Sealy, Dave Evans, Jackie Rawlings, Christopher Stokes, Vera Kellock, Ann Aitken, Philip Nichols, Victoria and Jeremy Stratford, Jackie and Richard Fidczuk.

I am particularly indebted to Dilys Brooks who not only reviewed the book but also took the time and trouble to fine tune the text and advised on structure and layout.

CONTACT THE AUTHOR

Thank you for reading "Fallen Hero. I'd really appreciate your comments. You can provide me with feedback either by: -

- completing a review on Amazon Kindle
- visiting the web-site www.vernonmedia.com and completing the "Contact Me" boxes. Or
- e-mail at glvernon@vernonmedia.com

42066021R00157

Printed in Poland
by Amazon Fulfillment
Poland Sp. z o.o., Wrocław